ONLY THE *small* BONES

ONLY THE *small* BONES

C.P. HARRIS

Page & Vine
An Imprint of Meredith Wild LLC

Paperback ISBN: 978-1-964264-32-5

Epigraph

"The marks humans leave are too often scars."
-John Green

CONTENT WARNING

Only the Small Bones **is intended for readers 18+ and includes heavy emotional and explicit content.**

Detailed warnings can be found at:
www.cpharrisauthor.com/care-warnings

CHAPTER 1

William

Traffic wouldn't have been an issue at this time of night under normal circumstances. The onslaught of rain and wind made the drive from the airport into the city twice as long though. Time wasn't a luxury I could afford tonight. I'd had to call Davidson twice to assure him I'd be at the hospital soon. He confirmed someone would be waiting to escort me upstairs.

"How much longer?" I asked the Uber driver.

"GPS says ten minutes."

I nodded, resuming my pensive stare out my window while pressing a palm against my knee to keep it from bouncing. Lightening arced across the night sky, and the roar of thunder drowned out the sound of my pulse pounding in my ears. My nerve endings were firing up, twitching with anxiety for what lay ahead. The heartache would soon follow.

My phone vibrated with an incoming text from Xavier, jarring me from thoughts of guilt and impending pain.

Xavier: Are you okay? Is everything alright?

I'd had to rush out in the middle of a performance after receiving the urgent call from Davidson, leaving Xavier to fill in for me while I raced to catch the short flight home. I hadn't even stopped at the hotel to change out of my tux and collect my things, or scheduled my usual car service to pick me up at the airport. I should've hired an assistant to handle those types of things, but I feared it would make me feel as important as everyone else believed I was.

According to Davidson, a trailer truck was found idling a few miles inside our border. Upon further inspection, border patrol discovered several young Americans inside—bound, gagged, and barely lucid—hidden behind crates stuffed with cargo.

So no, I wasn't okay, and nothing was right. In all fairness, I hadn't been okay, and life hadn't been alright in a very long time.

Xavier knew he'd never get the answer he truly wanted from me, so I ignored him instead of lying, like I ignored everything else in my life in these situations. I was a man determined to burn for his sins. No one could stop me.

"Where should I drop you off?" the driver asked ten minutes later.

Leaning forward, I squinted past the rapid back-and-forth motion of the windshield wipers, reading the signs posted along the hospital's exterior. "Straight ahead. That building just past the main pavilion."

He eased the car toward the spot. Two unattended police cruisers were parked, forming a barrier that prevented us from pulling in close to the entrance.

I thanked him then hopped out of the sedan, narrowly avoiding a huge puddle as I jogged for the protection of the building's portico.

One of the uniformed cops holding court inside the vestibule let me in out of the rain, but wouldn't permit me to go any further until I'd shown identification. "Tenth floor, east wing," he said, handing me back my ID and pointing down an empty corridor. "There's a bank of elevators around that corner."

"Thanks." I set off at a quick pace in the direction he indicated, as the other officer reported my arrival through his comms unit.

I jabbed at the elevator call button repeatedly, as if doing so would make it come faster. I used the same flawed logic once I stepped inside, pressing the number ten and the 'door closed' button simultaneously until the elevator started moving.

This never got any easier. In fact, the heartbreak I experienced with each call seemed to deepen to a point where it felt like the organ in my chest might give out. My mother said it was the empath in me. That I'd never known how to not absorb someone else's pain. She said it was one of the qualities that made me rare and special. I didn't see an ounce of good in myself, so I'd had to take her word for it.

Most of the activity on the tenth floor came from the Federal agents and officers positioned around. Some were giving orders, while others were carrying them out. I recognized one of the men as someone Davidson considered a friend. He tipped his head to me, expression grave. I returned the sentiment. Wins like these were always hard to celebrate when they were accompanied by so much devastation.

The squeak of my wet shoes against the linoleum echoed as I trudged to the double doors up ahead. Davidson came into view as I pushed through them.

"This way," he said once I'd caught up to him. "How was your flight?"

"Agonizingly long." I'd only been airborne for a little over an hour, but it might as well have been days.

"Yeah, well, I appreciate you coming." He squeezed my shoulder.

"Of course."

Medical staff chatted in hushed tones behind the nurses' station, combing through what looked like patient charts. Machines hissed and beeped from behind doorways and curtains.

I followed Davidson to a closed room at the end of a hall. He relieved the officer stationed there, motioning for me to look inside once we were alone. I stepped up to the plexiglass window but didn't look in. Not yet. I needed to gather my strength first.

"I would've called you sooner, but it's been non-stop madness ever since."

"It's okay. How'd you get them here?" I peered around at the skeleton crew of people.

"We airlifted them here after determining their external injuries were minor."

"You'll be moving them all to Safe Haven, I assume."

"Yeah," he confirmed. "Hopefully, until we can track down their families. Right now they're being treated for dehydration. The doctors are also running a battery of tests to make sure there aren't any other health concerns that need immediate attention. They'll live, though," he assured me, opting not to say they'd be okay. They'd learn to live with what happened, but they'd never be okay again.

He motioned to the room again, face solemn. "This is the one I told you about over the phone. We can't get him to cooperate. Wouldn't let anyone touch him. Whatever he'd been given to make him compliant wore off by the time we arrived here. He turned feral shortly after. Thought you might be able to work your magic."

Noticing me stalling, looking everywhere but the room on my right, he took on a fatherly tone. "Living a life in service to others can be hard, but what you're doing here matters, William. It helps to focus on all the people you're helping, rather than dwell on the many still out there."

Davidson had it wrong. It wasn't what I did now that mattered. At least not to my conscience. It would forever be what I didn't do *then* that haunted me. I wondered what he'd think if he knew it wasn't a life of service I lived, but one of penance.

When the outside world looked at me, they saw a successful, ambitious man doing good for humanity. They didn't see the truth beneath the facade. The real me would emerge the moment I entered that room. It always did. My guilt made it difficult to hide from them.

I swallowed hard, nodding before turning to the window. My breath caught in my throat, and without thought for the barrier blocking me, I moved closer, the toe of my shoe grazing the door.

A young man with a shock of jet black curls and pale skin waited inside. I couldn't see his eyes. They were focused on the wall in front of him. From what I could see of his profile, though, he couldn't have been any older than his mid-twenties.

His clothes were askew, dirt and dried blood covering the arms of his white shirt. His angular jawline too. I didn't want to know where the blood came from.

My gaze dropped to his hands. They were handcuffed to the railing of the gurney he was sitting on. "You *restrained* him? Was that necessary?" My hand flew to the door knob like I could run in and save him. But I knew it would take much more than being free from his restraints to be saved.

"He attacked one of the nurses trying to take his vitals." Davidson sighed when my head whipped toward him. "He doesn't want to be touched," he explained. "They had to sedate him before we could get the cuffs on. He's still coming around from it."

"So he'd been drugged by his captors, and then drugged again for trying to protect himself," I hissed.

"We didn't want to do it," Davidson said. "He left us no choice."

"There's always a choice." Turning back to the room, I noted how lifeless and slender he looked. "Is he hurt?"

"No. At least not that we can see. The blood isn't his." A male nurse walked by then, wearing a bandage over his brow. Davidson gave me a pointed look.

"Has he said anything?"

"No. Other than snarling, he hasn't said a word."

"So we don't know his name, then."

"Ryan," Davidson said, and I threw him a questioning look. "A few of the others told us, and he responded to it."

We both faced Ryan now, contemplating him. Davidson brushed aside the lapels of his department issued windbreaker, sliding his hands in his pants pockets. "And we may not be dealing with captors here. Or at least, it may not be that simple."

"What do you mean?" I wanted to turn to Davidson, to give him my full attention, but I couldn't take my eyes off Ryan. I'd promised myself I would remain objective moving forward, not be blinded or guided by my personal demons. Against my will and better judgment though, my heart reached for him. It reached in a way it hadn't ever done before, and I hadn't even said a word to him yet.

"The rest of the victims couldn't give a description of the people who'd transported them here. They'd kept them blindfolded the whole time. From what we've gathered, they were abducted and sold some time ago. But they were recently re-sold, then brought here." He shook his head before adding, "Someone spent a lot of money, and went through a lot of trouble to bring them here, then abandoned them in the middle of the road to be found. The question now is, do we have traffickers on our hands, or vigilantes?"

"Maybe both," I whispered, knowing what it felt like to have a change of heart.

"The surveillance footage from the border was useless. The men wore hats and sunglasses, and kept their heads angled away from the cameras. They had all the right documentation to get through. We were able to determine the victims were smuggled into Ontario by sea. Canada's looking into a cargo ship possibly used. All we know right now is that the vessel's port of origin was somewhere in East Asia. That lines up with the statements we've obtained so far." He nodded toward Ryan. "Other than responding to the sound of his name, he gave us nothing."

Davidson was a middle-aged, graying man in good shape, both mentally and physically. He'd worked with my organization for years. The fight to put an end to all forms of human trafficking was as important to him as it was to me. I was grateful for him, but he wasn't as educated about the psyche of someone who'd been trafficked. I, on the other hand, lived and breathed the subject.

"He's likely been in captivity longer than the others," I said. "He's given up hope. His trust would've been completely shattered by now. And as horrific as it may sound, he's likely grown used to what has been done to him. Freedom probably feels more like the enemy now."

"We can run his prints. See if he pops up in the system," Davidson suggested.

"No. Treating him like a criminal will only make the situation worse. I'll see what I can do."

Davidson's phone buzzed from somewhere. Pulling it from an inside pocket he glanced at the screen. "I gotta take this. It's headquarters. I'll be out here if you need me." He stepped aside to take the call, his tone all business. I counted out five deep breaths before entering the room.

Ryan's shoulders stiffened, the only sign that he'd heard me come in. I let the door close gently behind me before taking the few steps needed to put me against the wall he was staring at. His eyes were as black as his hair, just as wild too. The lashes framing them were long and thick. I always asked for details on the survivors before I arrived. He was just as Davidson described over the phone—down to the beauty mark on his cheek. He was striking, and it took me a moment to remember how to breathe.

His sluggish gaze dropped to my shoes then moved upward. The more of me he took in, the more agitated he became. By the time he reached my face, his breathing had become audible.

My size tended to work against me in these situations, but it never took long for their apprehension to recede. Maybe because they sensed I was more broken than they were.

"It's okay," I whispered. "I'm not here to hurt you or make you do anything you don't want to do." Carefully, I dragged the rolling stool over with my foot before easing onto it, slouching my shoulders to make myself appear smaller, insignificant. Making my outside match the way I felt on the inside.

We were quiet for a while, and in that silence I worked to keep what I felt in my heart from showing on my face. I fought to contain my pain, to hold back the tears that his own pain inspired. I wanted to nurture him, to tell him I was sorry for everything that happened to him, and that it would be better from this point on. I couldn't do that, though. He wouldn't have welcomed it, and there were people here who would've been confused by my reaction to him.

"My name is... William," I breathed, hesitating for reasons I didn't want to contemplate. His lips thinned, cheeks flushing pink with anger, I assumed.

I couldn't blame him. I also couldn't hold his gaze.

"I'm a music composer. I compose for symphonies, opera, film..." I trailed off, fiddling with the wrinkle creasing my pants. "I used to conduct for the orchestra. Every now and then I still do, but playing will always be my first love." I chanced a glance up at him, feeling thoughtless. Telling him about all I'd gotten to accomplish in my life while he'd had to endure the horrors of his was the worst idea possible. Even though I would have traded those accomplishments for a chance to bear his burdens in a heartbeat. For an opportunity to have switched places with him.

His eyes bulged, the blood along his jaw a brutal reminder of how cruel the world could be. I cursed inwardly for not demanding the keys to uncuff him. I hated seeing him restrained.

I cleared my throat. "More important to me than all that, though, is my foundation: Freedom Fighters." I paused for his reaction. The pitch of his breathing no longer threatened to drown out my voice, but his hands still clenched and unclenched in their restraints.

"We work to raise awareness about human trafficking, and we provide resources for those affected by it. There's a place just outside of the city called Safe Haven. It's a sanctuary, of sorts, for adult survivors." Recovered minors were taken into custody by state child agencies until their families were located, but we offered external resources to them as well.

"You'll have a room of your own there. Counselors to talk to—or not talk to," I rushed to add when his eyes grew wider with obvious panic. I remembered Davidson said they couldn't get him to speak. "We'll help you with everything you need. Most importantly, you'll be safe there."

The speed at which his chest rose and fell gradually slowed, but he twisted his already raw wrists within the cuffs as though trying to slip them free. His bones were small enough, and that, coupled with the sight of his desperation made me internally flail with anger on his behalf.

"Please, stop," I begged, my heart hammering at my rib cage. My fingers curled into the fabric of my pants to stop me from reaching out for him. I should've been more put together than this. I shouldn't have been falling apart at the seams, but seeing Ryan this traumatized did something to me that the others before him hadn't. I wondered if he could sense that. I wondered if he *knew.*

His hand stilled, and I closed my eyes in gratitude.

"Will you go to Safe Haven? Agent Davidson can take you. He's one of the agents who brought you here. He heads the human trafficking division for the

FBI. You can trust him."

Ryan didn't answer verbally, but the way his fists balled told me his answer was a resounding no.

"Your options are to stay here—I'm sure they can keep you a few days for observation— or... Agent Davidson can take you into custody." I wasn't sure if the second option was true. Ryan hadn't been charged with any crimes. He wasn't guilty of anything. But maybe Davidson could pull strings to get him into some sort of protective custody. Find him comfortable accommodation. To be honest, I didn't like any of those ideas.

"You can't save them all, William."

I shook my head, clearing it of Xavier's frustrated voice. I didn't want it to prevent me from making—what he would call—a poor decision. I fought past every red flag that went up in my mind, bulldozing right over my good judgment to speak. "Or you can come home with me."

DAVIDSON WRAPPED UP his call when I exited the room. "Well? Did you get him to agree to Safe Haven? Did he give you information about his family?"

I hadn't even asked about his family. I drew my shoulders back, preparing for his disapproval. "He's coming home with me. And before you start—"

"You can't keep turning them into charity cases, William." Now he sounded like Xavier.

"That isn't how I see them and you know it. But this is different from the handful of other times."

"How fucking so?"

"It just is," I argued.

"Did you forget what happened the last time?"

"I'll be careful. I'll reach out for help at the first sign that I'm in over my head." I hadn't done that with Jacob—the last survivor I'd allowed to stay at my place while Davidson worked on tracking down his family. I had a three-inch scar on my shoulder to show for it.

"The sign is right there in the room behind you," he said, jabbing a finger at Ryan's hospital room door. "He had to be sedated and restrained," he reminded me. He was worried about me. Worried about Ryan, worried about them all. The ones found—dead or alive—and the countless others still missing. The ones taken on foreign soil, and the thousands being trafficked through coercion and other unsavory means right here in our own backyard.

I couldn't be moved, though. Not about this. Not this time. Davidson sighed, turning in place with his hands on his hips.

"Did he say he wanted to go with you?"

"He didn't *not* say it. But he didn't react to it as terrified as he did the other options."

"I'll find him someplace to stay until we can get him to agree to Safe Haven. We'll search the missing persons database. Find his family. Maybe we can—"

"He won't go with you," I said, speaking over him. I glanced back to see Ryan staring blankly at the wall again. "Just give me a few days. My building is secure. He'll see that he's safe. He'll open up. They always do."

He couldn't argue with me on that front. Jacob had been mortified by what he'd done to me while in the throes of a nightmare. Soon after, he'd agreed to go to Safe Haven until his family arrived. The outcome had been worth the lingering scar.

"Fuck it," he said sounding exhausted, looking at his watch. "Okay. I've officially been awake for twenty-four hours. If anyone asks, I'll blame it on being sleep deprived. I need to wrap a few things up. I'll get you two an escort home. And answer your phone when I call to check on you in the morning," he warned, before striding off and speaking into his comms unit.

It took Davidson notifying Ryan of his options to get him moving. He hadn't said it unkindly, but I still leveled him with a scowl after Ryan went into the en suite bathroom to change out of his grimy clothes into a pair of scrubs. I was already protective of him.

He crept out of the bathroom, leery and shivering. I removed my tuxedo blazer, laying it across the gurney before returning to my spot near the door.

"Please, wear it. It'll keep you warm until we get outside." I slipped into the hall and closed the door when he didn't move. Maybe some privacy would make him more amenable to wearing it. He emerged with it draped across his shoulders.

We rode in the backseat of an unmarked car. Ryan pressed his body against his door to create as much space as possible between us. The roads were still clear of traffic, but the sound of the windshield wipers going, the occasional horn honking, or the tires hydroplaning over puddles, caused Ryan to flinch in his seat. The cacophony of the weather outside felt almost akin to the emotional storm brewing inside the car. When he wasn't leaping out of his skin, his teeth chattered despite the muggy summer night. Was it from shock? Or fear? The agent had been kind enough to turn the heat on, causing the interior to swelter.

We pulled up in front of my place in record time. When Ryan glanced up at the luxury high-rise, I felt the odd need to explain why I would live here. "It came with a recording studio. The previous owner was a musician. Enables me to do much of my work from home." Embarrassment and shame formed a knot in my stomach. I lived like this, while he, and others like him, were out there fighting to survive terrible circumstances.

How did I explain to him that I filled my life with meaningless things in an attempt to fill the gaping hole inside me? How did I tell him that *nothing* ever worked, that I was less than empty inside? Would he even care?

"It doesn't make me happy," I said when he just stared at me. "None of it."

I got out first, circling to his side and holding the umbrella open for him to step under. He refused, as though it would put us too close to each other.

Once inside the lobby, I considered introducing him to the security guard stationed near the revolving doors, since he was one of many responsible for keeping the building safe. I thought better of it. Overwhelming Ryan with new people right then wouldn't have been wise.

Instead, I pointed him out, letting Ryan know there was always someone on post.

"No one is allowed past the lobby without identification and approval." I gestured to the concierge desk where visitors checked in as we made our way to my personal elevator. "And there are cameras everywhere."

Ryan simply looked at the floor as if in a daze. His movements were listless, and he seemed on the verge of collapsing from sheer fatigue. I dug my nails into my palms to keep from reaching out to him, to stop myself from scooping him into my arms and carrying him the rest of the way.

We stood in front of my open apartment door while he assessed the interior hallway, deciding if he felt safe enough to step inside. "This is the only apartment on this floor." It was technically a duplex. "So you don't need to worry about other residents or their visitors roaming around up here. You need a code to ride the elevator up, and I'm the only one with that code." I let that sink in. "I can send the elevator down to anyone visiting using an app on my phone, but only after the concierge has seen their identification and contacted me. I give my code to no one," I assured him.

I never had many visitors anyway. I didn't even employ household staff, preferring to handle my chores myself. It kept me humble.

Ryan crossed his arms, a clear defensive movement, my blazer swallowing him.

"We go in once you're ready. Not a moment sooner. And if you're not comfortable with this arrangement anymore, just say the word. We'll figure something else out." What that something else would be I had no clue, but what he needed came first.

Taking an unsteady breath, Ryan hesitated with one foot over the threshold before physically forcing himself over it.

"Breathe," I instructed when he leaned against the wall, wheezing. "It's okay. I won't let anything happen to you."

Ryan's gaze turned sharp on me. I replayed my words, guilt weighing heavily on my shoulders. I didn't know the particulars, but something had already happened to him. Something tragic and unfair.

"I'm sorry," I whispered, wondering if he knew my apology held weight, that it wasn't just some platitude offered because it fit the moment. I was sorry for what happened to him. My sorrow ate away at my core.

I made a show of bolting the door and activating the alarm system. If the added security helped with the anxiety of being in a strange place, he didn't show it. But just in case it made him feel trapped, I walked him through how to disarm it. He'd never be a prisoner again.

He struggled to keep his eyes open, so while I wanted to prove that nothing sinister lurked here, the full tour would have to wait. I showed him to one of the guest rooms.

The room was spacious but the decor sparse to minimize the high stress levels that came with chaos and clutter. The furnishings were done in earth tones. Unlike the white walls throughout the rest of the apartment, the walls in this room were painted gray—like the color of storm clouds on a rainy day.

Ryan smoothed a trembling hand over the wall, looking over every inch of it. Did he hate the color? Did it mean something to him? My mouth went dry as I waited for the answer. Noticing my gaze on him, he snatched his hand away, his expression turning to steel.

I closed the drapes of the floor to ceiling windows in case the view of the city overwhelmed him. The whole apartment was encased in glass with panoramic views of the city.

"You have your own bathroom through there." I pointed toward the door adjacent from the four-poster bed. "It's fully stocked. And you can find clothes that should fit you in here." I headed for the walk-in closet.

A few minutes passed where I thought he wouldn't come into the closet, but then his head poked in, his gaze traveling the carpeted space before he fully crept inside. His childlike hesitancy tugged at me.

Opening the top drawer of the closet island, I withdrew a pair of sweats and a t-shirt. This had been the first stop for others like him before transitioning to Safe Haven, so I made sure to keep a few items on hand. “We can order you some more things tomorrow.”

Ryan ignored me, drifting back into the bedroom with me not far behind. He pressed his fingers into the mattress, as though testing its softness, before tentatively sitting down then curling onto his side. He let out a long breath, his blinks slowing more and more with each one.

I wanted to help him out of his shoes, to insist he change into something more comfortable before tucking him under the blanket he lay on. I didn’t though. However thoughtful, those actions would have reversed any progress we’d made. I had to remember that space would be my best ally right now. I’d need to fight against my urge to hover.

“My room is down the hall,” I said from the doorway. His eyes opened, letting me know he’d heard me, but he kept them fixed straight ahead instead of focusing them on me. “I’ll leave my door open in case you need me.”

I waited until he fell asleep before venturing to my bathroom to shower the day off me. Afterward, I slipped into my own pair of sweats and a t-shirt then set my phone on the charger. I pulled the covers back, but I couldn’t get into bed, not before checking on Ryan one last time.

Taking my inspiration from him, I slowly poked my head in first, then entered fully with my heart in my throat. The pillows and blanket were scattered on the floor. My jacket had been discarded there too. The sheets were torn to shreds in certain places, and Ryan was nowhere in sight.

I rushed for the open closet door, coming to a halt once the other side of the bed came into view. What I saw made my knees waver.

Ryan was sleeping on the floor with two strips of bedding tied to his wrists like manacles. I noticed now that the ends were secured to one of the bedposts. He’d created chains and shackles for himself. He looked comfortable in a way that anyone would when doing something they were used to, even if they hated it. Like it was the one familiar thing in his new world.

I backed away, bile and horror rising inside of me. Once back in my room, I let the door close softly before slumping against it and sliding to the floor. My head and my heart ached, and my already fractured spirit splintered a bit more.

Anguish consumed me, and suddenly I resented the bed I’d been about to sleep in a few minutes ago. How dare I?

I got to my feet once the shaking subsided, cracking the bedroom door open before dragging myself over to the bed. One by one, I dumped my blanket and pillows onto the floor—then thought better of it. They were too soft. I needed to suffer like they had. Like *he* had.

Laying down on the hardwood floor, I drew my knees up like Ryan had. I fell asleep vowing to help as many survivors as I could, but especially Ryan, because he was different.

"You say that about all of them." Xavier's voice filled in my head again.

I didn't listen to it. I refused to. I'd stay the course, like always. Maybe this time I'd get it right. Maybe this time I'd earn the one thing I always wanted. Maybe helping Ryan would finally make me worthy of redemption.

CHAPTER 2

William

Ryan slept through the following morning and afternoon while I cleaned in between hovering—something I said I wouldn't do. How could I not? I checked more than once to make sure he was breathing. My own breathing leveling at each sign of life. A twitch of his limbs, a tug on his makeshift chains. Even the terror-stricken thrashing that left him trembling against the hard floor, as though something unseen had been tearing his insides apart.

It was hard not to untie him, not to set him free. But I knew the chains that truly bound him weren't the ones he wore on the outside.

He hadn't woken up once, not even to roll to his other side, or to eat or use the bathroom. I wondered if the latter was a sign of dehydration. He hadn't allowed the doctors or nurses to examine him at the hospital. Was he healthy? Should *I* have encouraged them to hold him for observation?

I, on the other hand, hadn't gotten much sleep at all. It had little to do with the escalating pain in my shoulder and hip due to the unforgiving floor, and everything to do with the pain in my heart. Had he been subjected to this every night? I'd been tempted to create my own set of chains to get the full experience. Just to hurt a little more.

I abandoned my post outside his bedroom to venture into the living room, resting my palms against the windowed wall. It was hurricane season somewhere, because the storm from last night hadn't ebbed one bit. Thunder roared, and the gray, ominous clouds cast shadows over the whole apartment.

What had I gotten myself into? What had I *always* gotten myself into? I wasn't a physician, or a therapist, or anything resembling someone who could help Ryan. Not with the things that mattered.

"You're easy to connect with."

My mother's assurances rang out in my head. I never understood that. All I had to offer was deep rooted sorrow and crippling regret.

"There's also your rare but beautiful smile, sweetheart." She'd cradle my cheeks and say, *"Let me see it."* I had to give it to her, it worked every time.

My phone sounded from somewhere behind me. I tracked it down to the kitchen, right next to my untouched bagel and coffee from this morning. My stomach growled, reminding me that Ryan wasn't the only one who hadn't eaten yet.

Davidson's name flashed across my screen. I glanced down the hall to Ryan's door before heading for the library—which doubled as my office—on the other side of the apartment.

"How's it shaking, kid?"

"I'm thirty-one, Davidson. I haven't been a kid for a long time now," I reminded him, sinking onto my desk chair.

"Yeah, well, when you get to be my age, anyone under forty is a kid."

I huffed, unable to manage a fully formed laugh.

"How's it going?" He lowered his voice as though he didn't want anyone overhearing. The buzz of activity in the background told me he was either in the office, or his kids were in town. Knowing Davidson, his kids were probably in town, but he was in the office anyway.

"I honestly don't know," I admitted, shifting to face the window. "He hasn't woken up yet." I left out the details about Ryan's heartbreaking sleeping method.

"He's been through a lot in just the last twenty-four hours, and I can only imagine the hell he's been through before then. Plus, the sedative is probably still purging from his system. I wouldn't worry too much." He knew worrying was my favorite pastime. I didn't let on that I knew we shared the same hobby. There would be at least three more calls from him before this evening.

"Anyway, I gotta go. I've got a shit-ton more paperwork to do. Let me know if you get him to talk. Maybe he heard or saw something that could help the investigation. It'd be great if we could question him about it."

I leaned forward, not liking the idea of Ryan being interrogated. "He isn't a criminal."

"I know, kid, but we want to get the people who did this."

"Well, what about the other survivors? Have you spoken to them again?" I wanted the people who did this caught too, I just wasn't sure if I wanted Ryan traumatized further to make it happen. He wasn't in any condition to help bring anyone down.

"We've gotten all we can from them for now. He may know things they don't."

"What did they say?"

"Nothing I can share with you." He'd probably shared too much as it was.

"Okay. I understand. I'll keep you posted on Ryan."

"Hey," he called out before I hung up. "Maybe bring your mother in on this, yeah?"

I sighed, not wanting to go that route. She had a stealthy way of getting me to face realities I'd rather ignore. Hazards of a job that could easily bleed into our mother-son relationship if we weren't careful.

"We'll see." I ended the call, turning to drop the phone on my desk. My hand bumped against my favorite book. I'd been in here reading it before leaving town a few days ago. I must have forgotten to put it back on its coveted shelf.

I headed for the bookshelf now, the one at the end of the room next to the display case full of meaningless awards. Running reverent fingers over the book's worn spine and edges, I gripped it to my chest, bringing it to my nose and inhaling its aged pages. Hoping, and not for the first time, that I could siphon Gargantuans strength into my body, as if the process were akin to osmosis.

Xavier would never let me hear the end of it if he knew my favorite piece of literature was a children's book—one that I could recite by heart now. Another form of self-punishment my mother would say, if she knew.

Tucking it back into its hiding spot, I turned to find Ryan watching me from the doorway. My brain glitched, my mouth opening and closing, words nowhere to be found. How long had he been there? What had he heard or seen? What had he discovered about me?

Overnight, a purple bruise had formed on his cheekbone, right under his beauty mark. Was it the result of an injury sustained during the tussle at the hospital, or prior? Or one obtained while he slept chained on the floor? Either way, I found myself wanting to ask if it hurt, and wanting to make the pain go away if I could.

"Good morning. I mean, ah, afternoon?" I hadn't intended for it to end as a question, but I also couldn't recall what time it was. "I had some groceries delivered this morning. I didn't know what you liked, so I got a little of everything. You must be starving." I scanned his frame again, realizing starvation wasn't new to him. He seemed about twenty pounds underweight. His broad shoulders hid the worst of his malnourishment.

"I'm not that great at cooking, but I've mastered the toaster. I can toast a bagel to perfection. Frozen waffles too. And boiled eggs. I can also make boiled eggs. I have a coffee machine as well. I bought Gatorade and some protein drinks, in case you can't handle solids right now. The doctor suggested it. Or we can order in, or..." I knew I was rambling, but his blank expression unnerved me. Or maybe the blame belonged to his piercing eyes. They seemed to see right through me.

"Are you hungry?" I whispered. "Or maybe you want to shower first? Feeling refreshed helps sometimes."

He blinked, flushing before subtly angling his head to the right and sniffing himself. I hadn't meant to imply that he smelled, but who knew if they'd been allowed to bathe during their long journey here. I thought it might help to shower all that off of him. He backed away, the stain of his embarrassment still blemishing his skin.

"I didn't mean to—"

He darted away in the middle of my apology. I followed after giving him a head start, but he'd already closed his bedroom door by the time I made it there. I called his name. He didn't answer, didn't so much as grunt in response. I knocked next, and the door creaked open under my fist. The sound of running water trickled over to me from his bathroom, and I debated the pros and cons of stepping into his space without permission.

My gaze landed on the strips of white cotton dangling from the bedpost. I thought about hiding them, about cutting them free and tossing them in the trash. There were more sheets where that came from, though. I also didn't want him to think I disapproved, that I judged him. However he needed to cope, I'd let him—to an extent.

Deciding not to intrude on his territory, I eased the door closed and headed to the kitchen. It felt pointless to wait for him to tell me what he wanted to eat since it seemed he wouldn't speak. I made the decision myself.

Ignoring the clock, which said I should've been making dinner, I dropped two waffles and a bagel into the toaster. While that heated up, I piled some fruit into a bowl, and filled a glass with milk.

I plated the food then set it on the island before grabbing the syrup, butter, and cream cheese. At the last second, I placed a bottle of water next to his milk, and dropped a granola bar near his silverware.

Ryan didn't make any noise when he walked, but I could feel his approach. I considered rushing over to the couch and feigning interest in the deluge of rain coming down outside. Anything to not be caught in the kitchen and deter him from eating. The kitchen overlooked the living room, though, so he'd still be on display. I needed him to eat, which meant I needed to be out of sight. Left with no other options, I crept around the corner and into the dining room, pressing my back to the wall there.

The silence stretched as I held my breath, wondering if I'd imagined sensing him coming down the hall. He should've been seated by now, yet the stool legs hadn't scraped against the floor. I pictured his first bite being tentative, but he should've taken it by now.

The illogical part of my brain said I should've heard the crunch of bagel or waffle, the sip and swallow of milk or water. There was nothing but the sound of rain hitting the windows and my heart beating too fast.

The air grew thick with tension, and the sensation of being watched—of being caught—made my palms grow sweaty.

I knew what I'd find if I came out of hiding. Knew what I'd come toe-to-toe with. Turning slowly, I tapped my forehead against the wall and internally groaned. Maybe I could've waited him out, but the suspense had me on edge.

When I stepped into view, Ryan's eyes were already pinned in my direction. He probably sensed me in the same way I'd sensed him. His chest rose and fell with his shallow breaths as he looked between the food and me. Clear distrust and confusion sparked in his raven colored gaze.

"I thought you'd want some privacy," I said, sticking to the archway. "I guess I should've just asked." It seemed so simple then. I made a note to never assume anything on his behalf again. "So, *would* you rather be alone?"

I crossed over the kitchen's threshold, still keeping my distance. He sucked in a sharp breath, shuffling back.

"You have to be hungry," I whispered. His stomach let out a growl. Ryan stiffened, pressing a palm against his abdomen. His fingers curled into a fist, letting me know the pink blotches decorating his cheeks were from anger this time. I got the impression he thought admitting to hunger equated to a show of vulnerability.

"It's okay," I assured him, moving forward with caution. "You can eat. Eat as much, or as little as you want. Truth is, I'm hungry too. I was going to eat after you." Maybe he'd rather we ate together? "Actually, I think I'll make myself another bagel now." I'd already tossed my other one into the trash. "It's officially been twenty-four hours since I last ate. I'm feeling a little lightheaded." How long had it been since he ate? One day without food probably made me sound privileged from his perspective.

Ryan's curls were wet and heavy, dipping below his ears. Droplets of water fell from the ends, soaking into the t-shirt I'd pulled from the closet dresser for him last night. This close, I could see the wet shimmer of his eyelashes too. Striking had been the wrong word to describe him. Ryan was beautiful, but in a wild animal sort of way.

It was hard to tell with the constant hard set of his features. Whatever softness he may have once possessed, life had beat it out of him.

I grabbed the sleeve of bagels from the bread basket on the counter, splitting one in half before popping both ends into the toaster. "I like cream cheese on mine," I said, making easy conversation as I moved around the kitchen, pretending his suspicious gaze wasn't trained on me.

With my fresh mug of coffee and bagel plated, I settled onto a stool and dug in. Anxiety made it difficult to swallow down the bite, but I did it, washing it down with a sip of steaming French Roast.

Ryan took his first reluctant step closer to the island, then rocked back as though his mind and hunger weren't in agreement. I faked being too consumed with my food to notice, nearly choking on my next bite of bagel when he nudged his plate of food toward me.

"Um, I don't think I can eat all that." I set my bagel down and dusted the crumbs off my hands. "Besides, what will you eat if I do?" There was plenty where that came from, but I had to try *something* to get him to eat. I pushed it back in his direction, but he shoved it back in mine, his face set with determination. That's when it hit me... Ryan thought I'd drugged his food.

"You think I've put something in your food?" I couldn't keep the shock from my tone. Of course he thought that. It was how they got you to comply, especially when they needed to move you. "I would never do that to you. You can trust me." I winced at his vacant, but somehow mocking glare. He *couldn't* trust me. I hadn't given him much reason to yet.

Reaching over, I poured syrup onto one of his waffles, meeting his eyes as I bit down on one corner, chewing and swallowing before moving on to the bagel. The sip of water was welcomed, but unless it was in coffee, milk made me gag. I guzzled down half the glass anyway. Lastly, I scooped up his butter knife and added some of his condiments to my partially eaten bagel before taking another bite.

His ragged breathing began to slow the longer I remained clear-eyed.

Ryan sat, staring at his food with something other than suspicion now. He looked at my coffee mug, then over my shoulder, then back to me.

I stood to fulfill his wordless request, trying to play it cool while blood raced through my veins with every beat of my heart. "I'm not sure how you like it, but I'll make it the way I take it." I added a splash of milk from his cup, since I'd already tested that, then grabbed the sugar bowl. I dipped a finger in, licking it clean to prove it wasn't tainted before adding a teaspoon to his mug. I did the same with the powdered cocoa and drizzle of hazelnut syrup.

With everything now set in front of him, I waited. I began to get nervous when he didn't make a move, but then he glanced up at me, then behind him to the living room, and back at me. This seemed to be the way he liked to communicate. I took the hint, leaving him alone while I feigned relaxation on the couch, reaching up to grab the newspaper off the coffee table.

One end ripped in my tight grip as I watched him through the reflection in the window. His back bowed, curling protectively over his plate, like he thought I might return to take it from him. His arms moved frantically as he scarfed his food down. His cup clinked on the table, his silverware clattering to his plate as he rotated between eating and drinking. At a certain point he abandoned his utensils altogether.

I wanted to warn him that eating too much too fast might make him sick, especially if he wasn't used to eating a high quantity of food at once. I couldn't bring myself to interrupt him, or the heartbreaking scene before me. It was as though the simple act of eating was an emotional journey.

He stayed there a long while after, his shoulders trembling. My heart squeezed within my chest. I wanted to take him in my arms, to stroke his hair and his tears, to shed my own tears for him. I stayed put, though, once again knowing my attempts at comforting him would do more harm than good.

Eventually, he stood, turning to the living room and flinching at seeing me there. He'd forgotten about my close proximity. Syrup stained his chin and shirt, and in an instant the lost look he wore changed. His puffy eyes had gone stone cold again. I didn't speak, although an apology rested on the tip of my tongue. Ryan's pain made me feel sorry for even existing.

I thought he'd head to his room. He'd looked that way. Instead, he moved in a trance-like state to the window, flattening a palm over the rain battered glass. A squeaking noise echoed through the room when he slid to the floor, his hand dragging down the window as he went. The trail of condensation he'd left behind must have come from wiping away his tears.

I perched on the edge of the couch now, not moving a muscle. He curled up onto his side, bringing his knees up to his chest. The knots in his spine were prominent in that position. My insides twisted with rage at seeing his frailty, and it made me want to do unspeakable things to the people who hurt him.

It didn't take long for his soft snores to fill the space. Some of the tightness I'd been carrying in my limbs since yesterday—since long before then—left my body, seeing him rest. I hoped it was peaceful, that nothing hurt him in his dreams. I couldn't protect him there, but I'd do whatever I could to protect him in reality.

Tip-toeing over to him, I covered him with the soft throw I kept on the back of the couch. My eyes grew damp as the corners of my mouth rose. I traced my smile with shaky fingers, thinking my mother would be happy to see it.

"Celebrate the small victories," she'd say, and so I did. Because while he still slept on the floor, at least he was out of his physical bondage.

CHAPTER 3

William

I jerked awake with a gasp, barely managing to keep the name clawing its way up my throat from exiting my mouth in a scream. The nightmares were back. It had been a blissful few weeks without them.

Shoving the blanket off me, I wiped the sweat from my neck while attempting to orient myself with my surroundings. Moonlight pierced through the glass wall as the rain raged on, and the newspaper I'd been holding earlier lay on the floor near the coffee table.

Dropping my feet to the area rug, I dug the heels of my palms into my eyes, trying to rub away the final dregs of sleep in hopes of gaining clarity. The last thing I remembered was Ryan drifting off to sleep on the floor, and me watching him from this very spot. *Ryan.* I shot to my feet, looking around to see if he might be sitting in the kitchen or at the other end of the expansive room. I was alone.

Ambient light shone from the hallway leading to the library. I looked around for my phone to check the time, but then remembered I'd left it on my desk after speaking with Davidson earlier. I set off in that direction.

The brass picture lights hanging over the bookshelves illuminated the room in a soft golden hue. Ryan stood in front of my award case with his back to me, skating a finger over the engravement of one of my gold-plated statues.

"Être *dans la lune*," I pronounced softly, not wanting to scare him. He wheeled around like I had anyway, wearing a caught-red-handed expression.

Not caught touching something he had no right to, but caught caring about something. The way his eyes fell from my face to my shoulder made me believe that. Recalling how he responded to me hearing his hunger made me sure of it too. Ryan didn't want me knowing anything about him, specifically anything he perceived to be a weakness. I looked toward the accolade he'd been trying to read. He was curious about me. I found the idea both moving and terrifying.

"It's a French film. *To be in the Moon.* I won that one for Best Original Score."

He swallowed, his breathing irregular.

"I didn't mean to scare you. I woke up and you were gone... I wanted to make sure you were okay."

He'd pressed his back into the case when I entered. I retrieved my phone from my desk, then returned to the doorway to put him at ease. After checking the time I did the math in my head. I slept for three hours. Had he been awake for most of those? I slipped the phone into my pocket after seeing I had a few missed calls and texts from Davidson and Xavier.

"I've been meaning to box this stuff up." I scanned the meaningless trophies, feeling no pride in having won them. "I showcase them for my mother's benefit, really. To keep her from worrying about me. She worries when I choose not to focus on the good. When I minimize it in preference of the bad."

Ryan turned away from me as if he didn't want to hear about what might not be good in my life. I didn't blame him, not when imagining what his life had been like prior to yesterday. My martyrdom suddenly resembled ungratefulness.

"I was thinking of having my mother over for dinner one night. She's a great cook, and we could use some variety around here. Plus, the longer I try to keep her from visiting, the more insistent she'll become." I didn't know how long Ryan would be here. The others had been ready to transfer to Safe Haven after a week or two. I wouldn't rush him, though. It would take as long as it took. I did have people in my life that would want my attention, though. Primarily my mother and Xavier. If Ryan was going to be here a while, I'd need to start warming him up to the idea of them.

"She's a great listener too," I added without revealing what she did for a living. I didn't want to pressure him. "I'm guessing after a few days we'll get tired of eating breakfast for every meal." I knew he wouldn't eat take-out. Everything would need to be prepared in front of him before he ate it. I supposed I could have just sampled everything first, but cooking would be the way to get my mother in here, so I'd stick with that reasoning.

"Did you sleep well?" I whispered. My question sent his nostrils flaring. Nothing I said seemed to be the right thing but I'd keep talking anyway. It worked with the others—although where they'd been mostly scared, anger seemed to be Ryan's primary emotion. I began second-guessing myself, unsure if I was equipped for this. The empty pit in me expanded further, letting me know my demons agreed.

"How about a tour of the place?"

Ryan peered up looking guilty before bowing his head so his hair hid most of his face. I froze up thinking of all the private things he could have seen on his exploration. Things I didn't ever want anyone seeing.

"Ryan?" Fear scrambled my brain as his haunted, yet honest, eyes returned to me. I relaxed then, somehow knowing he hadn't pried into anything that could have exposed me.

"How about the recording studio then?" You needed a code to get in, so he wouldn't have been able to venture in there. His eyes glittered with something close to excitement before the spark died again, as though there was still too much bad weighing down any possibility of good in his life.

I led the way, ascending the staircase at the far end of the living room with Ryan in tow. I punched the four-digit code into the panel, saying the numbers out loud so he could memorize them. "Not sure why the previous owners wanted to secure the room, but it seemed easier to leave it than to have someone come in and remove it." I shrugged, waving my arm over the threshold to activate the motion sensor lights. "After you," I gestured for him to go in ahead of me. I wanted to see his reaction, even if it'd be from behind.

He hesitated, as if not trusting that I wouldn't lock him inside, but then he contorted his body to ensure we didn't touch when he breezed past me. With slow and steady steps, Ryan bypassed the control room, his gaze fixed on the live room. It was large enough to record a chamber orchestra, and held the instruments needed to do so.

He ran a hand over the soundproofed door, then the acoustic panels on the wall, frowning at me over his shoulder.

"To contain the sound. The insulation is top notch. You barely hear anything when the door is closed."

He moved past the piano next, jumping when his trailing fingers pressed one of the keys. It was adorable. I bit the inside of my cheek to stop myself from smiling. Ryan stared at me expectantly, and I took a gamble that he was asking me if I played.

"I'm no concert pianist, but I get by. It's actually the instrument I started with as a kid. I moved on to something else after being inspired to." I waited with my heart in my throat for him to ask about my inspiration. It wasn't something I talked about. *Ever.* He didn't seem to care and his gaze lifted to the Decca Tree ceiling mounts keeping the microphones suspended.

His disinterest in the matter filled me with relief, but not for the reasons one would think.

"My grandfather is responsible for my love affair with the symphony. He'd babysit me while my mother took night classes at the community college—after having served tables all day at the shabby diner down the block," I added, wanting him to know my life had never been easy. I hadn't expected him to pause his exploration to give me his undivided attention. I couldn't read his expression. Something told me he was working hard to make sure of it.

"Uh," I started, scratching my brow trying to remember where I'd left off instead of focusing on how exposed he made me feel. "My grandfather couldn't sleep without some sort of white noise in the background. Something about it drowning out the sound of bombs striking overhead." Post traumatic stress disorder, I'd later understood.

"My mother could only afford a studio apartment, which meant the bedroom and the living room were one and the same. So if grandpa listened to white noise, then so did I. He'd let me choose, but his battered radio didn't have many options. It was either static or the classical music station, WKTS. Static kept me up all night," I said wryly. "Still does."

I rubbed at the back of my neck, feeling silly all of a sudden. I couldn't get a read on whether or not Ryan cared, or if he was just being polite.

"I found it fascinating that songs without words could inspire such strong emotions. That I could go from happy, to sad, to outright petrified depending on the piece. On the chords or notes struck. Some nights I thought my heart would beat right out of my chest as the symphony reached its crescendo. Some nights I'd cry myself to sleep from the sheer beauty—or terror—of it all." I'd peeled back a layer of my soul with that last confession, and I waited for Ryan to make me regret it. He didn't.

"I fell in love with film too, realizing the score dictated whether you laughed or seethed or hid behind your hands in fright." I huffed, getting lost in my memories as Ryan watched on. "'*Under The Skin*, *The Lighthouse*, and *There Will Be Blood*' were some of my favorites. The score for '*Suspiria*' was an assault on the auditory system. One fan described it as making a slow walk down a hallway feel like a rollercoaster ride. I wholeheartedly agreed."

I paused, checking the level of my excitement, wondering if this was all too much for him, if it would have a negative impact on him. I got the sense he wanted me to continue as much as he wanted me to stop, because while his expression still told me nothing, his arms hung rigid at his sides, hands bunching in the sweats he wore.

"Ever since I could remember I dreamed of playing in the Philharmonic," I whispered. "While other boys my age played in the dirt, or shot hoops, or were obsessed with video games, I spent my spare time living and breathing the symphony. It was the only thing that saved me when..." I couldn't finish, and his facial expression shifted then, to something resembling anger and disappointment. Did he know I was a coward? Did he know that while I wanted him to be brave, to not let what happened to him define him, that I couldn't do the same? I was a hypocrite. Did he know it? Did he not speak because he heard and understood more in the silence?

I didn't take a breath until he turned away, in fear that its shakiness would give away whatever I'd managed to keep in. Whatever scrap of truth I'd managed to hide.

He ambled through the lineup of instruments as though he had all the time in the world, never stopping again to give me that questioning look he had with the piano. It was like he'd seen me, summed me up, and was no longer curious about what made me... me.

He plucked a few strings on the cello before wandering on to do the same with the harp. He hadn't done it with any skill, just an absent sampling of sound as he perused.

I wished I could see his face, wished I could see if anything in the room meant something to him, or if it was a temporary fascination with something he'd never been this up close to before.

I got my answer when he made it to the violin. He stared at it for a while before reaching for it. He drew his hand back before making contact, making two more attempts before seeing it through. Removing it from its stand, Ryan examined every inch of it before bringing it to his chest and sagging. It clearly must have sparked a memory in him, and I desperately wanted the details. Something good? Something that brought him comfort, or something that caused him pain?

I got my answer to that too when the air in the room turned stifling. The ache radiating from his trembling shoulders hit me square in the chest. I brought a hand to my throat as the phantom blow morphed into a type of pressure I couldn't breathe through. All that he experienced in that moment,

I experienced too, as if his pain had become *our* pain.

It was too big for me, so it had to be astronomical for him. How was he standing there surviving it? How was he not a crumpled heap on the floor?

The sniffling started then, and I took two steps forward, my arms opening, ready to embrace him. I stopped myself, the abruptness of it audible on the shiny hardwood floor. I couldn't touch him. Not without his permission. Not when I didn't know what that touch would mean to him. The way he'd skirted around me to enter the room left little to the imagination.

I backed into the control room before spinning and exiting completely, closing the door to allow him and his pain some privacy.

Downstairs, with nothing to do but worry, I decided to cook for him. Bagels and waffles again. I had everything set up once he reached the bottom landing, and I did him the courtesy of not meeting his eyes. I wouldn't have been able to hide my own emotions at seeing the aftermath of him crying, and the last thing I wanted was for him to think I pitied him.

I took a few bites of everything, waiting long enough for him to see I hadn't died before leaving him alone again.

Entering the library, I pulled my favorite book from its shelf, then sat at my desk, reading it twice. I would've gone for a third round but it became hard to read past the tears in my eyes. It wouldn't have mattered anyway. No matter how many times I recited the words, I'd never be as mighty as Gargantuan. I'd forever be weak.

Ryan wasn't in the kitchen when I returned, and his dishes had been cleaned. I checked the trash bin, but other than my first uneaten bagel from earlier, and a few other miscellaneous items, it was empty. He'd eaten all his food. At least we were making progress on that front.

I flopped onto the couch feeling useless and defeated, but determined to be better the next day. I owed it to him. I owed it to them all.

Lost in thought, I idly stroked the knit throw's frayed edges, remembering how hot I'd been when I woke up with it draped over me.

My fingers stiffened. Everything came to a halt at once. My negative thoughts, my concerns, and the heavy exhaustion pulling at me. I looked over to the spot on the floor where Ryan had fallen asleep earlier, then peered down at the blanket in my hand. The blanket I'd covered him with. The one I'd been covered with.

Slowly, I got to my feet, inching toward the hall and staring at Ryan's closed bedroom door. The faintest hint of a smile spread across my lips as I realized that with this small, insignificant gesture, he'd taken care of me. He'd returned the favor.

CHAPTER 4

William

The sky held onto its gloom, and the puddles were large enough to take a swim in. At least the rain had eased up enough for me to resume my morning runs. I'd left before sun-up and hadn't wanted to wake Ryan that early, so I left him a note on the refrigerator. The non-stop second guessing, questioning if that would be enough caused me to double back halfway through my usual circuit.

We'd crossed the one week mark, and there had only been one minor change. I no longer had to sample Ryan's food before he ate—because now he meticulously watched me prepare everything. I think it was more about him enjoying the process than him not trusting me. For breakfast, lunch, and dinner, he'd perch at the edge of his favorite stool, engrossed while I worked the toaster and coffee machine.

We still hadn't graduated from Eggos and Everything bagels. The sight of both now made me gag.

Ryan was particular about how much syrup made it onto his food. Too much and it made a mess, not enough and he choked from the dryness. Cream cheese was another matter. I couldn't spot his bagel beneath the amount he slathered it with.

I could see he'd put on a few pounds. His long arms were still thin, his broad shoulders still boney beneath his shirt, but the hollows of his cheeks were less pronounced. I didn't suspect he'd get too big, though. He seemed naturally lean, his frame a close match to Colson Baker's.

He needed more nutrients though. We both did, which was why I'd been teasing the idea of my mother's cooking bit by bit. When I'd mentioned she'd be coming by in less than a week, he hadn't stormed away from the island like he did the day before.

Pushing through the building's revolving doors, I slowed at seeing Xavier speaking with Steve at the concierge desk. *Fuck.* I'd been brushing him off all week. Him showing up unannounced meant he'd finally had enough of it.

Spotting me, Steve smiled and said something to Xavier. Xavier turned as I made it into the lobby, panting and wiping sweat from my brows. I wore compression tights and an equally form fitting tank, my typical running gear. Xavier had never made a secret of liking it. He gave me an appreciative once over before coming to meet me halfway.

"I know it's not the most attractive thing to show up on your doorstep uninvited, but you left me little choice." His annoyance made his Spanish accent thicker, his 'R's' rolling.

"Xavier—"

"You left me in the middle of a performance with nothing more than a shout for me to cover for you, and a mention of something urgent needing your attention back home." He handed my leather duffle over, packed with the items I'd left at the hotel.

"I'm sorry—"

"Then you ignore my calls and texts. What the fuck is going on, William?"

To be fair, he wasn't the only one I'd ignored. I cleared my calendar of all upcoming appearances, and I'd left Freedom Fighters in the hands of the capable people I'd put in place to run it. It helped that I wasn't responsible for the day-to-day. My other work commitments didn't allow for it. Davidsons' was the only call I'd returned, because I was invested in his investigation.

"Is everything okay?" Xavier pushed. "Is your mother—"

"She's fine," I cut in, laying my hands on his shoulders to calm him. I'd really screwed this up. His deep-set hazel eyes implored me to explain what was going on with me. I pulled him to the side as morning rush-hour foot traffic picked up in the lobby.

"I'd gotten a call from Davidson. They found a group of Americans they believed were trafficked."

"Jesus," Xavier exclaimed quietly, inching closer. "That's amazing, William. I mean not—"

"I know what you meant."

"That doesn't explain why you needed to rush back. Or why I haven't heard from you since."

"Davidson needed my help with one of the survivors. They couldn't get him to speak or accept medical attention."

"Oh," Xavier said, taking a step back. He peered toward the bank of elevators. "Let me guess. You're the only one who can save him." His expression was guarded now.

Xavier and I worked together, he'd been my replacement as concertmaster after I'd taken the position as conductor and music director of the New York Philharmonic. We became friends, and he eventually began working on outside ventures with me. He was talented. He was also attracted to me.

The attraction went both ways, but Xavier wasn't the type who could handle a no-strings attached fling, no matter how much he professed otherwise. He'd lapsed into discussion of a possible future for us more than once. I couldn't be who he wanted, who he deserved. There were limitations to what I could offer him.

I'd been upfront with him from the start, and he'd told me he could handle it. That it wasn't my job to manage his expectations, and that if he fell, he wouldn't blame me for it. He did fall, and I knew he believed it was my fault.

I heard it in his voice every time I had to leave in the middle of a work session, or cancel plans to tend to something related to Freedom Fighters. I felt it every time he forgave me after going pliant beneath me, screaming out his pleasure while stuffed full of my cock.

Xavier wanted more, he wanted to be my priority, and he couldn't comprehend why that was impossible. He didn't know that every spare part of me was abandoned in a field alongside my broken promises. I had nothing left for him.

My non-existent dating life didn't help matters. My apathy toward romantic involvement with anyone else kept his hope alive. He believed I'd one day grow tired of running and choose him. We were stagnant in our own ways, and maybe subconsciously I encouraged his need to hold on. Because if it were to be someone one day, then why not him?

I'd broached the subject of ending our work relationship after putting an end to our intimate one. The mere suggestion had caused a huge argument. From Xavier's perspective, if I couldn't give him my heart, then I could at least help him fulfill his professional dreams. We'd won our first Academy Award shortly after.

"Well, what about work?" he asked, folding his arms over his chest. "We have deadlines to meet, William. Maybe you don't mind putting *your* life on hold whenever someone in need comes calling, but I still have goals I'd like to meet. What you do affects me too."

"I know that," I said, taken aback by his clipped tone. For the most part Xavier had a mild temperament, and rarely needed to raise his voice or sharpen his tone to get his point across. "He should only be here for another week. Two at the most." Even I heard the uncertainty in my voice. Seven days had passed and Ryan still hadn't spoken. I didn't even know if he could.

Xavier shook his head, muttering something in Spanish before running a hand through his wavy hair. He was beautiful, sensual and elegant. Especially when reduced to begging me for mercy in his native language while I used his body to the brink of collapse. Life would've been easier if he was enough to make me different, to make me forget about my past.

"Do you have an hour to spare now to run through the final edits I sent you last night?"

"You know that isn't possible, Xavier."

"Why not? He can't expect you not to work."

His jealousy and frustration made him insensitive. This wasn't normally who he was. He seemed to be on the cusp of an explosion. I took full responsibility for that.

"Because you're a surprise, and surprises aren't ideal. He needs predictability right now." We'd gone through this before, but each time he made me repeat it again. Maybe hoping I'd 'see the light' at some point, or hoping each occurrence would be a reminder to him of what I would always put first, assisting with him getting over his feelings for me.

He chewed his lip, looking helpless and lost, as if hearing the familiar words hadn't lessened his feelings at all.

"I'll have to rearrange our current schedule, yet again," he said with undisguised irritation. "Two weeks?" he asked as though needing me to promise. I couldn't, because it would only make things worse when in two weeks not much had changed. We both knew that could be the case.

Xavier had a point, though. We had important deadlines looming, and he'd need to be here for us to meet them.

"I plan on having my mother over for dinner at some point. I'll tell him about you. Let him know you may be joining us. I'll let you know how it goes."

"Okay," he said, before nodding and walking away. He stopped after a few steps. "I'm really happy for you, William. For Davidson, for the people recovered. I know how much this means to you." Except he didn't know how much it meant to me, not really. Because he didn't *know* me. No one did.

I KNEW SOMETHING was off the moment I entered the apartment. That sort of feeling you get when something bad is about to happen, or has happened. The hairs on the back of my neck rose, my heartbeat pounding in my ears.

"Ryan?" I set my duffle bag on the floor before taking off for his open bedroom door. The mattress and bedding were on the floor, one of the bedside lamps lay on its side, the other one shattered. The chipped paint on the wall confirmed how it'd been broken.

"Ryan?" I called louder, jogging down the hall. "What the..." I peered around the kitchen. The cabinets were thrown open, dishes smashed to pieces along the counters, stove and sink. Something crunched under my shoe. Broken glass.

Panic set in, locking my brain and my limbs. A muffled sound of pure agony sent me spinning around, and I had to grab hold of the wall to avoid slipping on the debris littering the floor.

Ryan stood heaving in the far corner of the living room, crushed against the window. Fist sized blood stains peppered the glass, like he'd been trying to beat his way out. He made that guttural sound again. A trapped, primitive baying that came from somewhere deep in his chest. Calling it a sound almost minimized it. A more apt description would've been misery. That's what it sounded like to my ears.

"Ryan," I breathed, still unable to comprehend what the hell had happened. His hair hung around his face, his gaze vicious. He looked dangerous, unhinged, but most of all... scared. Utterly, heartbreakingly scared. But why?

I searched my brain for a reason, finding an obvious one. Because I'd left him. I *left* him.

Swallowing down the acrid truth of that, I took a step in his direction, needing to find the source of the bleeding and make it stop. He shrank back deeper into the glass. I halted. "I left you a note," I said, turning my head toward the kitchen. The note was torn to shreds, scattered among the mess.

I thought over the seven words I'd written down. "*Went for a run. I'll be back.*"

The last three played on a loop in my head, making my insides hurt. *I'll be back... I'll be back... I'll be back...*

"Did you think I wouldn't come back? I live here," I said instead of the pointless drivel I'd been about to say. *I wouldn't do that. I wouldn't abandon you.* "My things are here. My life is here." *You are here.* A rational mind would have understood these things, but I had to remember unaddressed fear would overrule logic every time. I'd need to be more mindful of what could potentially be a trigger for him.

Seeing droplets of blood hit the floor threatened to tear apart my patience. I needed to get to him. I needed to find his wound, to find the source of the bleeding and make it stop. As though sensing my intentions, he hid his hands behind his back.

"How hurt are you?" I continued. "If you won't let me look at it, then at least let me get you the first aid kit so you can clean and examine it yourself."

He still said nothing. I thought about all the things I could have done differently. Thought about what I would've needed from him, right now, if our roles were reversed. I also recalled something I'd said to Xavier downstairs.

"He needs predictability."

We had a routine going here, and he'd come to count on it. Maybe even trust it without realizing it. And then he woke up, and I was gone. He'd depended on me being here for him, and maybe he hated realizing that.

I exhaled and closed my eyes briefly before opening them and offering him a deeper look inside me, a peek behind the curtain no one else had ever gotten before. "I'm constantly trying to outrun the unrest inside me because I know what happens once it catches up to me." Flashes of blades and blood filled my mind. I shook my head to clear it.

"I spent a good chunk of my adolescent years in therapy. Some of my adult years too. One therapist suggested running to help reduce my stress levels. With nothing to lose, I tried it and fell in love. I can literally see my demons in my mental rearview as I race through the streets at breakneck speed. If I get far enough ahead of them, I earn a couple days worth of peace before they're biting at my heels again." Peace might have been an exaggeration, but I didn't want to scare him with the unfiltered truth.

"Wash, rinse, and repeat. It's been a week since I ran. I hope you can appreciate what that means."

Ryan's breathing evened out at a gradual pace. The only sign that my honesty might have gotten through to him.

"I should've waited until you woke up and explained all this before leaving. I should've invited you. I should've done a number of things to prevent this." I looked around at the destruction again. "I'm not a perfect man, Ryan, but I'm doing the best I can."

I grinded my molars together as I listened to the drops of blood hit the floor behind him. Time ticked by, and I thought I might scream, but then he began to relax. His eyes softened first. His jaw unlocked next, then his shoulders lowered. With some hesitance, he held his left hand to his side, letting me know it was the injured one. He snatched it behind him again when I stepped forward, a warning that I'd taken it too far.

I nodded. "I'll get the kit for you." Racing into my bathroom, I searched under the sink until I found the red first aid kit. In the kitchen, I filled a bowl with water before placing it and the kit on the coffee table. It was the only area that didn't need to be sectioned off with caution tape.

Sitting on the arm of the couch, I watched as Ryan lowered to his knees across from me. First he dipped a hand in the bowl of water, clearing some of the blood away. The small gash at the center of his palm became visible then, already clotting. He must have cut himself with a piece of glass during his tirade around the apartment. The superficial cuts surrounding it scabbed over days ago, the ones he'd received during the struggle at the hospital.

"Sorry," I murmured, sitting back when he glared at me. I hadn't realized I'd leaned in to get a better look. I fisted my hands in my lap, hating that I couldn't help him, biting my tongue to prevent offering him unsolicited verbal assistance. He hovered his hand over the red water before dousing his palm with peroxide, gritting his teeth as it bubbled over the wound. There didn't appear to be any glass or porcelain splinters stuck in it.

Ryan worked as though patching himself up was second nature. I held back my questions as to why that was. I had enough heartache to work through at the moment.

By the time he finished bandaging his hand he looked exhausted, the adrenaline from his rampage fading. Still, he left and returned with his shoes on before retrieving the broom and dustpan from the pantry to start cleaning up the mess he'd made of the apartment.

"I can do that," I said, jumping up from the couch. Ryan ignored me, taking careful steps though the kitchen, hyper focused on the task.

"I'm going to take a quick shower," I said, scrunching my nose up as the stench from my sweaty workout clothes suddenly hit me. "I'll make us some boiled eggs after."

He didn't answer me, and I took in his bloody clothes, making a mental note to order him some more things. Maybe some running gear too, in case he decided he wanted to join me one morning.

Ruminating in my thoughts, I took way longer than I should have. I hurried to pull my t-shirt on as I headed for the hall. Two hard boiled eggs waited for me in the silent kitchen, shelled and cut into halves. I didn't have the opportunity to revel in the fact that Ryan had cooked for me. Not when I couldn't take my eyes off the torn sheet of paper resting near the bowl.

With an unsteady hand I lifted it, mouthing the one word written in a barely legible chicken-scratch. If I hadn't known any better, I would've said a child penned it. He'd scribbled it out and tried again numerous times.

I leaned back against the counter behind me, needing the support as my chest split wide open.

It wasn't the apology that killed me, but that he'd spelled "sorry" with one "r" and two "e's". A mistake a typical six-year-old might've made.

CHAPTER 5

William

As a boy I was prone to intrusive morbid thoughts. I'd see an old lady walking her dog, and out of nowhere visions of having my arm chewed off while I screamed bloody murder would overtake me. I'd fall down a rabbit hole of survival planning, thinking of ways to pry the dog off me, as the macabre scene took shape in my head. My insides would twist and turn imagining all the blood loss.

Picturing my future family was another favorite. Envisioning playing in the park with my kids—at least three, because I was an only child, a *lonely* child. Somehow, gazing at my children playing in the sandbox always ended with me throwing myself on top of them as gunfire erupted from somewhere close by. The random visions were detailed, down to their ages and the color of their hair, who would survive and who wouldn't. Sometimes the visions would be of me looking up from my phone to see that they'd been taken. I'd end up mourning these make-believe children for the rest of the day. Maybe my psyche had been preparing me for the unimaginable nightmare to come.

There were dark periods throughout high school. Days when I couldn't get out of bed, when fighting the bad voices became too tiresome. They'd tell me I wasn't a good person, that I didn't deserve the life I wanted, that I was a liar. I knew not to believe them. My mother and my therapist told me that. But sometimes it was hard not to listen to them. Not to trust they knew best.

For every negative statement the voices tossed at me, I came back with a positive one.

I am good.

I deserve to be happy.

I'm honest.

Some days the voices were stronger than me, though. Some days it seemed like their evil gave them strength, while my fight to push them back exhausted me. Sometimes I needed a moment to rest, to regroup and recharge. My weakness brought them joy, and in those moments, they pulverized me. Sometimes it took days—weeks even, to recover.

Through it all I had my instrument. I had music, and a stubborn determination to make things right. My resolve got me out of bed most days, and helped me to excel in school. It gave me purpose. A reason to fight, to survive, because what happened to me had to have been for something.

JACKKNIFING UPRIGHT IN bed, I slapped a palm over my mouth to catch my scream, gaze flying to my bedroom door. I wondered if there were any words shouted that I hadn't intercepted. Words I wouldn't want Ryan, or anyone else, to hear.

I lowered my hand, breathing hard, blinking into the dark room. I hadn't meant to fall asleep. Last thing I remembered was cleaning up the pieces of glass Ryan missed, and scrubbing down the rest of the apartment while doing laundry and waiting for him to come out of his room. He hadn't, so I'd made him a late lunch before coming to my room to think.

"Christ," I muttered, taking in the sweat covering my arms and staining my tank. The bedding beneath me was soaked through with it too.

Rolling to my feet, I poked my head into the hall. The tray of waffles I'd left by his door was gone. I hoped he'd eaten it and not thrown it away.

The sun had set, and a check of my phone showed it was a little after nine. I'd be up for the rest of the night now. Davidson had called while I slept. I listened to his voice message asking for proof of life. I shot him a text letting him know me and Ryan were okay and asking if there'd been any progress on the investigation.

After changing the bed linen, I headed to the bathroom for a long, hot shower. I got the water running before contemplating the bottle of pills on the sink. I'd dug them out earlier, but ended up not taking them. I couldn't recall the last time I'd needed to.

I popped one into my mouth now, swallowing it dry before shrugging out of my clothes and stepping under the hot spray. I leaned my head back, letting the water pour over my face while I waited for what felt like an hour for the medication to kick in. My limbs began to loosen as my anxiety melted away.

With some of my issues now moving to the back-burner of my brain, it left room for other needs that I'd neglected for some time. My blood began to warm, and it had nothing to do with the water temperature. I turned the lever to the right anyway, sighing when the coolness met my heated skin.

Bypassing my burgeoning erection, I soaped myself up, repeating the process before shampooing my hair. I stalled for as long as I could because the end result would be more powerful after a little self-deprivation.

With only my cock left to clean now, I did so with as much indifference as possible, biting my lip to hold in my moan.

I felt most at peace with myself during sex, but even that became affected when the dreams and voices became relentless.

By the time I dried off and slipped my shirt on, the ache of ignoring my arousal had become too much to bear. Gripping the edge of the sink and panting, I looked at my reflection in the mirror. I took in the dullness of my normally vibrant green eyes, and the dark circles beneath them. When I could finally sleep again, I needed it to be good. That wouldn't happen until I found release.

I slipped a hand down to grasp my hard length. I examined my crown, taut and shiny like stretched leather, my shaft a shade darker than my light brown complexion. The wetness at the slit shimmered under the overhead light. The heavy sack below my base drew in, as if to say this was happening with or without my cooperation.

Licking a landing strip up my palm, I lifted the hem of my shirt to my teeth, biting down before grabbing hold of myself. I closed my eyes as a low groan escaped me. Toes curling into the bath mat, I let my chin fall to my chest as I gave in to my need. Now that I'd committed to it, I couldn't remember why I'd thought it was a bad idea to begin with. I could already feel the angst and uncertainty evaporating as my orgasm took shape, winding itself like a vortex at the base of my spine.

Swiping pre-cum from the head, I jerked off like I meant it now, ass cheeks clenched and unyielding. I pressed a hand against the mirror, my palm slipping across the surface as my biceps flexed, and the veins along my neck pushed against the skin.

Xavier's hazel eyes flashed in my mind. I tried to hold on to it, tried to remember all the times we were together like this. The times when his hand replaced mine, when his body replaced this lonely experience. The image shifted, and suddenly cool black orbs bore down on me. So dark and cold, so bottomless, haunted and afraid.

I tried to stop it, attempted to shake my head clear, but all it did was fast forward the reel until a delicate beauty mark on a high, pinked cheekbone came into view. This felt wrong. It felt forbidden, and completely out of my hands.

The muscles in my back rippled, my calves burning as I rose onto my toes and held there, trembling. "Fuck," I breathed around the cotton between my teeth. My jaw tensed and I came on a groan of excruciating pleasure.

Cum bathed my fingers and the porcelain sink, a rope of it splattering the faucet. I worked my cock even after it was spent, shivering through the overstimulation, my body bowing.

I let my shirt fall back into place, blinking several times before the bathroom came into focus, then took my time licking my hand clean. My mouth went slack and I met my blissed-out reflection in the mirror, any remnants of the man riddled with pain nowhere to be found.

Looking past myself, I noticed the bedroom door was ajar. Panic replaced satiation as I thought back on whether or not I'd closed it after peeking into the hall. Had I? I *had*, I was almost positive of it.

Snatching my towel up off the floor, I wrapped it around my hips and rushed into the room to close it.

"Damnit." I tapped my forehead against the wood, then pushed away, hurrying to get cleaned up and dressed before stepping into the hall.

Ryan's door was shut. I tiptoed over and rested my ear against it, hoping for some sign that he wasn't awake. While I was concerned about the possibility of him having seen me jerk off, there were other things to be seen that worried me even more. I'd had a shirt on, but the front had been lifted to my mouth. Had that caused it to hike up enough to provide a partial view of my back? Even a small portion of it on display would've been too much.

I gazed down at my pant covered legs like I could see the skin of my inner thighs through them, wondering if from my doorway he would've been able to see them too. My legs were spread wide enough, but the scars—although raised—blended in with the color of my skin. I couldn't even remember the excuse I'd given Xavier for them. Whatever it was, the pitying look on his face said he hadn't believed me.

Thankfully the medication prevented me from spiraling into an overthinking frenzy. That would only hold until it wore off, though.

Grabbing a bottle of water from my mini-fridge, I settled into the chair on my bedroom balcony, sipping as the city lights and sounds kept me company. The air still smelled of petrichor, but the fog from earlier had evaporated.

I thought back on the note Ryan had written. ***Soree.*** I thought about how it oddly felt like he'd spoken to me for the first time. My heart ached with wanting him to speak to me again. I'd assumed his silence boiled down to a trust issue—which could still be true. I figured he'd eventually say something after getting used to me. I hadn't once considered that maybe he just didn't talk at all. That he'd lost his voice, in the literal or figurative sense, because of whatever trauma he'd gone through.

Now that my mind had made room for something other than guilt and misery, a bright idea came to me. I jumped up, nearly knocking over the small table holding my water in my mad dash back into the bedroom.

Entering the walk-in closet, I beelined for the back of it where my satchel hung on a hook. Flipping it open, I tugged free the pad of paper it held, then rifled around the inner pockets for a pen. I came away with a pencil. *Good enough.*

Back on the balcony, I kicked my feet up on the railing, pencil poised over a fresh sheet of paper, wondering what to say. I'd start by addressing his apology.

Don't be sorry, I wrote, then put his version of the word in parentheses so he knew what I meant. Hopefully doing so wouldn't offend him. I didn't think he was stupid. Far from it.

I got back to my letter. ***I was the one who did something wrong.*** I paused, taking a deep breath before writing the last part. ***I shouldn't have left you.***

I wasn't sure if he'd be able to read any of this, but I took a chance. Whatever he didn't understand, I hoped he'd allow me to help him with.

I slipped the pad and pencil under his door, careful to be quiet about it in case he was asleep. Returning to my room again, I spent a couple more peaceful hours on the balcony, enjoying the late summer breeze. It was after midnight when I began to feel tired. A good tired, not a brain-in-overdrive tired. I looked forward to getting the best sleep I'd had all week.

Halfway to the bed I heard a rustling sound at the door. Ryan was on the other side of it shoving the note pad underneath. Shock overtook my body, locking me in place. Deep down I hadn't believed I'd get a response, and definitely not this late. For all I knew I still hadn't received a reply. Maybe he'd seen my note on the way to the bathroom and decided to return it unanswered.

Keeping quiet, I waited until he'd gotten it all the way through, and until

I heard the faint click of his door closing, before crossing the room to scoop it up. A good chunk of the pad was missing, as though he'd torn out several pages after trying over and over again to get his reply right. Had he spent the last two hours on this?

My brows dipped at the single word on the paper.

Chikin.

"*Chikin,*" I whispered in confusion, my frown disappearing when the misspelled word sounded exactly as it would have spelled correctly. *Chicken.* But I tried to relate that back to what I'd written to him and couldn't. Had he misread what I wrote?

Sitting on the edge of the bed, I turned the word over in my head, searching for some hidden meaning. *Chikin.* I perked up, remembering when I'd spoken to him through his door earlier, trying to lure him out. I'd babbled about my mother's impending visit, asking if there was any food he liked in particular—as if he'd answer me. He hadn't.

I read the word again and smiled. *Chikin.* Retrieving the pencil he'd returned, I began writing.

Chicken is the best. I spelt it properly. ***What else do you like? She can cook just about anything.***

I snuck it under his door, feeling like a kid as I slid under the covers and turned my lamp off. The anticipation of hearing from him again made it impossible to fall asleep, so I'd still been wide awake when the rustling sound returned over an hour later.

There was only one sheet of paper attached to the backboard of the notepad now. I'd need to order a bulk supply, stat. With dizzying excitement, I read the short list he'd scribbled and could almost picture him doing so with the utmost focus and concentration.

There were a couple of things I noticed right away. He'd written within the lines this time, his words no longer bleeding above or below them. He'd also spelled chicken correctly. He learned fast.

Chicken.

Beens.

Ryss.

Potayto.

I hurried to my satchel again, praying I had another pad of paper in there. I carried them around constantly, as work inspiration tended to strike me at the most inconvenient times. I struck gold.

Too impatient to go back into the room, I wrote on top of my chest of drawers.

I like beans and rice too. Not a huge fan of potatoes, though. What's your absolute favorite meal?

Sliding it under his door, I decided to give sleep a real try this time. It helped knowing I'd hopefully have something good to wake up to. I couldn't blame the smile making my cheeks ache on the white pill I'd taken earlier that night. It was almost two in the morning. The effects of it would've worn off by now.

CHAPTER 6

William

Sunny days made owning a high-rise apartment worth the hefty price tag. The yang to that yin was that dreary days felt all the more depressing from this high up.

We were on our fifth consecutive day of rain, and any respite we'd had since Ryan arrived didn't come with a break in the clouds. Still, I moved about the kitchen whistling a cheerful tune while Ryan showered after having slept in that morning.

I hadn't woken up to another note from him, even though I'd taken my odd dreams filled with ancient quills and rolls of parchment as a sign that there would be. I'd opened my eyes with a start, sitting straight up in bed, my gaze going to the floor. It was a wonder I'd gotten any sleep at all. I'd been highly conscious of our exchange even within my dreamscape.

I placed an order for more writing materials and groceries before climbing out of bed to get my day started with an at-home workout. Two hours later, I met the delivery guy at the door, and with nothing left to do but wait for Ryan to emerge from his room, I got started on breakfast.

He liked to observe, but I'd gotten some chicken tenders and fries I wanted to surprise him with. If we could eat bagels for dinner, then why not chicken for breakfast? Not burning the place down in the process would be the trick. I didn't have a good track record with stoves.

Slipping the package of precooked tenders and fries into the preheated oven, I set about putting the rest of the groceries away and tidying up.

Twenty minutes later, the timer dinged. I grabbed the mittens, hoping I'd followed the directions correctly.

The tenders were a bit too crispy along the edges, but were otherwise golden as pictured. The fries were soft in some places and hard in others. I took another look at the cooking instructions for both, cursing under my breath. The fries needed to cook longer than the chicken. I should've had them baking first, or maybe went with the option to fry. I bit down on a soft end and nodded. They weren't perfect, but they were edible.

I got everything plated, and had just placed Ryan's food on his side of the island when he appeared at the kitchen's archway. He'd tied his damp hair away from his face, making his surprise more evident.

"Hey," I said, my mood brightening further, despite my nerves. Ryan looked from the food to me, his gaze turbulent. I couldn't tell if that was a good thing. "I know you like to watch..." I trailed off when his sudden blush and swift turn of his head confused me. Then I recalled the incident in my bathroom last night. He'd seen me.

My words took on a whole new meaning then. Dread and disgust filled me as I contemplated the old wounds on my body again, wondering if he'd seen them from his vantage point outside the door. It was highly unlikely, but that was how shame and paranoia worked. It made the impossible seem plausible. There was also the issue of him witnessing the act in itself. Had he stuck around for it all? Did it trigger him in some way? I still didn't know what he'd been through. Did it scare him? And if he *had* seen it through to completion, if it *hadn't* triggered or scared him... Then what had it done to him? I didn't allow myself to contemplate that answer.

"I wanted to surprise you." I went back to the meal I'd prepared. "I made something different. Hopefully it's edible. The fries are...okay."

Ryan continued to stare at the food.

"I can taste it first. Prove there's nothing more than flour and way too much salt in there."

Ryan's gaze returned to me, his cheeks crimson free, his jaw now set like stone. He seemed angry. At himself? At me? My smile ebbed as he took a step back, and continued to fade with each backward step until he was gone, taking whatever joy I'd found with him.

I stared at the empty space he'd left behind, asking myself what I'd done wrong. I wanted to believe it was something to do with the food. Or maybe his embarrassment over my unintentional double entendre. Something told me the truth was much worse than that, though. I couldn't help feeling like Ryan saw my momentary lapse into happiness and decided to punish me for it.

WE DIDN'T COMMUNICATE over the next four days. I spent most of my time upstairs working in the studio while Ryan made the library his home. For three of those days he made his own bagel and waffles. The loss of that role affected me more than I'd have liked to admit. Preparing his meals made me feel needed in a way I hadn't experienced in a long while, and he'd taken that from me.

Him having the power to do that made me realize I'd lost sight of the main objective. To get him to Safe Haven. He needed to see a doctor, needed to talk to someone licensed and equipped to deal with his trauma. He needed to start rebuilding his life. *I* needed him to start rebuilding his life.

Today he hadn't eaten at all. Earlier, I'd waited as long as I could before tapping on the library doorway to ask if he was hungry.

"It's almost dinner time and you haven't eaten anything today."

He'd been sprawled out on the floor, books and reams of paper surrounding him as he traced letters with resolute concentration. He scowled at me, making no move to get up. I broke first, walking away.

My emotions were tethered to those of the people around me. How someone else felt usually dictated how I felt. I'd always been that way. It was something I constantly worked on. I had another side too. A side that lashed out when hurt, or when my overthinking grew to a breaking point where I said "fuck it," not giving a damn about anyone or how they felt. Those moments were closely followed by remorse, and an even deeper dive into self-dissecting. Was I wrong? Were they right? I could feel one of those moods coming on as midnight approached and Ryan still hadn't eaten or given me the time of day.

After picking at a couple pieces of the bland tenders still in the fridge, I decided to go to Ryan and speak honestly instead of stewing over how things were. I had to be the one to keep making the effort, and I wouldn't get any sleep knowing he still hadn't eaten, and that it was likely because of me.

He sat at the window seat now, huddled over a notebook. I watched him from the dark hallway, the dim light above the closest bookshelf to him extending over his top half. He guided his pencil in slow, careful strokes over the sheet of paper, his brows drawn together in concentration.

Suddenly I didn't want to interrupt him, but the floorboard creaked when I took a step back. His head turned in my direction, trapping me with his hostile gaze. His expression blanked, as though he didn't want to give me anything, not even his rage. As though he knew I craved anything other than indifference.

I entered, drawing in closer than usual. His features didn't shift, he didn't recoil in the slightest, but the hand holding the pencil to paper trembled. I inched back once the lead tip snapped, not proud of myself for needing a sign that he cared. Even if he only cared about keeping me away.

"Something went wrong between us," I said, "and I don't know what it was."

Ryan didn't seem moved by my words. I sighed, slipping my hands in my pockets. I cleared my throat, continuing with the truth this time.

"Actually, I think I have a good idea. The thing is, I have a habit of over analyzing things and creating scenarios in my head that don't exist." I waved a hand at my head before pocketing it again. "I don't know if I can trust what my brain says is wrong." Looking at him made me feel seen in both good and bad ways. Like he understood me but also hated me because of it. It was a feeling I couldn't explain, or maybe I could if I wasn't afraid to.

His large, black eyes burned with something old and familiar, something that took me back to a time I hated to remember, but couldn't stop myself from reliving every day. It would've been easier for us both if I hadn't let him in. If I'd left him in Davidson's hands that day at the hospital.

My heart rejected that thought the moment it filtered down to it. He was here for the same reason the others had been. Ryan served a purpose. A purpose I'd been running toward for as long as I could remember.

"I got excited when you wrote back to me the other night," I whispered, careful not to let a sad smile break free. Sad or not, I now felt protective of any small amount of joy I possessed, of showing any emotion that could be confused with happiness in any way. The fiery hate in his gaze faded a bit. Or maybe that was wishful thinking on my part.

"I can't recall the last time I'd felt... happy," I said, for lack of a better word that would've put me somewhere neutral. "You saw that didn't you?"

Ryan dropped his gaze to the scribble on his notepad, as though he had seen it and felt terrible about it. I took that as confirmation, feeling bolder now that I knew my inner voices hadn't been playing tricks on me.

"I think it offended you, or upset you. Maybe even scared you. I can only imagine why."

His fingers curled around the notebook's spiral binding. I pondered if his reaction was out of anger at me having it all wrong, or fear because I'd gotten it right. Because if I had gotten it right, then that meant I saw him too, that our understanding of each other went both ways. I could see how that would be scary when I sensed we both would rather hide.

"My brain settled on a conclusion," I went on, walking to a shelf to grab a book I wasn't the least bit interested in. I just needed to move, needed to remove myself from his line of sight, needed to hold something in my hands to stave off the strange desire to touch him. Maybe if my fingers were busy with something else, they wouldn't want to reach out to him.

Cursing my cowardice, I shoved the book back in its slot, returning to my spot a few feet away from him. Some things were worth facing directly, worth squirming through.

"You were happy too," I said. "But maybe you can't trust that happiness. Or you don't want to. Maybe you hadn't realized our guards were lowering until then, and now yours are back up again."

Ryan twisted away from me, staring out the window now. I made do with his pained reflection.

"I get it. But I'm only trying to help you. You can stay as long as you like, Ryan, but it's been nearly two weeks. If you don't want my help, then what *do* you want?"

He didn't answer, didn't grab another pencil from the pile next to him to write down what he couldn't verbally say. Through the glass, I could see he'd reverted to his stoney mask.

I took a deep breath then I let it go. I'd done my best for the night. I'd try again tomorrow. "Just eat something before bed, will you? The tenders and fries aren't amazing, but at least it'll be something in your stomach. Zap them in the microwave for a minute or two, or make waffles and bagels. Just please, eat something."

His stomach growled, like it had before. It took every ounce of strength to turn away from the sound. A scary thought hit me then. Was he using his hunger as a weapon against me?

"Oh," I said, pausing at the doorway. "My mother's going to stop by for dinner in a few days. She agreed to make enough food to last a whole week." Still nothing. I hesitated before adding, "My business partner, Xavier, may join us. He's a good guy. Trustworthy. If his being here will be a problem for you, I can tell him not to come." Still nothing. I lowered my head and left.

I was halfway through the living room when the sound of paper ripping hit my ears. I waited for it to stop, but it continued on for some time, followed by labored breathing. *Don't,* I warned myself. *Don't turn back.* But what if he needed me? I remembered the state of the apartment when I'd returned from my run the other day and doubled back to the library.

Avoiding the creaky floor plank, I held my breath and approached the room. Ryan sat on the floor atop the mountain of torn paper he'd created. He'd wrapped his arms around his legs, his forehead lowered to his knees, his shoulders shaking. My heart reached for him, the ache in my chest intensifying. He seemed so broken. A bird without its wings.

I hurried to my bedroom before I got any stupid ideas about consoling him. Letting him see me right then would've been the worst thing I could've done to him.

After staring at my ceiling for what felt like hours, a shuffling noise at my door caught my attention. I sprung up, seeing a crumpled sheet of paper waiting for me.

I stood there reading the three semi-neat words, trying to sort through what it could mean.

Chicken tenders and fries.

Smoothing the paper out on the wall near the light switch, I tilted my head, squinting to make out everything that came before it. It was one of the sheets we'd written back and forth on many nights ago. Everything in me sank when I read the last thing I'd asked him. He hadn't responded to it then.

What's your absolute favorite meal?

The paper dropped from my numb hands as I realized my mistake.

Opening my door, I shuffled to the kitchen on shaky legs, pulling the saran wrapped pan of leftover chicken tenders and fries from the refrigerator before dumping it in the trash. Gripping the edge of the counter, I dropped my head forward, breathing through the panic and paranoia, failing at bringing an end to it.

Back in my room, with no memory of how I'd gotten there, I popped one of my pills. The ones that made the voices tired. I fell onto my bed, not bothering with turning off the lights, and waited impatiently for oblivion to take me away.

CHAPTER 7

William

"Momma," I sighed, stepping into the hall and scooping her off her feet into a bear hug. She grunted, unable to hug me back because her hands were ladened with grocery bags. Xavier often made fun of me for not outgrowing the term momma, but I never cared. It was comforting, made me think of cold nights sleeping in her warm arms when she couldn't afford to pay the heating bill. The word "Momma" meant safety and unconditional love, the epitome of everything she was.

She smelled like rose water and peppermint, a mix of her favorite perfume and candy. I inhaled, welcoming the feeling of home I only got when around her.

"Hi, baby," she squeezed out as I placed all five feet, two inches of her back on the ground. She dropped a peck to my cheek, and I straightened with a crooked smile knowing she'd left her lipstick stain behind. "I missed that smile." She graced me with one of her own. "Well, are you going to help me with these bags or what?"

"Oh, yeah." I shook my head, taking the bags from her.

Pushing inside the apartment, I stood against the door to hold it open for her. She stepped inside, looking me over with brown eyes almost as dark as her skin. I got my moss green eyes from my European father. My complexion was lighter than hers thanks to him too. I used to hate that I resembled him. Still did. But my mother never looked at me like all she saw was the man who'd abandoned her in the delivery room.

After confirming I looked whole and healthy—at least on the outside—she peered down the hall.

"He's in the shower. He knows you're coming, but I didn't mention you were a therapist."

My mother once dreamed of being a Chief Nursing Officer, but I hadn't been the only one inspired to change direction after life had its way with us. She specialized in family therapy, which didn't make her an ideal candidate to work with Ryan. It wasn't what she was here for anyway. She was good with people. Good at making them feel comfortable, safe. I hoped she could crack Ryan's shell a little bit. Maybe help me with getting him to give Safe Haven a chance.

"You're here to feed us." I held the bags up.

"I won't lie to him," she warned. "If he asks, I'll tell him the truth."

"Trust me, he won't ask you anything."

She frowned at my remark, her gaze brimming with concern. I should've told her everything the last time we spoke, but I hadn't realized then that Ryan being non-verbal went deeper than him not wanting to speak to me. I still didn't fully understand it. Maybe he'd speak to her. "What aren't you telling me, William?"

Sighing, I glanced toward Ryan's closed door before gesturing with my chin for her to continue to the kitchen.

Setting the bags on the counter, I spotted a whole chicken in one of them. At least it wasn't tenders. "He hasn't spoken. I'm not sure if he can."

She slipped out of her blazer, setting it on the back of one of the stools before crossing her arms. "There could be a number of reasons for that. I'd need to spend more than an evening with him to be sure."

"This isn't a session," I said. "I don't want him to feel like he's being observed, but..."

"But you want me to observe him."

"Yeah, basically."

She patted my cheek, something she'd been doing since I was a boy.

"Is Davidson coming?"

"No, but Xavier might stop by." As soon as I said it I realized I'd forgotten to tell him he could come over. I'd told him I'd let him know. My mother seemed intrigued by the news. "We work together. That's all."

"Does he know that?" She strolled over to the pill bottle I'd left on the counter in my rush to let her in. I'd been about to take one. I groaned inwardly, not knowing which was worse, her probing me about my love life, or her worrying about my mental health.

"You're taking these again?" She was no longer concerned about me and Xavier. Her gaze and her tone were soft, her profession making her good at hiding her fear for me.

"Work's been stressful," I lied, as if I didn't know she'd see right through me.

She moved in closer, her heels clicking on the floor. "Work is what you usually do to *relieve* stress." She eyed my facial expression. I kept it as neutral as possible. "What's really going on, baby? Is this about—"

"No," I cut in harshly, not wanting to hear her utter the words. Exhaling, I planted a kiss on her forehead in apology before whispering, "I already have a therapist. I just need you to be my mother."

"Mothers care, you know." She swatted my chest when I gave her a who-are-you-trying-to-fool look. She'd been well on her way to doctor-mode, and we both knew it.

"I'm fine," I tried to assure her. She gave me her own skeptical look. The sound of a door opening saved me. We turned in the direction of the hall, and a moment later Ryan's head nervously peeked into view, the rest of him becoming visible soon after.

We stared at each other, and maybe his silence rubbed off on me because I couldn't locate my words. He wore a pair of charcoal slacks and a white button down. The two top buttons were undone. I'd ordered him a decent number of items for any occasion just in case. Better to be prepared than not. I hadn't expected him to dress up for dinner, though.

He'd slicked his hair back, his cheeks still rosy from the shower. It always took time for him to cool down. I often wondered how he still had skin on his bones when I imagined the molten lava degree of the water he bathed under. It was almost as if he were trying to burn something away. Something that went beyond skin deep. Something he couldn't quite get to.

I felt underdressed in my loose, paint splattered jeans and threadbare t-shirt. This wasn't a formal dinner, but I guess he didn't know that, and I didn't think to mention it. I'd felt lucky enough that he hadn't had a fit about her coming over. Good thing my mother was wearing her work clothes. It made it so I was the oddball out, not him.

"Guess we're being left to make introductions for ourselves," my mother said, eyeing me with mock disappointment. "I promise you I raised him with manners." She smiled over at Ryan. "I'm Maxine. Most people call me Maxie, though." She didn't wait for him to answer. Didn't put him in a position where he'd feel rude or embarrassed by his limitations. "You must be Ryan. I hope you're hungry, because I brought enough food to feed a village." She shooed me out of the way to get to the bags of groceries. "How about you help me get started, Ryan. Let's place the veggies in one pile, and everything else in another pile."

Gratitude consumed me. I hadn't gotten around to mentioning that he liked to watch his food being prepared, but it seemed she knew the one way to get him to warm up to her was to get him involved.

"You look nice," I said, emerging from my brain fog to compliment him before adding "You both do," because I didn't want it to seem weird that I'd singled him out.

Ryan ran a hand down his shirt, then looked me up and down.

"I, ah, haven't gotten dressed for dinner yet."

"Chop, chop," my mother said to Ryan, her urgent tone meant to activate him. She'd used it on me enough as a child for me to know. "Everyone's got to work for their food. Mr. No-manners over there brought the bags inside, so I suppose he's done his part." She lowered her voice to a conspiratorial whisper as Ryan made his way to the opposite end of the counter. "I wouldn't trust him to do more than that, to be honest. If it can't go in a toaster, he can't make it." She winked, and Ryan's mouth softened at the corners.

Ryan started unloading the bags, reluctantly at first, then with more confidence when my mother began to hum, seemingly ignoring him as though she trusted him to do his part. I knew she was fully aware of him and already gathering information for her hypothesis.

I stepped out of the kitchen, then waited until I'd caught her eye to beckon her over. She said something to Ryan, probably telling him she'd be right back, before heading toward me.

"Don't tell him anything I wouldn't," I murmured. I gave her resulting saccharine smile a stern look.

"If you were my patient," she muttered under her breath, "we'd be bound by this pesky little thing called doctor-patient confidentiality. As it stands, I'm just a mother who'll use every opportunity to brag about her son." She patted my cheeks and headed back into the kitchen, starting up a one-way conversation with Ryan, who had already created three piles.

"So, I hear you love chicken," she said to him as I made my way to the library.

SETTLING ONTO MY desk chair, I booted up my computer, deciding to kill time by tackling my emails. I'd been avoiding my inbox. There were numerous messages, most of them marked urgent and leaving me unsure where to start. I took a deep breath, fighting the anxiety churning in my gut.

I filtered by sender, choosing to go through the correspondence from my agent first. I knew Mihaela's emails would be work related, which at this point in time equated to stress. I didn't want anything taking me away from home. *Away from Ryan.* He needed me, and I needed that more than my next "big deal."

All things related to Freedom Fighters would lift my spirits, so I'd save those emails for last. I called them my stress relievers. Stress first, relief later.

Mihaela's enthusiasm bled through her message. Every sentence ended with an exclamation mark, and she used phrases like "once in a lifetime opportunity," and "more money than you could count." All of which she knew typically motivated me, but not for the reasons she believed.

Once in a lifetime opportunities led to more exposure, which ultimately led to me making more money. But it was all done to grow my foundation. It enabled me to do more, to bring higher awareness to the cause, which aided in the recovery of the missing and the taken. Finally, it allowed us to provide the resources they needed to thrive in spite of what happened to them.

According to the email, Foxhound Studios had received the green light and funding needed to move forward with what would no doubt be the next box-office record breaker. They'd signed Dillan Malben—the latest Hollywood heartthrob—to play the starring role.

"The studio heads and director would like to fly you out to L.A. ASAP for a meeting! Can you believe this?!"

Falling back in my seat, I rubbed at my temples. They wanted me to drop everything and hop on a plane? I couldn't do it, the idea threatened to send me into a spiral. What would I do with Ryan? I couldn't kick him out, and he wouldn't stay here alone.

I bypassed taking a look at the attached premise for the story. It wouldn't have changed my mind. I hit reply, fingers flying over the keys as I extended my gratitude for having been considered for the opportunity. I cited a conflict with a similar project I was set to start with a competing studio as my reason for graciously declining.

I hit send, realizing too late that I'd replied to all. Xavier had been copied on the email.

"Fuck," I bit out. I hadn't even thought about him. I'd made the decision without consulting him first. This wouldn't go over well. And I'd lied. There was nothing keeping me from accepting the job offer, or at least from taking the meeting.

Mihaela would see right through it too. After all, she'd have been the first to know about a conflict, because she would've been the one who'd brokered that deal.

"Get your head on straight, William," I snapped at myself, then decided to worry about the blowback later.

I skipped past the other work related emails—having reached my stress limit—and opened the one from my foundation's Chief Financial Officer. The subject read "Freedom Fighters - updates."

We'd received another sizable donation. Our third one that week. My budding headache began to recede.

The next email contained Safe Haven specific news. Construction on the rooming expansion would be completed earlier than expected. We'd be able to house more people now, and for longer periods of time. The second phase of construction would start on the other end of the property soon after.

The following email came from the head of the foundation's public relations department, reminding me of the upcoming charity gala. We had one every year. I pulled up the calendar. We were seven weeks out.

Before I knew it, an hour had passed, and the library was filled with the hearty scent of roasted chicken with herbs and spices. My mouth watered and my stomach rumbled, the delicious smell pulling me away from my computer.

My mother's soft voice stopped me before I turned the corner leading out to the living room and kitchen area. I crossed my arms and leaned against the wall, my heart warming as I listened to her talk to Ryan as she worked.

"I worry about him sometimes," she said, then amended, "make that *all* the time—but don't tell him I said so. Me worrying about him too much makes him pull away. I hardly see him enough as it is."

I straightened. *Did* her worrying cause me to pull away? I'd never looked at it that way. In my mind staying away equated to putting a shield around her. It meant she'd be protected from my darkness. I'd never viewed it from her perspective. Did she feel left out of my life? I rounded the corner, able to see them now, even though they couldn't see me.

"The worrying starts the moment you become a parent," she continued, then paused to show Ryan how to cut the potatoes correctly. "Your turn. There you go," she praised. "The smaller they are, the quicker they'll boil. So, what was I saying? Oh yeah," she said after a few seconds with no response from him. She asked him questions knowing she wouldn't get a reply. Instead of accepting he wouldn't speak, she kept the opportunity open for him to do so if he decided to.

"Parental angst is what I call it. Now that I think about it, it actually started for me the moment the drug store pregnancy test came back positive." Her wry chuckle ended with a sigh, as though the conversation had taken her back to those hard times.

"Do you think your parents worry about you, Ryan? About where you are?" She gazed at him the way she did when seeing me in someone else's child. The kitchen went silent. No more knives striking cutting boards, no more drawers opening and closing.

He wasn't going to answer her. I knew that, but I still tightened my arms around myself in vain hope, even if his answer was no. I feared the pounding of my heart would give away my presence.

My mother moved over to the sink, rinsing her hands, blocking my view of Ryan. "Well," she began, "how about I worry about you then? Would that be okay?"

My heart lurched in my chest. Had he answered her? Had it been a whisper? Something so low my straining ears hadn't heard it? Had he mouthed it? Shaken his head—something I'd never seen him do. Or had she come to her own conclusion? I craned my head to try and see him, but she still stood near the sink.

"Good," she said, an evident smile in her voice. He must have nodded, because I definitely hadn't heard anything that time, unless his whisper hadn't made it past the drumroll of anticipation in my head. "Now you have two people worrying about you. Two people who care." She let that sink in before lowering her tone. "You know, when Malcolm was a boy—"

"Who's Malcolm?" My voice was a little too loud and panicked when I marched into the kitchen. The warning masked as a question was for her, but my eyes were on Ryan. His body language told me nothing and he went back to cutting the potatoes. I worked on keeping my expression respectful, while showing my displeasure as I turned to my mother. She answered with a knowing look.

She wouldn't have said anything private, anything I wouldn't want her to. But sometimes what seemed innocuous to one person, could be the missing piece to someone else's puzzle. Ryan had enough to deal with. He didn't need someone else's traumatic childhood baggage added to his plate. At least not certain parts of it.

"*William,*" she stressed, before adopting her usual carefree tone again. "See," she said to Ryan, patting my cheek in reassurance before heading for the oven, "I told you he'd be in here any minute now asking for an ETA on dinner."

"Hey, I haven't asked," I feigned offense, keeping my eyes on Ryan. He seemed intent on keeping his off of me. "But now that you mentioned it..."

My mother laughed, basting the chicken before shutting it back into the oven. "Soon you heathen. Now go set the table and..." she looked at my casual attire, "get dressed for dinner." She winked, knowing I'd had every intention of sitting at the dinner table like this before seeing Ryan all dressed up.

"Now, let's get those potatoes in the water," she said to Ryan as I backtracked the way I'd come and went into the dining room.

Rummaging through the buffet drawers for the utensils and fancy dishware, I made fast work of getting the table set before taking a quick shower and changing. My phone rang as I'd been about to head back to the kitchen. It was the concierge desk letting me know I had a visitor. *Xavier. Shit.*

I gave the okay to send him up, clicking the module that would unlock my private elevator before hurrying into the vestibule to wait for him.

"Hey, I was going to call you," I started, jumping right into damage control as soon as the elevator doors opened. He'd likely seen the email to Mihaela, and would soon realize my mother was here for dinner. The dinner he was potentially supposed to be invited to.

"Were you?" he asked in a cynical tone. "How dare you decline an offer that big without consulting me first. What the hell is going on with you, William?"

"Will you lower your voice," I hissed, peering over my shoulder at the ajar apartment door.

"Sorry." He continued in a less hostile, hushed tone. "Foxhound Studios? This is a big deal. Why would you lie about a conflict?" He sounded as if he truly wanted to understand. He always sounded like he wanted to understand me.

"I can't drop everything and fly off for a meeting. Not right now. I have obligations here."

Xavier glanced at the door, knowing exactly what I meant by obligations. Knowing *who* I meant. "What about me, William? For fuck's sake, what about *you*?" He flung a hand in my direction.

"I'm fine."

He'd been referring to my dreams, to the ambitions I once had, not my wellbeing. Those dreams and ambitions were only there to facilitate the ultimate goal, though. Freedom Fighters would always come first. He couldn't understand that, because he didn't know why.

"Look at where you came from, and look at where you are now. You overcame hardships and adversity to get here, and yet you sometimes treat this like it was easy. Like you can take or leave it."

I didn't come from a life of money and privilege. I grew up in a single parent household in a crime infested neighborhood. I had to work twice as hard, be twice as good as some of the other applicants vying for a coveted spot at Berklee College of Music. All things he'd heard me say in an acceptance speech. Acting as if none of that mattered now seemed to offend Xavier.

"Look, I'll give Mihaela a call. You know she hasn't gotten back to them yet. She'll try to twist my arm before turning the studio down. I'll agree to a virtual meeting, and if the terms sound alright, I'll negotiate for you to take the lead on this."

Xavier's mouth parted in surprise. "You would do that?"

"I would." No reason for him to suffer because of me, and he'd been working hard for a chance like this. He deserved it. "Are you ready?"

"Yes," he said with confidence. He wasn't, but I'd help him as much as I could.

"You'll need work on your—"

"I will. I won't let you down."

"I know."

He looked at me as if I'd hung the moon, and I felt like I'd done something good for once in my life. I also felt guilty because of what else lurked behind his smile. Something intimate I couldn't return.

Xavier sniffed the air, his lighter disposition faltering. "Have they invented chicken flavored waffles?" he asked with a dose of sarcasm.

"Oh, ah..." I looked at the door again. "My mother's cooking dinner. That's also why I'd been about to call you. Because you were invited."

Xavier folded his arms. "Would've been nice to be told I was invited."

"I could've sworn I told you already. Did you not get my message?"

"No."

"Huh," I feigned confusion. "Maybe I forgot to hit send. I told my mother you'd be here. And Ryan. I told him too."

Xavier huffed a disbelieving laugh. "You've always been a shitty liar."

If only that were true.

Right then my mother pulled the door open, eyes beaming when she saw Xavier. "Xavier!" she called. "You're finally here. William said you'd be coming."

Xavier's expression turned apologetic. I could've picked her up and spun her in my arms at that moment. Instead, I settled for mouthing, "*thank you.*"

They shared hellos and hugs. "Alright, come on now. Dinner's getting cold."

Ryan was setting the bowl of mashed potatoes in the center of the table when we entered the dining room. He looked between Xavier and me, but otherwise showed no sign of curiosity or uneasiness with him being here.

"Ryan, this is Xavier. Remember I told you about him? We work together."

Ryan said nothing, of course, but his eyes did drop to my shoulder—the one that brushed Xavier's because of how close he stood next to me. I scooted over a bit. My mother noticed.

"Xavier, this is Ryan."

"Nice to meet you, Ryan."

Ryan hadn't taken his eyes off my shoulder, as if it were somehow tainted now. His dark eyes flicked up to mine, a battle waging behind them before he opted to take a seat, ignoring Xavier's pleasantries.

"Sit, you two," my mother said, settling into a chair herself and gesturing for us to take the seats across from her and Ryan. She'd left an unoccupied spot between them. She said grace, and then ordered everyone to dig in.

Things were tense, and I didn't know why. My instincts said it had to do with Xavier being here, but I couldn't say for sure. Ryan being angry and withdrawn could've just been par for the course. He behaved the same way when we were alone.

The awkward silence worsened as time moved on. Ryan pushed his food around his plate, Xavier kept sneaking glances at him as though he were some science experiment, and the nerves in my stomach had waged an assault on me. The only one who seemed unaffected was my mother. She had years of experience at remaining cool under pressure, though.

I did wonder why she hadn't stepped in to fill the void of conversation. She must have had her reasons. I noticed her keeping tabs on Ryan. She'd been observing us all. Her watchful eye was more subtle than Xavier's, though.

"So," Xavier said, deciding to cut through the tension. "I'm sure William has told you all about Safe Haven. Do you plan on visiting any time soon?"

I cut him a look he ignored.

"It's a great place," he said casually, taking a bite of chicken. Ryan looked up at him, his irritation obvious—at least to me. I'd become well versed in the nuances of his blank stares.

"Xavier," I muttered under my breath. He continued, ignoring the reprimand in my tone.

"I'm sure being around others who have similar stories to yours would be beneficial. Listening to their testimonials could go a long way in helping you."

"There's no rush," I said to Ryan, then turned to Xavier. "He'll go when and if he's—"

"Being cooped up in here can't be good for you," he spoke over me.

I dropped my utensils to my plate, facing him before biting out, "That's enough."

Xavier recoiled at my volatile tone. I'd never used it on him or in defense of him before, yet here I was wielding it for a man I barely knew. My reaction stung. I could see it in the dimming of his eyes, hear it in his shallow breaths. Our gazes were locked, and I didn't know where to go from here.

Xavier swallowed hard before addressing Ryan. "I, um... I'm sorry if I upset you. It wasn't my place to say all that."

Ryan shoved back from the table, shocking me as he stormed from the room. I stood to follow him, but my mother held up her hand, stopping me.

"Let him sort himself out," she said. "Sometimes a little time alone to think helps."

"What if he uses it to consider what Xavier said?"

She looked at me as though asking: Would that be such a bad thing? I lowered onto my chair, closing my eyes in embarrassment because the pitch of my voice suggested it would be a terrible thing. It revealed that there was more going on here. More going on with me. When I opened my eyes, she and Xavier were staring at me like they knew it.

Xavier's gaze held warranted pain and anger. My mother's gaze expressed a deep love and understanding. The only difference was she knew more about me than he did, but even still, she didn't know enough.

CHAPTER 8

William

"I'll let you know how my talk with Mihaela goes," I said as Xavier stepped onto the elevator, anger making me sound gruff. I was upset with him, but I was more upset with myself. He placed his hand on the doors, keeping them open.

"I know it wasn't my place to say—"

"No, it wasn't. You could have set him back."

"Are you saying he was close to leaving here?"

"Why are you in such a hurry for him to leave?"

"The real question is why aren't you?"

"I am," I snapped, "but it needs to be when he's ready, and not a moment sooner."

Xavier stepped off the elevator, letting the doors close behind him. He stared into my eyes as if searching for something he'd never been able to find before. Like maybe he'd give trying to figure me out one last shot. Everything he needed to know was right there. I carried it with me, rarely able to get a moment's rest from it. He just didn't know what to look for, so the truth would forever be an elusive thing to him.

"What about his family, hmm? I'm sure there's someone out there who misses him, who hasn't stopped looking for him. Do you even care about them? Have you asked him about them?"

"I..." I couldn't answer him. My answer would've been damning. I hadn't thought much about his family. I'd only been thinking about him. "He doesn't talk."

"How convenient," he drawled. "It's been weeks. Has he even gotten any fresh air? Gotten some sunlight? Or have you kept him trapped in this beautiful prison?" He waved a hand toward the apartment door.

"Sun?" I scoffed. "Have you seen the weather the last couple of weeks?"

"You get the point I'm trying to make, William. God, just take a moment to look at yourself. Have you asked yourself what it is you're doing here? Are you being honest with yourself?"

I set my jaw, speaking through clenched teeth. "I'm trying to help—"

"You're trying to fix them," he interrupted me. "You can't fix them, William. You can't save them all." He drew in closer, resting his hands on my stubbled cheeks whispering, "And they can't save *you*."

What he didn't realize was that I didn't need to save them all. I only needed to save *one*.

He pressed the call button, and the elevator doors opened. We watched each other until they closed, neither of us knowing what else to say.

I found my mother in the kitchen dishing food into Tupperware containers.

"I made enough to last a full week, as promised. And there's a whole chicken in the freezer already seasoned. Thaw it and pop it into the little rotisserie oven I got you whenever you're ready for it."

"Thank you." I kissed her forehead before loading the dishwasher. While we worked, she hummed the lullaby she used to sing to me when I was a kid. It always calmed me, even when I became too old for her to still be singing it to me. She hummed until my movements turned fluid, her voice putting me in a daze.

"They're all the same, you know. The survivors who come through here," she explained when I stopped wiping down the counter to shoot her a questioning look. "Even the ones who don't. They're all the same."

I leaned against the counter as I thought over that. "They look nothing alike."

"No, but the way they are drawn to you, is the same." She came around the island to stand near me. "Your mournful nature intrigues them. They see a kindred spirit when they look at you, and I think that makes you safe in their eyes."

Ryan possibly preferred me to the alternative, to being with a group of strangers versus one, to having to face reality over being able to lock himself in his room here. But drawn to me? Kindred spirits? For once I thought she may be wrong about something. I didn't stop to correct her, though. In truth, her words made me hopeful.

"Xavier obviously wants you to open up to him. Whatever battles he's faced, he wants to share them with you, and he wants you to share your scars with him. He's jealous that they get to know you in a way he doesn't, even if the truth is that they don't know you either. None of us do. Not really." She cupped my cheek to soften the sting. "I think for Xavier it's enough that you care about this part of your life more than you care about him. You wear your brokenness on your sleeve, but you keep the reasons why locked away in a place no one can reach."

I closed my eyes, finding sanctuary in her soothing touch. "I'm sorry," I whispered.

"I know, baby," she whispered back. "I know. Sometimes I still wonder if—"

"It wasn't your fault," I said resolutely, and not for the first, or even the hundredth time. "You were never the one to blame."

She nodded, clearing the emotion from her throat before taking the dish towel from me. She continued where I'd left off with wiping down the counter.

"Why didn't you jump in when Xavier was saying all those things to Ryan?"

"You didn't ask me here in an official capacity. It wasn't my job to mediate. And because sometimes it takes a little disruption to move things forward. You weren't going to be the driving force. You're too close to this. You always have been." She shrugged. "All in all, Xavier didn't say or ask anything harmful."

I had nothing to fight back with. "What should I do?"

Finishing up, she tossed the towel into the sink and rested her hip against the counter. "Do you want my professional, or personal opinion?"

"Depends. How much will your professional opinion cost me?"

She grinned. "For you it's free of charge." She sighed, both of us sobering. "I accidentally bumped into him while we were cooking earlier. I had to count him down from a panic attack, William."

"He doesn't like physical contact. I don't want to push him."

"All that's understandable, but it's time to set boundaries and encourage healthy compromises. He *needs* to talk to someone equipped to handle what he may have gone through."

"He doesn't speak," I reminded her.

"Talking isn't only defined by sound."

"I'll need to consult Merriam-Webster before agreeing to that statement."

She placed a hand on her hip, unimpressed by my obtuseness. "There are other ways to communicate, and you have some of the best therapists in varying practices on payroll at Safe Haven. Boundaries and healthy compromises," she repeated, and I nodded.

"Out of curiosity, what would your personal opinion have been?"

"The same," she said simply, grabbing her blazer off the back of the stool. I would have laughed under different circumstances. "Come on, walk me out."

"Are you sure you don't want to stay the night? Traffic out of the city is brutal at this time." My gaze lingered on Ryan's closed bedroom door as we made our way out of the apartment.

"I can't. I've got an early start tomorrow. I'd rather wake up knowing I only have a short walk to the office versus the almost one-hour drive in rush hour traffic from here. I'll text you when I make it home, baby." She kissed my cheek before the elevator doors closed.

I made my way up to the music studio, then poured myself a stiff drink at the bar cart in the corner. I spent a couple of hours there fine-tuning a few cues I'd needed to work on for weeks but hadn't. Now that Ryan and Xavier had been introduced, I didn't see any reason why he couldn't come over to finish work on this project. I could let him in from this level, avoiding Ryan all together, if need be. He didn't seem to like Xavier, but he didn't seem to like me much either, so there was that.

Figuring I'd given him enough alone time, I rubbed my tired eyes, refilled my drink and made my way downstairs. The moonlight guided my way through the darkened apartment, and I stopped short at finding Ryan's door open.

Stepping in, I whispered his name. No answer. The tangible emptiness in the room told me checking the bathroom and closet would've been pointless. It was the same palpable emptiness I felt whenever we were more than a dozen feet apart.

Closing in on his bed, I glanced hesitantly over my shoulder into the hallway. I didn't want to be on the receiving end of his glare if I was caught. Running a hand over the carved wooden footboard and grabbing hold of one of the posts, I scanned the room he'd made his own.

His pajamas were neatly folded on the nightstand, ready for when he returned for bed. I opened one of the drawers, my breath stuttering at the familiar strips of cotton inside. Setting my drink down, I picked them up and ran them through my fingers. Sorrow filled me. Did he still use these to chain himself at night? Or had he just forgotten they were in there? I wanted to strike a match and watch them burn, but it wasn't my place to. Not when doing so might have done more harm than good.

"He needs to talk to someone equipped to handle what he may have gone through."

Dropping them back into the drawer, I closed it.

The library would be the only other room he'd be in. He didn't ever hang out in the living room, and only spent time in the kitchen to eat. As expected, I found him on the window bench, a book in his hand and several in his lap. His brows were furrowed in what looked like equal parts concentration and frustration.

He knew how to read and write, if only at around a first or second grade level. Fluency, speed, spelling, good penmanship, and comprehending complicated text was where he struggled—from what I could tell by observing him, and from the notes we'd exchanged.

I'd downloaded a phonics tutor app on my phone for him. It would allow him to type words in from the various books he seemed to take interest in. The virtual assistant would then give the proper enunciation and definition. I hadn't told him about it yet, though. I didn't think he'd want my help. Or maybe because I wanted to be the one to personally teach him, if he'd let me.

He looked up from his book, the dark circles under his eyes adding color to his normally pale skin.

"You're tired," I said, an unintentional bite to my words. I hated seeing him sad or angry or scared. And apparently, I hated seeing him tired too. "You should get some rest." I'd softened my tone. "The books will be here tomorrow."

He gave no indication that my concern meant anything to him, but his gaze did lower to the tumbler I held.

"It's just a little something to help me relax." I managed not to sound ashamed or defensive—both of which I felt to my core.

He returned his midnight eyes to mine, and it took me clenching every muscle in my body to not squirm under his intense scrutiny. Slowly, he closed the book in his hand and set it to the side, doing the same with the others on his lap before unfolding his crossed legs and dropping his bare feet to the floor. He did this while peering into me, and again I couldn't help taking notice of his beauty.

Ryan did everything with so much passion. From the way he wrote, as though the blank page offended him, to the way he ate. Even down to the way he sometimes seemed to hate me. His scowls contained enough heat to singe the hairs off my body from across the room.

That passion gave him a sensual quality I was positive he wasn't aware of. The more fire he displayed, the more fascinating he became. I was beginning to find myself captivated by him, and he hadn't even spoken a word to me yet.

Speaking of which, I wanted to hear his voice more than I wanted my next breath. I had to know if his tone matched the soft appearance of his skin, and the delicacy of his cheek bones, or the exoticism of his beauty mark. I shouldn't have been wondering about any of that, but I couldn't help myself.

Ryan reached out, removing the tumbler from my hand, careful not to touch my fingers. He waited a few seconds—as if giving me time to object—before taking a tentative sip.

I couldn't have objected if I wanted to. Like him, I couldn't find my voice. He swallowed, his cheeks glowing red from the burn.

"It's rum and coke," I breathed, heart beating a staccato rhythm. "More rum than coke."

Other than the sweet color spreading over him, he hadn't flinched or winced. Perhaps being intoxicated wasn't new to him.

He took a more generous sip before handing it back to me and licking his lips. Something deep within me clenched, and I felt an overwhelming need to apologize for it.

I needed to clear the lump forming in my throat, but that reaction would've exposed how he'd affected me. "I ah... I'll let you get back to what you were doing." My feet didn't get the message, because I hadn't moved.

Ryan went back to his book, flipping to the dog-eared page he'd left off at.

"The Pain and the Great One," I read, angling my head to make out the title. "I used to love that as a kid. I never had a sibling, but I'm pretty sure if I had, I would've been The Pain." It was one of the new books I'd ordered for him. I'd left them somewhere easy for him to find rather than making an announcement about it. I had a feeling he would've avoided them out of spite if I had.

I'd been about to leave, but then he turned the book around, pointing to a word. "Ordinary," I said, taking a chance he wanted me to sound it out for him. "It means—"

Ryan slammed the book shut. I took it as him saying he hadn't asked me what it meant. When he was sure I understood the rules, he opened the book again, turning to a new page and pointing to a different word.

"Pokey," I said and stopped. This time, though, he kept his finger on the word long after. "It means slow, carefree, in a sense. Not at all moved by the demands of time."

He looked at the word, rubbing his finger over it as if he wanted the letters to seep into his skin, never to be forgotten again. We went through this a few more times, and I got good at knowing when to elaborate, and when to simply tell him how to sound out the word.

He picked up another book by the same author, and we continued on. I didn't dare smile, or show my amusement in any way for fear he'd do something to shut down my blip of happiness. Like maybe burn my library to the ground. In many ways he didn't trust me, and when it came to my rare declarations of joy, I didn't trust him either. Joy was such a fragile thing, and he'd already proven he had the power to rob me of it at will.

After a while he yawned, stacking all the books together and placing them back on the shelf. He glanced back at me like maybe he wanted to say something, but then his eyes filled with that familiar rage again. He left without so much as a wave goodbye. I stood there wondering about his anger, wondering if I should take it personal. No, it wasn't about me, I told myself. He'd be angry with anyone after what he must have survived. I was just lucky enough to be in his vicinity when he needed a punching bag.

I showered for the third time that day, shaving at the sink afterward, making a mental note to make an appointment with my barber. The mixed texture of my hair was starting to stick up straight in some places and coil in others.

Crawling into my enormous, empty bed, reminded me of my loneliness. If I wanted to, I could have called Xavier over, snuck him in while Ryan slept, and made love to him all night. My body craved that connection with someone, even if my heart would keep its distance throughout the whole ordeal. It had been too long, and I was starting to feel the effects of deprivation. I couldn't bring myself to do that to Xavier, though. Things were messy enough between us as it was.

Spitting into my palm, I reached into my briefs and withdrew my cock, already hot and hard. I bit down on my cheek to stifle my moans as I worked my shaft, moving closer to the crown. Swiping up the precum with my thumb, I envisioned a tight warm body on top of me, taking me to the hilt and whispering my name. The loneliness swelled further, until my skin felt like it might burst.

Needing this to be over with, I bent my legs and spread them wide to slip a finger from my free hand into my opening, stopping at the first knuckle and coming instantly. I couldn't even manage to get up to clean myself off. I pulled the sheet over me, letting the cotton absorb my cum.

I fell asleep with my teeth buried into my pillow, a precaution to keep from howling the name that haunted me every night now. It would always remain my dirty little secret.

THE NEXT MORNING, I awoke to a sheet of paper at my door. I hurried from the bed to snatch it up. It was a sketch. The most beautiful piece of artwork I'd ever seen.

It depicted a man facing the horizon, the sun exaggerated in the distance. Simple, yet no detail had been spared. Not his curls, his straight nose, nor the scowl he perpetually wore. He'd managed to capture it all, even in profile.

I backed up, falling onto the bed once the backs of my knees met the mattress. Too many things floated through my mind at once.

Ryan's an artist.

What does this mean?

Ryan's... an incredible artist.

What the fuck does this sketch mean?

Is he trying to tell me something?

Is it just a random sketch?

Am I overthinking this?

And finally... *Ryan's an artist.*

Then I remembered something Xavier said before leaving yesterday.

"Has he even gotten any fresh air? Gotten some sunlight? Or have you kept him trapped in this beautiful prison?"

Could it be... "No," I whispered, striding for the door, forgetting I wore nothing but the boxer briefs I'd fallen asleep in. I was too excited by the possibility of what this could mean to even remember to check if dry cum stained my chest. I pulled my door open with more force than needed. I exhaled shakily at what waited for me.

Ryan was sitting against the wall across from my room, dressed in the running gear I'd bought for him. He held a sheet of paper up, three words scrawled across it.

I want sun.

CHAPTER 9

William

Ryan climbed to his feet. He'd chosen to wear the compression tights I'd ordered him. The same ones I preferred to run in. I'd gotten him every option I could think of. Tights, shorts, pants, tanks, t-shirts. He likely picked the tights because the weather was changing. With the first day of fall a week away, the mornings were cooler. Or maybe he chose them for the same reason I did. To keep my legs hidden—one area on them specifically.

He wore the running shoes I bought for him too. I'd purchased them after checking the size of the battered shoes he'd worn here.

It took me a moment to realize he was looking me over. I'd been too consumed with taking him in to notice. I looked down at my chest, releasing a sigh of relief at finding it cum free. The bedsheet had absorbed all of it. My long-legged boxer briefs covered my inner-thighs, so that was one less thing to feel humiliated about.

I cupped my hands in front of my crotch. "Sorry. Give me a few minutes to get dressed."

Ryan met my eyes again, but there was nothing but mild boredom in his dark gaze. At least the sight of me hadn't traumatized him.

Mindful of being shirtless—and the other parts of my body I wanted to hide—I backed into my room, closing the door before turning for the bathroom.

I washed up quickly at the sink then brushed my teeth, hurrying before

Ryan had a chance to change his mind. He'd overheard my conversation with Xavier in the hall, which meant he had to be eavesdropping. Xavier's words lit a spark in him. They'd mattered for some reason. What about everything else Xavier said? Did that matter to Ryan too?

"I'm sure William has told you all about Safe Haven. Do you plan on visiting any time soon?"

He *should've* visited Safe Haven, and I should've wanted him to. I *did* want him to. So why couldn't I meet my own gaze in the mirror?

Not wanting to delay us any longer, I got dressed and strode out of my bedroom. Ryan wasn't in the spot I'd left him in.

Creeping down the hall, I listened for movement behind his closed door before finding him in the living room. He peered out over the darkened city, hands clasped behind his back. We were still an hour away from sunrise.

"Ready?" My question hadn't pierced through his thoughts. I understood being overwhelmed by thoughts. So consumed by them nothing outside of myself penetrated until they were done with me. I repeated the question louder this time. Still nothing. Did he not want to go anymore? Did the world outside scare him?

Since I couldn't count on him to verbally tell me what was wrong, I analyzed his body language. The hand clasping his wrist squeezed and released repeatedly, his lithe back and long legs tense. In the reflection of the glass I caught him watching me draw my own conclusions.

His lips pressed together in a thin line, as though he had a problem with me looking at him. Like he had a problem with me in general. We were playing this weird game of cat and mouse, it seemed. For every step forward we took, no matter how insignificant, we retreated two back. Or he did, at least. I was just the masochist puppet, my strings being yanked in multiple directions.

"We can take our time. I don't expect you to be marathon ready. We jog, we walk, we walk slower, or we stop altogether. So long as we get out, get some fresh air into our lungs, and start to move forward, it doesn't matter to me." Because we were stuck in place. "Can you do that?"

He turned to me, but gave me nothing else. I wanted to beg for a nod, a shake of his head, a mouthed "yes." Something. I wanted whatever he'd given my mother in the kitchen that for some odd reason felt like he was purposely withholding from me.

He swallowed, mouth parting to let out an unsteady breath. That small show of something would have to be enough.

I waited by the front door to give him space to make up his mind. I wanted to smile when he appeared at the other end of the hallway, then proceeded to meet me where I stood. Not wanting to find out what my show of excitement might cost me, I kept my expression clear.

The cool morning air ruffled his hair as we jogged along the West Side. Not my usual route, but foot traffic tended to be lighter, with mostly other runners occupying the pathway at this time of morning.

Cars whizzed by along the highway, but it seemed to be the people that concerned Ryan most. He couldn't relax until he'd confirmed, with enough glances over his shoulder, that whoever had jogged past us was no longer in view.

I kept our pace light, and within ten minutes he was panting loud enough to wake the dead. We walked briskly the rest of the way to the pier, making it there in time to see the sun make its way above the horizon. I hung back as Ryan eased toward the railing.

The moment matched his sketch, and my heart constricted when he reached his trembling hand toward the sunshine like he wanted to grab hold of it. He held his position as rush hour struck, blind to the students and working people zipping past to get to their destinations.

It was as if the darkness had cleared from his vision, and now he only had eyes for the light.

WE WENT OUR separate ways to shower and change when we got home, then I made us protein shakes—under his watchful eye. I tossed the package of waffles onto the counter when he looked at the freezer meaningfully.

"I guess your love for Eggo's trumps your love for my mother's chicken, huh? Don't worry, your secret's safe with me."

Opening the refrigerator next, I noticed three of the containers my mother stuffed with food were gone. "I take that back," I murmured. He must have binged them in the middle of the night. His appetite had returned in full force.

I heated up her leftovers for myself. I couldn't stomach another waffle or bagel. We ate in silence, as always. Everything with Ryan was done in silence, causing me to fixate on him, to obsess over his non-verbal signals.

"I was thinking," I began, going for light and casual even though my nerves were on edge. "Maybe I could help you with your reading and writing. If you want." I ripped a paper towel from the holder, wiping my mouth and fingers. Ryan glowered at me.

"I mean, you don't have to—"

He shoved his stool back, nearly knocking it over in his urgency to get away from me. I bit out a curse, pushing my plate aside and dropping my head into my palms.

I'd lost count of the seconds passed after reaching fifty, a semblance of stillness calming the overactivity in my head. Something hitting the island startled me. My eyes popped open on Michael Ende's *The Neverending Story.*

Ryan shifted his weight from one foot to the other, averting his gaze.

"This was my favorite book as a kid," I said, gliding my hand over the tattered cover. "It started my love affair with reading." Caught up in my nostalgia, I'd forgotten the number one rule.

Never say the wrong thing.

Breathing past the panic, I scanned his face for a sign that what I'd said meant something to him. I picked up on his indecision as his fingers twitched toward the book. I held on to it tighter.

"I've been wanting to read it again," I said, hoping he'd still want me to read it to him. I opened it to the first page, deciding to jump right in before he had a chance to disappear. He retreated from the kitchen before I could.

Instead of storming to his room, he went over to the couch and stood there waiting.

I scrambled to my feet and followed, sitting in the middle while he stared down at me. Ignoring his stunning, terror filled eyes, I started reading, my tone welcoming, my excitement hidden.

By chapter two he'd settled onto the edge of the couch, more than two arm lengths away. By chapter five he'd reclined onto the pillows, and by chapter eight he was close enough to lean over and point to words he didn't know the meaning of.

I took my time, enunciating everything because I wanted him to understand, but also because I didn't want the moment to end.

Before I knew it, the sun was setting and my mouth had gone dry from the length of time I'd spent reading aloud. Ryan slept curled up on his side, less than two feet away from me. I slipped the book onto the coffee table, then did the same with the notepad he'd gotten to fill with words and their definitions. I'd helped him write some down to save time.

Covering him with the throw, I watched him sleep for an unhealthy amount of time before closing myself into the music studio. I picked up the instrument I'd been avoiding for weeks. The instrument that had saved my life. The one I played in homage to someone special. Because of my hours just spent with Ryan, Bastien, Falkor and Atreyu... I was suddenly in the mood to play again. In the mood to remember why I'd begun playing to begin with.

RYAN WOKE UP the next morning too sore to get out of bed. He felt good enough to go for a jog the following morning, and was less sore than the first time after that. After a week we were able to sprinkle in a few thirty-second sprints. By the second week we had a well-oiled routine. We ran, he ate waffles while I ordered in, I read to him, and he wrote for a couple of hours before disappearing for his sacred alone time.

Having finished breakfast after our recent run, I cleaned up while he ventured to the library for a new book. We finished *The Lord of the Flies* yesterday. Ryan shared my love for the classics, he'd also reignited my love of reading. I'd returned to the tradition of keeping a book on my nightstand, and staying up way too late before drifting off with the open book still in my hand. I hadn't done that in a few years. Life had gotten too busy.

He returned this time with *Where the Red Fern Grows*. An idea hit me then.

"How about we switch things up and watch the movie version? It's pretty old, but I'm sure it's streaming somewhere." I closed the dishwasher as he thought about it. Didn't take him long to nudge the book he'd placed on the counter. His way of saying he'd rather not make any changes to the new system he'd come to depend on now.

"Let's give it a try," I encouraged. "I'll put the subtitles on, that way you can see the words as they speak them. It could help in a way listening to me read them can't." I wasn't sure about that, but it sounded good, and I needed to get him closer to the end goal.

"It's time to set boundaries and encourage healthy compromises. He needs to talk to someone equipped to handle what he may have gone through."

My mother's words trickled into my thoughts. She'd called to check on us a few times now, and every time she asked if we'd gone to Safe Haven yet, my answer had been no.

Thankfully, securing the contract with Foxhound Studios for Xavier had bought me an extension on his patience with our unfinished project. But with our deadline looming, his patience would wear thin again. I'd told him he could come by for a work session next week. I still hadn't mentioned it to Ryan.

He tapped the book cover, making his preference clear.

"Okay, but I'm going to have the movie going on mute, just in case you change your mind." I snatched up the book and went into the living room, opening the coffee table drawer for the remote. I found the movie, got the subtitles going, and muted it as promised.

We were maybe a few chapters in when from my peripheral I noticed his attention shift from me to the movie, then back again. This continued while I read. The stints of time he spent listening to me shortened until it became clear I was reading to myself. I quieted, unmuting the TV when Ryan got to his feet and moved closer to it. He stayed there until the last credit rolled and the screen went black.

The next day I offered him caramel popcorn while we watched *Glory*. He turned it down with a cute scrunch of his nose. It took three more nights and a Denzel Washington marathon to get him to give it a try. I'd had to order more by the boatload after that.

Ryan hated change. Every new idea clashed with his resistance, but I came to realize he could be reasonable. If my explanation for the change made sense, he'd come around. Not instantly, but still. Also, some alone time did wonders for his stubbornness. I waited a couple more days before proposing something else. Something big. Something I knew he'd hate.

We were rained-in again, so we didn't take our morning run. I spent time checking in with Freedom Fighters, and finally returning Davidson's calls. He was eager to speak with Ryan, and I was eager to protect him. I didn't think he was ready to deal with it. Davidson said that wasn't my call to make, and so I agreed to talk to Ryan about it.

He'd been in his room for most of the afternoon, a full shelf worth of books in there with him. I'd been pacing the length of the living room when the sound of his door unlatching traveled down the hall.

He walked into the living room as though something had drawn him there against his will. Like he'd felt my need to talk to him, felt my crippling anxiety about the topic all the way from his room. Ryan exhaled and folded his arms.

"I was about to knock on your door. Feeling okay?" I asked, stalling. "I can make you waffles if you're hungry."

Ryan didn't bite.

"Sit, please." I gestured to the end of the couch he stood closest to while I took a seat on the other end. He chose to stand.

"I spoke with Davidson earlier. He's the agent from the hospital, remember? The one who helped you and the others."

Ryan dropped his arms, fully alert now.

"He'd like to know if you remember anything about how you got here. Can you give any names? Descriptions? Did you see or hear anything that may be useful to their investigation? Did the men or women speak English? Have any tattoos? Is there *anything* you remember?" I didn't mention Davidson's interest in how and when he'd been taken to begin with. I told myself it would only overwhelm him more. "It could be important."

Ryan's lips set in a stubborn line. If he did know something, he wouldn't be telling me. He turned to walk away.

"It's time to set boundaries and encourage healthy compromises. He needs to talk to someone equipped to handle what he may have gone through."

"Wait!" I called out, my insides recoiling at what I planned to address next. "I think it's time we visit Safe Haven, Ryan." I didn't want him to think I was punishing him for not cooperating with Davidson, which was what his shocked gaze suggested, but he needed to talk to someone. As much as I wanted that someone to be me, I needed to accept it couldn't be.

"I'm not punishing you, or putting you out. You can stay here as long as you want." I noted the rapid rise and fall of his chest. "But you can't stay here as a prisoner from the world, or your problems." I wanted to take it all back. I wanted to barricade us inside the apartment and keep him safe from all harm, but that would've only satisfied my selfish needs.

"We have therapists there who can help you deal with the things that make you scream at night," I whispered. It was more of a caged sound than a scream. Like yelling underwater, or trying to speak past lips glued together. It didn't happen as often as when he first got here, but it still happened. He balled his fists, face heating from embarrassment or anger. Maybe both.

"You won't have to talk, if that's what you're worried about. They'll meet you where you are. Just give it a chance," I implored. My assurance got me nothing. Not even a shake or a nod of his head. "Ryan—"

He stormed off, a look of fury and determination etched across his ethereal face.

"Ryan," I tried again when he returned, but he threw himself onto the couch and began scribbling furiously on the notepad he'd gone to get. He grunted with impatience when his rage got the best of him. Sheet after sheet rained down around him as he wrote and tore the paper away to start again. His fingers white knuckled the pencil, and he gripped the edge of the pad with brutal force. He couldn't calm himself enough to get his thoughts written down.

"Ryan..." His whispered name got lost in the sudden strike of thunder.

"Ryan," I tried a little louder, "it's okay." Without thinking I reached out to comfort him, to tell him I take everything back, that we could stay locked away from whatever was making him feel like this. I wanted to tell him that I understood why the idea of speaking to a therapist scared him, because the idea of it scared me too.

His pencil and paper slid across the coffee table as he leapt up, stumbling away and falling. He scurried backward, away from the threat of my outstretched hand. He panted heavily through clenched teeth, spit flying as he practically foamed at the mouth.

"I'm s-sorry," I stammered. "I wasn't thinking."

His chest pumped up and down at a speed too quick to keep track of.

"I'm sorry," I repeated, voice breaking. He looked like an animal that had been beaten and was now cornered, waiting.

"God," I breathed, unsure if it was the beginning of a prayer, or the start of a curse. I sat there drowning in self-hatred. I did this to him. It was all my fault. My heart hurt, and I dug the heel of my palm into my chest, trying to get myself under control.

"You don't..." I'd been about to tell him he didn't have to go, to promise I'd never suggest it again. I got sidetracked when his gaze fell to my feet. To the sheet of paper that had landed there when he'd made his explosive escape from me. I made a slow show of picking it up, giving him ample time to let me know if he didn't want me to.

When he didn't, I looked at the page, the corners crumpling in my fists as I read the horror smeared across it.

Burned!

Stab!

Cut!

Drugged!

Slave!

Cold!

Hungry!

Chained!

Floor!

Beat!

And the last one, written three times...

Broken!

Broken!

Broken!

"No," I breathed, close to tears, looking him over as though I could see through his clothes to the scars his words screamed were beneath them. He'd told me what happened to him. He was telling me he wouldn't talk about it with anyone, but in doing so, he'd shared it with me.

He must have realized that, because his eyes watered as he shook his head and scrambled to his feet. He'd never given me a head gesture before, and it felt almost like he'd finally said something to me. I wished it wasn't this. I wished he'd gotten to live a normal life, gotten to fall in love, wished he'd gotten away. I wished he'd never been taken in the first place.

"Wait!" I called when he turned for the hall. "You don't have to go to Safe Haven. You don't have to..." I clutched the paper I still held, my blood boiling, demanding the immediate hunting down and torture of the people responsible for all this. I shut down the voices attempting to take those thoughts a step further, my guilt didn't need any more ammunition. "You don't have to tell anyone about this, if you're not ready to. But I need you to see a doctor."

He spun toward me, nearly falling over again.

"I know you don't want to be touched, but what if..." I looked at the paper again, noticing the absence of the four-letter word I dreaded seeing, hoping it wasn't because he hadn't gotten a chance to write it down. "What if something is medically wrong because of what they did to you? Something we can't see?"

Ryan wasn't examined at the hospital. Davidson said he wouldn't let anyone touch him. He'd had to be restrained and sedated after having a meltdown when they tried. I strengthened my resolve before meeting his tearful eyes again, because I couldn't afford to back down now. I couldn't let my need to make everything right for him cloud my judgment. Not about this.

"My doctor makes house calls. I'll get examined too, if it helps." It was almost time for my annual check-up anyway. "It doesn't have to be today, or tomorrow, but you *need* to do it. This is my compromise."

His face blanched at the seriousness in my tone, and he clutched his t-shirt as though already fighting to hold on to his autonomy, to hold on to his right to choose. I wouldn't force him, regardless of what I'd said. I just hoped he would agree.

"Don't let them keep you chained," I whispered, still seated for fear my legs wouldn't hold me up. "Don't let them win."

Ryan stayed in his room for two whole days after that. I went back to leaving trays of food by his door, and notes that went unanswered. I went back to taking my little oval pill again.

CHAPTER 10

William

I'd been taking my anxiety medication on an as-needed basis, but recently that method hadn't been as effective as in the past. If I called Dr. Stein, she'd tell me what I already knew but didn't want to hear. That I was only treating one symptom of a bigger issue.

She'd urge me to get treatment for my dysthymia, which had obviously returned. I'd ignored her professional opinion when she cautioned me about what could happen if I didn't keep up with my maintenance treatment. I didn't keep up with it because sometimes it didn't seem fair to be self-content, after all the things I'd done. Sometimes not suffering for it all felt too much like forgetting.

She would also want me in her office, and once there, she'd want to know what changes had interfered with the carefully cultivated structure of my life.

I'd then have to tell her about Ryan, or lie, which would be pointless. Then I'd have to sit there while she took the scenic route to getting me to realize this situation wasn't ideal. That it wasn't good for either of us—myself or Ryan.

I'd never admit that, because despite how it looked—and sometimes felt—Ryan was the best thing to happen to me in too many years to count.

So rather than address the depression wreaking havoc on my sleeping pattern, I found things to keep me busy in the small hours of the night.

Setting the clippers on the bathroom sink, I drew in close to the mirror, brushing a hand over my scalp to clear away the loose bits of hair. Making it to my barber didn't seem possible at the moment, neither was having him come to me. Doing it myself would have to do. It was a struggle, but I managed to take it down to a light-caesar while avoiding bald spots in the process. Clearing away the stubble along my cheeks was much easier. Ryan lucked out. He never had to shave, and the wilder his hair got, the more gorgeous he looked.

I took my time sweeping up the mess before taking another hot shower for something else to do. With that done, I slipped into a pair of loose basketball shorts and a t-shirt, grabbed a cold beer and stepped onto my balcony. We were at that sweet spot of fall where nights were cool but not yet unbearable. The chilled air felt good against my overheated skin. I welcomed it as I slouched in one of the chairs.

The baggy legs of my shorts slid down to my hips when I propped my feet up on the railing. I hadn't put on any underwear, so my scars were visible. Taking a swig of my beer, I counted each jagged line, then ran the cold neck of the bottle over them, leaving behind the condensation.

I repeated the process on both thighs, getting lost in the old habit when the sound of movement caught my attention. I craned my head around in time to see Ryan step through the sliding door, homing in on my scars when he stopped near my shoulder. His hair stuck up in various directions, and the circles under his eyes were darker than I'd ever seen them.

The bottle nearly slipped from my hand, and my legs shook with the need to slam them shut. Instead of closing them, I took a steadying breath and spread them wider.

Maybe it was the silent yearning to let someone in that made me do it. Maybe I wanted him to *see* me. If only a little bit. Or maybe I needed him to know I'd been suffering a long time too.

"I..." I didn't know what else to say, what else to do as I sat there more naked and exposed than I'd ever been. Would this scare him? Disgust him? Give him ideas? I felt uneasy. Repulsed by my own audacity.

We both breathed raggedly, and the railing vibrated when my shaking became a full body thing. More than ever I needed him to understand me, to take the seat next to me and hold my hand. It wasn't his job to, though. I wasn't his problem. Fundamentally I knew that, but it still felt like he'd slid a blade between my ribs when he turned and walked away.

I dropped my feet to the floor, doubling over and dry heaving as the bottle slipped from my fingers and shattered.

I needed to scream but couldn't. I needed to hit something, but couldn't do that either. Ryan had to come first, and losing my shit would only further destabilize what he'd hopefully come to see as a safe place.

What he didn't know couldn't hurt him, though. I could do all those things without letting him hear me. I'd lock my door and scream into my pillow until my voice gave out, punch the mattress. *Anything.* I just needed to let some of this pain go.

Pushing my way past the curtains to get into my room, I skittered to a stop at the sight of Ryan perched on the edge of my bed. He stared at the wall in front of him, back straight, knees touching, fists planted against his tensed thighs.

Releasing a shuddering breath, I sat on the opposite end, keeping my eyes trained on the wall as well. The bedside lamp was bright enough to see clearly by, but dim enough to give my demons the illusion of privacy. But the truth was, none of that mattered. We could've been shrouded in darkness and I'd still feel just as exposed as I had on the balcony. The hem of my shorts were already at my knees, but I tugged on them anyway.

He'd stayed. He hadn't run away. What did that mean? I didn't give myself time to second guess. If he was here, it meant he wanted something from me. I could only think of one thing.

"I was abducted when I was a kid," I whispered. My mother had cautioned me about a lot of things growing up. Gangs, guns, drugs, what the color of my skin would mean in this world... She'd never once mentioned human trafficking. "I still can't walk past a park without freezing up. It's one of the reasons I bought this place. The nearest park is fifteen blocks away."

Ryan didn't run for the door. Didn't flinch at my confession. Did he already know? Did I have survivor's remorse written all over me?

Either way, I took it as permission to continue. "Luckily, I was... rescued before anything too traumatic happened to me." A phantom throbbing started up between my thighs, a painful reminder that my true trauma began once I returned home.

"I started cutting freshman year of high school. The deeper I cut, the quieter the inner voices got. It's like they'd redirect their attention to surviving my physical pain, instead of doing what they did best—inflicting mental and emotional pain on me. My head would go so quiet.

"The coping mechanism took on a life of its own, though, and when my mother found out, she got us both into therapy. Therapy saved my life." From the corner of my eye I watched as Ryan loosened the tight hold he had on himself. He flattened his palms over his thighs, and relaxed his shoulders. I did the same, my mental binds slackening now that I'd purged some of the poison.

"My mother was right. The more she worries, the more I distance myself." Now he knew I'd listened in on them in the kitchen. I didn't care. This moment was bigger than my eavesdropping. "I can't bring my pain to her. It triggers her guilt, no matter how much she tries to hide it. I know all about guilt." I gave a mirthless laugh. "Some mornings I'd wake up feeling guilty to be alive. They don't tell you about how hard it is to come back to your regular life. They don't tell you that you'll never be the same. That you'll never look at people the same. Everyone becomes a stranger, even the people you already knew." I wanted to say more on that topic but couldn't. Some truths—and lies—could never be exposed. I'd accepted that in some ways I'd always be a coward.

"Most people look at me and see someone driven and ambitious. Someone who's accomplished so much at such a young age. They don't know most days I have to claw my way out of bed. They don't understand that professional and financial success doesn't equate to happiness, or confidence, or having it all figured out," I rasped, my gaze still glued to the wall. "They don't get that sometimes it simply means you've found the one thing that makes you want to hang on for just a little while longer. Sometimes life is a series of holding on. Most would assume music is what keeps me going. That hasn't been the case since before..." I stopped there. Any more would've been too much.

"I won't say I understand how you feel or what you're going through, but you're not alone, Ryan. With me, you're not alone."

My shoulders sagged as exhaustion hit, and I finally turned toward him. Ryan faced me too now, his eyes soft and free of judgment. He stood, and I thought he'd leave, that he'd had enough for one night. I wouldn't have been upset by it. He'd given me an ear to talk to, he'd sat a few feet away from my pain and listened. It was more than enough.

I'd been about to whisper goodnight, but then with jerky, hesitant movements—as though his heart and mind were engaged in battle—he pulled his shirt over his head. I couldn't swallow past my devastation.

Ryan inched closer to my side of the bed before sitting down again, facing me. Scar tissue formed a map across his skin. Some of the old wounds were about an inch or two wide, others were longer and meaner looking, like someone had attacked him with the intention to kill. My hand shook with the need to touch them, and my mouth trembled with the need to apologize for them.

Deep crimson flooded his cheeks then spread to his ears and neck.

"Breathe, Ryan," I whispered. "Breathe." I took my own advice.

His shoulders twitched a few times, as though he wanted to turn around, but couldn't fight past self-preservation instinct. I somehow knew the worst was yet to come.

When he did turn, I bit my cheek to stop a gasp from escaping. The skin along his spine looked gnarled and melted, like someone had taken a blow torch to it. My breath fanned across his flesh as I leaned in. I had no idea what my intentions were, but I pulled back when he arched away from me.

Ryan hurried to slip his shirt back on before facing me. He searched my face with suspicion. Did he think I'd pity him?

Every bone in my body felt brittle. I ached for him. I wanted to trade places with him. But I'd never pity him.

I'd shown him my wounds, and he'd found the courage to share his in return. It made me feel less alone. It was the kindest thing anyone had ever done for me, and I did my best not to appear broken by it.

"Can I hug you?" I questioned whether my intent was to console him, or to have him comfort me. Whether I wanted to soothe the little boy in me, or the one within him.

He shook his head, and I sucked in an audible breath.

"Do it again," I breathed, and he shook his head again. I studied the movement, committing it to memory. The way his hair moved, the way his brow scrunched like my request confused him. "It feels like you're talking to me," I explained. It was the smallest gesture but it meant something to me. "Why won't you talk to me?" I could hardly keep my eyes open now. "I just want you to talk to me. Or yell at me. I don't care." Or maybe I did care, because there was a certain level of safety in his silence. Who knew what he'd say if he put words to his anger.

Ryan swallowed, looking sadder than I'd ever seen him before. I asked a question knowing if he answered it I'd be shattered and unable to hide it. I had to know, though. I had to know how deep his well of pain went. Had to know the moment he felt broken by it.

"How..." I licked my lips and tried again. "H-how old were you when you stopped speaking?"

He caught his bottom lip between his teeth, his leg bouncing. Ryan closed his eyes for a second, then began to count using his fingers, over and over again. Once he was sure he had the number correct, he held up both hands. One had five fingers lifted, the other just one. *Six.* I was not okay.

The room began to spin, and I fisted the blanket to keep from falling onto the floor. I blinked past the moisture building in my eyes. Ryan watched me with wide-eyed concern. The fact he remembered that far back broke my heart. I wanted to ask what caused it, wanted to know the moment it happened, but I was terrified of making him relive whatever it was. Terrified of making him remember, if he'd forgotten. I would've given anything to forget my pain, even a little bit of it. "I'm s-so sorry."

He pointed to the head of the bed, then more urgently when I continued to sit there.

I snapped out of it, hauling myself closer to the headboard before curling onto my side. He motioned for me to roll over. I did so on auto-pilot, too far gone to care why. His harsh breathing filled the room, and then he pushed a pillow up against my back. Before I could figure out what was going on, I felt the pressure of his body against it. We laid back-to-back with the pillow between us, keeping his body from touching mine. I didn't know where the sound of his breaths began and mine ended, but after the surprise wore off, gratitude followed.

I fell asleep with my fist lodged between my teeth, praying it stayed there throughout the night, that no secrets slipped free.

I WOKE UP later that morning to find the space empty of him. A sketch of himself blindfolded on what appeared to be the deck of a ship rested on the pillow. I assumed it was the ship he and the others were brought here on. Below it he'd written: ***I didn't see anything.***

I blew out a breath. Whether it was true or not, he'd made it clear he had nothing to say about it. I'd let Davidson know.

Ryan didn't come out of his room, and I didn't bother him. We went through a lot last night. I respected his need for solitude. I heard his television going, heard the same scenes playing over and over as if he were rewinding his favorite parts, so I knew he was okay. Or alive, at least.

I'd skipped breakfast, choosing to get some cleaning and laundry done instead. Truth was I didn't have an appetite, and forcing myself to eat lunch turned out to be an epic fail. Opening the trash can to dump the sandwich I'd ordered, I almost dropped the whole thing on the floor. I pushed harder on the pedal, watching the lid open wider. Strips of cotton rested on top of trash. Strips of a bedsheet to be exact.

I set my plate and fork on the counter behind me, then reached in to pick up Ryan's chains.

I whispered a thank you toward the ceiling. If God was up there, I hoped he heard me. Alone and feeling safe to smile, I did so. A small thing that eventually took over my whole face.

That night I woke up to a pillow against my back again, and the weight of Ryan leaning against it. His first night without his chains. It couldn't have been easy for him.

His scent surrounded me, making it hard to go back to sleep. I stayed up for way longer than I should have just breathing it in. Before drifting off again, I noticed my phone on my nightstand. It had been next to me on the bed. He'd rested it there before claiming his spot. *His* spot. How quickly I began to think of it as that.

By the fourth night he'd backed the length of one leg against mine. By the fifth, the pillow was gone.

CHAPTER 11

William

With Ryan's approval, Dr. Baptiste came by to conduct our physical exams. He, and one of his nurses, transformed the kitchen into a work area while waiting for Ryan to come out of his room. I figured letting him go first would be best. We could get it over with before he had a change of heart.

"Give me a second." I made my way to Ryan's bedroom, knocking a few times but he didn't answer. Testing the knob and finding it unlocked, I cracked it open. The overcast skies darkened the gray room.

"Ryan?" It felt wrong to enter without his consent. The bathroom door stood ajar, its light trickling into the room. I called his name a little louder before announcing, "I'm coming in."

I called his name through the partial opening, spotting him standing in the shower with the water off, fully dressed. His panicked breaths filtered through the door.

Pushing inside the bathroom, I opened the shower door and stepped in front of him, careful to leave enough space between us. He wore a thick sweater with what looked like at least three layers of shirts beneath, and his lower half was twice its normal size. He had to have on a whole pack of socks as well. He'd layered up to protect his skin from their touch, and I couldn't tell if the sweat on his brow was from the panic attack or the amount of fabric he wore.

"Turn around," I whispered. He shook his head, hands flexing in front of him. "Please, trust me."

His chest expanded with his inhale, but then he faced away from me. I allowed myself only a second of uncertainty before pressing my back to his. Ryan stiffened, both of us no longer breathing.

We slept in this position for over a week. We'd done so with nothing but our clothes between us the last couple of nights. I never initiated it, though. Ryan was the one in control, the one to decide, and he would sneak into my room and do so *after* I fell asleep.

Ryan wasn't in the mood for physical contact, but I'd taken the liberty anyway, hoping for me he'd make an exception. He relaxed into me after a minute, and I did the same.

"They'll need to take your blood pressure. The nurse will do that." My voice echoed around us. "She'll secure the cuff around one bicep, then press a button to inflate it. It'll temporarily block the blood flow in your arm. That'll allow her to measure your blood pressure. She said she can do this without touching your skin," I pointed out, and his shaking subsided.

"And your weight. You'll step on a scale for that. She'll need to take a few vials of your blood for testing. She'll tie a tourniquet around your arm, maybe ask you to make a fist, then she'll search the crook of your elbow for a good vein before inserting a thin needle into it. It'll feel like a quick pinch," I hurried to say when he grew agitated again. He'd felt a needle prick his skin before. They'd had to sedate him at the hospital, and I was sure he'd been drugged in that way in the past.

"She'll wear gloves," I added, hoping it helped. "No skin-to-skin contact. But she will need to touch you." I pressed further into him in an attempt to absorb his fear, whispering for him to take a deep breath.

"They'll ask you to pee in a cup. That's always fun," I said in a wry tone. "I end up needing to run the faucet and think about waterfalls to get my body to cooperate." I looked back to see if he'd smile or laugh at my joke, but he did neither.

"They'll ask questions about your medical history. Your family's medical history too." I moved on quickly. "They'll want to know what types of medications you're on, if there's been any changes to your health since your last exam... Things like that. I've already told Dr. Baptiste that getting those answers won't be possible this time. He understands."

His posture softened, so I turned and waited for him to look at me. His big, ebony eyes shimmered like they did sometimes when his emotions were too heavy for him. If only I could hold him.

"They may do a few other things, but it'll be okay. They won't hurt you," I promised. "I'll go first, if you want. And I'll stay when it's your turn, if you want that too."

Ryan wiped the sweat from his forehead with the sleeve of his sweater, before nodding once. I'd never grow tired of that. Now that he'd deemed me worthy of his gestures, they never stopped coming. Nods, head shakes, a palm extended when he wanted me to shut up. I tended to ramble, and even though he didn't speak, he made it clear his ears worked just fine.

I left him to unbundle himself, and was sitting on a stool with the blood pressure cuff around my arm when he crept into the kitchen. He looked from the empty tubes lining the rack on the island, to the nurse concentrating on my pressure reading.

"Good morning, Ryan," Dr. Baptiste greeted from where he sat in front of his open laptop. Ryan startled at his voice, he hadn't noticed him sitting on the other side of the kitchen. The doctor stood. "I hope you don't mind me calling you Ryan. William assured me it would be okay."

It hadn't occurred to me until then that I didn't know Ryan's last name. Ryan didn't answer him, but Dr. Baptiste wasn't offended by it. He knew enough about Ryan not to be.

"Natasha will take your vitals once she's done with William. I'll step in to review those results, and to go over what we'll be testing you for. I'll check to make sure everything sounds nice and healthy internally, and to answer any questions you may have."

Ryan looked at the pencil and paper I'd left on the island for him.

"There are a few forms I'll need you to sign first, though." Dr. Baptiste gave him a warm smile. "And William expressed that you'd like him to be present for it all. Is that correct?"

Ryan nodded, a curl springing free from his elastic tie.

Dr. Baptiste pointed to the small stack of paperwork on the counter. "Everything's there for you whenever you're ready. I can explain anything you have trouble understanding, but it's pretty straightforward consent and privacy stuff. William can confirm that as well." He retook his seat and slipped his glasses back on, splitting his attention between his screen and the file in his hand.

It didn't take long for Natasha to finish up with me. She passed me a specimen cup and asked me to fill it to the indicated line. "I'll be right back," I whispered to Ryan, who still stood several feet away from all the activity.

Returning from the bathroom, I handed the cup over to Natasha, looking

Ryan over to make sure he'd made it through my short absence unscathed.

"Remove your shirt and have a seat," Dr. Baptiste said from behind me. I whipped my head around in panic to find him inserting his stethoscope plugs into his ears. He gestured toward my stool, rubbing the bell against his lab coat to warm it.

My back burned in all the spots I wanted to keep hidden. "We keep our shirts on."

Dr. Baptiste didn't argue. I'd never declined removing my shirt during an exam before, so he likely assumed I did so now in support of Ryan's needs.

I sat, and he reached under the hem of my t-shirt with the bell, placing it against my skin and instructing me to take deep breaths in and out. He listened to my lungs next.

Dr. Baptiste added a few notes to my file, then looked over the rim of his glasses at Ryan then back to me.

"It's okay," I said, knowing he wanted confirmation before discussing my medical history in front of Ryan. We went over my current medications and the status of my runner's knee.

"And you'd like to be tested for *everything*, is that correct?" He glanced at Ryan again.

"Yes," I replied. It seemed like a lifetime ago since I last had sex, but I always had them run the full works on my blood and urine samples anyway. I didn't see the harm in being thorough. They'd be running all the same tests for Ryan, especially considering his situation.

"Okay," Dr. Baptiste said, "it's your turn, Ryan."

He took his time stepping to the counter where the forms waited, tremors overtaking his hand as he picked up the pen.

"Do you need me to read them to you?" I asked under my breath. Natasha busied herself with getting everything ready for him, and Dr. Baptiste had gone back to tapping away at his keyboard. Ryan hit me with a hard head shake loaded with stubbornness and attitude.

It took him a while to get through them, but Baptiste and Natasha did a good job of pretending they had a lot to do while they waited. He drew a squiggly line near the signature request at the bottom, then exhaled before taking up my vacated stool. I stood next to him like a bodyguard until Natasha politely asked me to wait several feet away. Unhappy about it, I obliged, moving to lean against the refrigerator.

Ryan kept his gaze on me the whole time, either afraid I'd leave, or maybe needing me to anchor him. My stomach cartwheeled at the idea it could be the latter. *Careful, William.*

He grimaced when the needle pierced his skin, crimson blooming beneath his beauty mark.

We'd made it through Natasha's portion of events. Dr. Baptiste stepped in next. "Okay, I'll need to slip this under your shirt," he said, moving in with the stethoscope in hand. Ryan gripped the edges of the stool, recoiling and turning his face away.

"No!" I barked, holding a hand up. Everyone jolted. "Over his clothing," I said in a lower tone.

"That will dull the sounds," Dr. Baptiste advised.

"It doesn't matter," I said, holding Ryan's frantic gaze and repeating, "Over his clothing."

I WALKED THE doctor and Natasha to the elevator, promising I'd help Ryan get set up on the portal so he could access his results in a few days. Locking the front door and resting my forehead against it, I closed my eyes for a beat, trying to shake off the tension. I'd been on edge all morning, nervous that at any moment Ryan would call it quits or freak out and end up needing to be restrained like at the hospital.

Taking a deep breath, I turned to head for the living room. I stopped, noticing Ryan watching me from outside his bedroom door. He'd jumped off the stool as soon as they were done with him, hurrying to scrub away their touch. His hair hung damp around his shoulders, his shirt wet and clinging to him as though he hadn't dried off before dressing. He looked as tired as I felt.

"I'm proud of you," I said. He averted his gaze. We stood there a while, me staring at him, him staring at a spot on the floor. I didn't mind. It meant I got to drink him in without worrying about what he'd see written across my face.

He eventually did look up, and we watched each other until our blinks were in sync, until our chests rose and fell in unison, until our breaths turned into sweet music to my ears.

Ryan's fingers twitched at his sides, and he raised a hand to the juncture of his arm, where the needle had been. Next, he closed his palm over his bicep, where the blood pressure cuff had been placed. Then he rubbed a hand over his chest, as though he could still feel the bell of the stethoscope there. The lump at his throat shifted with his swallow. I shouldn't have been able to see it from this distance, but my vision seemed to be supernatural when it came to him. A slow nod followed.

"You're welcome," I choked out, in response to his demonstration of gratitude. Something tender passed between us while our staring match continued. I could've stood there all-night gazing at him. I could've composed the greatest song ever, inspired by the look of confusion and curiosity in his eyes.

But then it was over, our connection broken when he slipped into his bedroom, closing and locking the door behind him.

I hurried to fall asleep that night, knowing he wouldn't come to me, wouldn't press his back against mine if he knew I was awake. I counted numbers and sheep and all the lies I'd told myself since he arrived, but it was hours before oblivion found me.

I woke in the middle of the night with a jolt, my palm over my mouth in the role of dream catcher. My nostrils flared as I clamped down, squeezing my lips closed to keep the name from my past trapped inside. I knew if I turned on the lamp and looked down at my hand, I'd see the letters scorched into my skin.

Rolling over, I scrambled up after noticing the spot next to me empty. Ryan never came. I clicked on the lamp then, removing my sweat slicked shirt and pleading with my heart. "Just once," I whispered. "I promise." One brief moment to remember, to feel his name on my lips. A small indulgence.

The pain in my chest and my head competed as they bargained with one another. One wanting to protect me, the other demanding total obliteration. Scurrying into my closet, I stopped in front of the tri-fold mirror, alternating between staring at my back, and watching my tears fall as I prepared to rip myself to shreds. I should've known better. Perhaps I did. Maybe I just couldn't live with ignoring it anymore.

Bracing myself for the ache and the guilt and the continuing life of turmoil ahead... I said it. I gave life to the name that haunted me.

"Asher."

CHAPTER 12

William

Xavier: I'll be at your place in two hours.

The message was time stamped an hour ago. I flopped back onto my pillow groaning. I hadn't mentioned our scheduled work session to Ryan yet. Between our new sleeping arrangement—which may have ended, since I slept the whole night alone—and our new routine of running, reading, and watching movies, I hadn't wanted to rock the boat any further. Not to mention the tense lead up to the doctor visit and the stress of the physical exam.

We could both use a few days to breathe, but Xavier wouldn't agree to another delay. Thanks to me, we now had days to meet a deadline that would've normally taken us a couple of weeks. We'd have to work day and night to get it done.

After a quick trip to the bathroom, I went in search of Ryan. A sliver of sunlight broke through his bedroom doorway. The murmuring of voices caught my attention, and my footfalls slowed as I neared his open door. I'd been about to knock on the doorframe, but got distracted by the sight of him sitting cross legged on his bed, a note pad pressed to his knee as he wrote something down before erasing it and trying again.

Frowning, he grabbed the remote and lifted it toward the television. I assumed it was to rewind the drama he was watching in order to get a second look at the subtitle. He paused with it suspended mid-air when he spotted me.

"Morning. You left your door open." I tried to remember a time when he'd done so whilst inside the room. Other than his first night here I couldn't think of any, which made this occurrence feel intentional. It felt like an invitation.

Was he letting me know we were okay? That him not showing up to my room last night didn't mean he was shutting me out?

He lowered his arm, staring at me. Suddenly Xavier's visit was the last thing on my mind. All I could think about was how much I missed having Ryan in my bed.

"I woke up alone, your side of the bed was cold. Are you upset with me?" I regretted it the moment I said it. Implying he owned one side of my bed felt presumptuous, or like I'd gotten ahead of myself. Ryan didn't owe me anything. Obligation or pressure were the last things he needed to feel right now. Still, I couldn't take it back.

He kept me in suspense for a few moments before shaking his head.

"Did you sleep well?" Without thought, my gaze went to the bedpost, and so did his. There were no chains. He nodded.

"Are you sure?" I hedged, strangely feeling hurt by his answer and unable to keep the truth from spilling out. "Because I didn't."

Ryan tilted his head, assessing me. Did I look as desperate as I felt? As confused as I sounded? Did I owe him an apology for both? I wasn't sure what he saw while he stared through me, but his gaze softened as he amended his previous answer, giving me the hand gesture for so-so. I shouldn't have felt better, but I did.

I leaned against the door frame, aiming for nonchalant. "I've been neglecting work for weeks. For good reason," I added, hating to see guilt overtake his expression.

"Anyway, I've had the final cut on a film I scored for a while now. The director has some concerns about the number of cadences used, and the register of some of the instruments in the more sentimental moments. He has some experience with music composition, which always leads to way too much feedback. It's why I prefer working with music-illiterate directors. It allows for more artistic freedom on my part." The speed of my speech increased, signs of an oncoming ramble. Ryan's frown deepened.

"He wants everything to be big, dramatic. But you need to take the emotions of a scene into account, you know? How you want the audience to feel, even if they aren't in said scene. Do the characters have any desires, where does the scene lead? Where—" I stopped when Ryan held his hand up. I'd explained all of this to him over dinner some nights ago. He'd sat riveted and appalled as I told him it was a film's score that dictated what the audience felt. That it had little to do with the acting or dialogue.

He'd immediately made us watch three movies in succession, wanting to prove me wrong. It took everything in me not to smile when he turned shocked eyes on me after leaping in his seat at a jump scare. It hadn't been the zombie appearing out of thin air. It was the slow build of halting, off-kilter piano keys at the highest octave that sent his heart rate into the stratosphere. It had been the music reaching its crescendo with an explosion of horns and dark notes, dominating the scene and signaling the approaching danger was now here.

Ryan motioned for me to get the point. I straightened.

"Xavier will be here soon. He'll be here most of the day for the next few days while we hammer things out."

His lips tightened.

"I should have mentioned it days ago, but there was a lot going on."

Ryan climbed off the bed, his movements as graceful and fluid as water. It stunned me to think he'd been afraid of his own shadow just a month ago. He seemed nothing like the man who'd hid in the shower yesterday. With every day came a new change, a bolder Ryan in some way, even though he avoided making the biggest change of all. The one that would bring him closer to being whole. With his pencil and notepad in hand, he walked over to me.

"I didn't want to pile anything else on you," I continued, my mouth going dry. Why was I looking at him in this way? A way that made me feel wrong, and even more of a bad person than I already felt.

He stopped a couple of feet away and began writing, then held the paper out. I squinted to read what he'd jotted down.

Do you want him here?

"Do I... *want* him here?"

Ryan nodded.

"Sure. We work together. I don't mind having him here. It's the perk of having an in-home studio."

His pink lips pressed together.

What am I missing? I studied him closely. Two red blotches appeared on his cheeks. "Are you asking if I hate that he has to be here, because I wish it could just be us? You and me?"

He looked at his feet, but then peered up at me through thick lashes.

"No," I breathed. "I don't want him here."

He tucked his hair behind his ear, nodding once before shooing me backward. I cleared his doorway, and he shut the door in my face. I went back to my room to get showered and dressed for the day, feeling better than I had in a while, and for once not questioning it.

I LET XAVIER in from upstairs to avoid a possible run-in with Ryan. It seemed best. We'd just finished going through our game plan for today's work session when the short beep and release of the door's keypad lock sounded.

Xavier and I looked up to find Ryan standing in the doorway. He seemed unsure of himself, or unsure of his presence in this space. His gaze asked if he was welcome.

"Come in," I said, feeling the heat of Xavier's disapproval at my back. Ryan let the door close behind him and looked around, studying the mounted TV displaying the opening credits of the film we were working on. "You can hang out over there while we work." I pointed to the loveseat adjacent to us.

"William," Xavier cautioned under his breath. "It's a breach of contract to allow anyone to watch this."

"He won't tell anyone," I said, not taking my eyes off Ryan as he maneuvered around the various equipment. I glanced over at Xavier to find him gaping at me. "It'll be fine," I assured him, jumping back into my concerns over the scene one cue.

It took us four hours to work through the first quarter of the film. Ryan watched and listened as we brought it all together. After getting to the midway point, we decided to roll it back to the beginning. I wanted to watch with no interruption before making adjustments this time.

Ryan scooted to the edge of the loveseat, looking between the door and the TV, his bottom lip tucked between his teeth.

"We'll wait for you," I said, pretending I didn't sense Xavier's displeasure.

"We don't have time to wait," he said once Ryan left the room.

"It's fine," I shot back. "We could all use a little break." I headed for the bathroom before he could respond.

When Ryan returned, he had a bowl of caramel popcorn in one hand, and a bottle of water in the other. He set both down in front of me, not meeting my eyes before retaking his seat. I hadn't eaten all day, and felt faint because of it. He'd brought me my favorite sweet snack, and ensured I had something to wash it down with because popcorn made me thirsty.

Had he left just for this? Or was it an afterthought? He hadn't disappeared for long, though, so maybe...

"Can we continue or do you need another minute?" Xavier asked in a tight voice, shaking me from my preoccupation with Ryan. I gestured toward him with the bowl. He had to be hungry too.

"No thanks."

I glanced over at Ryan in time to catch his displeased expression.

I had to practically sit on my hands to avoid making tweaks while we watched the romantic drama. Certain spots needed more work. I didn't know how I managed to notice with my attention diverted to Ryan and his enjoyment of the movie.

By the time Xavier and I had dug back into the edits, I'd started ignoring the score's time codes in exchange for taking my prompts from Ryan's emotional responses—or lack of. If he straightened during an adrenaline-charged moment, I elevated the action cue, causing the screen to erupt in kinetic energy.

If he seemed bored or distracted when he should feel drawn in and connected, I made a note to double back and strengthen the musical signatures that echoed throughout the entire film. The idea was that the musical motifs would imprint on the audience's subconscious, weaving together a sonic tapestry between characters, objects, or concepts. A reminder of what was at stake and what had already been suffered through and endured due to a love separated by war.

And when he looked flushed during a scene involving a simple kiss, I scaled back completely, letting raw honesty color the moment. I did so by ensuring the music played as a backdrop to the sensual sounds coming from the characters before the screen faded to black. In such a short time, and completely unaware of it, Ryan had become my muse.

"What are you doing?" Xavier asked during the film's climax. "You were supposed to cut out as soon as the sun set."

"I'm trying something," I whispered, my gaze on Ryan. Xavier had to notice, but I couldn't pull my eyes away long enough to confirm it.

"We're not getting paid to try something new. This isn't the rough cut. Everything's been decided. We have to stick to the codes."

"We'll do a playback. If it isn't better, we'll do another cut."

"Are you also going to beg for more time on a project we've already gotten a generous extension on?"

"If I have to," I said, finally looking at him. Xavier looked between Ryan and me, his expression full of disbelief and jealousy.

"Fine," he bit out, rolling his eyes when I nudged his shoulder playfully. Xavier took his job seriously. We both did. It made us great working partners.

I rewound to minute ninety-eight and hit play again, concentrating hard to pick up what wasn't working. I wanted Ryan to melt from the melodrama, wanted him to pump a fist in the air or flutter an eyelash or two after the long-lost soldier fell into his lover's arms. After all, they'd been apart for many years. He did nothing, and I wanted to see if I could fix that.

"The key didn't extend long enough," I said, hitting pause again. "That's the difference between watery eyes and a tear actually falling."

"Trust me, the tears will fall. It was a microsecond, William."

"Even microseconds count."

"Okay, we can extend it digitally, then."

"We can't mix digital in with this."

"No one will be able to tell. We're probably the only fools in the business who still go through the trouble of recording with a live orchestra."

"Which is why everyone's clambering at our door. Remember that." I headed for the live room. "Mics," I shot back. Xavier's frustrated curse cut off once the door sealed shut. I sat on the piano bench, waiting for everything to fire up and for Xavier to give the thumbs up.

"You can't be in there," I heard Xavier say over the intercom. I turned on the bench as Ryan walked in.

"He's fine." I pressed a finger to my lips, letting Ryan know to be quiet. He studied the instruments before stopping at the violin just as he had before.

The red light above the door flashed. Xavier's signal to start. I wouldn't have won any awards for my skills as a pianist, but I knew enough to get by, enough to make the ending of this film something my audience-of-one would never forget. Ryan's approval would mean everything.

I pretended to need more time in the live room than I actually did. I refused to move until Ryan finished his silent exploration.

Once we were back in the control room, I asked Xavier to rewind the ending. This time when the characters embraced, engaging in the most breathtaking kiss, I felt it deep in my core.

I turned to Ryan, trying to keep my expression neutral. I frowned at seeing his glare pinned in Xavier's direction. My bewilderment faded when I realized why.

The atmosphere in the control room thickened, the tension awkward enough to make me shift in my seat as my gaze fell to Xavier. A level of regret I'd never reached before ate away at me. Xavier was watching me with heartbreak and longing in his eyes. He knew. He *knew* what I'd been trying to hide from myself.

CHAPTER 13

William

It was well after four in the morning when the closing credits rolled for the last time, and to my surprise we were done. I'd have to review things once more after getting some rest, but Xavier didn't need to return for that part.

"Do you want him here?" Ryan had asked.

"No."

Had I subconsciously worked myself to the bone so we could be alone again? I wouldn't have stopped to eat if it wasn't for Ryan. Had I powered through my work so we could get back to our isolated existence?

Xavier yawned, rubbing at his eyes while Ryan slept on the loveseat with his long limbs tucked under himself.

My conscience told me to ask Xavier to stay instead of allowing him to leave at this hour. It was on the tip of my tongue to do so, but then Ryan's question replayed in my head again, and my answer hadn't changed. *No.*

"Let me call you an Uber." I pulled up the app as we stepped into the hall.

"Already done." He slipped his jacket on. "It'll be here in fifteen."

Xavier looked me in the eyes. I felt as though he were digging around in my soul for some clarity. I sighed, knowing he wouldn't leave until he'd spoken his mind.

"He doesn't like me." He tipped his head toward the room. Ryan didn't need to like him, because this wasn't about Xavier. Seemed too cruel to say that though, when I already knew this conversation would end with his feelings hurt. Until Xavier made peace with what I could give, our relationship would be overshadowed by his bitterness and my guilt.

"He can be a little standoffish." I didn't mention the part where Xavier made him feel cornered with his questions at dinner. That hadn't helped. "Give him some time."

"Time won't help. He'll never like me, because he knows that *I* like you."

"What?" My disbelief turned the word into a laugh. "Are you saying—"

"That he has feelings for you? Yes, that's exactly what I'm saying. I recognize another man's jealousy and possession over you when I see it, William."

I gazed at Ryan's sleeping form through the door's window. "You're wrong," I whispered. "He's just—"

"Used to his routine? Doesn't like surprises? Or change?" Xavier stepped closer. "Tell me, William, is sitting in there watching the same film, over and over again for more than twelve hours, part of his daily routine?"

"I..." I had nothing to say. I felt thrown off balance, unsure if Xavier was the one confused. Ryan didn't have feelings for me. Most days it seemed like he hated me. He'd been through a lot, refused to speak, and couldn't stand to be touched.

Except... we did touch. At night, while I slept, and then again in his bathroom before he faced Dr. Baptiste. But that only meant he was getting comfortable with me. Right?

"You don't even see it, do you?" Xavier said, clearly frustrated with my ignorance. "You're so broken inside that you can't see what's happening right in front of you. You think so little of yourself that you can't comprehend someone wanting you more than they want their next breath." His own breath seemed to catch in his throat with his words. "I guess that's part of your charm." It came out low and sardonic, as though meant for himself.

"He doesn't want me, and I don't want him in that way. Nothing's going on between us. I wouldn't do that."

He brought his steepled fingers to his lips, as though praying for patience. "Why can't you see it's already happening?"

"You're imagining things," I snapped, not wanting to hear another word. "You're letting your emotions get the best of you."

"He knows how you like your coffee, William," he continued undeterred by my unfair assessment of him. His eyes implored me to not do this to him, whatever *this* was. "*I* don't even know how you like your coffee, because you'd never let me make it."

We'd taken a break several hours ago so Xavier could scarf down his takeout. I'd slouched in my chair, resting my eyes. I hadn't meant to doze off.

I'd woken up to the smell of coffee. Ryan hovered above me with a mug of it, and half a toasted bagel. I'd been so grateful I almost forgot not to smile. *Almost.*

I never let Xavier make my coffee because the recipe was too complex, and him getting it right would've felt like I let him in. I couldn't allow that. Ryan had gotten it right, though.

"That's because he sits in the kitchen while I make breakfast for us. He's seen me make myself coffee countless times." I realized my mistake as soon as the words left my mouth.

"Breakfast," he said as though he'd been gut punched.

"Come on, Xavier. I've made them breakfast before."

"*Them,*" he stressed. "But now you're using words like "us."" His phone chirped, probably an Uber notification. He ignored it.

"Every time you allowed someone as broken as you into your home, you would swear to me they were *different.* That something about them spoke to you in a way it hadn't with the others. You'd let them in, give them the time needed to find the strength to move on with their process. Whether it be to find family, or return home, or to Safe Haven." He huffed a sad laugh, placing his hands on his hips as he paced a small circle.

"'This one's different,'" he said in a mocking tone, throwing my words back at me. "Well, I believe it now." He turned for the door leading to the elevator.

"Xavier, wait," I hissed, giving chase and grabbing his arm.

He whirled on me, snatching his arm away. His phone chirped again, but he didn't seem to care. We were both out of breath due to fear not exertion. Fear sat on my chest, crushing the life out of me. And I knew him well enough to recognize the signs in him as well.

"You know," he started, "until now, I never took your unwillingness to open up to me personally." He held a hand up, stopping me before I could speak. "I know. You warned me, and I promised I could handle it. Turns out I couldn't. Sue me." He lowered his hand. "As disappointing as it was, deep down I knew the problem was you. And I think... I *know* I've just been waiting for you to come around." He glanced toward where Ryan slept, then back to me. "But it *is* me—"

"It's not," I swore. "The problem is *me.*" I tapped a fist against my sternum to emphasize the point, the action made my heart race faster. "Never you. It was never you, Xavier."

"He takes care of you. I mean... caramel popcorn?" He ran a hand through his wavy hair. "Jesus, I sound like a lovesick teenager. But really, why didn't I know you loved caramel popcorn? You inhaled it like you preferred it to air."

Popcorn and coffee. Those things were shallow in the grand scheme of it all. I thought about the scars Ryan had seen on me. Thought about the reasons I'd given him for their existence.

"I was abducted when I was a kid."

I hadn't even scratched the surface of what shaped me, on why he should be avoiding me, not living with me. Ryan would never know the depths of me, would never know what corroded my heart. No one would.

Xavier thought Ryan had some special insight into me, but at the end of the day, they were both on the same playing field.

"He doesn't know me."

"He's getting to know you," Xavier bit out like I was a complete idiot. "Why can't I get to know you too?"

"I could try," I said, tossing my hands up. "I can try and open up to you more. As friends." It wouldn't work, but I had to say something to end his suffocating anguish. It bore down on me, causing my lungs to constrict.

"Friends?" he asked, his tone equal parts dubious and exasperated.

"Yes. I could try to do better."

He moved closer, laying a hand on my cheek, his gaze fluttering over my face. "As your friend, do I get to know the origin of the graveyard on your back?" he whispered.

It wasn't a graveyard, but the sentiment was spot-on because I felt buried beneath it. I tried to retreat in defense of the memorial I wore, but he brought his other palm up, clamping my face between both hands to hold me hostage. "Do I get to know the story behind the name you call out in your sleep? Hmm?"

"Don't."

"Who's Ash—"

"Don't!" I repeated, the word cracking. I pulled free of him, my fear fortifying my internal walls.

"You live your life like you're waiting for something, or for someone. Like you can't *truly* live until whatever or whoever it is arrives. I'm done living the same way, William. I'm done waiting for you."

"I never asked you to." My voice sounded small, lining up with the way I felt.

"No, you didn't," he confirmed, "but you loved it all the same." He allowed me to digest that truth for a minute before hitting me with his parting words on his way out. "I can't work with you anymore. I quit."

REENTERING THE CONTROL room, I made my way over to Ryan, admiring the way his long lashes fanned out across his cheeks. Sweat dotted his nose. I reached over to the thermostat, turning the air on.

Despite being cramped on the love seat, he seemed peaceful and sweet. His missing scowl did wonders for his natural beauty.

I thought about waking him, but I couldn't bear losing this version of him yet. I considered carrying him to bed, but couldn't risk him having a violent outburst because I'd touched him without his consent. Whose bed would I have taken him to anyway? The voices in my head replied: *"Mine."*

Maybe Xavier's unadulterated truth had cut through some of my denial, because for once I agreed with the voices. My bed would've been the preferred option.

Unwilling to leave him here alone, I settled onto the floor with my back against the loveseat, scooting down until my head rested on the edge of the cushion.

I wouldn't let myself believe Ryan had feelings for me. Perhaps Xavier's jealousy caused him to misinterpret things on that front, to see non-existent things.

I did, however, allow myself the deconstruction of one lie. I had feelings for Ryan. The inappropriate kind. I could be brave enough to admit it to myself. Taking it a step further, I didn't blame my sleep deprived brain on the admission.

I have feelings for Ryan. The man I promised to protect until he was strong enough to reacclimate into the world. I refused to contemplate what type of monster that made me. Refused to think about when those feelings began. The answer to both would be too incriminating.

CHAPTER 14

William

I woke in the dark, disoriented and with a crick in my neck. It took a minute or two for my vision to adjust. The frame of the loveseat dug into my back, and the blanket covering me slipped past my shoulders, settling in my lap. Ryan must have covered me with it.

"He takes care of you."

I remembered another instance where Ryan draped a throw over me. I'd seen the gesture as a form of care, or perhaps an act of kindness, but now Xavier's opinions filled my head. I didn't know what to think.

The faint squeak of a stringed instrument caught my attention. I strained my ears toward the sound, trying to pick up the familiar melody. "Mary Had a Little Lamb." The song most violinists learned to master first.

It wasn't the playing of a complete novice I listened to, speechless. Ryan played like someone who hadn't played in years but had only mastered the basics. He played like someone being reacquainted with an old love, testing the waters.

It made me emotional and unable to move under the phantom boulder crushing my chest. The reasons why weren't unfamiliar to me.

He could've used help with his pitch, and guidance in depressing the correct strings at the right intervals. Call me biased, but it was still the most beautiful piece I'd ever heard.

The live room door could be stubborn sometimes. It tended to need a good hard push to seal all the way. Ryan likely believed he couldn't be heard from this side of the insulated room.

Getting to my feet and groaning as I rubbed the kink out of my lower back, I followed the music.

Ryan played with his back to me. A blessing. It meant I got to observe him from a place of honesty. A pleasure I'd lose the moment he saw me and shyness—or anger—set in. He took it from the top. I wanted to tell him he'd started in the wrong key, but I wanted to remain inconspicuous even more. At least for a while longer.

He clicked his tongue, surprising me. Other than his trapped screams fighting for freedom while he slept—or the morning he cut himself—I'd never heard him utter a sound.

I tried to gauge the timber of his voice from the small molecule of sound. Would it be high pitched like a tenor, or contain the warmth and depth of a baritone? Would it be low and rich, capable of sending chills down my spine? Or maybe soft and breathless. My body began to warm at the idea of the latter, and for once I didn't stop the heat from spreading.

Ryan whirled around at the sound of my rough exhale, nearly dropping the violin in his surprise. He panted, eyes wide, trembling.

"Sorry. I could hear you from the control room. I've been meaning to get the door fixed." I pointed a thumb over my shoulder. He considered the instrument in his hand, then its stand, as if contemplating setting it down.

"You need to start with the second finger on the D string," I instructed. "Can I?" I moved closer with my hand out. His brows dipped. Either my request for permission seemed odd to him, or he wasn't convinced I could play. He handed the violin and bow over, then waited.

Holding it by the neck, I sat the body along my collarbone before gently resting my jaw on the chinrest. I kept my movements slow enough for him to study them. Next, I aligned my index finger over the first stop on the fingerboard while the remaining digits hovered over each successive note in the major scale.

This particular violin hadn't been crafted by a master luthier from the finest of woods, but it held sentimental value to me. I'd had it restored and upgraded to produce the best quality sound possible while not making it unrecognizable. I wanted to maintain what made it special in the first place. It was the violin I exclusively played. It was well loved by me.

Ryan watched me closer as I ran the bow back and forth over the freshly tuned strings. I ran through the nursery rhyme twice—calling out each note shift—before closing my eyes and getting carried away by a haunting number that never failed to crush me. A song about loss and finding salvation.

I forgot about my muse, my audience-of-one. Forgot about the voices in my head, and all the tragic stars that aligned to bring me to this moment. I just played. Something I hadn't done enough of lately. The one thing that would send me as close to heaven as God would allow—given my past sins.

The sorrowful piece escalated near its climax, the long, sustained notes adding intensity and emotional depth. The music became a third being in the room, joining us as something tangible with its own heartbeat. The sound reverberated under my skin and down my arm as I moved to create a vibrato effect. I felt the quiver deep in my bones, and I allowed myself to get lost in the ache both there and in my heart.

I played until I could no longer hear my soul weep beyond the wailing of the music. I played until the pain melted away, until I was lost. I passed the bow over the strings one last time, drawing it out, not wanting to let the last note go.

Everything I thought I'd outran came crashing back into me when I opened my eyes to see hate and betrayal pulsing in Ryan's angry stare. He didn't need to speak, didn't need to utter a single word. His feelings had never been clearer.

I'd gotten to play while he hadn't. I'd gotten to perfect my craft while he—and so many others like him—had been stolen from theirs. Life wasn't fair by a long-shot, and I wanted to tell him he didn't need to waste time and energy hating me for it, because I already carried that burden.

I've got it, I wanted to whisper. *You can let it go.*

The first time he entered this room he'd cried over seeing the violin. I'd made a vow right then never to mention it was the instrument I played. It seemed cruel to do so. But seeing him in here tonight, trying to recapture something he'd so obviously lost... I had to help him. He needed to know he could get it back, that it wasn't too late. I could teach him. *Save* him.

My ribcage felt like it expanded to the point of cracking with every harsh breath I took. I could see it in his eyes, in the pooling of moisture in them. I was losing him. Whatever ground I'd gained, he was taking it back from me, just like he'd taken my once-in-a-blue-moon smiles. He had no idea how much power he had over me.

I reached out a hand to him, not sure what I intended to do with it. Ryan retreated a step, and then another before making a wide arc around me, storming toward the door. He knocked the cello over in the process.

“Please don’t be angry with me,” I said, voice cracking. “My heart can’t take it.”

Ryan came to an abrupt stop as though he might actually care about what I’d said. Or maybe he was at war with his own heart. I refused to think about the reasons why.

Later on, I’d wonder if that was the reason he stayed. The reason for the change in him after that night. Perhaps the remainder of the ice around his heart was melted away by my plea. Maybe he finally understood how sorry I was, and decided he’d had enough of punishing me.

I set the violin down. “Look at me,” I whispered. *See me.*

His shoulders tensed as though he was fortifying himself for the task. He turned to me, eyes awash with pain and beauty, both equally as stunning and fatal. He looked so young and fragile as he weaved his way through the lineup of instruments to get back to me.

Ryan’s fingers clawed into the fabric of his sweats, but he advanced on me as like he’d dared himself not to stop. We were closer than we’d ever been while awake and eye to eye. So close my breaths were his, and his were mine. Close enough for me to make out the single teardrop clinging to his lashes. It was either touch him or die from wanting.

I held my palms out to him like I would to a frightened animal, letting him know I meant him no harm. His tongue darted out, wetting his full lips, making them glisten. A nervous habit of his.

I brushed a lock of hair from his forehead, halting at his minute backward shift. “I’m not going to hurt you,” I breathed between us, my stomach tightening when his eyes fluttered. He inched forward again.

My fingers moved upward, getting lost in his curls. His breath smelled like caramel and hazelnut, like he’d secretly sampled both my popcorn and coffee when he’d prepared them for me. I wanted to taste him, to slip my tongue past the opening of his parted mouth and explore the flavor of him. I settled for gliding my digits behind his ear, the pads of my fingers caressing the lobe before descending to the column of his neck.

Ryan’s skin warmed, blooming crimson as I trailed past his collarbone to his shoulder where the loose neck of his t-shirt hung.

“Breathe,” I whispered, reminding myself to do the same as the intensity of this moment threatened to overtake me.

Ryan took a step back. The teardrop fell, traveling down his cheek.

He was shaking. I could almost hear the rattling of his bones. His gaze lowered to the erection pushing at my zipper, and then to his own tenting the front of his sweats. I couldn't deny it another second, not when the proof was staring me in the face. Ryan's interest went deeper than just a general sense of care, gratitude, or the pursuit of shared comfort. He was attracted to me, and I didn't know whether to feel happy or regretful about it.

When he lifted his head up again, a wave of sadness filled his eyes.

"I'm sorry. I went too far." I stepped back, giving him more room when what I really wanted to do was hold him in my arms. "It won't happen again." My erection deflated as shame overwhelmed me. I looked around for somewhere to sit, suddenly feeling ill.

Ryan held up a hand this time, stopping me. He took several deep breaths to calm his erratic breathing, then swallowed before closing his eyes and baring his neck to me.

I couldn't get my brain to function, to figure out what he was asking of me with the gesture. "I don't know what you want, Ryan." I sounded helpless. He pressed forward until our toes touched, eyes still screwed shut, neck exposed to me in offering.

He couldn't mean... *Could* he?

Taking a chance and hoping I didn't damn us both, I lowered my nose to his shoulder, filling my lungs with his scent. Traveling to the fluttering vein at his throat, I collected more of him, then ascended the same pathway of skin, repeating the process until his low whine stopped me.

We separated again, and this time instead of tears cresting his eyes, sweat shone along his brow.

I'd had plenty of sex in my lifetime. Empty, meaningless sex. Never had I experienced the level of intimacy I'd just shared with Ryan, and we hadn't even kissed. We were afraid, broken, and trying to work our way through both. I felt even less alone than I did when he showed me his scars, and I hoped he wasn't about to take that feeling away from me. All it would've taken was a regretful or hostile glare before leaving me there without a backward glance.

He moved over to the violin stand, fingers gliding over the scroll and peg box before making their way down to the bridge. He glanced at me with such longing that the minor repair made to my heart threatened to undo itself.

"I'll teach you," I promised. "I'll teach you everything I know."

He nodded, picking the instrument up and hugging it to his chest.

"Keep it," I said when he set it down again. He shook his head, but I insisted. "Really, keep it. I was holding it for someone, but..." It was my turn to shake my head, not wanting to go down *that* road. "It's yours." My voice was rough with emotion as I made the decision for him.

He nodded his gratitude before collecting both the instrument and bow, staring at me like he had so much to say.

"Goodnight," I said. "Or good morning, I guess."

He glanced back once he got to the door, his expression soft and reassuring. It made being in there alone, after he walked out on me, not feel so bad.

CHAPTER 15

William

I assumed things would be weird between us after that. At the very least, I believed Ryan would avoid me for the rest of the day. But when I entered the living room that afternoon, he was there, idly plucking his violin strings while gazing at the dark clouds in the sky.

"Hey," I whispered, my voice unrecognizable from sleep. He hadn't startled, which meant he'd heard my approach. He took a deep breath before he faced me.

We watched each other from across the vast space, his intense disposition and the dismal weather setting the tone in the room. It felt like we were balancing on a knife's edge.

"Are you okay?" I asked. "Are *we* okay?"

He didn't so much as blink an affirmative.

"Do you regret what happened?" I decided not to skirt around what took place in the studio. We hadn't kissed, we'd barely even touched, but it was the most intimate and vulnerable I'd ever felt with anyone. The sweet, dark scent of him stalked me in my dreams. Even now, I could feel the baby soft texture of his curls on my fingertips.

"I don't regret it," I added, choosing to be brave. "But I'm worried that I hurt or triggered you, maybe?" Although he'd initiated it, my nearness hadn't come without sacrifice on his part. The caress of my nose along his skin had been wordlessly asked for, but I couldn't deny the erotic element of the act. It had affected him.

The image of his hard length pushing toward mine filled my head until I ordered it away. Still, with all he'd been through, I couldn't help wondering if I'd caused him more mental harm. I thought about the scars on his body, then some of the words he'd shouted at me on paper.

Burned!

Slave!

Cut!

Broken!

"You have to communicate how you feel, or felt, about it. You can't leave me guessing. Not about this." I scanned the coffee table, and then the kitchen behind me for a notepad. I'd purchased too many for one to not be laying around. I spotted one on the counter near the stove, and thought about getting it, but then I'd have to take it to him. I didn't want to get too close until I knew it was okay to.

"Damn it, Ryan. Nod, or shake your head, or cut a hand through the air... *Something*. Just let me know you're okay."

The muscles in his jaw ticked. He looked so pale in the sunless room. A marble statue under a mass of inky hair. The fitted tank he wore covered the roadmap of horrors along his chest, but it exposed his broad shoulders and the supple flesh I'd had the pleasure of scenting. The loose jeans had holes at the knees, and his toes peeked out from the baggy hemline. Ryan was tempting, even now, and I felt horrible for noticing at a time like this.

Circling the couch, I flopped onto it, sinking into the pillows and scrubbing my hands over the scruff on my face. I needed a strong cup of coffee. "What are we doing here?" I whispered to myself, throwing an arm over my eyes. I couldn't look at him. Couldn't take how my feelings were changing and deepening when he could never be mine, when making him mine shouldn't be the goal. It confused the hell out of me. I had a hard time remembering why I'd brought him here to begin with, because my reasons for keeping him here were less clear than they were before.

Damn Xavier for forcing me to see the truth. I felt selfish. Maybe I'd always been.

I'd slept in shorts, so the sudden brush of denim against my bare shins gave me goosebumps.

Lowering my arm to the cushion, I opened my eyes to find Ryan standing above me. I didn't blink. Couldn't stop my heart from racing and tripping over itself, because all my energy went into remembering how to breathe.

Ryan sank onto the coffee table, setting his violin beside him. I wanted to sit up. I wanted to inch forward until my knees touched his, but I couldn't run the risk of pushing him away.

His Adam's apple bobbed as he maintained eye contact with me. Lifting a hand up, Ryan tugged the strap of his tank off his shoulder. The movement slow, adding a sensuality to it, the tight fabric made a tearing sound as it stretched.

I dug my fingers into the cushions to keep them off of him, waiting for his next move.

Ryan chewed on his lip for a moment, then sighed before lifting his chin. The move elongated his neck, and he watched me with full autonomy from below his lashes. He was terrified, but he wanted this. *That makes two of us.*

Choosing a position of submission, I slid to my knees in front of him, securing my hands behind my back. "You're in control," I whispered, leaning into what I knew would forever be my favorite part of him. The place my rebellious heart tried to convince me could be mine. My mind kept me in check, though. *He can never be yours.*

Like earlier, I breathed him in, running the tip of my nose over his shoulder—now shaped by muscle. I moved higher in a lazy, zig-zag motion, not wanting to neglect even one pore. I wanted to experience every inch of supple skin perfumed by cocoa butter soap and an aroma belonging only to him.

Ryan shuddered when I reached the space between his collarbone and jaw. My lips felt like they'd go up in flames as they coasted over the quivering vein in his neck. I placed a ghost of a kiss to the lump at his throat, feeling his swallow.

I straightened, not wanting to push my luck. Every part of him trembled, even his curls, and his lips were swollen from all the nibbling on it he'd done. I'd never seen his cheeks so red before, or his pupils so blown.

Bliss radiated within me, spreading through all the decrepit places, bringing them to life in its wake. I couldn't show any of it on the outside, though. The sadness of that almost threatened to reverse the healing made to my soul. I dropped to my haunches, turning away.

Ryan's finger met the corner of my chin, pulling a hitched breath from me. He brought my gaze around to his, tilting his head, looking *into* me. He must have found what he'd been probing for—what I'd tried to keep locked down—because after glancing down at his shaking hands, he brought both index fingers to the corners of my mouth and lifted them into a smile.

He removed his fingers with caution, like he thought the smile would slip without his support. It didn't slip, it'd been begging for too long to be set free, begging to be seen. "Can I?" I showed him my two fingers and gestured toward his lips.

Ryan shook his head. But then he smiled on his own. No show of teeth, just a small, timid life of his lips.

My own smile fell, and I gripped the edge of the coffee table to stop myself from falling over. "You... You have dimples," I breathed, eyes so wide they hurt. Ryan bit his lip and blushed. "You have *dimples*," I repeated. "They're beautiful."

He tucked his hair behind his ears before checking on his violin.

"H-how about a movie?" I asked, sensing this part of our afternoon nearing its end and not wanting him to disappear. I eased onto the couch.

Ryan shook his head no, shoving the violin at my chest, scowling. I chuckled, and he seemed okay with that too.

"*After* a lesson," I amended. Ryan could have whatever he wanted. He'd returned my smile to me. From then on we included violin lessons into our daily routine. We now had a jam packed schedule with no room for anything or anyone else. I went to bed every night afterward with one thought on my mind. *I could survive like this.*

Of course, life would have other plans for us.

"THAT WAS MY mother." I entered the kitchen and slid my phone onto the counter. Ryan was busy making omelets and breakfast potatoes. We'd started watching cooking shows at night. He seemed interested in this particular recipe and nailed it on the first attempt. "She said to tell you she hasn't stopped worrying about you."

Ryan flashed his little smile again. I'd seen it a few times since its first appearance. It never ceased to floor me.

"Ugh," I groaned, screwing up my face and pulling my sweaty shirt away from my body. "I should at least change this." After a run, we normally showered before we ate. Ryan's fascination with the fall leaves overtaking the sidewalk delayed our return, so we were ravenous.

He'd picked his way through a pile of them in search of the perfect one to sketch. He'd studied the shape, color, and veins of it with a critical eye, paying attention to every detail. It felt safe to assume fall was his favorite season.

I changed my shirt, then got everything set up on the island. We settled in, scarfing down our food while I stole glances at him, pondering when would be the right time to bring up the fundraising gala. Other than our morning runs—when the streets were clear of people and traffic—we hadn't ventured out to do anything else. Ryan preferred an isolated existence. If I were being honest, so did I. I couldn't remember the last time I'd brought up Safe Haven.

Skipping the gala wasn't an option, though. It might not have seemed like it lately, but my foundation meant everything to me. The black-tie charity event provided an opportunity to raise more funds and awareness for the cause, and to catch up with those we'd helped—and those we were still aiding. It was a way of saying thank you to all involved in the success of Freedom Fighters. I wanted Ryan there.

After a while, Ryan dropped his fork and gave me an "out with it" expression.

"The Freedom Fighters charity gala is in two weeks. I'd like you to attend it with me."

Ryan leaned back on his stool, I could already see him preparing to tell me no.

"My mother will be there. And Davidson. He works the gala every year, handling the security. No one gets in unless they're on the list, and there will be places you can disappear to if you feel overwhelmed and need a moment to yourself. We call them serenity rooms. Or you can stay with me," I rushed to say when he frowned. "I'll need to mingle a bit, but I'm not the primary focus of the night, so I won't be too preoccupied. It's important. It's how we're able to help so many people like yourself. It'll be good to get out, and—"

He made a stop motion with his hands, and I quieted. He lowered them once satisfied with my silence.

His lips thinned, then relaxed, then thinned again before he motioned toward his body, still clad in his sweaty running clothes.

"There's time to get you a tux." I kept my excitement from my tone. "I'll take your measurements." It would've been best for my tailor to take them for accuracy, but Ryan wouldn't let anyone touch him. I wasn't even sure he'd let me take them. Aside from baring his throat to me on occasion, as though attempting to build up his tolerance for physical contact, we didn't lay a hand on each other. He didn't even sneak into my bed while I slept anymore. "We'll make it work," I promised.

He considered me for an excruciating minute before going back to his food, stopping every now and then to add something to his sketch-in-progress. I did the same, eating and bouncing my knee under the island until I thought

I might crack from the angst.

Eventually, Ryan flipped the page on his sketchbook, writing something out before pushing it my way.

Yes, his note read.

"Yes?" I asked. "Yes?" This time I let the excitement break free, and Ryan rolled his eyes. "Yes!" I whooped, leaning over the island to cup his face between my hands. I planted a quick kiss on his mouth, recoiling once I realized what I'd done. My stool rocked back, and I clung to the island to keep from falling with it.

Ryan gritted his teeth, the vein in his forehead bulging.

"I-I'm sorry," I spluttered. "Ryan... I didn't mean to—"

He closed his eyes and unclenched a fist, holding a finger up to halt my incoming onslaught of words. Splaying his palms on the island, he tapped each finger until he got to ten, then repeated the process.

Opening his eyes, he picked up his fork and started eating as if nothing had happened. He didn't storm off, not to be seen for days. Didn't shrink in on himself, or glare at me either. After having enough of me staring at him dumbfounded, he jabbed his fork toward my plate, telling me to eat.

In a daze, I righted my stool, licking my lips and finding it hard to feel bad about having the taste of him on me. I kept my mouth shut after that, knowing when he needed a moment to even himself out again.

When we were done, he scooped up our empty plates, depositing them into the sink before going to his room. Blowing out a breath, I gave my heart time to come down from the shock before heading for the shower.

Balancing happiness with regret proved to be difficult, like enjoying the beauty of a rose in your hand and feeling the pain of the thorns. Ryan agreed to go to the gala, but I'd screwed up in a big way by kissing him. I didn't know whether to smile as I scrubbed myself clean, or stop and listen to the voices telling me how stupid I was. *You're sinking*, they said. *You have no business trying to keep anyone else from drowning.*

I'd just stepped out of the shower, facing the mirror and tightening the towel around my hips when the sound of a hiss behind me sent dread slicing through my body.

"Fuck, Ryan!" I shouted, whirling on him. "You can't just barge in here without knocking first!"

I realized too late he could still see my back through the mirror. Bile rose up my throat. I slammed the door on his baffled expression, pressing my forehead to it as I battled to keep my anger contained.

Peering at the damaging mural Ryan had gotten a perfect view of, my blood chilled and bone deep worry set in. I couldn't face him. I couldn't face myself, so I avoided him for the remainder of the afternoon, eating and taking meetings regarding the foundation in my room.

I HALF EXPECTED him to be long gone when I emerged from my room, or have a dozen or more questions. The city had gone dark by then, and Ryan sat on the living room floor, propped up against the window admiring his violin. I loved the way he cherished it. Made me think if I was ever lucky enough to have him, maybe he'd cherish me in the same way.

I'd never have him, though. Not when I reacted in such an abysmal way to him seeing the most damning thing about me. Not when I stood there too afraid to explain myself, too afraid of his reaction to my explanation. To his *rejection* of it.

He pointed toward the kitchen, lit only by the stove's overhead lamp. The oven was set to warm, the scent of pasta breaking through the fog in my head.

"You cooked for me?" I whispered. "After how I treated you?"

He shrugged a shoulder, shuffling over to the coffee table for his bow before sitting on the arm of the couch to practice. It was odd. He behaved as though the incident never happened or he'd forgotten about it. But it had happened, and he hadn't forgotten. He just seemed over it.

Otherwise he'd be asleep, or alone in his room, or taking over the library with his notepads and books. He wouldn't be out here babysitting the dinner he'd prepared for me. His rapt attention on his instrument was an act. He'd waited up worrying about me like my mother often did when I'd lived at home.

"Thank you," I said, hoping he also heard the apology in my tone. He paused mid note but didn't look up at me, then continued to draw the bow over the strings.

My stomach cramped as soon as the first bite of food hit it. As much as I wanted to eat, my anxiety made the task near impossible. My lunch from earlier was still on my nightstand.

If I forced myself to eat now, I'd likely spend the next few hours bent over the toilet. I placed the leftovers in the refrigerator, then leaned against it to listen to Ryan play a little longer before making my way back to bed.

Moonlight poured in from the balcony, illuminating the spot on the wall I'd been staring at between meetings all day. A light knock sounded on my bedroom door, forcing me upright. "Come in."

Ryan closed the door behind him before resting against it. I could smell his soap and shampoo from the bed, and the ribbed pajamas he now sported clung to him.

"You knocked," I whispered, wavering between remaining calm or destroying everything in my vicinity. He shouldn't have to knock. Not with me. I wish I didn't need him to, but there were too many scars, triggers, and landmines still unaddressed. I'd need to tackle those first. I needed to find the courage to be totally honest with him. Not tonight, though. Tonight I wasn't brave enough to do it.

He pushed off the door, taking baby steps toward the bed. His lips moved as he counted, the way my mother taught him to do when feeling anxious. Once he got to the foot of the bed he waited, maybe for me to make the next move. My heart began to race as I pulled the covers back.

Ryan rolled his shoulders, clenching and unclenching his hands.

The mattress dipped as he sank one knee into it before crawling over to the unoccupied spot. We situated ourselves on our sides, hands tucked under our cheeks as we gazed at one another, still a good distance away.

As the minutes ticked by he drew closer, until we shared the same air, exchanging panicked breaths. Soon the apprehension faded, and intoxication set in.

Ryan's gaze traveled from my eyes to my parted mouth and back. I sank my fingers into my pillow to keep from shoving them into his hair. We nudged our heads forward at the same time, reducing the space between our lips.

"If you want this," I breathed in a husky tone, "you'll have to be the one to take it." I couldn't afford to get it wrong again. He'd need to make the final move.

We both clutched at our pillows now, bodies ram-rod straight and untouching.

Ryan licked his lips, the tip of his tongue accidentally brushing my mouth, pulling a strangled moan from me.

"Ryan," I groaned. I'd never been this turned on by a moment so pure in all my life. I'd had sex on private planes, been fucked on the deck of a yacht in broad daylight, and had threesomes with foreign delegates. But none of that compared to having Ryan—my beautiful, broken counterpart—in my bed, not laying a hand on me, yet touching me in ways no one ever had.

I could barely see through the haze of anticipation. I felt fulfilled and his lips hadn't even brushed mine. Satisfied, and my cock hadn't even spilled a drop. The rush of excitement, fear and lust made me dizzy. But the best part of it all, was the feeling flooding my heart.

"I don't need more," I breathed. "This is enough. *You* are enough."

My words lit a fire in Ryan's eyes. He breached the miniscule gap, covering my mouth with his. I let out a low whimper that should have embarrassed me, but I couldn't think past my shock to focus on that.

Neither of us moved, other than to continue strangling the pillows clamped between our hands. It was a soft press of our lips, barely any pressure at all, but I felt it in every corner of my mind and body.

Ryan pushed a little harder until my lips were pressed against my teeth. Our eyes were open.

Tentatively, he parted his mouth, and I followed his lead, allowing his shy tongue in. We groaned in unison, Ryan's grip moving to his shirt collar, as my toes curled beneath the blanket.

He tasted minty, and my gums tingled in the wake of his tongue's exploration. I grew hot as he became greedy, and I ripped the duvet away as his back arched, body leaning forward instead of away.

Our legs writhed as the kiss deepened, our breathing escalating to dangerous heights. Abruptly, Ryan pulled away, my lips puckering in chase of his. He rolled to his back, staring up at the ceiling. I followed, willing the fire spreading through my body to recede.

"Will you stay?" I whispered after a while. With the moment now cooling, remnants of what I'd been feeling before he knocked on my door started to creep back into my mind. I felt raw, and I needed him. From the corner of my eye I saw him nod.

"Thank you." I shifted to my side, facing away from him, tracing my kiss-warmed lips.

My hopes were low for getting any sleep, but with him there with me it didn't matter. Maybe he sensed my turmoil, or perhaps he was dealing with his own, but I could've wept when he inched closer.

I sighed, wondering if he knew how much it meant to me right then to have his back up against mine. To have his *bones* up against mine.

CHAPTER 16

William

We slept together every night after that, and kissed before bed. We ensured only our lips touched, because physical contact in more than one way at a time overwhelmed Ryan. It took all his energy to keep the panic at bay while he kissed me. Having to focus on anywhere else our bodies touched would've been too much.

We'd kiss, then he'd let me bury my nose in his neck, where I breathed him in before skimming my lips down to his shoulder. Then, we'd roll over and fall asleep back-to -ack.

There was kissing and scenting during the day too, just not as all-consuming as when our bodies were aligned in the dark. A surprise peck on my cheek as I ate dinner, or he'd trail a finger down his throat while we watched the rain from the living room floor. A not-so-subtle request for my lips to be there.

Ryan could be demanding too. If I was in the library reading or responding to emails, or engrossed in a movie we were watching, he'd sit on my desk—disrupting my paperwork—or toss popcorn at me to get my attention. I'd stalk him while he backed into a corner leaving himself with nowhere to go. Then he'd close his eyes and raise his chin as he parted his lips for me. I'd make the kiss count, knowing it would be mere seconds before he retreated.

I'd leave him flushed and visibly aroused, then back away with a smile, because I couldn't seem to stop smiling lately.

I didn't prey on his reactions, or take advantage of what I thought his body wanted. His mind held the control, and it never hesitated to shut things down once he couldn't handle any more. I'd simply excuse myself to take care of my own needs in private before returning. It had been the best two weeks of my life.

"Are you almost ready? It's a thirty-minute drive across town, more if there's traffic. We're going to be late," I complained from outside Ryan's bedroom door. He'd been in there getting ready for over an hour. I never got impatient with him, but I was already on edge because he'd logged into the medical portal for his test results and had yet to confirm if everything came back okay.

I didn't ask. He had a right to his privacy, but he'd avoided it for over a week after learning they were available. Relief flooded me when he held up a note with the words I'd been waiting for scrolled across it.

I'm ready.

I showed him how to create the online account, then stepped away so he could set up his password and log in. He then stared at the screen for an agonizing amount of time before logging out and leaving me standing there to think the worst.

I'd printed out my results the moment I got the email saying they were ready. I'd shared them with him, hoping it would give him the courage to face his, and also to explain how to interpret them once he did.

"Take your time," I said. Entering a ballroom gala with close to a thousand people in attendance would be staggering for anyone, let alone Ryan. He had a right to take all the time in the world. "No rush."

I'd made it to the end of the hall when his door opened. My shiny Oxfords squeaked against the floor as I spun around.

"*Wow,*" I breathed, drinking him in. The all-black tuxedo fit the contours of his slim, yet defined, body. I'd been nervous the measurements I'd taken were incorrect. Getting them had been a challenge, and he'd walked away when I'd asked if I could double check for accuracy.

His beauty had a youthful quality, but his broad stature and time-worn eyes lent credibility to his manhood. He carried the weight of many hardships on his shoulders, and he'd seen, experienced, and survived things no one ever should.

His shoes were shiny too, but he'd gone with the Venetian-style loafer. They looked great on him. He wore his hair in a neat bun, which put his slightly larger ears on display. Of all the things he seemed self-conscious about, his ears were never one of them. I found them sexy as hell.

Seeing him dressed in all black pleased my senses. His attire complemented the shock of black hair and black eyes set on a canvas of pale skin. The beauty mark staining his cheek could've been seen as an imperfection, but it only made him more gorgeous. I wanted to do things to him I wasn't proud of. Things I hoped he'd one day be ready for.

I held myself in check, looking him up and down while he waited for a response from me. "You look..." I trailed off, searching for the right word. *Beautiful, sexy, arousing...* "Nice," I ended up going with, but it didn't feel like enough. "You look more than nice. You look amazing, Ryan. Handsome."

He tugged on the cuffs of his sleeves, the tips of his ears turning a pretty shade of pink.

"Your bow tie is crooked. Is it okay if I fix it?"

He nodded as I approached, holding his head up for my adjustments.

I stepped back to take in my handy work. "Better."

I pulled his wool coat from the closet, holding it open so he could slide into it. He did the same for me.

"Are you nervous?" I asked, fixing my lapels. Ryan blew out a heavy breath then nodded. "Don't worry, I won't let—" I caught myself before promising not to let anything happen to him. Those words felt empty to me. "I won't let you out of my sight. We stick together."

He nodded again, then held up a finger while he dug into his pocket for a folded piece of paper.

"What's this?"

I'm okay, it read.

"I'm okay," I repeated under my breath before snapping my head up. "You're okay? *Really*?" I wanted to be extra sure. He pointed to the two words again. "So why did you keep me in suspense all day? Do you just live to torture me?" I joked.

He smiled. A wide smile showcasing his straight, pearly whites, and his dimples. I'd never seen that smile before. My expression must have shown it, because he actually chuckled. With sound! It was low and gone as fast as it came, but I'd heard it.

"Do that again," I whispered, but he sealed his lips as though he knew he'd given me something precious and was now unsure if I deserved it. I'd already stored it in my memory bank, though. I'd never forget it.

It sounded like a beautiful but chaotic musical scale. A succession of rumbly, husky and hoarse. It sounded untried. It was the sweetest music I'd ever heard.

❧

AFTER HANDING OUR coats off to the attendant, we stopped near the wall fountain along the perimeter of the room. I wanted to give Ryan time to adjust to the grandeur of the ballroom before we did more than dip our toe in it.

His jittery gaze roamed the room, absorbing everything in it from the gem-cut chandeliers, to the extravagant floral arrangements at the center of every table. I tracked his perusal of the finely dressed attendees as the stringed section provided ambient music from the curved stage.

"There are sanctuary rooms around every corner. We invite all the residents and staff from Safe Haven, and other survivors who we've helped. This," I said, in reference to the flurry of activity happening in front of us, "can be a lot for some of them to take in. We set up the rooms as a place they can escape to when they need to be alone. They're insulated from sound, they lock from the inside, and they're filled with every comfort you can imagine." I waited for him to look at me. "If you feel at any time that you need to get away from this, you let me know. Even if you want to go home." I hadn't meant to say home. I should've said my place. But it did feel like home. *Our* home.

I gestured toward each exit, pointing out the security personnel dressed to blend in, discreetly manning each door. "Most of them are off duty or retired cops. They're trained to handle any emergency situation."

Ryan turned to me abruptly, leaning in for a kiss. I stepped back. He frowned, his confusion obvious.

"We shouldn't do that here," I whispered, hating that I couldn't anchor him, that I couldn't provide some normalcy. "There are people here who may question that." Xavier being one of them. I'd spotted him chatting on the opposite side of the dance floor. I supposed the end of our working relationship didn't mean the end of him supporting an important cause. I would've expected nothing less from him.

A hand eagerly waving in the air caught my attention. I smiled as my mother beckoned us over to the chocolate fountain. Davidson stood next to her in a black and white tux. Ryan went rigid.

"I already told him you aren't ready to talk. He can't force you."

Ryan nodded after taking a deep breath. We let a server pass before diving into the fray.

"William!" Mark Delaney called, weaving through the throng of people to get to us. He was an older, stocky gentleman who ran one of the largest film studios in Hollywood. He was also one of Freedom Fighters most generous donors.

"Mark," I replied with as much enthusiasm as I could fake. I had three unread emails from him in my inbox, and several from my agent ordering me to get back to him.

"You're a hard man to get a hold of these days," he said, skipping the small talk. I appreciated it. Ryan stepped as close to me as he could without actually touching me, his head turning in every direction.

"Have you had a chance to look at the script I sent you? You're the first person I thought of when it crossed my desk. It was like kismet," he chuckled, accepting a champagne flute from a server. "Who better to handle the screen composition for something like this?"

"I'm flattered, truly, but I'm taking some time off from work right now."

"Yes, your agent said as much. I knew she couldn't possibly be serious, though." He laughed. "You're in the prime of your career. You're on the wish list of every idiot in Hollywood holding a camera, for Christ's sake. You'd be insane to pull away now." His laughter died when I didn't join in. Ryan stiffened beside me, his gaze burning into the side of my face.

"You... You can't be *serious*?"

"I am. Now if you'll excuse us—"

Mark stepped left, cutting off my path to my mother and Davidson. "Now hold on a second." He hadn't sipped from his flute yet, and I was close to snatching it from him and downing the contents myself. This wasn't something I wanted to address in front of Ryan.

"Just read it, will you? It's about the kidnapping of the Kiwanika girls. I thought this topic was close to your heart. We spent hours talking about it over lunch the last time I was in town on business."

The Kiwanika reservation sat just shy of the Mexican border. After a string of young girls went missing over a three-month period, the authorities decided to take the situation seriously. At first, they believed they were dealing with a case of rebellious teen girls who'd run away from home. Then reports came in linking the disappearances to a sex trafficking ring. The investigation ended up hitting a wall—until one of the girls managed to escape.

Ryan twisted his whole body toward me, but other than a quick cursory glance from Mark, we both ignored him.

"It is important to me," I said, trying not to show my urgent need to end the conversation. "But as I said, I'm on hiatus at the moment. I can bring it to

Xavier. He's more than capable of filling my shoes."

"I'm sure one day he will be," Mark said. "But we don't want Xavier. We want you." He sounded disappointed now, making a final request before striding off. "Look, just read it and give me a call if you change your mind."

I turned to Ryan then, my heart absorbing the blow of sadness his gaze unleashed on me. "Come on," I rasped, "or my mother will eat all the chocolate." My joke didn't land well, and for once his refusal to speak didn't leave me conflicted. I had a feeling I knew where his thoughts had gone, and I didn't want to hear it.

"If it isn't the man of the hour!" a familiar voice declared from somewhere to my right. Ryan and I were on the outskirts of the excitement now, about twenty feet from where Davidson and my mother chatted with one another.

"Senator Roberts," I greeted. I relaxed my jaw as he came to a stop in front of us, managing to make my next words sound welcoming. "Happy you could make it."

"Are you kidding me? I'd never miss it. What you're doing here is amazing."

"Thank you. I don't mean to be rude, but my mother's waiting for us." I looked over, and bless her heart, she stared back looking concerned.

"Ah, yeah, she looks like she's ready to come over and chase me away." We both laughed at that, only mine was forced. "Real quick before you go, we're introducing a new bill to congress next month. One that will grant stiffer penalties for anyone involved in the trafficking of people—at *all* levels. You'd be surprised how many officials are accepting bribes at our ports and borders. Think you can make it out to D.C. in support? Maybe bring a few residents from Safe Haven? It'd be good to show the faces of those who've been affected by this. Maybe they can even share a few words—"

"I'm sorry to interrupt Senator, but I'm unfortunately unable to travel at the moment. If the offer still stands, I can see if someone from our staff would be willing to represent Freedom Fighters. Just reach out to me with the details."

"Someone from your staff?" He frowned. "I do think having you there personally could make all the difference."

"Sorry, but I can't." I got Ryan and I moving before he could add anything else.

"What's wrong?" I asked when Ryan came to a halt. He looked to the table where Senator Roberts now sat next to his wife, then back at me. "Let's just meet up with my mother and Davidson so we can get to our table."

Ryan grabbed the hem of my jacket when I passed him, stopping me. He crossed his arms, stubbornly refusing to move until I told him what was going on with me.

"I can't leave you," I whispered. He dropped his arms to his sides, that heartstopping sadness gracing his handsome face again. "I don't want to."

We met up with my mother and Davidson, Ryan offering them both a small smile before we were ushered to our tables. The awards and performance portion of the evening was about to start.

I couldn't enjoy or concentrate on any of it. Not even the testimonials made by so many survivors, or when I took the stage to thank them all for their show of courage and perseverance. Not even when Davidson hopped on right after to give an impromptu speech in my honor.

Thoughts of Ryan plagued me. I needed to know what ran through his mind while he stewed in the seat next to me. I released an audible breath when the music started up, and the Emcee ordered everyone to the dance floor.

Davidson leaned over to me. "Hey, can I talk to you for a minute?" He'd attempted a whisper, but he had the kind of booming voice that couldn't quite pull it off.

I glanced at Ryan who now listened to my mother chattering on the other side of him. "We'll be fine," she said, pausing to address my look of concern. "Won't we, Ryan?" He nodded once without looking at me.

Davidson and I excused ourselves, but we didn't go too far. I had to keep an eye on Ryan, to be able to get to him quickly if I needed to.

"We go together."

I let my eyes drift shut on those words as they floated through my head, taking me to a place I didn't want to be.

"We were able to piece together more information," Davidson said, bringing me back to reality. I stood taller.

"Anything you can share with me?"

"Most of it is public knowledge by now. Some of the Americans found had been taken while studying abroad. Others while on vacation. A few were abducted right here on our soil, They were forced into labor mostly, but some were passed through the underground sex trade. Residential brothels, online ads and escort services, fake massage businesses... A few were purchased by wealthy sadists to be kept for personal use. Those stories are the worst."

I wondered where Ryan fell into those categories. *Labor,* my mind supplied. It had to be forced labor. The other possibilities were too painful to consider.

"William?"

"Huh?"

"I said they were all rounded up and resold to the same benefactor shortly before we found them. None of the survivors can provide an accurate description of the man." Davidson looked at me as though he wondered if Ryan could.

"I told you, he can't help you right now."

"You know, I would think you of all people would—"

"I want these people caught," I said, stopping him right there. "But he isn't ready to talk about it, and by law, you can't make him. You've got plenty to work with from the others. Chances are Ryan knows just as much, or as little, as they do."

"They've all got their own story," he said. "They've all faced their own individual horrors."

What else did he want from me? Did he want me to tie Ryan down and force him to give us answers?

Davidson gave a slow nod when I didn't engage further. "Have you gotten him any closer to agreeing to go to Safe Haven?"

"Uh, no. I'm still working on it." I smoothed my hands down my jacket front.

"Uh, huh," Davidson said, tone indicating he didn't buy my casual act. On top of everything else, this was the last conversation I wanted to have tonight. Davidson was also the last person I wanted to have it with. If anyone could see through my bullshit, it would be one of the FBI's top agents.

"Has he communicated anything about a family? People who may be happy to know he's alive?"

"No. He hasn't."

"Has he given you his last name? Something we can plug into the missing person's database?"

"No."

Davidson glanced at Ryan before bringing his shrewd gaze back to me. "Have you *asked* him?"

"Is this an interrogation?" My guilt made me defensive.

"No, but the fact that you think so is concerning." He sounded offended. Davidson was a father figure of sorts. He knew what made this cause personal to me, even if he didn't know all the particulars involving my abduction. He cared about me, about the work we were doing. He had a right to his questions, and he was smart to be worried.

"I don't think pressuring him for those answers would be helpful."

"What are you, a shrink now?" In addition to caring, Davidson could also be direct to a fault.

"He'll be okay. I'm helping him."

Davidson moved into my line of sight, blocking my view of Ryan. "He's fine," he said when I tried to look around him. "He's with your mother, and there's more than a dozen armed men stationed at every entry point."

I stepped back to let a giggling group of women pass between us, then closed some of the distance again. "Say what you need to say, Davidson."

"I know you don't have bad intentions, because that's not the kind of person you are. But I'm aware you have your demons. Sometimes demons influence our decisions." He pursed his lips before continuing. "You have feelings for him."

I didn't see any point in lying, and it wasn't a question anyway. Davidson had seen right through me. All I could do was nod.

"And how does he feel?"

"The same." I assumed anyway. Ryan hadn't spelled out his feelings for me, but he'd more than shown them. Some of those feelings were good, and depending on the day, some not so good. I felt it beneath his soft, seeking lips every night. "It's complicated."

"I imagine it is," he mused. "And now you're *helping* him." He'd stressed the word as if quoting me. We were quiet then. "Did I ever tell you how my marriage ended?"

"No," I said, clasping my hands behind me to keep from fisting them. I despised Davidson blocking my view of Ryan, especially when he seemed intent on giving me a rude awakening via a cautionary tale.

"This was during my tenure with the police department. She walked into my precinct pretty banged up. Her boyfriend had done a number on her. He'd been beating on her for years." His jaw clenched at the memory.

"Even through all the swelling and bruises, she was beautiful. I wanted to bury the guy. We brought him in and booked him. He had a few outstanding warrants and ended up doing some time. She had nothing. She'd been completely dependent on him. I went into hero mode." He glanced over his shoulder at Ryan as if to say I was in that mode now.

"Long story short, we fell in love. I bought her the dream house, complete with the fucking white fence, gave her the 2.5 kids and a dog. The whole bit." He lowered his voice, but it still carried over the music and hum of conversation around us.

"I gave her anything she wanted, she never had to work for anything. With what she'd gone through, I'd built a wall of protection around her instead of encouraging her to deal with her issues. It was mostly unintentional," he admitted. "I thought I was doing the right thing. Giving her what she wanted. Keeping her safe. But part of me didn't want her to be dependent on anyone but me. I didn't want to lose her, but in the end, she'd only traded a shitty cage for a gilded one. But a cage is a cage, kid, and eventually your little bird will want to break free." He let that sink in before adding, "That's if you don't start resenting him first, because if he's caged, then so are you."

"It's not like that," I swore, feeling his words wrap around my neck and squeeze. "He'll get better. It takes time. He's already more comfortable with me."

"With *you*." He said it in a way that didn't make me feel so accomplished. I'd measured Ryan's progress by the progress he'd made with me. I'd made it all about me.

"That's great, kid." His tone suggested the opposite.

He moved out of the way, and Ryan stood there, my mother not too far behind. He seemed pained, turmoil creating fine lines across his features. How much of Davidson's lecture had he heard? Even the tail end of it would've been too much.

"Ryan," I breathed, but he'd already made an about-turn, knocking into a server and sending the contents of his tray crashing to the floor. A collective gasp spread through the immediate area as glass broke and champagne splashed onto the people loitering nearby. My mother reached for him, but he shrank back, bumping into a table, toppling it, the silverware, and floral arrangements to the floor. He had the whole room's attention now. Even the music came to a halt.

Flushing bright red, he ducked his head and hurried in the direction of the sanctuary rooms.

I glanced over to Davidson, whose gaze was sympathetic, but also seemed to say: *He may be getting comfortable with you, but what about the rest of the world?*

CHAPTER 17

William

The apartment was cold when we arrived. November nights could be brutal, and I hadn't left the heat on. Or maybe the chill came from the man in front of me. He'd been in a dark, quiet mood the whole drive home.

"He's wrong," I whispered into the darkness. We hadn't turned on a single light, as though in silent agreement that illuminating our problems would only make them worse. Ryan sighed, removing his coat and slinging it over a kitchen stool before striding in the direction of the dining room. The moon and city lights illuminated his way.

I bowed my head, bracing myself for what lay before me. Discarding my coat as well, I followed his trail.

He stood at the drink cart, staring out the window with his back to me.

"His ending doesn't have to be ours," I said, coming up beside him. "You can stay here as long as you want, take all the time you need before making any big decisions. Our home isn't a cage, and I'll never resent you." *Our home.* I'd said it deliberately. Did he enjoy the sound of it?

Ryan glanced over at me, the blank stare I hated so much in place. Since he never talked to me, I relied on his expressions. For now it seemed he wanted to hide from me.

He uncorked the decanter of scotch, pouring a few fingers into a tumbler before swallowing it down with a wince. I'd seen him drink once before, when he'd taken a couple of sips directly from my glass. This felt different. This felt like preparation for something terrible.

He poured another, the sound of liquor spilling into the glass made my stomach tense.

"Ryan—"

He offered it to me, becoming more persistent when I shook my head. Red mahogany liquor swished around the tumbler as he shoved it into my chest.

I took it, holding his challenging gaze as I knocked it back in one go. He left me holding the glass, picking up a fresh one for himself before filling both tumblers halfway. Our eyes locked, his blazing with defiance.

"We don't have to do this," I said softly, but he'd already downed the contents by the time the last word got out. He exhaled the burn, then nudged the bottom of my glass until it reached my lips, not relenting until I'd ingested the last drop.

Ryan nodded his approval, then poured us another with twice the amount as the first two. This wasn't the cheap stuff, it was potent and fast acting. My limbs were already loosening, my common sense gearing up to abandon me. The way Ryan's eyes shone, like a star held under water, said he was experiencing the same. He wanted us reckless, I realized.

"Ryan, that's enough," I said when he helped himself to a fourth. He made a show of holding my stare as he inhaled it in one gulp. He dragged the back of his hand over his mouth before setting both our tumblers aside.

"You don't have to prove anything." I assumed that was his intention. To prove he was no longer a victim to his trauma, that he could push past his limits. "I'll take whatever you can give me. I'll never ask for more."

Ryan gave me a forlorn look similar to the one he'd given me at the gala. Like I'd said the saddest thing he'd ever heard.

He backed up so he could see all of me, his stance relaxing as he took a visual tour of my suited body. What I'd said hadn't made a difference.

The temperature of the apartment didn't bother me anymore. I was so hot I could practically feel steam rise from my skin. Maybe I'd imagined the cold.

Removing my jacket, I tossed it away from me, uncaring about where it landed. My bow tie went next. I popped the top two buttons on my shirt as I strode to the other side of the dining room, leaning a forearm against the floor-to-ceiling window. Dangerous carelessness threatened to take over me as the liquor passed through my bloodstream. I began asking myself questions like: would this be so bad? Began telling myself things like: we both just want a little comfort, that's all.

My cock throbbed behind my zipper, and my head pounded to the beat of my heart. "I don't know what you want from me, Ryan." I shut my eyes at the ache building behind them. "I wish you could just tell me. Or show me." Was that truly what I wished for?

The silence stretched long enough for me to regret not taking another drink. All I needed was one more to finish me off, to put me to bed and out of my current misery.

Shoes tapping against the floor made my chest tighten. Ryan's steps were sure, unfaltering, and picking up speed as they headed for me. I was terrified of what would come next, even while wanting whatever it would be.

I kept my gaze fixed on the moon shining over the river, even when his footfalls quieted, even when his scent wrapped around me from behind. Ryan's long, elegant fingers wrapped around my bicep, and I let out a sound of both shock and pained relief. He'd never grabbed ahold of me before, never gripped me as though he didn't want to ever let go.

All sensation rushed to that location, to the flame his hand ignited below my shirt. The touch wasn't much, yet I felt branded by him.

He pulled me around until I met his nervous but determined stare. He'd made up his mind to push himself tonight. I wondered how much of that could be blamed on the Rare Cask he'd just breezed through. I'd had enough myself that I was content to see how this played out, falling into his trap.

The antique grandfather clock struck twelve, the chime startling us both. A new day, a new beginning. A new opportunity to start over, to change our minds and make better decisions. Ryan watched me as if I were a specimen under his microscope, wondering what to do with me. I'd be his specimen, his pet project, his guinea pig... I'd be whatever he wanted me to be, so long as he touched me right then.

As if sensing my desperation for him, he raised an unsteady hand, the other hand fisted at his side. Starting at my brows, he mapped out my face, the trembling easing the more comfortable and confident he became. I wanted to shut my eyes, to focus all my attention on how his hands felt on me, but his caress was feather soft, so I needed the sight of him to know this wasn't a figment of my imagination.

He took the most time with my lips, tracing the outline before grazing the groove below my nose. My mouth parted to release the pent up air, blowing aside a wisp of his hair. I considered pulling the rest free of his bun, but kept my hands to myself.

Ryan's fingers tickled past my chin, and I lifted my head, clearing the path to my throat. The notch at my collarbone fascinated him, he swirled his finger there, seeming content to stay for a while.

"Why does your touch, your gaze, your anger, and even your spurts of joy always feel like... more?" I asked, my brows drawing together as I tried to answer my own question. "How is it that you own me so completely, and I haven't even had all of you, yet?" The insertion of "yet" made me come off presumptuous. That wasn't my intention, but maybe it was his. Maybe he wanted me uninhibited tonight. I looked at the remnants of scotch in the crystal decanter, my gaze hot and unafraid when it returned to him.

Both of his hands were on my face now, the backs of his fingers ghosting along the scruff I hadn't shaved. I could've sworn I'd seen a glint in his eyes when it grew in, so I left it.

Ryan had a pattern of teasing his affection, keeping me on edge and wanting more. An addict receiving his dose in tiny increments. Just enough to keep me functioning, but never enough to leave me satisfied. I harbored a constant craving for more, the unfulfilled need made this intoxicated version of me want to snatch him up by the hair and punish him for what he did to me. For what he *didn't* do to me. Even now, he taunted me without knowing it, unintentionally dangling himself from a string while I fought to enjoy it instead of reaching for him.

My mind hadn't been completely obliterated by the alcohol, so my conscience shouldered its way through the procession of lust, inappropriate thoughts, and anticipation. I pushed down my carnal needs for a moment while I attempted to do the right thing.

"Ryan, I-I haven't been honest with you." My eyes rolled back as his blunt nails raked over my scalp, not quite digging in. "Your being here is about more than me wanting to help you. I've been selfish," I whispered, ashamed of myself. "I *am* selfish—"

The delicate stroke of his lips against mine put an end to my momentary lapse into guilt.

Ryan cradled my head with the faintest touch of his fingers. His mouth trembled but parted, mine opening too as his tongue tentatively entered.

Like always, his kiss was soft and shy, his moan an extra shot of both. The spicy duet of vanilla and woody notes added a hint of masculine rebellion to his flavor. I lapped at the inside of his mouth, issuing my own low rumble as every nerve ending in me came alive.

He retreated a step, and something in me snapped, red clouded my vision at the thought of losing this. At the thought of losing him. I banded an arm around his waist, hauling him into my chest and deepening the kiss.

I clamped a hand over the back of his head, holding him to my mouth as I launched a full-frontal assault on him.

I spun us, pressing his back against the window as I lined my body up with his, slapping my palms on either side of him, caging him in. I was losing myself, losing all self-control, and a part of me begged for Ryan to stop me.

His fingers bunched into the collar of my shirt pulling me closer as his body vibrated beneath me. I got lost in him. Lost in taking his breath away, lost in my inability to find my own.

"Fuck," I panted against his damp lips before sending my tongue in again, swiping it across his and dominating the moment. We were on fire, or maybe it was the world around us that burned, searing all our inhibitions to ash.

I jutted my hips forward, my throbbing erection rubbing along his zipper seam, searching for proof we were on the same page. As though my desperate search were a call to action, his own length began to rise to the occasion. I increased the friction, increased the pressure of the kiss, increased the grip of the hold I now had on his hair.

Something changed then. Ryan froze, then began pushing me away instead of pulling me in. He jerked his hips back sharply, shoving his back into the glass.

My senses weren't returning fast enough, I still kissed at his mouth, following him after he'd retreated from me. It took a punch to my shoulder for me to jump away. Ryan slumped forward, catching himself with his palms on his knees.

"*Fuck*, I... I..." Everything hurt. My head, my heart, my balls and my cock. I stumbled backward, throwing my hands out for something to break my fall. I bumped into the table, sending it and a few chairs screeching across the floor.

Ryan watched me from his bent position, his hair now wild and free, chest heaving.

I needed to say something, needed to do something to fix this, to help him, but I couldn't even see straight. My arousal still had a hold of me, like the part of my brain in charge of my desire had malfunctioned.

"S-sorry. I'll b-be right back," I stammered, taking uncoordinated steps toward the archway. There was movement behind me, then something crashed to the floor. I whirled around to find Ryan near the head of the dining room table, anger bleeding from his eyes, a chair toppled over on its side.

I spun away again, needing to escape so I could handle the need raging through me. Between the alcohol, the months spent locked away with him here, and the rough encounter we'd just had, I thought I might explode.

Ahead of me, something hit the wall with an explosive crack, and glass shattered everywhere. I stared at the shards in disbelief, turning slowly to find Ryan by the drink cart, the other tumbler in his hand. But I wouldn't give him what he wanted. I wouldn't give him a fight.

I made for the entryway again, this time quickening my pace. I heard the whistle of the tumbler passing before it connected with the opposite wall. I ducked, covering my head to protect myself from the sharp projectile.

My own hostility took over. I whirled around to him and roared, "What do you want from me?!" I charged over to him. Ryan nearly tripped over the wheel of the cart to avoid being run down by me. "Tell me what you want," I gritted out, placing my hands onto the sides of his head and shaking. "Tell me what the hell you want!" I could only remember being this upset once before in my life. And like then, the anger was mostly misplaced. "You can't give me more, but you don't want me to leave. Tell me what to do here, Ryan," I pleaded.

He knocked my hands away to swoop in and kiss me. I froze for a split second before getting on board. Ryan had never kissed me with such passion before. Our unabated mutual lust rose to inferno levels, but he pushed me away before we got a chance to incinerate everything to the ground.

"I'm going to my room," I said, my voice roughened by pent up arousal. "Don't stop me." I backed away a couple of steps while he panted heavily, his hair a halo of chaos around his face. He took a step forward, and I held up a hand to ward him off as shards of glass crunched beneath my shoes. "I can't do this with you. Not tonight. Don't—"

He was on me before I'd finished my warning, his hands fisted in my shirt as he slaughtered me with his kiss. I growled, fisting his tuxedo jacket to keep him on his feet as I used my larger body to back him up. We were against the window again, both of us manic, the kiss chaotic, animalistic, raw.

Ryan slapped at my chest, and I reared back instantly, my lips curling in rage. He was playing with me now, egging me on as though trying to force a different version of me to the surface.

He sagged against the glass, blood smeared his top lip. I touched my fingers to my own mouth, they were red when I pulled them away. I couldn't say who bit who.

I was sweaty, exhausted, and horny as fuck. The effects of the alcohol deepened by the minute instead of fading. I needed to punch something, and

I needed my cock in my fist ASAP. I attempted to leave again. This time Ryan flipped the whole table over, the crash of the centerpiece smashing activating my body's emergency brake system.

I took in the destruction. "You're making a habit of destroying my shit," I said in a deceptively calm tone I didn't recognize.

Ryan stepped out of the way of the table and debris, circling the chair he'd previously knocked over and retreating to the darkest corner of the room. He'd increased the distance I'd have to travel to get to him. He was a wreck, but beneath the blood and sweat and harsh breaths, he looked pleased with himself. He had me where he wanted me.

The voices taunted me as I stalked him. They wanted me to put him down. To bend him over and fuck him until he fell apart.

I unbuttoned the cuffs of my sleeves, rolling them up my forearms as I approached. The ticking of the grandfather clock added an ominous tone to the violent and sexually charged mood.

"Oh, no you don't," I said with a menacing edge, hauling him back into his corner when he tried to slip past me. His spine slammed into the wall. "It's too late for that." I ripped his jacket away from his shoulders, yanking it down his arms and casting it aside before tearing open his shirt. Buttons flew in every direction. "This is what you wanted, right?"

Ryan's hiss of pain melted into a moan when I jerked his head back and dove in with teeth bared for his neck. He pushed at my chest again, and I bit down with enough pressure to still him, but not enough to break skin.

I sucked my mark into his flesh as he rose to his toes, keening at the back of his throat. "You'll be irrevocably mine when I'm done with you," I snarled, before latching onto a fresh patch of skin. He bucked into me, but I was stronger, and when he tugged at the neck of my shirt, I pinned both his wrists to the wall.

"This is how you wanted me, right?" I breathed close to his face, kicking his ankles apart so I could settle my cock against his. He turned his head away when I lowered to kiss him, my lips meeting his cheek. I bit down there too, stealing the kiss I wanted when he jerked his head back around. He tasted like blood, salt, and adrenaline, and I let go of his wrists to shred the tank top he wore down the middle.

Seeing his scars snapped me out of my craze. He covered himself with his hands and I grabbed hold of my aching head. "I'm sorry." I turned to dash out of there, but he yanked me to a stop by the neck of my shirt.

I snarled in frustration, going at him again, ducking my head to seal my mouth over one nipple. He made a wounded sound, his feet slipping on the hardwood floor.

I lifted him by the hips, his legs automatically wrapping around me even though his hands were now pushing at my face. "Why are you fighting me?!" I no longer recognized myself. I rutted against him, undulating as though I were already inside him. "Tell me what you want?! Tell me! Do you want me to take it? Is that what you want?"

My blood iced over in my veins, the wrongness of this whole situation striking me like a bullet to my chest. Even the voices abandoned me to my insanity. An insanity they'd instigated along with Ryan. I was the one to blame, though. This was all on me.

His feet hit the floor, and I backed away in abject horror. "Is that... Is that what you want?" I peered down at the buttons and pieces of torn fabric on the floor, then at my hands in disgust. Ryan didn't have to answer me, guilt covered his face in shades of red. Why would he want me to do something so vile? Why... The only reason I could think of made my stomach roll.

"Is that what they did to you?" I whispered, praying he said no. I wanted to fall to my knees and scream to the heavens, begging God to let the answer be no. My whole being, everything I was and used to be hung on by a thread as I waited for the answer I already knew.

I ransacked my memory for the words he'd written down on paper. It seemed like eons ago now. I went over all of them in my head.

Burned!

Stab!

Cut!

Drugged!

Slave!

Cold!

Hungry!

Chained!

Floor!

Beat!

Broken!

He hadn't written down rape, and I'd held onto that delusion. I'd convinced myself his aversion to physical contact stemmed from another form of abuse. I'd told myself the only abuse he'd endured was on that page. Any or all of those eleven words were the reason. I let myself believe that because I knew I'd never recover from the truth.

Ryan busied himself with righting his shirt and fastening the only remaining button. It was enough to cover his scars, the most vulnerable and revealing part of himself. I didn't miss the look on his face before he lowered it. *Shame.* I knew firsthand how it made the eyes dull, how it made the mouth lax and the breath leave you on a heartbreaking exhale.

I paced away from him, punching my fists through the air, screaming, needing to expel my rage somehow. I charged over to the buffet, swiping the decor on top of it to the floor. I ripped the portrait of A Dying Man's Melody hanging on the wall above it, breaking it over my knee before throwing the pieces aside.

Ryan stood still in his dark corner while I destroyed everything I could put my hands on, adding to the pile of rubble. Between the two of us, the room had become a war zone.

My throat was as dry as scorched earth by the time I was through, the air burning in my lungs felt hotter than lava. I paced a tight circle, kicking debris out of my way. The spots clouding my vision began to clear, and I laced my hands behind my sweaty neck as I gazed up at the chandelier.

"I don't know what to do," I said, utterly dejected. "I could say I'm sorry for what happened to you, because I am. I'm so fucking sorry, Ryan. But it won't fix it. No matter how many times I say it, it'll never be enough."

Davidson's words came back to me, highlighting how naive I'd been.

"What are you, a shrink now?"

"No, I'm not," I muttered to myself.

I took a step in Ryan's direction. I needed to get to him. To hug and protect him, even though it was too late for the latter. He shrank back, molding his shoulders to the wall.

Kicking a chunk of the portrait out of my way, I walked over to the table, righting it before leaning against it. I scanned my useless brain for something to say, for encouraging words aimed to soothe. I thought about what happened here tonight, thought about all the nights we kissed in spite of our fears and pain. Thought about what Ryan had been trying to do through those kisses. He'd been trying to repair himself. Trying to find the beauty in something that had only ever caused him pain.

Had he never been touched from a place of kindness after having been sold? Had he never experienced pleasure in his own body? Did he only associate sex and intimacy with brutality and non-consent? I'd hoped somewhere along the way, someone in the sick and twisted world he'd lived in handled him with care. But it seemed nothing but savagery had tarnished every corner of his life.

As I watched him curl in on himself with his hands drawn protectively to his chest, I decided to do something about it. To take a different route, one that hopefully led to his heart. To the damaged bits of it. I'd educate him.

"Sex can be stimulating," I started through a scratchy throat, "invigorating, exhilarating, and about a dozen other things. When done right, and with the right person, the experience can even feel spiritual." I checked to see if I was scaring him. His hands slowly drifted to his sides.

"Sometimes the right person isn't always the person you're in love with. It could mean someone who cares about you, someone who respects you. Someone who's just as concerned with your pleasure as they are with theirs. Although, I hear sex with a soulmate can feel like you've died and gone to heaven. That the connection goes way beyond two bodies coming together. They say the experience can be so life affirming it reduces you to tears." I huffed. "I read that in a magazine once. I'll have to take their word for it. I've had plenty of sex, but I've never been in love. Sounds amazing though, doesn't it? To feel that much for someone else? For the orgasm to be secondary to the strengthening of a bond?" Did he hear the wistfulness in my tone? The longing?

"Sex used to be my form of escapism. Something I used to take my mind off of my pain, or if I needed to shut down the voices haunting me." I tapped a finger to my temple. "My first time wasn't as romantic as the movies would have you believe it'll be. It hurt a little at first. And sometimes, if I go too long without bottoming, it can feel like the first time all over again."

I wasn't sure if I was helping matters, or making it worse. I was rambling again, but I spoke from the heart. Hopefully that made sense through the mess I was making of things.

"But the pain of first-times gives way to a euphoric, all-consuming and spellbinding gratification. The touch of your own hand can do the same." I scooted higher onto the table, leaning back on my palms. "Granted, jerking off can sometimes feel like you're only taking the edge off your desire. Killing the flames but still choking on the smoke. I got that horrible metaphor from a magazine too. I'd be lying if I said it didn't feel good, though. It has its own appeal."

I couldn't make out his face as it was hidden in the dark, but I could see everything from his neck down clearly. His feet shuffled a fraction closer.

"No always means no, Ryan. And just because that wasn't your reality then, it doesn't mean that it isn't now. You don't need to be afraid or ashamed of your arousal, and when you're ready, just know that sex can be the most beautiful thing you've ever taken part in. And if you're never ready, that's okay too. Sex doesn't need to be the measuring stick used to determine if you're whole. To determine if you're worthy. You already are." I pressed my lips together to keep them from quivering.

I wanted to give him something. I wanted to *show* him what it could look and feel like if he ever chose to explore his own body.

Hopping down from the table, I used a shoe covered foot to herd the broken glass near me into a neat pile several feet away. Then I returned to my spot and began to strip, painstakingly slow. I kicked off one shoe, waiting for some sign that he couldn't handle this before removing the other.

"Sometimes I get so turned on when I'm around you," I said nervously. What if I scared him further? What if my honesty made him terrified to be near me? Ryan eased forward another inch, his chin now exposed to the moonlight.

I unbuttoned my pants, taking my time to lower the zipper. He took another step toward me. "Sometimes jerking off once isn't enough. Sometimes it takes a couple orgasms before I can be in the same room with you." I shoved my pants down, kicking out of them and cupping myself through my boxer briefs. Ryan hadn't retreated, so I continued.

"Anything can set me off. Like watching you struggle with a note during our violin lessons. You do this cute thing where you scrunch up your face, and you stare at the instrument like it's your mortal enemy." My cock grew heavier, firming up as I spoke.

"See?" I whispered, gesturing to the imprint of it beneath the tight cotton. The lower half of his face was exposed now. "This is what you do to me, Ryan." My cockhead reached for the waistband of my underwear.

"Sometimes it's the way the tips of your ears heat when you're embarrassed, or the way you slam your door when you're tired of my rambling, or when you just need to be alone. You're mercurial, and I fantasize about having you through each and every one of your moods." I swallowed. "I come the moment my hand touches my dick on those occasions." I started on the third button of my shirt, the top two already undone.

"The way you run, so efficient and graceful. The way you eat like you haven't eaten in days. With so much gusto and... hunger. The way your curls are tighter around the nape of your neck, but looser near your crown. The way you never seem to think about a haircut, or fuss about the clothes I buy you, or the bath products I choose for your bathroom. You're low maintenance. Your outer beauty means nothing to you, but it means so much to me because it matches your inner beauty."

I hesitated after undoing the final button, but then I reminded myself he'd seen my back before and hadn't made a big deal out of it. I peeled my shirt away, my chest filling with arrogant pride when the volume of his breathing increased.

"I want to show you what you do to me, Ryan," I whispered. "I want to show you how an orgasm, how self-pleasure, should look and feel. Let me redefine this for you."

I peeled my boxer briefs off, then stretched out on the center of the table, planting my feet flat on it. Spitting into my palm, I wrapped it around the base of my shaft and stroked upward. My other hand gripped the edge of the table as I let out a needy moan.

I continued to work myself in an unhurried rhythm, raising my head at the sound of Ryan's footsteps. He emerged from the shadows, stepping into the moonlight, his eyes shimmering with unshed tears and curiosity.

"Fuck," I bit out letting my head fall back, a desperate need to come blurring my vision. I felt the muscles in my neck grow taut as my body jerked and clenched all over.

Chair legs scraped along the floor, and I glanced between my spread legs to see Ryan seating himself at the head of the table. He watched with intrigue, splaying his palms flat on the wooden surface as I beat my dick.

"I won't l-last long," I bit out, hand pumping faster as my balls drew close to my body, "with you s-staring at me like that." I swiped a thumb over my sticky slit, swirling a finger over the sensitive tip before jerking just the top half of my cock. The fingers of my other hand dug into the underside of the table.

"Lick your lips," I ordered. Ryan's gaze flew to my face, eyes widening. "Lick those luscious lips for me. Yes, that's it," I praised when he obeyed. He blushed, then went back to obsessing over my dick, his eyes went wide when a rope of precum squirted out.

"It feels... so... *good*," I said, my voice rough with lust. Ryan sat like a man before a feast, and the sight made me even hotter. Sweat glistened all over my body, and I dug my heels into the table as my climax began to take shape.

Spitting on my middle finger, I relaxed my body enough to squeeze the thick digit inside my hole, hissing at the burn as I plunged it in and out of me. "*Fuck...*" I groaned, striking my prostate over and over again.

Ryan's stare bounced between my face, my ass, and the painful erection I damn near strangled. I tugged my finger free, crying out from the loss of it before wetting my index finger and shoving them both in. I arched off the table, whipping my fist up and down my cock as I came all over myself. I barked out something unintelligible, toes curling as I forced a third finger in, feeling the ache but not giving a damn.

I played with myself through the aftershocks, my bicep getting a workout as my asshole clenched around my fingers.

My body dropped to the table when it was over, limbs falling in every direction and I blinked slowly, struggling to see past the fireworks my orgasm set off.

Ryan pushed up from his chair, strolling the length of the table, drinking in every available inch of me, his fingers dragging along the edge of the surface as he went.

I felt his gaze like a soft wind along my feet, then up my calves and thighs. I wondered for a split second how he perceived my scars in this moment, but inwardly sighed with relief when the sight of them didn't make him falter.

He paused near my hip, captivated by the mess dripping down my groin. Some of it slid down my ball sack as well. A final drop dribbled through my slit as he watched. I pinched my cockhead, helping the thick, pearly white bead of cum erupt over the tip.

Ryan reached a quivering hand toward it, then pulled back.

"It's okay," I whispered, sated and drowsy. "You can touch me if you want."

He scanned my upper half, and I resisted tensing up under his perusal. Going back to my cock, which now relaxed on its side, softening, Ryan reached his fingers out again. They traveled up from my hip, then through the trimmed hair surrounding my pubic area.

"Your fingers were made to torture me." I shuddered under his touch. I was spared the overstimulation when he stopped before reaching my dick. He coated a finger with my release, examining it before bringing it to his nose for a sniff. He then sampled it with the very tip of his tongue.

"It's an acquired taste," I breathed as he explored the flavor of it.

Ryan scooped up a bigger helping this time, sending two fingers to the back of his throat before pulling them away clean. His eyelids fluttered, his expression starved.

"Fuck, Ryan," I groaned.

He flushed, drying the digits off on his shirt. Doing so disturbed the flaps, exposing the hard bulge at the front of his pants. He followed my gaze to it, then tugged the long hem back into place.

"Touch it," I said, my tongue thick, mouth dry. Between the scotch, the destructive rage, the mind-blowing orgasm, and hurricane of emotions that'd wreaked havoc on me, it was a wonder I could keep my eyes open at all. For this, I would. For him, I'd do anything. "It can't hurt you. Your cock isn't your enemy, Ryan."

He took several steps back, his breathing ragged when a quick glance down showed he hadn't outrun his erection. It had followed him. It always would. He had to deal with this.

"It's okay," I crooned, slowly sitting up, swinging my legs over the table. I wanted to go to him, to calm him with my touch, but that would've only made things worse. I rapped my knuckles on the table in a slow rhythm, counting with each tap until he relaxed.

I didn't ask him to touch himself again. Pressuring him wasn't my goal, and I no longer wanted to live in a fantasy world where I alone could fix him. "It's okay."

Ryan chewed on his lip, but then he pressed a hand into his hip before drifting it over to his cock at a snail's pace. He kept his eyes on me. They widened in time with his mouth parting. I curled my fingers over the edge of the table.

His loose, shaky grasp on himself tightened as he snaked his hand up and down his shaft. Within seconds he climaxed, cheeks warming and body bowing on a soundless gasp. Ryan threw his free hand out to grab one of the dining room chairs, using it for support as his orgasm ripped through him.

He dropped his chin to his chest, features tightening like he was in pain. I didn't know how much longer I could sit by and watch him hurting from experiencing something that should've felt good.

Please, don't let him be angry when this is over. Please, don't let him be ashamed. I waited on pins and needles for him to regain his control, hoping this wouldn't cause a setback.

Ryan straightened, his hair clinging to his sweaty face. He blinked his watery eyes and a tear fell, stabbing me straight in the heart, but then his mouth trembled into a smile.

"You did it," I breathed, breaking into an emotional smile too.

His smile faded, and so did mine. Where did we go from here? And would we go there together?

"What is this?" I whispered. "This thing between us." More pointedly I asked, "Who am I to you?" I knew who he was to me, although I couldn't say it. How I felt about him, and why, would scare him off.

I feared I was nothing more than a starting point for him. A place he'd found safety and comfort in before transitioning to something, or somewhere else. He wouldn't be wrong for feeling that way. That should've always been the purpose. I'm the one who'd blurred lines. Who'd crossed them altogether. But now that I had, I didn't want to lose him.

Ryan strode from the dining room. I let him go, remembering how much he enjoyed time alone after dealing with something new. I'd deal with my unrealistic expectations on my own, some other time.

I needed to get cleaned up and get some sleep. I was so tired, though, and the ache in my chest made it hard to move. I slumped onto the table, rolling to my back, the firm surface sparking a twinge in my shoulder. *Just a few minutes. I'll close my eyes for just a few minutes.*

The muted notes of Ryan's violin captured me before sleep had set in all the way. He played near the window, the city serving as his muse.

I'd never heard the piece he played before. Must have been something he'd been practicing in private. It didn't occur to me to think about why he'd chosen to play it now, or here with me as his audience. By morning, it dawned on me that it was his way of saying thank you. I'd realized it was a breathtaking, haunting goodbye.

CHAPTER 18

William

Later that morning, I lay in bed trying to figure out how I'd made it to my room. I gave up once my headache started pounding. The last thing I recalled was falling asleep on the dining room table to the sounds of Ryan playing the violin. *Ryan.*

I rolled toward my nightstand for my phone, checking the time. A little past noon.

Tossing the covers off, I discovered myself naked and crusted with cum underneath. I took a quick shower and dressed before heading for my closed bedroom door. A note waited there for me.

I want to go to Safe Haven.

Ryan wasn't in his bedroom, so I hurried toward the living room, my steps faltering on its threshold. He waited by the window, staring into the rain with his wool coat on.

"Hey," I said in a soft voice, suddenly feeling sick. I held up the sheet of paper. "I got your note."

His expression wasn't neutral, but it wasn't emotive either. I couldn't decipher his thoughts, but I got the impression he wasn't holding back on purpose. He seemed resigned. He'd made up his mind, and the only thing left to do now was leave.

"I was actually going to talk to you about this today. I think it's the right decision." After the night we had, both at the gala and when we returned home, I knew it was time to broach the topic again. I thought it would've taken some convincing, though. Thought I'd get a few more days with him before we set off. Now I'd have to get used to spending most of my day without him.

"I could drop you off in the mornings." I walked into the room. "And pick you up in the..." my words stalled after rounding the couch and seeing the packed duffle bag near his feet. "...evenings." Realization hit me. He didn't have plans to come back home. *Has this ever been his home?*

He lifted the small notepad and pencil I hadn't noticed him holding. He'd anticipated needing them, knew I'd try to talk him out of this. He scribbled across a fresh sheet, moving faster than he had just weeks ago. He passed it to me.

I want to stay there.

"Yeah, I can see that." I tried not to sound bitter

about it. "Is this about what happened in the dining room? Did I do something wrong?" *Something you can't forgive?*

He shook his head no, his gaze now tender, but his shoulders still set in determination.

"Give me a few minutes to change, then we can go." I shut myself in my room, falling back against the door. *This is a good thing. This will be good for him. We can still be...friends.* All the convincing in the world couldn't erase the fear swirling around in my gut. I should've wanted this for him. I *did* want it for him. I tried hard to.

I swapped my thermals for a pair of jeans and a sweatshirt, then made a quick call to Safe Haven, alerting them of our impending arrival.

Ryan was already waiting by the front door, bag hanging from his shoulder, hand on the knob. He couldn't get away from me fast enough. I grabbed my coat from the hall closet, and we left without another word.

I took my time getting to Safe Haven, telling myself I needed to drive carefully in the rain. A convenient excuse to hold on to him a little longer.

Safe Haven was a gated community tucked away from the city limits, surrounded by acres of untouched land. Land I owned. Beyond the multiple layers of security required to enter, stood the three-story community hall—constructed to resemble a home—down to the gabled roof and shuttered windows. It was warm and inviting, and matched the aesthetic of the residential housing behind it.

I pulled into a guest parking spot, threw the car in park and shifted to face Ryan. I'd been about to tell him he could change his mind at any time. That all he'd have to do was have someone from the staff call me and I'd be here in the blink of an eye. But he was already out of the car, opening his umbrella as he rounded the trunk with his things.

I led the way into the community hall, the heart and soul of the place, and the first stop for any visit to Safe Haven. Everyone had to register here, and the only way to gain access to the rest of the property was through the courtyard—only accessible from the hall.

Ryan took in the scope of the place, eyes darting around as I dropped both our wet umbrellas into the holder near the entrance. From the cozy sitting area across from the lit inglenook fireplace, to the quotes about survival, hope, and strength framed along the walls.

Up ahead, past the plush, twelve-piece circular couch—where many of the staff and residents often communed for game nights—Peggy stood from her desk, meeting us halfway.

"Mr. Mayes," she greeted cheerfully, her Safe Haven nameplate pinned to her white shirt. "And you must be Ryan." She turned to him, exuding the motherly warmth she was known and loved for. She didn't take offense to his lack of response.

"This is Jackie," she indicated over my shoulder. The petite, younger woman approached, saying hello to us all. "If it's okay with you, Ryan, she'll help you get registered in one of the offices in the back. She'll answer any questions you may have, before showing you where you'll be staying."

Ryan gripped the strap of his bag, wringing it between his hands before nodding once. He avoided my gaze as he followed Jackie through a door.

"He's non-verbal," I told Peggy once we were alone. "He'll need lots of paper and pencils. *Pencils* not pens. He's still learning, and often needs to erase things to start over." I glanced at the door Ryan disappeared through. "Are there pencils back there?"

"Yes, Mr. Mayes," Peggy assured me. "I passed on your instructions to Jackie after our call earlier."

"Okay, good," I whispered, having already forgotten about the call. "He likes Eggos and bagels. Don't make either too crispy. And caramel popcorn. And—"

"Judy Blume books," she cut in, her smile warm and knowing. "We've got it from here, Mr. Mayes." She stepped closer and laid a wrinkled hand on my back, ushering me toward the entrance. I whipped my head around, as though I'd expected to see Ryan flying through the door, begging me to take him back home.

"You know the drill, right?"

"No contact for the first seventy-two hours," I muttered. There were certain exceptions to the rule. We'd never keep anyone from their family. But typically, family members weren't tracked down that fast, and if they were, the survivors often went home with them instead of coming here.

The rule mostly applied to the authorities, who sometimes wanted to ask follow up questions. If the individual agreed, we allowed it. If not, we protected their right to decide. The rule also applied to me, who tended to be overly invested in the progress and recovery of the residents who stayed with me before transitioning here.

My check-ins became a sort of security blanket to them. So I understood. They needed to get used to their new environment. I guess this was how parents felt when dropping their kids off at school for the first time.

"He'll be fine," Peggy said softly, rubbing my shoulder.

I sighed. "Yeah, I know." I wasn't so sure about myself.

I RETURNED TO a quiet apartment. And not the type of quiet I'd grown used to, the kind where I was the only verbal occupant. It was the kind that whispered: "*You're alone.*"

What did I do with myself now? I could already feel the voices waking up.

Kicking off my wet shoes, I headed for the one place—the one thing—that might help. I went to the library to check in with Gargantuan, texting Davidson with an update on my way there. He replied instantly.

Davidson: I'm glad to hear it. Safe Haven will be good for him.

I couldn't find it in me right then to agree. At least he hadn't outright made it about his investigation.

Davidson: How are you holding up?

Me: That's to be seen.

I didn't bother reading his follow up text. I wasn't in the mood to be cheered up, or to share my feelings on the matter. I exhaled as I entered the library.

I hadn't read my favorite book in weeks. Months even. I hadn't needed to. I had Ryan. The book wasn't on the shelf dedicated to it. The one that didn't get much sunlight, sandwiched between two dense textbooks no one cared about. The spot I'd kept it hidden in just for me.

I dragged my fingers along the spines of every book on the shelf, and the one above and below it, reading each title I passed. Maybe I'd put it back in the wrong place. No such luck.

Rushing over to my desk, I flipped through the piles of paper there, then ransacked each drawer in search of it. I came up empty. I charged for my bedroom next. I'd started reading at night again, maybe it sat in my nightstand or closet. I dug around, but the book wasn't in any of those places.

I strode down the hall, at a loss for where the hell it could be. As though the book summoned me, I paused near Ryan's bedroom door. I checked his closet, upending the dresser drawers. I looked under his bed, tossing his slippers and shoes out of the way. I even searched the cabinet below his bathroom sink, dumping the contents onto the floor. Nothing.

Feeling weary, I fell onto his made bed, bringing one of his pillows to my nose and inhaling. My lungs filled with his scent, making me miss him even more. I'd been about to toss the pillow down and leave, but I did a double take at finding the book resting in its place.

I took my time flipping through its pages, looking for dog-eared corners or highlighted passages. Anything to indicate what he thought about it, or if anything resonated with him. Mostly I wanted to know if he realized how much the story meant to me. And if he understood why.

I grew restless, hopeless, and scared. Signs of an oncoming episode. I curled onto my side, gripping the book to my chest. For the next three days, I allowed the voices to have their way with me.

Peace. I wanted peace more than anything else. My mother once told me true peace could only be gained through devotion to living a life of honesty. Living a lie was a soul-crushing job, but the harder I fell for Ryan, the harder it became to tell him the truth.

I RETURNED TO SAFE HAVEN on the third day. Dusting the snow off my coat, I looked around the busy community hall for Ryan. Some of the residents were chatting by the fireplace, others were engaged in conversation on the couch. None of them were Ryan.

Upon seeing me, Peggy shot up from her desk, her short legs carrying her over to me. "Mr. Mayes," she greeted. "How are you?"

"I'm fine." *I'll be even better once I see Ryan.* "I'm here to see Ryan. Is he available?"

"Ah, no, he's in a therapy session with Dr. Shwartz right now."

"Okay. Can you let him know I'm here once he's free?" I walked over to the sitting area, not realizing Peggy had followed me until I sat down. I raised a brow at her. "Is something wrong?"

"He has literacy tutoring right after. He seems to love it and won't want to miss it."

"Will he have a few minutes to talk in between?"

She cleared her throat. "I hate to be the one to tell you this... Oh! Here's Dr. Shwartz now. I'll let you two speak." She walked away before I could get another word out.

"Katherine," I greeted, standing for a hug. I'd hand-picked her to run the therapy clinic myself after having worked with her on the Freedom Fighters charity circuit. She'd known about Safe Haven since its inception. She'd been a champion of my purpose from the moment we met.

"William, how's everything?" She pulled back to gaze up at me. Between her sharp eyes and medical experience, it'd be useless to pretend with her.

"I've been better. I'm here to see Ryan. Is he okay?" Peggy's odd behavior left me worried.

"He's fine, all things considered. He's an amazing young man. Very resilient."

"Has he spoken to you?" The idea bothered me more than it should have. I selfishly wanted to be the one to hear his first words.

"No, but we've found other ways to communicate. He's open to getting help, and I'm sure we have you to thank for that." The compliment was sweet but I knew the signs of being built up to be let down.

"What's going on, Katherine?"

"I think it's best if you wait until Ryan reaches out to you before visiting him."

"*You* think it's best? With all due respect, shouldn't he be making that decision himself?"

Her amber eyes filled with compassion, making me flinch. "I'm speaking on his behalf, William."

"Oh," I replied, my feelings hurt. "Did he say why?"

"He wants to stand on his own two feet. And by the look on your face, I think a little time might be good for the both of you." She gave my forearm a gentle squeeze. "You got him this far. Give him a chance to cross the finish line under his own steam."

My heart sank, but I knew she had a point. "Sure. I can do that." I searched for the inner tools I'd need to accomplish the task.

"Can you give this to him for me?" I handed her the small bag I held. "I bought him a phone." With no longer living together, he couldn't pass me notes anymore. We would have zero communication outside of me visiting him, and now I couldn't even do that. I'd planned on spending the afternoon teaching him how to text.

"Sure," she said, relieving me of it.

"I saved my number in it, but someone will need to show him how to use it." I didn't know if he already knew how to work a cellphone. I hadn't thought to ask because he didn't speak. The chances of him calling me were pretty much non-existent. "Can you have someone teach him how to send a text? In case he wants to reach me. No pressure though."

"Of course. I'll show him myself. Depending on the model I may need to enlist Peggy, but we'll get it done."

"Thank you." I made no move to leave.

Katherine squeezed my forearm again. "He'll be fine, William. I promise. Let us do what we're here for. What *you* put us here for."

I SPENT THE next seven days checking my phone for missed calls or text messages from him. I'd decided not to give up on him calling. If he was working on himself, that meant he might've been working on finding his voice too. There were never any messages or calls from his number.

It'd been ten days without Ryan. Did he not miss me? Need me? *Want* me?

Sick of my own wallowing, I carried my weary body to the music studio. Maybe work would shake me out of the funk I was in.

But as I entered the code to the door, I remembered I didn't have anything to work on. I'd canceled everything I had lined up, and turned down all incoming offers against the advice of my agent and manager.

I pushed into the live room with plans to play the piano for a while, since I had yet to replace the violin I'd given Ryan.

His violin. It perched on its stand. He hadn't taken it with him. A folded note was stuck between the strings. I'd never been so excited and so scared to read something in all my life.

I plucked it from the violin, unfolding it with trepidation.

I can't let you change my mind. I want to be fixed. Hold this for me.

It all made sense now. Why he'd been packed and ready when I woke up. Why he'd waited by the door while I got dressed, and why he hurried from the car once we got to Safe Haven. He couldn't risk me changing his mind. He knew I could if I'd wanted to, and I did want to.

"He'll be back," I whispered to the instrument. "He'll be back for you." *And maybe for me too.*

I moved over to the piano bench, needing to sit down before my legs gave out. I grew weaker and weaker by the day. His words should have bolstered me, given me hope, but they didn't shake the blue mood I'd been sinking further and further into. I'd hit a wall. I needed help.

If Ryan was strong enough to get help, then so would I. But first I needed something else. I needed *someone* else.

Slipping my phone from my pocket, I dialed the most important person to me. She answered on the first ring.

"Dr. Mayes speaking, how may I help you?"

I smiled at hearing her comforting voice. The voice that both lifted me up in love and prayer, and firmly put me in line when needed. She didn't typically answer her office phone, not unless her receptionist wasn't around. She must be on her own today.

I inhaled a deep breath, trying and failing to sound strong when I answered her question. "It's me. Momma, I need you."

CHAPTER 19

William

My mother took one look into my bloodshot eyes and pulled me in for a hug. She then gave me something for the headache I couldn't hide before tucking me in and humming me to sleep. Her voice, her love, and the light strokes over my hair were better than any pill I could've taken to shake the insomnia.

Night had descended by the time I woke up, and the apartment was clean. I hadn't taken out the trash since Ryan left, or cleaned up the mess I'd made while searching for my book. And even though she didn't bring it up, I knew she had questions about the state of the dining room. I felt terrible that she'd witnessed the aftermath of me and Ryan losing our cool.

"When's the last time you ate?" she asked as I shuffled into the kitchen.

Concentrating had been impossible lately, so I didn't even bother trying to think back to an exact date. "I don't know." I settled onto a stool.

"I'm making your favorite. Your great-grandmother's secret recipe." She stole glances at me while she put the finishing touches on the jambalaya, fighting to mother me from a place of support instead of nagging. What was done was done. I hadn't eaten in who knew how long, so she'd feed me now, and then find a creative way to encourage me into treatment for what we both knew was going on.

"Have you run at all this week?" She kept her tone conversational. "We've had a few sunny days. I don't know what's been going on with all this rain lately. You've gotta get out there whenever you can."

"No." I could feel another headache coming on. Running helped. She knew that too.

She turned the fire down under the stock pot and set the lid on top of it. She'd made enough to last me a few weeks, maybe more. I'd need to freeze some of it.

"Well, I just so happen to be off for the next few weeks. I need the break," she said, waving off my silent concern. My mother loved to work. She never took more than a day or two off, here and there. "Plus, Thanksgiving is in less than two weeks." She rested her forearms on top of the island. "I figured you could come back to Brooklyn with me tonight. Spend some time out there, get a change of scenery. You could run with me and Delilah in the mornings."

I squeezed her hand. "I'm pretty sure what you and Delilah do is called power walking. She's too old for anything more." The Yorkshire Terrier had been with her for over a decade.

"I'll put her in the stroller then." We both laughed, though mine felt tinged with mania. The tears in her eyes said she'd picked up on it.

"You told me you were okay," she whispered. She'd checked in with me a few times, and for her benefit I pretended things were fine. "I'm worried about you, baby."

I sighed. "Did you close your office at the last minute because you were worried about me?"

"Absolutely," she said without hesitation. "You swore you were fine, but something felt off. I should've just shown up at your door like I've been wanting to, but my caseloads were this high." She raised a hand above her head. "I kept saying: tomorrow, tomorrow, tomorrow..." She shook her head, squeezing my hand in return. "I heard it in your voice today, William. You told me so. And so I did what I should have done over a week ago."

I felt the sudden need to cry. The urge felt crushing, debilitating. I wanted to be alone, even when I called her. I'd used my last reserve of strength to ignore my mind telling me I'd be a burden and to not to let anyone in. I couldn't trust my thoughts right now. "What about all this jambalaya you just made?"

She smiled, pointing to a clear tote bag filled with her infamous Tupperware containers. "We take it with us, or course."

I picked at my food and swallowed a couple more painkillers while my mother packed up the leftovers.

"Is what happened to the dining room the reason Ryan decided to go to

Safe Haven?"

I'd managed to tell her Ryan was gone before drifting off earlier. "No. I think what happened at the gala did that."

She didn't pry any further. "It was the right decision." She passed me another bottle of water from the fridge. "You need to stay hydrated."

It *was* the right decision, and I had the note he left behind to give me hope. It was impossible to feel hopeful though when I couldn't find it in me to face our biggest hurdle. I needed to be free of my painful past. I needed to unlock the shackles it held me in. Believing I deserved heartache needed to end. But how could I end what I did, in fact, deserve?

I'd lapsed into another one of my extended silences, staring at a vein in the marble of the island. My mother tapped the space in front of me. "Huh?" I snapped my gaze to hers, catching the look of worry.

"I said put the water down before you spill it, baby."

I'd uncapped the bottle, and held it tilted near my mouth. I set it down without taking a sip, massaging my forehead.

"You know, when you were about six, you came home from school one day in a rage." She crossed her arms and settled back against the counter. "You were always friendly and sweet, with a dash of melancholy. Your father suffered from the blues too," she whispered more to herself than me. "Your grandfather always used to say 'What you got to be tortured bout, Mally?'"

He used to call me Mally, his Geechee accent made it sound more like Molly, though.

Even as a kid I had a touch of sadness in me. I felt *everything*, even the things other people were feeling.

"You were in rare form that day," my mother said, not a hint of humor in her tone. I listened carefully, because this seemed different than a typical trip down memory lane. There was a reason she'd chosen this story. "The schoolyard bullies had found someone new to pick on, and you didn't like it one bit."

None of that rang a bell, but it was a long time ago. Six was a tricky age. Young enough for me to not remember certain events at all, but old enough for me to remember bits and pieces of others—especially if my memory was jogged. I swallowed at the thought—and what else it could apply to—before leaving it behind.

"So I was *jealous* because they stopped picking on me to bother someone else? That's... toxic." And it didn't sound like me at all.

"No, the whole reason they started bullying you in the first place was because you'd been distracting them from setting their sights on the new kid. He was the smallest boy in class, and he wore a knee brace. You would do silly things to draw their attention after school. Tell them video games are stupid, or show off your big, fancy vocabulary." She rolled her eyes.

"Samuel," I whispered. There was power in hearing a name. Memories of that time started trickling in. "I used to dare them to spell big words right."

"You used to double dare them," she corrected. "You were always such a bright boy."

Aside from music, I'd developed a love of reading from an early age. It started with my mother taking away TV time if I misbehaved. She'd tell me to read a book. I listened.

"Anyway, they'd chase you through the streets, clearing the way for Samuel to hobble home safely."

"He lived a few blocks away from the school," I frowned. "He was seven." Samuel was a latchkey kid, and on the days when my mother or my grandfather couldn't make it to the school by the time the final bell rang, so was I.

"All your classmates were a year older. You'd been skipped from first to second grade early in the school year. It leant credibility to your smarty-pants routine." She chuckled, then shook her head, sobering. "The bullies eventually grew bored of you. Guess it was no fun harassing someone who's literally asking for it. They cornered Samuel one day and pushed him to the ground, then kept pushing him down every time he got up. They didn't stop until he stayed there. A crowd had gathered round, mocking and laughing at him. His knee brace broke, and his parents ended up transferring him to a school across town."

"So I was upset they did that to him?" I asked, unable to recall my feelings about it back then. It angered me to hear about it now, though.

"You were upset because you weren't there to help him. You'd been home getting over the flu when it happened. By the time you went back to class, Samuel was gone." My mother stepped up to the island, her tone anguished, desperate even.

"The day you came home angry... I couldn't get you to eat dinner that night, and I had to threaten to take away your Faith Ringgold book collection to get you out of bed for school the next morning. I should've been more understanding," she added, no doubt believing my behavior to be an early sign of my depression. A sign she missed. I squeezed her hand.

"I came home with a black-eye that day," I whispered.

"Yeah, Mr. Jackson said you'd gotten a good swing in on the big one before they jumped you."

"Yeah, that I remember."

"You've always been a crusader. A champion for the underdog, even when you were the underdog yourself. It both inspires me and terrifies me, because you'll fight harder for others than you will for yourself—and at the detriment of yourself."

I let the first tear fall, and the rest soon followed. She came around to my side, and I twisted in my stool to face her.

"Seeing you like this is more than I can take, baby." She cradled my cheeks in her hands, her voice begging me to help her understand. "Tell me, what makes him so special?"

I breathed through all the pain I'd been holding on to, all the pain I'd nourished throughout the years before confessing, "He reminds me of someone I once knew." It wasn't a lie. It felt like the first real step I'd taken toward the truth.

I held onto her forearms for support, expelling another breath before whispering, "There's something I've never told you."

With one hand covering her heart, and the other one pressed to her mouth, she listened to the story I'd never told anyone before. Then I removed my shirt, showing her the tattoo on my back. The memorial to everything good, to the things I prayed Gargantuan would return.

My mother didn't try to diagnose me, didn't come up with a mental health gameplan like I was one of her patients. She'd shown up at my door as my mother. My momma. And that never wavered no matter how weak I became in front of her. No matter how afraid she became for me.

She cried with me, and then she did what she used to do every Sunday after church when I was a kid. She let me pick a couple of titles from my "most iconic movies" list, and listened while I dissected the instrumentation of the score—the heartbeat of every film.

I'd unlocked my dark prison and allowed someone else in, taking me one step closer to leaving those steel bars behind.

My mother built me up that night. She infused me with love and shared stories, highlighting the grit I forgot I possessed. She'd broken through my gray cloud and shined a light on the courage needed to carry me to the pinnacle of being whole. She taught me another important lesson that night.

"Sometimes guarding a secret gives us purpose. We find false honor in the keeping of it. We allow it to define us, because without it we feel as if we're nothing. The truth is letting go is where we find our true selves. So let go, William. Tell him."

CHAPTER 20

William

Thanksgiving came and went weeks ago, with Christmas now banging down my door. I had yet to hear from Ryan. I'd gotten a glimpse of him in the holiday group photograph the Safe Haven staff emailed me. We never spared any expense in making holiday celebrations special—although Christmas was one where we went all out. I sometimes attended the parties, but I wouldn't show up there again until Ryan confirmed it was okay. I'd respect his decision to heal under his own terms.

He'd gotten his hair trimmed, which made me hopeful for his progress. A month ago he wouldn't have allowed anyone that close to him. He gazed into the camera as though he knew I'd eventually see the photograph, like he knew he was looking at me. Ryan could be intense, so it could've just been natural for him to peer into the lens as if peering into a soul.

I'd gotten a lot done during the weeks I spent in Brooklyn. My barber was able to fit me in, so I no longer walked around with an uneven line-up. I'd started running again, and taking pleasure in the sunrise. More importantly, I resumed therapy.

Dr. Stein prescribed something stronger for my anxiety, but I decided to hold off on the antidepressants. Talk therapy, sticking to a structured routine, adjusting my diet, and integrating more of the things that brought purpose into my life worked before, so we'd agreed to try them again and see where things went from there.

Feeling stronger, I kissed my mother goodbye and headed home. I'd stayed much longer than I anticipated.

The apartment was warm, and every surface sparkled when I walked in. The air smelled like the cedar spice plug-ins I loved but ran out of. Even the bed linens had been changed. It explained where my mother disappeared to, yesterday evening. She'd supposedly gone grocery shopping, but returned empty handed.

"No good sales," she'd explained.

She now had the access codes to the elevator and apartment, and I'd added her name to my pre-approved visitors list. Prior to her finding me in the depths of one of my episodes, Ryan was the only other person with that level of clearance. It made her feel better knowing she could physically get to me if there ever came another time when she couldn't reach me by phone.

I spent some time reviewing the foundation's quarterly reports, and signing important documents. Next, I scheduled some time to meet with my team to get caught up on the things I'd neglected. I then did a little journaling before calling it a night.

My therapist suggested it as a tool for stress reduction and symptom control. Journaling helped with self-awareness, and dissecting and avoiding triggers. It was the biggest game changer for me so far.

I also slept better when I wrote down everything pent up inside of me before bed, instead of carrying it into my dreams. It also helped to see how far I'd come after revisiting prior entries.

My mornings were dedicated to meditation, affirmations, and exercise. She'd suggested that too.

A text alert woke me up. I felt around the nightstand for my phone, knocking a few things over in the process before grabbing it.

The bright backlight stung my eyes as the screen lit up. I extended my arm as far away as possible, squinting until my eyes adjusted.

Ryan: Are you there?

I shot up, fumbling the phone and tangling it in the sheets for a second before replying.

Me: I'm here.

I checked the time and sent another text.

Me: What are you still doing awake? Are you okay?

Ryan: It wasn't late when I picked up the phone to text you.

I huffed a short laugh, the sound sleep heavy. How long had it taken him to figure out the mechanics?

Me: Didn't Dr. Shwartz show you how to use it?

Ryan: Yeah, it wasn't that. I wasn't sure if I was ready to talk to you yet.

Ryan: I thought I needed to be all better first.

There'd been a brief interlude before he added that.

Me: Are you all better?

Ryan: No. I'm still just getting better. But I think I always will be.

Me: I think I'll always just be getting better too.

Life was a journey not a destination. We would always be a work in progress. Dr. Stein told me that.

Ryan: I miss you.

I hadn't expected that so soon, if at all. It was a welcome surprise, one I didn't realize my heart needed.

Me: I miss you too.

I gripped the phone, watching the screen for his reply.

Ryan: I like it here. Dr. Shwartz says I'm making great progress.

I wanted to know what their sessions were about, if they were anything like mine were years ago. How deep into his life had they gotten so far? How far back did her questions go? From the moment he was sold? Before he was taken? Or all that must have transpired in between? Had he forgotten anything that happened to him? Sometimes trauma victims block the most painful memories from their mind. I wished that were true in my case. But if it was true for him, would he ever get those memories back? The urge to ask ate away at me.

Ryan: My literacy tutor says I'm a fast learner.

I could see the proof of it through our exchange. His spelling had improved a great deal, and his responses were quick too. I wanted to ask if he'd spoken yet, but the question felt too insensitive. And I didn't want him to feel like the strides he'd made so far weren't more than enough.

Me: I can tell. I hear the excitement through your responses, and you text faster than I do. My fingers are too big for the keys.

Ryan: I've had lots of practice. It's how I communicate with everyone here. I use it in my therapy sessions too. So thank you.

Me: You're welcome.

I wanted to tell him he didn't have to thank me, but I understood gratitude was an important part of the process.

Ryan: I got a job in the kitchen. Waffles are my specialty. Chef Shawn taught me how to make them from scratch. If you come by for breakfast one day, I can make you some.

Me: I'd love that.

Ryan: Tomorrow.

I smiled, burrowing into my pillows. Either he didn't know how to play hard-to-get, or he simply didn't care to. Either way, his directness pleased me. It aligned with the way I felt, because I wanted nothing more than to cancel all my plans, to drop everything and go to him. That would've taken us backward, though, and I wanted to go forward with him.

Me: I can't. I've decided to meet with Senator Roberts to discuss the bill he'll be presenting to congress. I'll be in D.C. most of the day.

Ryan: I'm glad you decided to do it. Thursday?

Me: Can we make it lunch instead? I started therapy again. I have a session that morning.

Ryan: Those are important.

Me: So lunch, then?

Ryan: Yes.

Me: What should I bring?

Ryan: Nothing. But wear your green sweater.

My green sweater? The only green sweater I owned my mother had bought me last Christmas. It matched my eyes. She'd said it made me extra handsome, but I'd chalked it up to all mothers believing their kids were beautiful. I'd worn it around the house once, on a chilly day. *He noticed.*

Me: Are you saying you like me in that sweater?

I bit the inside of my cheek.

Ryan: Yes.

He added a blushing emoji, which made me choke on my laugh. Shy even in text exchanges.

Me: Good to see some things are the same.

Me: Sexy green sweater it is.

I added the zany face emoji.

The three dots appeared and vanished an agonizing number of times. I wanted to shout: *Send it! Send it! Whatever it is, just send it.*

Ryan: I miss kissing you.

Heat pooled low in my stomach. Was he trying to give me a heart attack? I needed a little warning before he said all the things I wanted to hear but never thought I would. I tried my own hand at being upfront.

Me: I miss kissing you too. I miss sleeping with you even more.

Ryan: Me too. Can I kiss you when I see you?

I kicked the blanket off me, suddenly feeling overheated. I stopped myself from telling him he didn't have to. I didn't want to revert back to my habit of making things okay for him. My habit of enabling his fears, which could make him second guess himself. He knew he didn't have to. I had to trust that. So if he asked if he could, it was because he wanted to.

Me: Yes, you can.

Ryan: Good. I wasn't sure if you and Xavier were friends again. I've been gone a long time.

I knew what he meant by "friends."

Me: There's no one else.

Ryan: "Okay. And I know you want to tell me I don't have to, but I already know that. I don't have to do anything I don't want to. No means no. And stop sometimes means no too. And I have a right to change my mind. Anyone who doesn't agree is the one with the problem, not me. That's what Dr. Shwartz said. I'm starting to believe her.

Me: I see you've picked up mind reading lol. Dr. Shwartz is right, though. And have I told you how freaking proud I am of you?

I got another blushing emoji.

Ryan: Did you get my note?

Me: Yes. I'm glad you didn't let me change your mind. And she's safe.

Ryan: She?

Me: Yeah, it just felt right from the moment I held her.

He sent through three laughing emojis. I wondered what he'd think if he knew I'd named the violin too. *Isabella.*

Me: My mother still worries about you.

A pink heart came through before a lull in the conversation. It was one in the morning.

Me: Are you still there?

Ryan: "Yea"

He'd forgotten the "h."

Me: Are you tired?

He sent a sleepy emoji.

Me: Get some rest.

Ryan: Bye.

Me: Goodnight.

I fell asleep counting down the seconds until Thursday.

CHAPTER 21

William

Safe Haven had a system in place for visitors. There were days designated for family and friends. But outside of that, no one without pre-authorization was allowed to just "drop by," or show up at the facility. Authorized visitors were sequestered in areas where visits took place, private rooms on the third level of the community hall, right above the floor where the classrooms and yoga studio were located. When the weather permitted, the courtyard and gardens were safe zones too.

Visitors weren't allowed to roam freely. They were provided a Safe Haven liaison to escort them to and from their meeting place. Most of our residents were hesitant to strangers, and our number one priority was providing them a safe place.

Residents were free to come and go as they wished. We weren't running a prison system, and saw it as a great improvement when they felt strong enough to venture outside on their own. It brought them one step closer to starting a productive life outside of our walls.

Many knew me as the founder, and were always grateful and happy to see me stroll through Safe Haven's doors. But there were others, survivors who'd more recently arrived and had yet to meet me. They would be leery. I didn't want to be treated differently, didn't want any special privileges. So I went through the proper protocols before showing up for my lunch with Ryan.

A group of young women I'd met before hung out in the sitting area playing cards. They smiled and waved as Peggy led me through the community hall lounge and into the dining area.

"You're soaking wet."

"I rushed out of the car without my umbrella. Felt pointless going back for it."

"An umbrella won't do you any good in this weather anyway. There's a coat rack in the kitchen." We weaved through the unoccupied tables toward the swinging doors in the back.

"As you know, communal lunch ended at one. If anyone wants to eat before dinner, they can do so from their residence. You two will be alone."

Ryan's strict instructions to get here after one made sense now. He'd wanted to make sure we were uninterrupted. I'd been too thrilled about seeing him again to pick up on that. He'd planned this out with purpose, and my stomach fluttered with excitement.

"He's nervous, you know."

"Wait, did he say that?"

"No, Mr. Fickle—as I like to call him—hasn't uttered a word. But I caught him staring into the rainy parking lot a couple times." She stopped with a hand on the kitchen door, lowering her voice. "And he changed his outfit *three* times." She smiled as though she were fond of him, then pushed the door open and gestured for me to go in.

Ryan sat at an intimate table for two in the rear of the kitchen, hunched over a piece of paper resting in a manila folder. From the way his pencil worked, as if he were shading something in, I assumed it was a sketch. The door closed behind me, leaving us alone.

"Hi," I said, and he scrambled to his feet, his pencil rolling onto the floor. He'd been too preoccupied to hear me enter. "What are you drawing there?" I craned my neck to see as I hung my satchel on the coat rack. Ryan frowned, slamming the folder closed, amusing me.

"I miss your frowns," I said, then remembered the nickname Peggy called him, "Mr. Fickle."

Ryan looked at the door and his features turned tender. He had a soft spot for the older woman too.

I hung my wet trench coat next to my satchel. Ryan studied the green sweater I wore at his request. There was no denying the heat in his gaze when our eyes met again.

"You look nice," I said. He wore a vintage Stone's t-shirt with the short sleeves rolled above his shoulders. He complimented the look with slim fitting jeans and black loafers. I'd only ever seen him in the clothes I'd picked out for him. Sweats and basic-tees mostly. This new, stylish look suited him. He seemed comfortable in his own skin.

He whipped his phone from his back pocket and typed something into it. My phone chirped behind me. I fished it out of my bag.

Ryan: I got my first paycheck last week. Peggy helped me get a prepaid debit card, then showed me how to shop online. I thought it looked cool.

"It looks *really* good. Shows off your muscles." I wiggled my brows and felt satisfied when he grinned.

Ryan: I'm lifting weights with Shawn now.

"You and Chef Shawn seem to be getting close," I said wryly. Ryan's lips twitched.

Ryan: Jealous?

"Of course. Shawn's a good looking guy." I aimed for playful, but only halfway succeeded.

Ryan: You've noticed?

"And you haven't?" I scoffed, laughing when he shrugged his shoulders.

We spent the next few minutes taking each other in, appreciating all the things we hadn't seen in a while, and taking inventory of the things that weren't the same.

Ryan: Your hair looks different.

"Ah, yeah. I let it grow for a few weeks, then got a haircut. This is how it was when you met me." I ran a hand over my fade. "Your hair's straight." It made his beauty mark more pronounced. Maybe because the typical wild state of his hair no longer hid his face.

Ryan: Lucy did it. She lives in the women's residence. We have the same tutor. She said it would make me look hot.

He dropped his gaze to his loafers.

"You were already hot. I love it both ways."

He'd gone to a lot of trouble for this lunch. I tried my best to feel deserving of it.

"You have to tell him." My mother's words rang inside my head.

"I will," I'd promised.

In our own ways he and I were in recovery. I needed us at our best, at our strongest before presenting him with the worst thing about me. We were better than we were over a month ago, but still fragile. I let all the negative thoughts go and refocused on the man in front of me.

Now that we'd taken in each other's smile, hair, and clothing, it was time to settle into the tension. It was there from the moment I entered the kitchen, but it lingered at the forefront now.

Was he thinking about the kiss he'd promised me? Or had he changed his mind? He had a right to, I just hoped not. I needed the feel of his soft lips on mine. I needed our mutual desperation to filter into my lungs and spread through my entire soul, nourishing me as it went.

Ryan broke eye contact, restoring the oxygen in the room. He slid the folder off the table, weighing it in his hand before holding it out to me.

"For me?" I grabbed it with childlike excitement. Ryan snatched it back before I could open it, gesturing behind me to my satchel. "What? You want me to open it later?"

He nodded, walking around me to tuck it into the satchel himself.

"Wait!" I blurted, but he was already withdrawing the gift I'd stashed in there for him. A stack of books wrapped in brown paper and tied together with twine. My excitement transferred to him.

"Yes, it's for you. But!" I called out before he tore away the wrapping paper. "You can't open it until I leave."

He scowled at me.

"I mean... I suppose I'm open to a compromise." I pointed to the folder tucked under his arm. He shoved the stack at my chest, freeing his hands so he could put the folder in my bag.

"Guess that means no deal, then, huh?" I sounded sadder than I was, but his sketches conveyed how he felt. Since I couldn't *hear* how he felt about me,

I was anxious to see it.

Maybe he felt bad for me, or maybe being so close to me made him crave my touch as much as I craved his. Ryan stepped into me, peeling his shirt collar down, exposing his neck and shoulder.

"Is this supposed to make up for me having to wait to open my present?" I lowered my nose to the spot below his ear, inhaling as I worked my way down. Ryan shivered, and I sank my teeth into his shoulder.

"I think I missed this the most," I whispered, before kissing the sting away. I didn't want to move from this position. I wanted to make a home against his skin. My arms itched to wrap around him, to hold him. Would this burning need for him ever cool down? No. I didn't think it ever would.

Ryan let his shirt fall back into place, and then he... hugged me. Not one of those informal hugs where you bend at the waist and the chests never meet. Ryan slung his arms across my back and squeezed, his chin resting at the base of my neck.

After the initial shock wore off, I returned the hug, rocking us gently as I soaked up the scent of his shampoo. I pressed my lips to the side of his head, and he didn't shrink away.

A timer went off, and Ryan extracted himself, hurrying over to the industrial sized stove.

"What's that?" I waited behind him while he pulled a pan from the oven. "Is that fried chicken? How'd you accomplish that without frying it?" The kitchen smelled divine. I would've noticed earlier if I wasn't busy noticing him.

Setting the hot pan on top of a metal trivet, Ryan removed the oven mitt and pulled out his phone again. I read from his screen.

"Oven-fried chicken?" I asked dubiously. He nodded, going over to the toaster oven and removing a rack of waffles. He'd been keeping them warm there.

Ryan bounced around the kitchen while I took a seat to clear his way. I watched in amusement as he got all the condiments together, then poured us fresh squeezed lemonade before sitting down across from me.

"Did you make this yourself too?" I took a sip, impressed when he nodded yes.

He urged me to dig in, nudging my plate closer to me. I laughed, reaching for my knife and fork.

"These are the best waffles I've ever had." Granted, we'd both survived on Eggos, and these were made from scratch. Still, they were amazing. More so because he'd made them for me.

"Okay, you're going to have to tell me how you got this chicken so crispy—in the oven." My eyes bugged out, and Ryan's shoulders shook with laughter as he texted me the sealed-lips emoji.

I pointed toward his untouched food. "Not hungry? Or too busy looking at me?"

Ryan tucked his hair behind his beet red ears and forked a piece of chicken into his mouth.

We were like love-sick puppies. Too scared to look away, but also too terrified to push for more. Whatever this was between us, it had been the slowest thing I'd ever experienced, with no finish line in sight. Under different circumstances, would I have wished for something different? Sure. But with him, I wouldn't have wanted it any other way.

After eating we talked for a long while. Well, I did all the talking—sometimes rambling—and he'd shoot me a text every now and then asking me to get to the point. Through it all, his eyes kept veering over to the counter where his gift rested.

"Go ahead, open it." I'd been joking when I said he had to wait anyway, torturing him the way he loved to sometimes torture me.

Ryan loosened the string and tore through the paper. He read through each title, his eyes widening as he went. Some were from my personal library. Books I knew he loved. A few were new.

One title in particular caught his attention more than the others. He returned to the table with it, holding it up to me while angling his head in question.

"*His Eternal Love*," I whispered. He'd already read the synopsis, so I didn't bother explaining the storyline. I didn't think he was asking me to anyway. "I thought it might be helpful to read about two men falling in love under the harshest of circumstances. How love could heal old wounds. I thought maybe you'd never seen love. This might help you comprehend how it could be. It's a true story." I wasn't an expert on love. I actively avoided it. But I'd been out in the world long enough to understand how it should work when it's good.

"You don't have to read it if you don't want to." I shook my head. I was being ridiculous. Why would he need me to expose him to literature about love? What made me qualified to determine whether or not *this* book was the best learning tool on the subject? All I had to go off was how it made me feel when I finished reading it last night.

I leaned over the table to take it from him, but he yanked it out of reach.

He went back to the counter, adding it to the pile before texting me.

Ryan: Thank you. I'll read it first.

I smiled, setting my phone down. "I heard the TV adaptation is even better. They say it's... spicier," I added hesitantly, wondering how cautious I needed to be.

Ryan: Will you watch it with me?

This time I typed my reply, afraid of what my voice would sound like if I spoke.

Me: Yes.

"I should go," I said when the sound of voices closing in caught my attention. I knew everything about Safe Haven. Knew the policies, the shift changes, and the Sunday brunch menu too. The afternoon cooks would be arriving to prepare for dinner. We'd be in their way.

Ryan's shoulders slumped, which only made my heart make more room for him.

He walked me out, and we stood under the protection of the eave as the rain pummeled the pavement. The cold air turned his breaths into clouds of smoke, and he rubbed his arms for warmth. I'd told him to get his coat, but he'd refused stating I didn't have a jacket on either. My coat was still too wet from earlier to wear, which I found odd. My sweater was warm enough to make the short dash to the car, though.

"I'll text you when I get home," I said, a bit agitated. I didn't want him outside in the cold. The thought of him getting sick dredged up painful memories I'd rather not deal with right then. He grabbed me by the arm, stalling my exit.

"Damn it, Ryan. If you get sick—" I stumbled, satchel and coat falling to the ground as he launched himself at me, stealing my breath with a searing hot kiss. I cupped his head, and he guided my palms to his cheeks, holding them there.

He dragged his blunt nails over my scalp. Deep enough to remind me I was alive. For the first time I wished I had long hair, so he could wrap his fingers into it and pull, showing me how much he wanted to hang on to me, how much he wanted to tear me apart.

We pressed our foreheads together when we were through, panting. It was so cold, and his wellbeing superseded my need to kiss him over and over again.

"Put this on." I fisted the hem of my thick sweater. Ryan stopped me before I tugged it over my head.

Kissing me once more, this time short and sweet, he hurried inside without saying goodbye. I grabbed my dripping coat and satchel off the ground before jogging to my car.

I'd used the key fob to get the engine running when we first stepped outside, so the interior was nice and toasty. Dumping my drenched things onto the rear floorboard, I pulled my now soaked sweater over my head, tugging the t-shirt I wore under it into place.

Flipping the front and back wipers on, I shifted the car into reverse before looking through my rearview camera. I couldn't move. Couldn't take my eyes off the spot we'd kissed in.

Maybe I should run back inside to hug and kiss him one more time before announcing I'd be staying for dinner.

I threw the car in park and cursed. I couldn't stay. And not only for all the reasons I'd mentioned earlier about Safe Haven's rules and procedures. I had a virtual work meeting scheduled, and I had emails and paperwork to go over.

I'd check my calendar and be intentional about building time in for him, if he wanted that. Spending time with him wasn't the problem. Neglecting my own life to do so was where I ran into trouble. I'd make more than enough room for him while still fulfilling my other passions, although none were more important to me than Freedom Fighters and Ryan.

Arriving home, I discarded my damp things by the front door, and strode for the living room with the folder in hand. I'd almost cheated and looked inside several times, but in the end, I wanted to keep my word to him.

Leaning a shoulder against the window, I withdrew the sketch he'd done of the two of us. We were wearing the same clothes we'd worn today, and we stood under the eave of the community hall kissing in the rain. He'd sketched this before I even got there. Peggy's words from earlier reemerged.

"I caught him staring into the rainy parking lot a couple of times."

She'd thought it was because he was nervous about seeing me, which I believed to be true, but he'd also wanted to make sure the finer details in his sketch were accurate.

"Wear your green sweater."

He'd planned this. I thought he'd changed his mind about the kiss. Instead, he'd created the most romantic gesture. Ryan had drawn a moment we hadn't even had yet based on hope and imagination alone.

Even the position of our hands was accurate. I remembered he'd brought my palms to his cheeks. I reached into my pocket for my phone.

Me: It's beautiful. No one's ever done anything like this for me. Thank you.

Xavier's past overtures were on a grander scale. A night out at the opera. Dinners at Masa and nightcaps at The Pierre. None of it ever hit the mark. He'd been trying to win a prize that wasn't his to attain.

I'd stared at the spot Ryan and I kissed in before driving off, trying to record everything to memory. I no longer had to. It was all right here.

I traced his bare, lean arms, pausing when a thought occurred to me. I picked up my phone again.

Me: Maybe next time draw yourself in a coat.

He sent three laughing emojis before a message came through.

Ryan: At least I remembered to pour water over your coat when you went to the bathroom.

I howled with laughter, falling back onto the couch pillows.

Me: I wondered why it hadn't dried even a little bit in all that time. If anything it seemed more wet. You could've gotten us both sick.

I got a frowning face emoji after that.

Ryan: I know. I wasn't thinking. When will I see you again?

Me: I'm not sure. I don't think it's such a good idea to make a habit of hanging out at Safe Haven.

My finger hovered over the screen as I considered whether or not to go through with my suggestion. *Screw it.*

Me: Maybe next time you can come to my place.

I'd been about to add "no pressure," but his reply came through at lightning speed.

Ryan: Tomorrow.

I grinned hard before checking my calendar to see if tomorrow was open. Other than my morning run, I was free.

Me: Tomorrow works. Just let me know what time to pick you up.

Ryan: Can I let you know in the morning? I need to finish my vision board for next week. Dr. Shwartz thinks creating a visual of my short term goals helps me to reach them. I keep the boards mounted on the wall next to my bed.

I loved this idea, and considered doing the same myself moving forward. I also couldn't help wondering if I was ever on his board.

Me: What was on your board for this week?

Ryan: Touch.

I reclined on the couch sporting a goofy smile.

Me: Touching me?

Ryan: Yes.

Five eye-roll emojis accompanied his reply, and I doubled over, chuckling until I couldn't breathe. We texted our goodbyes, then I headed for the library to get started on my tasks for the evening.

I carried his sketch with me, adding it to the pile I'd already collected in my desk drawer. There was the one he'd made when we took our first run together, the one of the autumn leaves, and the ones I'd snuck out of the trash bin when he wasn't looking.

Closing the drawer, I got down to my first order of business. I called my agent.

"William," Mihaela said upon answering. "I was just about to call you."

"Hopefully with good news. Did Mark get back to you regarding the Kiwanika movie?" I'd turned down his offer to work with him on it at the gala, and his ego bruised easily. He'd make me grovel now.

"Nope. He hasn't returned my calls either. You know how he is. Give him a few more days to come around."

"Yeah, okay." I could hear her pen clicking away in the background. I sighed. "What is it?" The clicking stopped.

"You think you know me, huh?"

"I do. Now what's on your mind?"

She cleared her throat. "I spoke to Xavier."

"Yeah," I sighed, knowing what she'd say next.

"He's striking out on his own."

"Yeah. It's for the best." I was surprised it took him this long to let her know. Maybe he'd been hoping I'd try to change his mind. Doing so wouldn't have been fair, or what was best for him.

"Are you sure?"

"I am."

"Well, he fired me before I could drop him." She chuckled. Representing us both would've been a conflict of interest and a disaster. Besides, Mihaela's loyalty would always be to me. "Raymond's going to work with him moving forward."

"Raymond's good. He'll help him get to where he wants to be." And I'd be there for him professionally if he ever needed me.

Mihaela and I went over a few more offers and goals for the new year before wrapping up the call. For a while I sat there in thought, my fingers steepled in front of me. Why did I have to wait for studios to bring projects to me? Why couldn't I create my own? Tell the stories I wanted to tell? I'd been in the business long enough to know how it worked. All I needed was the right team around me.

An idea lodged itself in my heart. I crossed the library in six long strides, untucking my favorite book from its shelf. *Gargantuan.*

Gazing at the cover, I ambled over to my desk again, dialing my manager.

"Miss me already?" Jamal said in a dry tone. I'd already had my daily check-in with him on the car ride home. I chuckled but got right to the point.

"I'd like to secure the film rights to a book."

"Uh, you don't have a film production company." His tone suggested he thought I'd hit my head.

"I know that. I'd like to create one."

There was a flurry of activity on the other end, drawers opening and closing, papers shuffling. I smiled, knowing whatever I came up with, Jamal would be committed to it.

"So what's your niche gonna be? Period pieces? War Films? Movies that focus on human rights? Documentaries?"

"Animation," I replied. I typically composed for the genres he'd rattled off. I still would, but I also wanted to bring another side of me to life. "I'd like the rights to a children's book. A series of them."

"Okay, animation it is," he said without skipping a beat. "First, let's make sure your company name hasn't already been trademarked. Then we can bring Estello in." Estello was my business attorney.

"Do you have any names in mind, or should I come by with Eggos and booze for a brainstorming session?" he teased.

"I'm never eating Eggos again," I vowed. Not after having Ryan's homemade waffles. "And I already have a name. I trademarked it years ago." I hadn't known what I wanted to do with it, but I needed it to be mine in case I one day thought of something worthy of using it for. That day had arrived.

"Well, don't keep me in suspense. What is it?"

I moved to the window, placing my palm against the glass the way Ryan loved to do when it rained. Something about the vibrations of the rain striking the glass calmed him. I closed my eyes, trying to siphon some of that calm into me.

"William? You still there?"

"Yeah, I'm still here."

"What's the name?"

I inhaled a fortifying breath before whispering on the exhale, "Asher Gray. The name is Asher Gray."

CHAPTER 22

William

Choosing an outfit had to be the most challenging thing in the world when attraction was involved. Any other day, I lounged around in sweats or basketball shorts without giving it a second thought. Ryan was coming over, though, so I'd changed four times, and now I stared into the mirror wondering if the white button down I'd settled on looked too formal for an afternoon in.

I untucked it from my khakis, thinking maybe it would give me a more relaxed look. But with the hem now wrinkled, it made me appear unkempt.

My phone dinged from atop the closet island. The distinct chime assigned to my elevator. Ryan had entered it. I'd offered to pick him up from Safe Haven, but he'd said Peggy would give him a ride on her way home.

"Shit." I unbuttoned the shirt, my fingers fumbling a few times before they were all undone. Jerking it off, I tossed it to the ground, reaching for the shelf holding my t-shirts. Tugging a plain black one over my head, I sped for the front door.

I shoved one hand in my pocket as I held the door open, trying for casual, the exact opposite of what Ryan would do. He'd keep it real without even knowing it.

Removing my hand, I drummed nervous fingers against the door instead. It felt more genuine. The elevator doors parted, revealing a bundled-up Ryan. He smiled at me with so much joy it nearly knocked me off my feet. I promised myself right then to never hide how happy he made me feel.

"Hey—" My greeting stalled in my throat when he moved into me for a brief hug. He pressed his cold nose into my neck, and I wrapped both arms around him, squeezing once before letting him go.

I hung his coat up while he kicked his Doc Martens off on the welcome mat. I then trailed him from a good distance away as he reacquainted himself with the apartment. I didn't want him to feel smothered or rushed. Hard to believe he hadn't been here in over a month.

Following behind him, I got to freely take in how sexy and gothic he looked in all black. The fitted crew neck sweater and matching jeans showcased his long limbs to perfection. The denim molded to his ass and thighs like paint. His curls were back, and just as rebellious as the day we first met.

He visited his bedroom, the kitchen—where we'd shared so many meals—before making a pit-stop at the dining room threshold.

Ryan peered over his shoulder at me, pain and apology in his eyes. The room had been cleaned, but the broken items were yet to be replaced. He moved on to the library next, plucking books from their places and flipping through the pages before returning them.

The nostalgia tour ended in the music studio, where Ryan quickened his pace through the live room to get to his violin. What if he decided to take it with him? I'd lose my only leverage in getting him to come back. *To come home.* Maybe I should have hidden it. Lied and said it was in the shop getting restrung.

I released those thoughts immediately, feeling the anxious energy they brought on melt away. Those types of thoughts were fear based, and would lead me nowhere good.

Ryan wasn't obligated to make this his home once he left Safe Haven. His life was his own, which hadn't been the case for a long time.

"Do you have time for a lesson?" I asked when he held it to his chest. He shook his head, placing it down with care before texting me.

Ryan: I want to watch His Eternal Love. I finished the book this morning.

"That was fast," I said, unprepared for his request.

Ryan: It wasn't a long book. Plus I didn't waste time on the words I couldn't understand like I used to. I had to get to the end of their story.

"Okay." I cleared my throat. "Have you eaten? I've got some food keeping warm in the oven."

Ryan's eyes widened.

"Relax, I ordered in," I assured him with a laugh. "I hope that's okay." I realized I hadn't asked, and just because he ate what the cook's prepared over at Safe Haven, it didn't mean he didn't oversee it.

> *Ryan: It's fine. They order pizza on game nights. I sneak a slice sometimes as I watch them play.*

I'd never felt prouder.

We ate, and then Ryan excused himself to change into something more conducive to watching television on the couch all day. He'd left some clothing behind. I used the time to switch into something more comfortable too.

He returned in sweats and a baggy t-shirt. The collar hung loose, and I considered he might have chosen that particular shirt because of the access it offered to my favorite spot on him.

Grabbing the giant bowl of caramel popcorn off the coffee table, he flopped onto the cushion next to me. He'd never sat this close to me on the couch before. Our bodies were no more than an inch from touching. He didn't seem to notice.

Ryan watched the show with the type of focus reserved for test taking. By episode three the two male leads shared their first on-screen kiss. Ryan moved in a trance-like state to the end of the couch, putting him closer to the TV. Unlike the film he'd seen Xavier and I work on in the studio, Ryan didn't watch this solely for enjoyment. This was an assignment to him.

The kiss lasted longer than any kiss I'd seen before, growing more fevered as the seconds ticked by. Ryan absorbed their palpable need like a star pupil.

The closing credits rolled on the episode after that, snapping Ryan out of his daze. He turned to me wearing an expression that made me adjust my shorts.

Reenacting the scene, he licked his lips and then swallowed before stalking over to me. He settled onto the cushion again, facing me, one arm spread across the back of the couch. If we were sticking to the script, that made me Gregory, the more emboldened one of the two characters.

I twisted in my seat and reached out for him, combing my fingers through his hair before pulling him into my lips—exactly how it went down in the episode. I kept the kiss gentle though, wanting to savor every moment of it.

Ryan's lips were swollen and shiny when I backed away, his eyes glassy and cheeks red. He smoothed his finger over my wrinkled brow, my pained expression melting away under his touch. I felt ready to explode.

He picked up the remote, skipping the intro on episode four before pulling the throw off the back of the couch and wrapping himself up with it.

The couple made love for the first time at the top of episode five. The blanket fell from Ryan's shoulders as he crept over to the screen this time.

The director had gone as far as he could without breaking any FCC censorship rules. Very little had been left to the imagination. The sounds alone coming from the men were carnal and explicit.

I couldn't say which positions they'd done, or what surfaces they'd christened during their night of lovemaking. I only had eyes for Ryan.

His body vibrated, his fingers tracing the sweaty lines of their bodies. At one point his panting became louder than theirs. He seemed stunned and heartbroken, and when his back bowed from some invisible strike of pain, I had to sink my nails into the cushions to stop myself from charging over to him.

Whatever this was, he needed it. I could feel the truth of it in my soul. So I watched and waited while he grappled with himself.

Once Gregory and Steven were sated, Ryan turned to me with an ocean of hurt in his eyes. There were a few familiar emotions there. Hate. Betrayal. Anger. But most of all, an ancient sadness.

He opened his mouth, then closed it, then gaped at me with his hands at his throat. He couldn't get the words out, and my anguish at seeing him struggle pulled me to my feet.

Ryan held a hand up, cautioning me to stay put. He looked at the TV screen then back to me. I wasn't sure what he wanted from me, but I went with my best guess.

"Yes, it can be that way. Loving and passionate and dramatic. It can be all things good." I'd told him as much before, but now he'd seen it—even if what he'd witnessed was just a fictional performance of the real thing. The portrayal of love and yearning had been spot-on. I'd gathered that much from Ryan's reaction to it.

"You're going to be alright," I vowed. He lowered his cautioning hand, allowing me to swoop in. He fisted the back of my shirt as I stroked his hair, whispering reassuring words until he was ready to finish the show.

Ryan slipped into a desolate silence afterward. Nothing I said helped.

I dropped him off at Safe Haven in time for his evening session with

Katherine. I hoped today wasn't a setback, but if it was, I had faith she could restore whatever progress had been lost.

I returned home and went through my nightly self-care routine before bed, letting the ritual of journaling stitch my frayed threads.

With the lights out and the covers pulled to my chest, I stared at my phone wondering if I should check on him. Maybe he needed space. The Ryan prior to Safe Haven would've needed time alone to process.

My phone pinged. Ryan's name popped up on the screen, saving me from having to decide.

Ryan: I can't stop thinking about Gregory and Steven.

Me: Me either.

It didn't feel like enough, but it was all I had.

Ryan: I jerked off tonight.

I scrambled upright, the phone bouncing in my hand.

Ryan: I guess my touch goal for this week didn't only include touching you.

Me: How did it make you feel?

The question felt insufficient, like maybe I should have said something else. *Asked* something else. Or maybe it was good enough. Maybe I didn't need to say the perfect thing, or have all the answers. Maybe I just needed to be there for him.

Ryan: I've done it a few times since being here. Tonight was the first time I didn't feel confused, or dirty afterward. It felt like I was the only one inside my own body for once. Does that make sense?

I pressed the phone to my forehead, consumed with pain and guilt. Guilt because I hadn't gone through what he had, and yet I suffered all the same. I needed a moment to feel it all.

"Let go, William. Tell him."

Me: It makes perfect sense. You're retaking control. You're refusing to let them win.

"Don't let them win," I'd once told him.

Ryan: I never enjoyed it. I didn't know it could be good for anyone but them. The ones who hurt and take.

I shoved off the covers, and dropped my feet to the floor. Every part of me felt hot and raw, growing weak and heavy. How did I respond to that? I couldn't, not when everything in me screamed I could've done more to prevent this. I should've spent less time wallowing in my own pain. I should've started Freedom Fighters a lot sooner. I should've diverted more resources into search and rescue efforts, instead of what my foundation was primarily known for—raising awareness and life *after* recovery. Somewhere along the way I'd lost the true purpose of the freedom fighters. We should've been fighting, working with investigators and the families of the missing directly, not waiting for the taken to be hand-delivered to us.

I'd made mistakes no amount of meditation, exercise, or journaling could make right. Now it came down to learning how to live with it.

I did my best not to sound like a fraud or a generic inspirational quote when I replied.

Me: Don't let what happened to you in the past define who you'll become in the future. You're on the right track.

What did that even mean? The words felt hollow. Maybe because I was still working on applying them to myself.

Ryan: There's so much I still don't know. So much I'm unsure about.

Me: The good news is you're doing the work.

Ryan: You sound like Dr. Shwartz.

I tried to infuse some levity in my reply.

Me: Sounds like she and my therapist subscribe to the same school of thought.

Ryan: Yeah. There's still a lot I haven't told her. A lot I can't even tell myself.

I wondered what those things were.

Me: Take your time. You'll get there.

The following silence felt like a moment of reflection, so I let him have it, determined to wait as long as it took for him to be ready to chat again.

Ryan: I'm tired.

Me: Get some rest, then. I'll talk to you tomorrow.

Ryan: Ask me something first.

Me: Something like what?

Ryan: I don't know. You never ask me things.

I shook my head in confusion, grinning as I settled against my pillows again.

Me: I ask you things all the time. You just don't answer me.

Ryan: I guess.

I decided I'd play along, keeping it simple because he was exhausted.

Me: What's your vision board goal for next week?

He'd said he needed to work on it before coming over today.

Ryan: I decided on more touch. I haven't touched enough this week.

We'd only seen each other twice this week, so I allowed myself to assume he needed more time with me to reach his goal. My body warmed from the anticipation.

Ryan: My goal for the following week makes me nervous, though.

Me: What is it?

The three dots appeared before vanishing and appearing again. My palms grew sweaty when he finally answered.

Ryan: Truth.

That had been my goal when I resumed therapy, but I seemed to be finding excuses for not obtaining it. I wondered what Ryan's truth would be, and how it would impact me. Would he be delving deeper into his past with Dr. Shwartz? Would doing so affect his feelings for me? Maybe he'd realize I wasn't good for him, that being with me would only add to his problems. Perhaps these vision boards weren't such a good idea after all.

CHAPTER 23

William

I shoved aside the mistletoe dangling from the silly hat Ryan insisted we wore to check my incoming text.

Ryan: Are we dating?

I gripped the top of the ladder to keep from falling off, then glared down at Ryan whose job was to decorate the tree while I hung the star on top. It seemed he'd gotten bored and decided to almost surprise me to death with his question.

"I could've fallen and broken my neck, you know."

Tomorrow was Christmas Eve, one of the hardest days of the year for me. I typically locked myself in my apartment and licked my wounds that day, then I'd somehow manage to find it in me to visit my mother and Safe Haven on Christmas day.

I didn't want to do that this year, but I also hadn't planned on decorating my place to rival Macy's festive window displays. Saying no to Ryan's request for a tree wasn't an option, though. I honestly didn't think he'd want to celebrate either, considering. The pickings were slim on such short notice, but I was able to secure a lopsided runt no one else wanted.

Ryan: Well?

He seemed anxious for a response. He'd been like this all day. Bouts of playfulness mixed in with moments of high intensity. Like when I'd caught him staring into the opened refrigerator as if his mind was millions of miles away. He'd told me it was nothing, but I didn't believe him.

I was guilty of being preoccupied and pensive too, and I had a feeling we were stressing over the same thing. Not only was tomorrow Christmas Eve, it also marked the start of a new week. The start of his new goal.

"*Truth.*"

We'd spent the last week relishing in each other's affection as he got more and more used to being touched by me. But I couldn't deny feeling like the clock was running down as this new week approached. I'd decided the truth would be my mission as well, no more stalling.

"Do you *want* to be dating?" I always went with Ryan's flow, did things at his speed. We hadn't officially put a label on our relationship, but I wasn't seeing anyone else, and every time he mentioned Chef Shawn I wanted to punch something. Hard. Ryan was it for me. That didn't mean I was it for him, though.

Ryan: Yeah. I think so.

Ryan: Yes.

"Your wish is my command," I laughed, climbing down. "I thought you'd never ask." I hauled him in for a kiss, my mistletoe catching him in the eye.

"*Ouch*," he mouthed, rubbing his eye and blinking a few times.

"These things are dangerous," I complained, tossing them both to the floor before dipping him backward for a kiss. I rarely got the opportunity to initiate affection. We'd spent a lot of time together during the week, and there'd hardly been a moment when Ryan's lips weren't already on mine, or on their way to mine.

He'd obliterated his touch goal—within reason. Hugs and kisses were safe zones. He'd also taken a nap against my shoulder yesterday afternoon. That was nice. We'd been on the couch watching the rain pour down when he'd wrapped his arms around my bicep and rested his head on me.

I gave him one last kiss before setting him on his feet. He went back to tapping away on his phone.

Ryan: If we're dating, then we should go on a date.

"Okay," I said with some hesitancy. "Maybe after the holidays. We can grab breakfast somewhere quiet and cozy." If he still wanted anything to do with me by then.

Ryan: Tonight. Let's do dinner.

With the exception of coming to my apartment, Ryan didn't venture outside of Safe Haven's walls. And he never got here by public transportation or even car service. I picked him up and dropped him off—with the exception of the one-time Peggy brought him here.

Sure, we used to run outside all the time, but at an ungodly hour where it felt like the streets were ours. He'd made great progress, but the last time we went out in public it didn't end well. The scene from the gala flashed through my mind. The idea of taking him into the New York City nightlife triggered my protective instincts. "We haven't finished with the tree, and we should give this more thought instead of acting on impulse."

Ryan: It's called being spontaneous. We have to go now.

"Why now, Ryan?" I cupped his shoulders. "What's going on?"

He shrugged out of my hold, pacing over to the window. He peered out into the snowfall for a moment before replying.

My phone chimed, and he then tapped furiously at his screen while I watched. By the time I took my eyes off him to look down at my phone, his message had been edited. In his mad dash to erase whatever he'd decided he didn't want me to see, he'd missed deleting one word completely. It was missing the ending vowel, but it didn't matter.

Ryan: I want to experience things befor

"Before what?"

He didn't look at me or type a response. A blush crept along his cheek, though. He'd either meant to erase it all, or at least the very end of his message. *Before it's too late*, I told myself, because nothing else seemed to fit. But too late for what?

I sighed, shoving my hands into my pockets and stepping up beside him. A few inches of snow had accumulated on the ground. "What aren't you telling me?" I whispered, acknowledging the hypocrisy in my question. I didn't want to guess because every scenario that came to mind caused me pain.

Ryan blocked my view, coming to stand in front of me. He rested a palm on my cheek, his gaze begging me to trust him. He held up his phone, an unsent message waiting for me to read.

Ryan: I'm ready to do this.

"What if it's too much for you to handle? It's dark out. Let's at least wait until day time."

Ryan placed a kiss on my lips, a kiss so soft and light I'd only felt it because I'd seen it happen.

He cleared the message field and typed a reply to that, holding it up to me.

Ryan: Don't be afraid for me. I'm afraid enough for myself. I can do this, and so can you.

I grunted, tugging on a curl that sprung from his bun. "You're so strong. I wished I'd been as strong as you."

Ryan frowned at my wording of the last part, but didn't ask for its meaning. I was glad, because I think I would have told him, and I wasn't ready to tonight.

"I know just the place."

His dimples deepened with his gorgeous smile. I often joked that he'd give me a heart attack one day, but as I read the new message he typed, I realized *this* time it was a real possibility.

Ryan: Good. And I want to ride the subway there.

WE SURVIVED THE subway ride into the East Village. I'd huddled Ryan into a corner on the bustling car, guarding him with my life, instructing him to focus on me and not the boisterous group of teens near us. Three train stops and about a hundred deep breaths later, we emerged from below ground.

Ryan's gaze flew everywhere. To the carolers on the corner, and the bells they rang. To the competing busker down the street playing the harmonica for spare change. The Christmas motifs strung from one light post to another seemed to overstimulate him too.

He'd never roamed the streets freely before. The last time he had, he'd been taken. So while there was obvious excitement mixed in with his apprehension, I had to do what I could to help him manage the terror.

Gripping his chin between my gloved fingers, I brought his wild gaze around to me.

I'd kept our destination a mystery, and I suddenly realized it was a bad idea. Knowing precisely where we were going and what we'd be doing would go a long way toward easing some of his anxiety.

"You breathe, I talk," I said, and he nodded, snowflakes settling onto his lashes.

"I'm taking you to a local bar called The Daisy. It's right down the street." I pointed in the bar's direction. "It's pretty popular, and there are a few locations throughout the city. I hear this one's the best, though. It's also the smallest. More intimate, *less* people."

Maybe I should have taken him to see a movie instead. An obscure foreign film no one else wanted to see. We'd have had the whole theater to ourselves. But I ignored that thought. I brought him here because I knew once he found out why, he'd be just as excited as he was afraid.

A few drunken college kids sporting NYU sweatshirts stumbled out of the bar we stood in front of, giggling and holding each other up. Ryan startled, but kept his gaze on me.

"They have an art studio in the back," I said, ignoring all the activity happening around us, "and I may have snagged us the last two open seats for tonight's figure drawing class."

Ryan's fear made room for curiosity now, and I held out my hand.

"You can do this." I reminded him of his own words.

Ryan took my hand, his death grip betraying what his smile didn't.

"We leave whenever you're ready," I swore.

Holding hands, we jaywalked across the street while I distracted him with bad jokes and even worse impersonations. We laughed at nothing and smiled at the world around us.

We unlinked our hands to let a few people pass us on the narrow sidewalk, but Ryan reached for me as soon as they went by. His fingers trembled through his wool mittens. I squeezed them tighter, pausing to plant a kiss on the tip of his frostbitten nose.

The Daisy had a rustic and friendly vibe. The type of place where the patrons were on a first name basis with the owner and staff. I hung our coats on the rack near the door, returning the greeting the blonde bartender threw our way. Ryan offered him a nervous smile.

Thankfully it seemed to be a slow night. It made sense with Christmas just a couple of days away.

"Ready to head to the back?" I asked. "There's enough time to order food and drinks before the real fun starts."

Ryan nodded, looking around once more before following me through the tables to the glass doors offering a glimpse of the art studio. The music from the bar area faded away as we stepped inside the cozy space surrounded by hung murals. A tall, older man appeared from around a corner to show us to our small table etched with daisies.

Between the table design, the bar name, and the paintings that contained the beautiful wild flower, it made me curious about the story behind it. They were etched into every chair too.

Ryan settled in next to me, his knee bouncing under the table while he observed the other couples engaged in hushed conversation around us.

"I'm Franky," said the man who'd shown us to our table. He handed us our menus. "And you two are?"

"William." Franky looked to Ryan next. "Ryan," I said. "His name's Ryan."

Franky's brows drew together. He likely wondered why I hadn't allowed Ryan to answer for himself. "William and Ryan," he mused. "We pride ourselves on remembering our regulars. Is this your first time here with us?" He addressed Ryan, but again, I jumped in on his behalf.

"Yes, it's our first time."

Franky glanced at me, his gaze shrewd. He seemed fit for dominating a boardroom, not waiting tables at a local bar.

"I'll give you a few minutes to look over the menu," he said before disappearing. Ryan's stare heated my cheeks, and I found him watching me with an expression I couldn't decipher. I tilted my head toward him, wordlessly asking if he was okay. His lips tightened before he rooted his gaze to his menu.

He was quiet while we ate. Too quiet. Not that he ever spoke, but he hadn't sent one text my way since we sat down, not even to order. He'd just pointed at the menu, and when his food arrived, he'd contemplated it for several long minutes before taking a bite.

"What's wrong?" I finally asked when our waitress cleared our empty plates away. He ignored me. I tapped his phone, but he snatched it off the table and shoved it in his pocket. *What the hell?*

I'd been about to push the issue, but our waitress returned, handing out tabletop easels and canvases. Ryan worked on getting his set up, pausing to accept the charcoal sticks she distributed next. She'd had to gesture for me to take mine twice because I'd been so focused on figuring out Ryan's problem.

"Thank you," I said to her. Sighing, I decided to let it go. He'd tell me when he was ready. Pushing him to communicate never worked. If we were back at my place, he'd probably be locked behind a slammed door by now.

The overhead lights brightened, but not by much. Enough to produce a decent sketch, but not enough to turn a romantic night out into a classroom setting. Ryan was probably the only thing close to Picasso in this room anyway. The rest of us would likely see this for what it was. Something fun to do on a date night.

The blonde bartender from out front took the small stage, surprising me when he introduced himself as Leland—artist extraordinaire and owner of The Daisy.

"Are you kidding me, Noon?" Leland said to the largest man I'd ever seen in my life. "This is the third night this week."

The giant he'd called Noon chuckled, wrapping an arm around a man with eyes a similar shade of green as mine. The man looked like a model. "You have Solace to thank for seeing my face again so soon."

Leland addressed the blushing blonde Noon had drawn closer to him. "You either really love this place, or you just want to see my man half-naked," he deadpanned. The crowd laughed. Franky rolled his eyes from his spot to the left of the stage. Leland winked at him, pulling a begrudging grin from Franky.

The waitress brought two stools on stage, setting up a larger easel and canvas in front of one of them.

"Okay," Leland turned serious. "Thank you all for being here. I'll be instructing you as we go, but it doesn't need to be perfect, it just needs to be fun. Our scheduled subject couldn't make it, so this handsome DILF over here agreed to step in." He flourished his hands in Franky's direction, and the crowd applauded him for being a good sport. Franky stepped on stage at

Leland's beckoning.

"I'll do the honors," Leland said, making a show of unbuttoning Franky's shirt. There were playful catcalls and low whistles coming from the audience. Once the shirt was off, he kissed a scowling Franky on the lips before ushering him to his stool.

"I'll pay for this later," Leland muttered, not sounding at all displeased by the idea before sitting in front of his canvas and directing us through the first steps.

"Wow, this is really impressive," Leland said to Ryan sometime later. Franky had made his exit off stage, and now Leland was walking around checking out the finished results. "Is this natural talent, or did you go to art school?"

"Natural," I said, and Ryan glared at me. His mood had only improved while he'd been lost in his work. It seemed to worsen with Leland's approach. "He, ah, lost his voice," I explained when Leland looked between us.

A guy poked his head in from the bar area, calling for Leland's assistance with something. He excused himself, setting Ryan's canvas back on its easel. Ryan fished his phone out of his jeans.

Ryan: Can we go now?

"Yeah, of course. Are you upset with me?" I rested a hand on his forearm when he went to stand without responding. He stared at me, his expression shifting from anger to a strange sort of resignation. He shook his head no, and worry snaked through me. The last time he looked at me that way was at the Freedom Fighters gala. "You've been acting strange all day." This time he did get up, exiting the studio.

We took an Uber home, my own mood deteriorating during the tense ride back to the apartment. I'd hoped this Christmas would be different. I thought I could erase the pain of previous years by making new, beautiful memories. Instead, I began to dwell on why this time of year hadn't been my favorite since I was a kid.

Ryan beelined for the living room, leaving me standing at the front door. I trailed after him, observing his pensive reflection through the window he stood in front of.

"I'll give you some space. Let me know when you're ready to head back to Safe Haven." I got halfway to the library when my phone chirped.

Ryan: You should want someone who can talk to you. Who won't embarrass you in public. Someone you don't need to translate silences for.

I turned back to the living room. Ryan sat on the edge of the coffee table now, head hanging, phone in hand. Kneeling down in front of him, I waited until he met my gaze.

"*You* are who I want, Ryan. *You* are enough, and so much more than I deserve."

He shook his head, pulling up the text screen on his phone.

"Yes, you are," I said adamantly, stopping him. *If only you knew.* "I could *never* be embarrassed by you. Never doubt that."

He rested his forehead against mine, stroking my neck and chest.

"What do you need?" I whispered, snapping the elastic from his hair so I could run my hands through the inky curls. I placed a kiss on his beauty mark, and he turned his head, catching my lips as I pulled away.

Ryan pushed me to the floor, falling on top of me as we kissed. He aligned his hips with mine, undulating against my cock, pushing his tongue deeper inside my mouth. I moaned, rolling up to meet his thrusts, untangling one hand from his hair to grip his ass. This was new, and I couldn't get my body under control long enough to question it.

We mauled each other's lips, getting sweatier by the second. It'd never been like this between us, our bodies touching this way, so close to the edge of everything. Moments later, Ryan tore his mouth away from mine, sucking in a razor-sharp breath, pinning me with his untamed gaze.

His hips continued to buck, and I held him to me with both hands now, increasing the friction. We were both on the brink of climax, one right move and we'd freefall into bliss.

A few more pumps and he threw his head back on a silent scream as he orgasmed, his nails biting into my shoulders. I'd never seen anything as raw and innocent and beautiful as Ryan letting go.

"Fuck!' I barked, following right behind, shuddering beneath him.

Ryan fell limp onto my chest, his breathing unsteady as I secured my arms around his trembling body.

"Pretty sure I haven't done that since I was fourteen," I said after regaining the ability to form words. I dropped a kiss to the top of his damp hair, loosening my arms when he craned his head around in search of his phone. He grabbed it from the coffee table before burrowing into my side.

Ryan: I bet more than that happened between you and Xavier.

"What?" I grabbed his wrist to bring the phone closer to my face. I needed to make sure I'd read that correctly. "Where'd that come from?"

He deleted that message to type a new one.

Ryan: Are you saying it isn't true?

"No, that's not what I'm saying. I just didn't expect to discuss it with you right... after." I resisted the urge to squirm in discomfort. He'd alluded to knowing the extent of my relationship with Xavier before, stating he wasn't sure if we'd become "friends" again during his first month at Safe Haven when we had no contact. He'd never been so outright about it before now, though.

Ryan: He practically drooled whenever you were near.

"Don't exaggerate."

Ryan gazed up at me, waiting out my deflection.

"You and I have more than Xavier and I ever had. Sex doesn't equate to love."

He propped himself up on an elbow, searching my face. I waited for him to call me on what I'd said, to ask if it was a general statement or something more. Something deeper. He didn't.

He sat up and urged me to do the same before fisting the hem of my shirt. He paused, waiting for me to grant or deny him permission. I raised my arms, allowing him to pull it over my head.

My heart raced, knowing what would come next. Ryan touched my shoulder, motioning for me to turn around. I swallowed my uncertainty. He'd seen my back before. Somehow, though, this time felt different. This time I got the sense he was looking for greater understanding.

I settled onto my stomach, the cum cooling in my underwear feeling unpleasant. I gritted my teeth through it, relaxing as best I could.

His fingertips landed on my shoulder blades, tracing the dense foliage of the tree canopies. His touch felt both condemning and absolving, both a reminder and permission to forget.

His fingers shook as they skated past the tree line to the field of colorful wildflowers and lush blades of grass. The view was attractive from a distance.

I closed my eyes with a sigh of surrender when the beam of Ryan's flashlight app clicked on. His breath tickled the middle of my back as he leaned in. Right under my rib cage, hidden beneath the soil and in between the beauty, lay the bones of everything stolen.

He tugged the waist of my pants lower. I lifted my hips to make it easier. Through the reflection in the floor to ceiling window, I watched as his light moved down my spine to my sacral region—to the mountain of skeletal remains holding up the field.

"That's the place where promises were broken," I whispered. "The place where innocence was lost." The smallest of the bones lay atop a wooden miniature coffin engraved with a name, a date, and my plea to Gargantuan.

Bring him back.

I shivered as he smoothed his hand over it.

Ryan's phone light went off, and he eased back. The loss of his touch and the warmth of his breath against my skin left me feeling cold and alone.

"What are you thinking?" I whispered into the silence, my heart racing.

His pensive gaze moved to the window where I watched his reflection with my hands folded under my cheek. Ryan licked his lips, and my mind clouded with negative thoughts, assumptions of what he must be thinking of me.

"Do you think it's morbid?"

He shook his head, and I licked my own lips nervously.

"Do you want to know who he is?"

Ryan appeared indecisive before looking away.

I wouldn't push him if he wasn't ready, because I wasn't ready either.

"You have to tell him."

"Do you think it's beautiful?"

"*Yes,*" he mouthed.

I turned over, sitting up to cup his cheek, brushing my thumb over his beauty mark. "Does it make you feel sad for me?"

"*Yes,*" he mouthed again, gently sweeping his lips over mine. He regarded me, his fingers outlining my sorrow. His lips formed a hard line of determination as he grabbed his phone again.

Ryan: Make love to me.

"No," I said with vehemence. His face fell, his cheeks turning red. "I'm sorry. I didn't mean it that way." I kissed him in apology, dragging it out so he knew it wasn't a matter of me not wanting him. "I don't want you to do something you're not ready for because you feel sorry for me."

Ryan: That isn't why.

"Then is it because of what happened earlier at The Daisy?" My mind was taking longer than usual to switch gears. How had we gotten here? "Because you've got nothing to prove, Ryan." I slid my hands along his neck, and he batted them away.

Ryan: I'm not trying to prove anything. I'm ready.

He'd been ready to go out tonight too, and look how that ended. This all felt rushed, every decision he'd made today held an edge of panic.

I got to my feet, backing away as my own fear and stubbornness reared its head. "I don't believe you."

Ryan shot up, storming over to me as he typed, shoving the device in my face when he was done.

Ryan: Why won't you believe me? If you don't want me, just say it!

"Because the last time you had something to prove, you left me the next day!" My lungs burned with every breath. "If we do this, when will I lose you this time? I can't risk it."

The tightness in his jaw faded, and his hand dropped to his side. A small smile filled with regret formed on his lips.

Ryan: This is different. Trust me.

"Why?" I breathed. "Why now? Why me?"

Ryan: Because it has to be now, and it has to be you.

His words were bold, full of conviction, but his chest rose and fell with shallow breaths. I shuffled back, creating more distance, because being this close to him made me want to take what he offered, made me willing to take a gamble on things turning out fine. There was also the matter of going further with him before bringing what hid between us to the surface. Doing so would make me a monster, or rather, more of a monster than I already was.

You have to tell him!

I turned away from him, unable to look him in the eye, struggling with what to do. Not wanting to do what I should have done long ago.

You have to tell him!

I stiffened when Ryan's lips met my back. He started from the top, kissing along my tattoo until he'd gotten to the bottom of it. I let my head fall, taking in his affection like the selfish man I was.

He wrapped his arms around me, holding his phone up so I could read the lit screen.

Ryan: Please.

You have to tell him!

"Tomorrow," I found myself whispering, unsure if it was in response to his plea, or the order being shouted in my head.

CHAPTER 24

William

The snowstorm raged outside, turning the view beyond the wall of windows white. From this high up, the howl of the wind was near deafening.

I increased the volume of the music playing throughout the apartment, but not enough to lose the ambient feel. The fingers of my right hand curved around a phantom bow when the sonata evoked a need to partake. The low whine of the violin closely mimicked a songbird's cry.

A text notification appeared at the top of my screen. With a sudden rush of adrenaline, I swiped out of the playlist to check Ryan's message.

Ryan: Almost there.

With the weather making it near impossible to drive in, I'd canceled our plans for tonight. Ryan had accepted the cancellation too easily. That should've been my first clue he was up to something. It usually took a lot of reasoning to get him to agree to anything.

An hour later I'd received another message from him stating I could remain safe in my glass tower, because he'd be catching a ride into the city with Peggy. She had to pass by here to get home. Sarcasm and determination aside, he'd been checking in periodically to let me know they were safe and that he'd be here soon. Lucky for me, I'd already gotten everything I needed for the night before the weather turned.

Maybe I should've let him stay over last night, but I didn't trust myself not to be swayed by him. I'd been in a vulnerable state, and Ryan could be very persuasive when he wanted something. We needed a night apart. We needed time to think.

He also had a session with Dr. Shwartz this morning that I didn't want him to miss. I'd hoped he'd run our plans for tonight by her, and that she could help him gain clarity on whether or not now was the right time.

Today also marked the start of "truth" week. Had he shared with her everything he'd previously withheld? Or did he plan to spread it out over the course of several days? Maybe he'd changed his mind altogether.

I hadn't changed my mind, though. I couldn't. Not if we planned on taking things to the next level.

Grabbing the box of matchsticks off the coffee table, I hustled around the room, lighting every pillar candle positioned on iron holders throughout.

I lit the candlesticks in the kitchen next, then fussed with the place settings on the island for the fifth time. I might've gone overboard, but I wanted this night to be special for him. The plan was to make love by the end of it—if the truth didn't end up costing me in the worst way possible. Even if it did, I needed him to know he was worth the effort.

I debated plating the food I'd ordered, but decided to leave it warming in the oven in case he wasn't ready to eat yet.

My nerves were frazzled, and it being Christmas Eve didn't help. Ryan had no idea what this day meant to me. He'd understand soon, though, and the idea of him looking at me differently afterward made my body feel weak. I gripped the edge of the island to steady myself.

Bell chimes rang from my phone. Three in quick succession, letting me know my elevator was on the move. *Ryan's here.*

Taking another look around, I hurried to the Christmas tree, turning the light setting to fade. I loosened the tuck on the turtleneck I wore, then adjusted my belt buckle before striding down the hall to meet Ryan at the door. Letting out a quick breath, I opened it with a smile.

Ryan wore a look I hadn't seen since the early days of him living here. *Anger.* He quickly covered it with a small contrived smile of his own. Something wasn't right. I could feel it. To be fair, I'd been feeling it since the day we met. Nothing had been right since then.

Ryan kissed me, his cold hands cradling my face. Our kisses tended to feel desperate or comforting—or a combination of both. This one felt like an escape or a distraction. Like he kissed me to get his mind off something. Maybe even to prove something. Ryan in the mood-to-prove was a dangerous thing. It didn't feel related to his desire to have sex, though. On some fundamental level, I knew this was separate from that.

Sure enough, when he pulled back, his smile seemed genuine. Whatever test that was, I'd obviously passed it. Or maybe he'd been testing himself, not me.

Slipping past me, he hung his coat in the closet while I watched him, my hand still gripping the door. I shook myself out of my confusion and closed it.

Ryan slid his arms around my waist. I relaxed, returning his embrace. Maybe what happened at the front door was nothing. Maybe I'd misinterpreted his anxiety. It made sense for us to be nervous. I let the incident go.

"You smell amazing," I whispered, massaging his back with my fingers. He wore a ribbed, long sleeved top. He seemed to prefer the fitted look. I didn't mind one bit. "You also look good in green." His outfit complimented my eyes, and my all-black ensemble matched his. "Great minds think alike, they say."

Ryan gave a muted laugh, but I felt the rumble of it between our chests. He tugged the neck down on my shirt, breathing in the cologne I'd spritzed myself with.

"It's new. You like it?"

Ryan nodded, kissing below my ear before pulling away. He checked me out, his gaze hungry as he took his time making his way down my body.

When his eyes returned to my face they were hard again, making my heart stutter with fear and confusion once more. He averted his gaze, angling his chin toward his shoulder.

"Hey." I waited until he'd turned back to me. His eyes were soft again, almost sad. "Are you okay?"

Ryan released a cynical sounding huff, sinking his hands into his straightened hair before strolling down the hall. He froze when he reached the living room, absorbing the scene I'd created. Careful not to crush the rose petals as he followed their trail to the center of the room, he spun in a slow circle, eyes wide.

He looked beautiful bathed in candlelight. The flames defied logic in his presence, flickering higher and seemingly arching toward him. Lured by the tortured parts that never truly abandoned him, not even in moments of happiness.

We weren't experiencing one of those happy moments now, no matter how hard he tried to project otherwise.

He faced the kitchen now, his sharp intake of breath cutting through the room upon seeing the recreated dinner scene from *His Eternal Love.* Long stemmed red roses lined the counters, and a pair of five-arm candelabras lit up the island.

Ryan's gaze crashed into mine, and his hands flew to his neck like he was choking on the words he couldn't get out. His fingers balled into fists, resting against his throat. Rage and sadness returned, eclipsing the spark of gratitude in his eyes.

My heart skipped a beat, watching him struggle, then felt as if it were failing me altogether when things began to take a turn for the worse.

Ryan charged at me, grabbing me by the shirt before assaulting me with an anguished kiss. I tried prying him off, but it seemed to intensify his frenzy. I gave into it, giving him what he needed—what we both needed—my desperation matching his.

He backed away once suffocation became a real threat, both of us reluctantly uncurling our fingers from each other's clothes. His eyes were squeezed shut, a dreamy sort of expression spreading across his face.

"Ryan," I breathed, feeling behind me for the wall that branched off from the hallway. I needed the support.

His eyelids popped open at hearing his name, and I wondered if it was the shameless plea in my tone that caught his attention. His smile turned shaky, then fell altogether. Despair extinguishing the fire in his gaze.

I realized it was my eyes. It was meeting my gaze that made him conflicted, that took away everything good in him. From the way his jaw ticked I assumed he saw something there he hadn't seen before, or maybe it was something he could no longer ignore.

He knows what you've done.

No, he couldn't possibly know, because I hadn't told him. It was on the tip of my tongue to say it. To put myself out of my own misery by getting it over with. I wasn't ready, though. Not quite yet.

"Your eyes are red," I noted. So were mine. "Were you up all night?"

He nodded once.

"So was I." The next logical question would've been to ask why he hadn't gotten any sleep. That ran the risk of me hearing something I might not have been ready to, though. Instead, I told myself his behavior came down to a lack of sleep and maybe hunger.

"Have you eaten today?"

Ryan shook his head, biting down on the corner of his lip.

"Neither have I," I rasped, pain spreading everywhere. I took the few strides needed to enter the kitchen. "I ordered lasagna from this great Italian restaurant close by." Slipping on the oven mitts, I lowered the oven door and withdrew the pan, setting it on top of the stove.

Gaining a bit of distance from him didn't help. I could feel his turmoil and confusion. I felt it even more when he stepped into the kitchen with me.

With my back to him, I took a few deep breaths, removing the mittens and focusing on the music playing softly overhead. I looked back at him, expecting to find his gaze on me, expecting it to be full of all the negative emotions he'd fluctuated through since arriving here.

Ryan was staring at the small cake peeking out from behind one of the vases.

"Dessert," I whispered. "It's double chocolate fudge, your favorite. It's the biggest one I could find." I realized my error after he'd stormed off, much like the mistake I'd made with the chicken tenders and fries.

With a forearm pressed to the window, Ryan watched the whiteout developing outside. It felt like we were looking into a snow globe. Soon we'd be surrounded by white fog, sealing us in from outside distractions.

I entered the living room, turning the playlist off and plunging us into crippling silence.

"How'd your session with Dr. Shwartz go?" I felt faint, and it had nothing to do with hunger.

Ryan shook his head.

"You... You didn't meet with her?"

He shook his head again.

"Did you meet with your tutor, then? Work out with Chef Shawn?"

Ryan didn't answer, clearly not in the mood for small talk or a game of twenty-one questions. I asked another one anyway.

"What did you do all day?" *And all night...*

That particular question seemed to interest him. He straightened, slipping his hands into the pockets of his slacks before turning to me.

A candle wick popped, breaking up the heart-pounding silence of the room. The flame went out altogether, symbolic in a sense. The scent of acrid smoke drifted through the air while I waited for something I couldn't have seen coming.

Where was his phone? I hadn't seen it since he got here, and I hadn't felt it on him when he'd pressed his body against mine. It must have been in his coat. I thought about getting it for him until I realized I didn't have to. Ryan gave me the answer to my question without it.

"Prac... ticed," he said in a voice that was deep but scratchy from disuse. "Prac... ticed," he repeated. The word came out disjointed, as though he were having problems connecting the syllables, turning the single word into two. He brought a hand to his throat again, rubbing at it.

It felt like someone had wrapped a noose around my neck. I fought for every breath, each one reducing the amount of oxygen I had left.

Ryan stared at me like we were strangers, like I was a hazard to his existence. He *knew.* He'd always known, and I'd been naive to believe otherwise.

"You ne... ver ask me things that mat... ter," he said, still massaging his throat. His words flowed smoother when he spoke again, only halting in one spot. "Not my last name, not my age, and noth... ing about my family." He winced. "Why is that?"

I didn't know whether to clutch my aching chest, or my throat where my own words felt stuck. "I-I didn't want to—"

"Truth!" he shouted, grimacing with both hands at his neck now. He closed his eyes, slowly lowering his hands and breathing deeply. He seemed more confident in himself when he opened them again, his voice steady. "I don't have any family. But you already knew that, didn't you?"

It wasn't a question. Not really. Everything he asked from that point on would be an accusation he already knew the answer to.

"Today's my birthday." He glanced over my shoulder to where the double chocolate fudge cake waited in the kitchen. "But you knew that too, didn't you?" he sneered.

I should've taken him up on his offer last night. I should have made love to him while I had the chance, should've told him I loved him while I had the chance, because I wouldn't ever get the opportunity again.

I'd been stupid, and all the good reasons I had for it were now lost beneath the mess I'd made. No, we wouldn't be making love tonight. We'd be saying goodbye.

"How old does that make me?" he asked, stalking me as I backed away. "I lost count early on. You'd be surprised how quickly you lose track of time when locked in a dark room for days, weeks, *months*," he seethed before taking a moment to breathe. "Not trusting my math skills didn't help. I don't even remember what year I was born."

"Ry—"

"Don't!" he shouted, cutting me off. "I'm done with lies. Today we're telling the truth. How. Old. Am. I?"

"T-twenty-six."

"Twenty-six?" he whispered, his tone rife with devastation and betrayal. Tears flooded his eyes, and it killed me that we were now close enough for me to catch them before they fell but I couldn't. I no longer had the right to. I never did. We'd always been on borrowed time.

He ran trembling hands over his cheeks and lips, as if searching for the truth in the smoothness of his youthful skin. "I-I thought I was older. I *feel* older." The weariness in his words gutted me. He stepped away, shaking as a waterfall of tears cascaded down his face.

"Say it," I breathed, my eyes and chest burning me alive. "Say it. Make it real."

He swiped the moisture away angrily, swallowing and raising his chin. "My name is Asher Gray."

CHAPTER 25

Malcolm

Nineteen Years Ago

My body felt heavy, and like the last few times I tried, I couldn't open my eyes more than halfway. I thought maybe someone had strapped bricks to them. Maybe one of the people who took me from the park. Did my mom know I was missing yet? Had she found my bike? They'd left it flipped on its side in the dirt. I remembered the back wheel spinning as they carried me away. Everything went black after that.

We were moving. I could hear the engine roaring, and my back hurt with every bump in the road we drove over. I groaned, trying again to open my eyes. My mouth tasted funny, and my neck still burned in the spot where the big man had stuck me with a needle.

Through the fog in my head, I tried to remember what happened. Tried to make sense of it.

I'd been talking to a nice lady who'd complimented the nameplate hanging from my bike seat. It read: Piano Man. I'd saved up my allowance for it. She said her son played and would love to know where she could buy him one. She kept smiling as my answer to her simple request turned into a history lesson on Martha Argerich—child prodigy and my favorite pianist.

My mother always said it'd be a waste of time trying to lure me away with candy or cash. Classical music was the way to my heart.

Somewhere between my comparison of Martha and a few of the other historical greats, the lady's smile turned mean, and she told the man who'd then grabbed me from behind to hurry and get me into the truck. I could still smell his cigarette smoke on me, could still feel his meaty hand over my mouth.

"Shhh," a small voice whispered. I froze, noticing I couldn't move my arms. "They'll give you more medicine if they know you're awake." The voice belonged to a little kid. A boy, I guessed. I tried to scream, but my tongue felt heavy too.

The truck stopped. "They're coming," he whispered. He sounded afraid.

I BLINKED AWAKE, my vision blurry and eyes stinging. I tried to rub them but my hands were tied behind my back. I pulled at the rope binding me, but it wouldn't budge. Fear filled my empty stomach, and then every other part of me once my vision cleared. I wasn't alone.

Up against the wall across from me, six girls—bound and gagged as well—trembled and cried. Their tears spilled over the silver tape covering their mouths.

I remembered the little boy who'd spoken to me. Where was he? Had they heard him speak to me? I scanned the damp space for him, finding him a few feet away from me. His terrified eyes were already on me. They were dark, watery and too big for his small face. Something about his helplessness bothered me, it made me want to get us out of here.

I leaned into the water pipes at my back, using them to push myself to my feet. I ended up slipping on the uneven floor and falling sideways onto my left shoulder.

My muffled scream of pain made the others stare at me with panicked eyes, like they were begging me to be quiet. It made me more afraid than I already was, because what happened if we weren't quiet?

"They'll give you more medicine if they know you're awake."

I managed to sit up again, glancing over at the little boy. His cheeks were soaked with his tears, his breathing too loud. I scooted closer. It was the only thing I could do for him.

We'd been separated from the girls. Maybe because we were the youngest, or because we were the only boys. Maybe both. They huddled close together like they knew each other, and they all wore the same Columbia University t-shirts.

I focused on our surroundings next. We were in a basement. The overhead lights buzzed and flickered, and a bug floated in the dirty puddle of water near a drain. One of the pipes above my head leaked, dripping water onto my good shoulder.

Our eyes snapped to the ceiling at the sound of footsteps, none of our breaths were quiet now.

The metal door up ahead screeched open, two large men dressed in dark clothes and boots stepped through. I looked at the little boy again. A wet stain was spreading over the front of his khaki pants.

The woman from the park entered the basement next. I had to tense up hard to keep from peeing on myself too.

She'd worn a flowery dress earlier while reading a book on a bench, and her long blonde hair had been pinned back by yellow clips. She looked nothing like that now. She wore all black.

The men looked us over. The girls drew in closer to each other, and without realizing it, I'd moved closer to the little boy too. The lady watched it all.

I didn't know what was going on, didn't understand why I'd been kidnapped.

They stopped near the girls first, one man crouching to brush strands of hair away from one of the girls faces. She shrank away, her friends doing the same.

They turned to me and the whimpering little boy next, their faces contorting at the sight of pee on him. The boy cried so hard I worried he'd suffocate if the tape didn't get removed. I wished I could distract them from him, even though I was crying too.

I couldn't scream for help, I couldn't fight, I could hardly breathe. I wondered if my mother was looking for me. I prayed to God, begging him to help us.

"Children are difficult," the dark-haired man said in a thick accent I'd never heard before. The lady looked between me and the boy, taking in how close to each other we were sitting. Her cruel smile returned.

"Not when they have an incentive to behave."

"There's a market for young Americans abroad." She clasped her hands behind her back. "But there's an even bigger market for young American boys."

The men took another look at us.

"Trust me. Have I ever steered you wrong?"

The men seemed to have a silent conversation with each other, because the taller one sighed before going to the far side of the basement to make a call. I couldn't hear what he said into the phone, but he kept staring over at me and the boy as he talked. The girls were quiet as mice, probably hoping they'd been forgotten about.

"We'll take him," he said when he strolled back over, flicking his wrist toward me. I shook my head frantically, tugging at my restraints. My trapped shout made my throat burn. "And him," he said next, gesturing to the little boy who began shaking in terror.

"And them," he added, pointing to the two youngest looking girls. The space erupted with our muted screams and thrashing.

"Get them ready while we arrange payment and transport," the other man said to the lady. She nodded, escorting them through the door while I went back to my prayers.

THE FOUR OF us were on the move again, and I wondered what would happen to the girls the men didn't want.

We were in the back of a smaller truck now, speeding down a quiet road. They'd removed the tape from our mouths, so I assumed we were passing through a deserted area where our screams wouldn't be heard.

I wasn't sure how long I'd been missing for. What if I'd been unconscious for days before waking inside that basement? I was thirsty enough for that to be true. The bottled waters they'd tossed into the truck with us hadn't done much to quench my thirst. One of the girls whispered something about the drugs they'd injected us with dehydrating us. Her mom was a doctor, she'd said.

I hadn't touched my bread roll. The queasy feeling in my stomach made it hard to eat.

It was dark out now, the air too cool for a Brooklyn summer night, and somewhere in the distance an animal howled.

They'd swapped the ropes on our wrists for cuffs. A second set at the end of a chain locked our ankles together. The girls were shaking against each other in one corner, and the little boy sat with his knees to his chest close to me. He smelled like pee, but that was the least of our problems.

I struggled to my feet. The loud metallic sound of my chains caused everyone to look at me with wide eyes. Pushing to the tips of my toes—nearly falling when the truck turned a corner—I strained to get a look through the metal grille letting air in. I wasn't tall enough to see anything below the mountain peak under the moonlit sky.

Mountains. No wonder the temperature felt cooler.

They were all looking at me when I sat back down. I shook my head. "I don't know where we are," I whispered. I could've mentioned the mountains, but I felt too sad to speak. What would it have mattered anyway?

I picked up my bread for something to do other than cry. I spun it around in my hands, noticing the boy scoot even closer. His watery eyes moved from me to the roll of bread in my hands. I held it out to him.

He snatched it from me, his hunger making him impatient. He took a couple of bites before he slowed down, hardly chewing before swallowing. Turning red, he looked down at the half eaten roll then back to me.

"I'm not hungry," I said, closing my eyes and dropping my chin to my chest. Something bumped against my chained hands, and I opened my eyes to see a corner of the bread resting in my lap.

"If you don't eat your blood sugar will drop," he whispered.

"Is your mom a doctor too?"

"No, my mom played the violin." The mention of an instrument made the back of eyes sting, but I forced down a piece of the bread.

"What's your name?" I asked a short while later, tired of referring to him in my head as "the little boy."

"Asher Gray," he breathed, his eyelids drooping. They popped open again when we hit another bump. "What's your name?"

"Malcolm." I thought about my grandpa, who called me Mally for short. I wondered how he'd handled the news of my disappearance. He and my mother would've been at the police precinct raising hell by now.

"Malcolm?" Asher called in a tiny voice. Leaving thoughts of my family behind, I stared into his puppy dog eyes.

"Yeah?"

"Are we gonna die?" He watched me like I had all the answers, like he'd believe whatever I believed. He needed hope, but I didn't feel all that hopeful. Maybe I could pretend to be for him, though.

"No," I said. "We're not going to die."

Asher yawned, resting his head against the wall of the truck, falling asleep. The girls were sleeping too, their arms and legs twitching.

I brought Asher's head to my good shoulder, and he stretched out his legs, settling into my side. I woke sometime later to the sound of the ocean, and sunlight pouring into the truck.

TWO MEN I'D never seen before forced us onto a cargo ship, shoving us past rows of stacked containers before dragging us—kicking and screaming—down a set of stairs.

"Let us go!" I yelled while Asher cried hysterically. I heard the girls shouting for help, but I could no longer see them.

The two men dumped us into a room, ignoring our pleas to go home, then a third man stepped in. He was smaller than the other two, but seemed more important. The two men who'd hauled us in flanked him.

The suit he wore hid his muscles, but I could see the shape of them through his black jacket. I panted from where I'd been tossed to the floor. Asher scurried over to me, gripping my shirt, trembling.

"We'll take the chains off if you promise to behave," the third man said from behind dark sunglasses. The tattooed wing of a bird peeked out from the collar of his shirt. "Make me regret it, and I'll punish you both."

Asher whimpered, burying his face in my shoulder. One of the men stepped forward with a small key, removing the cuffs from Asher first before moving on to me with a warning glare.

"W-where are you taking us?" I stammered, rubbing my sore wrists. "Why won't you let us go?" I hated that Asher had to see me that way. I got to my knees. "M-my mom will give you money. We have a lot of it," I lied.

The man in the suit turned for the door, signaling for the other men to follow him out. The sound of a bolt sliding into place made me flinch. I sank to the floor, a hand to my stomach as I tried not to puke.

"I have to use the bathroom," Asher panted, still wearing his stained khakis.

A few minutes later the door opened again. The two men returned, one carrying two pails of water and washcloths, the other a bucket and a roll of toilet paper. They set everything down before locking us in again.

Asher was too busy crying into his hands to notice me doing the same. I let my tears flow quietly, letting my fear get the best of me.

Drying my eyes with my filthy shirt, I scanned the tiny room. Two sleeping bags, a lantern, and a small stack of clothes rested in a corner. For now, sunlight filtered in from a small porthole too high for me to see through, but the lantern would come in handy at night.

My body grew heavy as I became more afraid. Where were they taking us? I turned back to Asher to find him sniffling, staring at me through swollen eyes.

"W-what do we do now?" he asked.

"Let's, uh," I glanced at the bucket and pails of water, "get cleaned up. My mom says feeling refreshed helps sometimes." It never worked for me, but he didn't need to know that.

Taking a deep breath, Asher pushed his hair from his sweaty face and wobbled to his feet. He stared at the bucket and pails, and I thought he might cry again.

"We're going to get out of this." I rested a hand on his shoulder. "We'll make it back home."

Asher's bottom lip quivered. "I don't have a home." He took cautious steps over to the bucket, and I moved to the opposite side of the room, facing away from him. What did he mean he didn't have a home? Did he mean he lived in an apartment? I did too, but I still called it home. It was where I felt safest, where the two people I loved most loved me back. It didn't need to be an actual house to be called a home.

"They left clothes next to the sleeping bags," I said over my shoulder.

Asher's sniffling continued as he peed into the bucket. "Don't turn around."

"I won't." The sound of him removing his clothes and shoes reached my ears.

"Finished," he said a while later. The long sleeve shirt brushed his knees, and he'd rolled up the legs of the sweatpants several times. I guessed they weren't used to having little kids on board.

I washed up and changed while he sat on one of the sleeping bags and stared at the wall.

"I've got an idea," I said, shoving the sleeves of the shirt to my elbows. "I can't see outside, but maybe I can lift you high enough for you to see."

Asher didn't move, didn't give any signs he'd heard me. I knelt in front of him, waving my hand in front of his face. "Hey," I whispered, and he blinked up at me. He looked paler than he did earlier, making the small mole on his cheek stand out more.

"I don't feel so good," he said. We hadn't set off yet, but the ship did sway a bit.

"Do you have motion sickness?"

"What's that?"

"It's when you get sick in cars or boats, or rides, or anything that moves,

I guess."

Asher shrugged.

"Do you feel okay enough to look outside? Maybe you can tell where we're at." It was a dumb idea. We were just out there not too long ago, and other than being on a deserted pier, I hadn't known where the heck we were. But maybe there was something I missed. A landmark or something.

Asher nodded, and I grabbed his shoulders when he swayed to his feet. I was taller and bigger than him, but I still only had kid strength. I crouched to wrap my arms around his knees and lifted him, almost sending us both falling to the floor.

"Can you see anything?" I gritted out, trying to keep him still.

"Just water. Lots of water." Which meant we didn't have a land view. Asher yelped when we jerked a bit. The ship was pulling away from the pier.

We sank onto our sleeping bags, staring up at the porthole in silence until the sun set and the room went dark. I turned on the lantern, watching Asher with concern. He was gazing at the wall again. I think I preferred it when he cried.

"How old are you?" I whispered. He didn't answer. "Asher?"

"Huh?" His eyes were sad when he looked at me. They shimmered in the lantern light.

"How old are you?"

"Six—but I'll be seven the day before Christmas," he said quickly, like he didn't want me to think he was a baby.

"I'm twelve, but I'll be thirteen on Valentine's Day." My birthday was months away. Would I still be around by then? "Around," sounded less scary than "alive." I breathed through the sick feeling in my stomach.

"What's your favorite color?" I asked when he faced the wall again.

"Gray."

"Like your name."

"No, like the color of storm clouds on a rainy day." His words sounded dull and recited, like he was repeating something he'd heard tons of times before.

I picked at a loose string on my sleeping bag, watching him watch the wall. "How did they get you?"

"I was walking down the street when the nice lady said hello to me. I was lost. I'd been walking for a while."

"By yourself? Where was your mom?"

"I'm tired," he said after a moment of hesitation. Asher slipped between the flaps of his sleeping bag, rolling away from me. He tried to cry quietly but I heard him. The sickness in my belly climbed higher until my throat burned from it. Seeing him sad made my own sadness ten-times worse. I'd always been that way.

"I'm sure your mom is looking for you," I said after some time had passed. "Between your mom, my mom and my grandpa, and those other girls' parents, we'll be found in no time." I bit my lip to keep it from trembling, and slid inside my sleeping bag too. There wasn't any noise outside our door. The silence on the ship didn't match the chaos happening inside of me. I tried to tell myself the bad guys were gone, and that we'd wake up tomorrow, open the door and be free.

"I live in a home for boys," Asher said, his voice scratchy from all the crying. "My family died in a fire when I was five. I've had a few foster moms since then, but no one ever keeps me." Asher rolled over to face me, then tucked his hands under his cheek. He looked so fragile beneath his big curls and wide eyes. I moved the lantern over an inch so I could see him better, then tucked my hands under my cheek too.

"They'll think I ran away, because all the boys run away sometimes. But I just wanted to go home. To see if maybe it was fixed. Maybe my mom hadn't died and she was waiting there for me to come back because she didn't know where to find me. I would've gone back to St. Joseph's if she wasn't there. I would've had nowhere else to go." His eyes flooded with tears again. That strange heaviness I sometimes felt when hearing a sad story made it hard to breathe. Asher reached his tiny hand out to me, and I untucked one of mine to take it. His nails were chipped, and he hadn't gotten all the dirt out from underneath them.

"Are you scared, Malcolm?"

"No." The need to make him feel safe was bigger than my need to be honest.

"I'm scared too," he said, seeing right through me. His eyes lids gradually lowered, and his breathing slowed down.

"Hey, Asher," I whispered in case he'd fully fallen asleep.

"Yeah?" he opened his eyes halfway, his hold on my hand tightening again.

"When we make it out of this, you can come home with me. I'll keep you."

CHAPTER 26

Malcolm

Asher turned paler and paler every day, and he slept longer too. One of the guys in charge of us tossed a wristband in the room and ordered him to put it on after I'd pounded on the door yelling for a doctor. It helped a little, but I couldn't shake the feeling that something else was wrong with him.

They fed us oatmeal and water for breakfast every day. The nasty kind with no flavor that my grandpa liked. I made sure Asher ate all his and a small portion of mine. He complained about it, but listened when I told him it would make him feel better.

I set Asher on his feet, rubbing the shoulder I'd banged on the floor of that basement. It didn't hurt much anymore, but holding him up to the porthole every day aggravated it.

"Am I darker now?" he asked, feeling around his face.

"Not really, but how do you feel?"

"Better?" He said it with a question mark at the end. I hoped the vitamin D from the sun would help. Other than sunlight, the only other things I had handy were the food they brought us, and the cold pails of water they refilled a couple of times a day. I'd wet a washcloth and lay it across his forehead while he napped.

"How does your stomach feel?"

"Better." He sounded more confident this time. "I don't think I'm gonna throw up again."

"Good." Voices trickled in from outside our door. I crept over to it, pressing my ear against it. As always, I couldn't make anything out. The steel was too thick.

The bolt on the door groaned, and I rushed over to where Asher stood, shoving him behind me. He peeked around me when the door opened, and I pushed him back again.

The man with the grim face stepped in, scrunching up his nose as he removed our bathroom, switching it with a clean bucket. I was sure the room had an odor Ryan and I could no longer smell ourselves. You got used to stench when forced to live in it. My grandpa used to say that about our neighborhood.

He refreshed our pails of water and dropped another stack of clothes onto the floor before removing the pile of dirty clothes from yesterday. Asher had vomited all over them. Next he brought in the bowls of oatmeal and bottled water. He was always alone.

"When can we go home?" I asked. He wouldn't answer. He never did. The door slammed shut again, the bolt sliding into place. I waited a whole minute to be sure he wasn't coming back before allowing Asher to step from behind me.

"I'm not hungry," he said, flopping down on his sleeping bag. Neither was I, and I didn't have the strength to force either one of us to eat right then. I laid down next to him, staring at the brown water stain on the ceiling.

"How many days now?" Asher asked.

"Four." We'd been using the sunrises to keep track of the days we'd been on board. Asher had a hard time remembering, and I didn't know if it had anything to do with him not feeling good, or him being six.

"Your mom should be close to finding us then, right?"

I'd told him she would do whatever it took to find me. "Yeah, she should be." I had to keep hope alive for one of us, because mine was steadily slipping.

"And you really think she'll let me live with you?" He sounded excited but also unsure.

I rolled toward him, the purple smudges beneath his eyes worrying me.

"Yeah, and she'll love you and worry about you just as much as she loves and worries about me. She *loves* kids."

Asher smiled at that. "Where will I sleep?"

"Well, we moved into a bigger apartment, but it's still small. There aren't any spare bedrooms, but you can have half of my room."

"You'd share your room with me? Like we were brothers?"

"Yeah," I shrugged. "Why not? I've always wanted a brother. And we can paint your side any color you want, and you can pick out your own bed too. And we'll take you shopping for sheets and clothes." My mom would take him in, that much I knew. What I didn't know was if she could afford all the other promises I was making. She had a better paying job now since she finished school, but she said she had one more degree to go before she started making the big bucks. I'd have said anything to make Asher feel better, though. Plus I had some left over allowance we could use.

"I'll paint my side gray."

"Like the color of storm clouds on a rainy day."

"Right." Asher nodded in approval.

"Did your mom used to say that to you?"

"Yeah." His eyes filled with tears. "I'm starting to forget her. I don't have any pictures of her to help me remember. They all burned in the fire. All I have is her violin." He shot up. "Her violin!" He started hyperventilating, scrambling to his feet.

"Hey," I got up as well. "What's wrong? What happened to her violin?"

"I-I don't have it. It's gone," he cried. "It's the only thing I had and it's gone."

I hugged him, his tears soaking into my shirt as I thought of something to say to calm him down. "Did you leave it somewhere? Maybe we can find it."

Asher pulled back, hiccupping. "It's under my bed. I always hide it under my bed."

"At St. Joseph's?"

"Yeah." He nodded frantically, tears falling to his chin.

"Okay, so it's hidden, it'll still be there when we get back." I realized I didn't know where he was from. I just assumed we'd all been snatched from the same area. I knew from the girls' college t-shirts they attended school in the city. But where was Asher from?

"They'll throw my stuff in the trash if they think I ran away. Or one of the other boys will take it."

"They won't think you ran away," I brushed his rebellious curls off his forehead.

"How do you know?" He swiped at the moisture on his cheeks.

"Do they know how much you love your mom's violin?"

"Yeah," he frowned.

"So the moment they find it they'll know you didn't run away, because you'd never leave it behind."

He thought about that for a second, shivering through his heightened emotions. "Yeah, that's true."

"Yeah, it is," I agreed. "Where's St. Joseph's anyway?"

"In Brooklyn."

"Hey, that's where I live." We smiled, the first smile we'd shared. I poked his cheeks. "You've got dimples. Nice."

Asher blushed, clearly flattered by my approval. We sank to our sleeping bags again, sitting crossed legged in front of each other.

"So, how'd you end up with your mom's violin? And do you know how to play it?"

"It was in the car. We were driving home from one of her shows. I could smell the smoke from down the street. There were lots of people outside in their pajamas, and I could hear sirens far away. My mom yelled for me to stay put while she ran inside for my nonna. They never came out." He continued before I could say sorry. "I was learning how to play. We hadn't gotten very far in my lessons. But I still practice what I know."

"Can't wait to hear you play."

"You won't like it. I'm not any good." He reddened. I hated that he felt embarrassed, but I was happy to see some color in his cheeks.

"Well, then we can both get better at playing our instruments together."

"What do you play?" he asked, curiosity lighting up his gloomy gaze.

"The piano. I'm better than "okay" but I'm no virtuoso. I will be one day, though."

"Uh, vir-too... what?" Asher scrunched up his face at the word. I chuckled.

"It means I'm not exceptional at it. Or not really, really good yet," I amended when he frowned at that word too.

"Oh," he blushed again.

"I'm just being a know-it-all." I downplayed my smarts. "I learned the word recently, and now I use it every chance I get."

Asher coughed into his hand. It continued for a few seconds.

"Feeling okay?"

"Yeah," he replied, laying down. I leaned over to rest the back of my hand across his forehead like my mother did when I was coming down with something. His skin felt cool. I took it as a good sign. "Do you have your own piano?"

"Yeah. My mom got me a hand-me-down one for Christmas a few years ago. The church was planning on throwing it away. She only had to pay for the delivery and tuning."

"Is it in our room?" Asher asked with a tired smile.

"Yup. It's an upright, so it fits against the wall. And there's plenty of space for your mom's violin."

He stared at a stain on his sleeping bag, his mind seeming far away. "Does your dad live with you?"

"No. I never met my dad."

"Me either." He sighed. "What will we do when we get home?"

I didn't know if he believed all the things I told him, or if he saw our talks as a fantasy that kept his mind occupied. I meant everything I said, but either way, I indulged him. It kept us both hopeful, and gave us something to look forward to. Without hope, we had nothing.

I leaned back on my palms, pretending to give his question serious thought. "We'll have dessert for breakfast, and dinner for lunch. We'll do everything backward and have nothing but fun for at least two whole weeks."

Asher's eyes and smile widened with excitement. "We'll have double chocolate fudge cake!"

"And for lunch my mom will make my great-grandma's famous jambalaya! I never met her, but her recipe is good."

"Do you think she'll make me chicken tenders and fries? That's my favorite."

"She'll make you whatever you want," I promised. "And we'll watch The Never Ending Story all day. I never get enough of that movie." The book was better, but we'd have fun watching the movie together.

Asher yawned. We hadn't woken up that long ago. "I can't believe you're gonna keep me. I can't believe I'll have a brother. Malcolm and Asher forever," he whispered.

"Malcolm and Asher forever."

He closed his eyes, and for several minutes I monitored his breaths, how loud and how often they came. I listened to his newly developed cough too.

I sighed once I believed he'd fallen into a deep sleep, shoulders slumping as I covered my face with my palms. I let myself be weak, let myself worry and be scared for a little while, because pretending to be strong took a lot of effort.

"Malcolm?" Asher breathed. I straightened, clearing my expression of the terror I felt inside. "What else will we do when we get home?"

I searched for something to say, pushing past the pain and sadness clouding my mind for something to keep him cheerful. "We'll start on our Christmas lists. We've got to give my mom and grandpa time to shop now that it's the two of us. And no Happy Birthday/Merry Christmas gifts either. You get a gift for each occasion. I already know what I'm getting you."

"Tell me." He forced his eyes open.

"Nope." My voice came out shaky as I watched him get sicker by the minute. "You'll have to wait. Go to sleep, Asher," I whispered, and when he glanced at the door, I vowed, "I'll protect us."

❧

"I DON'T THINK this is a good idea." Asher said, fidgeting with the shirt sleeves overwhelming his small frame. He was tinier than any six-year-old I'd ever seen. "We're too small."

I'd watched over him while he napped, even standing in front of his sleeping bag when the man I now referred to as our guard dropped off lunch. I'd told him that Asher wasn't feeling well and needed medicine, but he'd ignored me. So I'd come up with a plan to get us out of here.

"We have to try," I said, slashing the air with the plastic spork we'd been given with our food. "All you have to do is stand behind the door, and after I incapacitate him, you run and I'll be right behind you." I kept practicing my moves with my makeshift weapon.

"I don't know what in-com-pa-tate means."

"It means I'm going to take him down, knock him out. Or at least take him by surprise long enough for us to escape."

"He's too big, it won't work." He shook his head, panic in his eyes. "Maybe we should wait for your mom to—"

"Hey," I crouched in front of him. "Do you trust me?"

"Y-yes."

"He won't be expecting an attack. I'll get him in the eye. He'll fall to his knees screaming, and we'll run and lock him in here."

"Then what?"

"Then we'll find the other girls, grab anything we can use as a weapon and make our way up. I saw life vests when we got on the ship. Can you swim?"

"Yeah. I learned in summer camp."

"Me too."

He seemed to like that. He liked that we were similar.

"But you're not feeling well, and neither of us are at full strength, so the vests will help. We'll put them on and jump in the water before anyone else can stop us. Okay?"

"O-okay."

"Remember the whole plan, right?"

Asher nodded then coughed.

I looked at the porthole. Dinner usually arrived as the sun was setting. It'd be any minute now. I set the bucket we used as a bathroom near me, and waited for the door to open.

Minutes later the bolt whined, and Asher pressed himself against the wall, squeezing his eyes shut. I was grateful, because he didn't have to see me gag on my fear. I had no time to second-guess, the door opened, and I waited for the guard to step inside before I tossed the contents of the bucket at him.

"Fuck!" he shouted, dropping the tray of food he held and stumbling back a step. I lunged for him, bringing the spork down on his right cheek, missing his eye. The plastic teeth cracked, drawing a little blood but not doing much damage. He recovered quickly, grabbing me by the arms and shoving me further into the room. "You're gonna fucking pay for that," he growled.

"Run, Asher!" I fought viciously, scratching and punching as he took me to the floor. I looked over to see Asher staring at us, mouth hanging open, body trembling. "Run!"

The guard glanced over his shoulder at Asher. Asher bolted through the door, and was caught by the other guard. Asher screamed as the bigger man lifted him into the air by the collar of his shirt. "What the fuck is going on here?"

The guard above me pinned me in place by the throat, drawing his fist back.

"Declan, don't damage the fucking goods!" The man holding a thrashing Asher shouted.

Declan panted above me, his fist shaking. I tried to peel his fingers off me, my feet scraping against the floor.

"Declan," the other man warned. Declan released my throat and stood, jaw ticking, glaring down at me, the front of his clothes covered in pee. I coughed, sucking in air and reaching toward Asher who still struggled to break free of the other man's hold.

"Let him go, please," I wheezed. That was the wrong thing to say. Declan looked between the two of us, a cruel smile forming on his face. He strode over to the lantern and broke it with his boot. Only the light from the hall and the remaining bit of sunlight lit the room now.

"Malcolm!" Asher screamed, reaching for me. I scrambled up and ran for him, but Declan stopped me, shoving me to the floor. He stepped into the hall, taking Asher from the other guy.

"Please, no," Asher begged them. "Malcolm!" Fear locked my body in place.

"Let him go! No!" I charged for the door, but it slammed shut before I got to it. "No!" I yelled again, banging my fists against the steel and yanking on the handle. "Asher! Asher!" I punched and kicked at the door until my hands and feet ached. What had I done?

I screamed until my voice gave out, until it burned and the taste of blood hit the back of my tongue. Then I backed into a corner and sank to the floor, crying for all the days I hadn't before because I'd had to be strong for Asher. I cried for all the pain he must have been going through, all the fear he had to have been experiencing. I cried because I was alone in a dark room. I cried because I was just a boy, and I wanted to go home.

CHAPTER 27

Malcolm

The sun rose and set for three whole days before the door opened again. I was hungry, thirsty, and filthy. Most of all, I felt broken.

"Jesus fucking Christ. Get him hosed down and clean this room. And feed him! There's flies in here for fuck's sake. Are you telling me I can't leave you two in charge when I go off to handle fucking business?" The suited man in the sunglasses was back. Declan and the other guard listened to his tirade with their heads lowered to the floor.

I didn't understand what he meant by *leaving* them in charge, but then I remembered the helipad I'd seen when we first got on the ship, and the sound of a helicopter in the sky a little while ago. I thought I was hearing things that weren't there. I felt delirious enough for it to be true.

"A-Asher," I croaked from my dirty corner. My eyes were crusty and dry. I'd cried all the tears my body contained.

"Who?" the suited man said to me as the guards worked on clearing the dried food that had spilled days ago. I swallowed, trying to moisten my throat so I could answer him, but then he circled the room, looking around.

"Where's the boy?" he shouted, his rage making me curl in on myself. "I said, where's the fucking boy?!"

The two guards looked at each other, and my heart pounded so hard I thought it might burst through my chest. I held my hand there just in case.

"You've already cost us two packages," the suited man said, pinching the bridge of his nose. "If you tell me we've lost another one, I will kill you both right here and now."

"It wasn't our fault," Declan said, the cut on his cheek still healing. "They were sick. You know there's something going around on the ship."

The suited man stepped in close to Declan, grabbing him by the throat and asking in a low, scary voice, "Where. Is. He?"

It was the other guard who spoke up. "He's in the room that the lost packages were in."

I tried to stand, tried to beg them to take me to him, but I fell on my butt again.

"Why is he in there?"

"Because this one attacked me," Declan sneered, jabbing a finger at me.

"You were attacked by a scrawny kid?" He poked the cut on Declan's cheek, making him hiss, then shoved him away. "Get him a new room. This one needs to be sealed off." He pressed the back of his hand to his nose.

"The o-only other available room is yours," Declan said.

The man turned back to him, the room suddenly going cold. "Give him yours then. You seem to forget the main objective is to get them from point A to point B *alive*. I won't protect you from the repercussions of your actions. That goes for the both of you. Someone will have to answer for this, and mark my words, it won't be me."

ONCE THE SCARY man left, they grabbed me by the arms and hauled me on deck to hose me off. The force of the cold water was too strong for my weak body, and the direct sunlight too bright for my eyes. I ended up naked and curled onto my side with my hands shielding my face while I spluttered and shivered.

Afterward, I was handed a towel and taken below deck again. My new room had a small bathroom and a bed twice the size of my twin bed at home. A tray with something steaming in a bowl waited on a small table under the porthole. I began to panic when I looked around and didn't see Asher.

"Where is he?" I asked just as the door closed and locked. I jerked the handle, but it was pointless.

It took four attempts to get dressed in the clothes they'd left on the bed. Everything felt too heavy for me to lift, even my limbs.

I sat at the table, bouncing my knee, trying to sip at the hot soup. My body wanted the food, but my heart and my mind were too broken to cooperate.

"No," I whispered when a voice in my head told me to go to sleep and never wake up. Instead, I dragged myself to a corner, slid to the floor and rested my head on my knees.

The door opened a while later and the man in the suit ushered Asher in.

"Asher!" I cried out, stumbling to my feet. His skin looked gray, his eyes sunken in.

"M-Malcolm?" he stammered, like he didn't trust his sight or hearing. He tried to run to me, but ended up tripping over his feet. I caught him, both of us sinking to the floor. "They said you were gone," he cried hysterically, climbing onto my lap. "They said you were gone."

"I'm here," I hugged him back. "I'm here."

He'd been small from the start, but he was nothing but bones now. Asher sobbed my name into my neck, bunching my shirt into his tiny fists as I rocked him. He was hot enough to melt my skin away, and something in his chest rattled when he coughed.

The man in the suit watched us from the door, a curious expression on his face.

"He's sick," I said to him, peeling Asher off me so I could see his face. He made it near impossible, gripping my shirt tighter. "He needs a doctor."

The man said nothing, and I had to hold Asher's head up to keep it from drooping.

"Why are you doing this?! What do you want from us? *Please.* Help him. I won't try anything again. I promise. Just *please*, do something." I felt feral and scared and helpless.

The man snapped his fingers at someone in the hall, someone I couldn't see from where we sat. A moment later Declan strolled in holding a second tray of food with a bottle of water and medicine on it. He'd been standing there waiting for the signal to come in, and suddenly I knew that the man in the suit was the more dangerous one. He'd wanted to see my reaction to Asher first.

The man crouched down in front of us, and I angled Asher away from him as best I could. That made him smile a little. Asher had gone silent, breathing heavily into my neck.

"You've got at least thirteen more days on this ship," the man said, removing his sunglasses for the first time. His eyes were ice-blue, and he had a slash over his right eyelid. The scar tissue prevented him from opening it all the way. "I've warned my men not to harm you while I'm gone, but they aren't as civilized as me."

Somehow I didn't believe he was civilized at all, he just seemed better at pretending.

"What happens to him depends on you," he continued, gesturing to Asher. "No more bright ideas." He slipped his glasses on and stood.

"I brought a doctor back to look at him and the others." He jerked his chin toward the table. "Give him a dose of that after every meal, and make sure he stays hydrated." Without another word he left, the door slamming behind him, sealing me and Asher inside.

The "nice lady's" words in that basement made sense now, especially after hearing the suited man's warning.

"Children are difficult," one of the men looking Asher and I over had said.

"Not when they have an incentive to behave," she'd said.

They'd kept us together hoping we'd start to care for each other. And now they would use our bond to keep us obedient in fear of what would happen to the other if we weren't. It worked. From that day on, I never asked another question, never demanded we be let go again, and I made no more escape plans.

"OPEN UP, ASHER," I begged, patting his cheek. "Just a little more so you can take some medicine." I held the spoonful of broth near his mouth, tipping it into the small opening he'd made. "Okay, two more, then some water and medicine."

"I'm tired," he complained, his eyes fluttering open then closing again.

"I know, but the medicine's going to fix that." I looked at the bottle of pink liquid on the table. The man in the suit made it sound important that we stay alive, so I decided to trust it wasn't poison. I had no other choice.

We were still on the floor. Asher wasn't able to get up on his own, and the days I'd spent not eating made me too weak to carry him. Plus I had a bad headache, and my throat was starting to hurt when I swallowed.

I dropped the spoon into the bowl of soup to catch him when he slid sideways. "How about just one more spoonful then? Can you do one more?"

He licked his dry lips. "Water," he rasped. I uncapped the bottle so fast some of it spilled over my hands. I held it to his mouth, tipping it up as he sipped more than I thought he would. I went to the table for the medicine next, filling the little cup to the line inside, then pouring it into his mouth. He coughed some of it up, but kept most of it down.

"Can you make it onto the bed?" I asked, but he just groaned. Sighing, I pulled the pillows and blanket to the floor, laying us on our sides, my front to his back. Asher had another coughing fit, and I slid my arm around him when it was over, holding him close. His hair was damp against my forehead, but he didn't smell bad so I guessed it wasn't sweat. They must have hosed him down too before bringing him here.

He reached back to grab a chunk of my short hair, something he did in his sleep, like I was his security blanket. If it wasn't my hair it was my hand. Maybe he just needed to know I was still there while he slept. That I hadn't been taken again, leaving him alone.

I didn't mind. I liked knowing he was still there too. Having him snatched from our room and not knowing if he was dead or alive changed something in me, and my mind didn't feel as strong as it did before.

I couldn't sleep, not until I knew the medicine was working. I was scared I'd wake up and he'd be gone in a different way. Gone in a way he couldn't come back from. So I talked to him while he snored, hoping my voice reached him, hoping it made him want to hang on.

"My mom doesn't like me riding my bike in the neighborhood park," I whispered into the back of his head. "The older kids sell drugs there, and last summer a stray bullet hit a little boy while he was coming down the slide. We used to live across the street from there, but my mom got a job paying more money than the diner she used to work at, so we moved into a bigger, tiny place. My grandpa moved in too. His veteran's disability check helps pay some of the bills. Now we live a few blocks from the park, right on the border of the neighborhood." I scooted in closer to him when he shivered.

"My mom moved us a little further away from the violence, but we still live along the edges of it. She says we're going to own a brownstone one day. One of the fancy ones in Carroll Gardens. That's where she works now, and on her lunch breaks she likes to walk around the area imagining all the things we'll do once we live there."

Asher's hand twitched in my hair, and he coughed a few times before his snores started up again.

"Sometimes, when her boss is away, she takes me into the office with her, and we go on those walks together. She says my new bedroom will be big enough to fit a whole orchestra." I chuckled weakly at the thought before turning sad again. "Her boss was away the day I was taken. I was riding my bike in the park near her job when I saw the nice lady. It was early, so the park was pretty empty." I wondered if my mom still wanted to live there. There may not have been drug dealers in that park, but there were people hanging around there who stole kids. My grandpa always said the grass isn't greener on the other side. I got what he meant now.

"My grandpa's sick," I bit down on my bottom lip when it started shaking. "He coughs a lot like you do, but he does it into a rag, and there's always blood there after. He has cancer, but some days he seems like his old self. I bet he's looking for me too. I know he is. I-I need to get back to see him. I haven't gotten a chance to play the song I've been working on for him." I squeezed my eyes shut when they began to burn, holding Asher tighter.

"None of my friends will miss me, because I don't have any. I'm not like the other boys in my school. My mom said that's okay. But I have you now, though, and we're alike. We don't have fathers, we both play instruments, and we've both been stolen away. We'll always understand each other."

My sore throat began to feel worse from all the talking, so I pried Asher's fingers from my hair, patting his back to calm him when he began reaching and panting in his sleep. I quickly ate a little bit of the cold soup, then drank a full bottle of water while eyeing Asher's medicine. I was getting sick, and what good would that do us? If something happened to me, who would look out for him?

I took half the amount I'd given to him, because I wasn't as sick, and because I didn't want him to not have enough.

"Malcolm?" Asher whined, reaching his hand back again. I settled in behind him, guiding his fingers to my hair.

I started talking again, sharing the titles of my favorite books, the composers of my favorite songs, and my dreams of earning a scholarship to the Berklee College of Music. Then I ran down the list of famous Black maestros, promising I'd be added to the list one day.

I didn't stop talking. Not even as the days passed and he coughed less. Not even when he woke up long enough to eat more, or when he regained enough energy to shower. I'd talk because I realized the bad voices in my head were quiet when I did. The voices sounded like me, but they said things I'd never say.

The only time I went silent was when Declan showed up with more trays of food. He'd stare at me like he wanted to hurt me, like he hadn't forgotten what I'd done to him. I'm sure it didn't help that we'd been given his room. Was he forced to sleep in ours? Was *he* now using the bucket as a bathroom?

I didn't ask him if we were almost at our destination, never asked if Asher and I would be safe there, or ever get to go home. I simply curled over Asher's sleeping body protectively, not taking a real breath until we were alone again.

Five days passed before Asher seemed more like himself. “You talk too much, Malcolm,” he complained, letting go of my hair to sit up and rub at his eyes. “I can’t sleep when you’re talking.” He’d slept just fine while I talked for the last five days.

“I thought you liked talking to me,” I sat up too, brushing his hair back.

“Not when you talk all the time, and not when I’m sleeping.” He stretched his arms over his head then smiled.

“You woke up in a good mood. Or are you happy because I finally shut up?”

Asher laughed, surprising me, and I wanted to check to see if his fever had come back. “We’re gonna be okay,” he said. “We’re gonna get out of here.”

“We are?” I gave into the urge to feel around his face for warmth.

“Yeah,” he pushed my hands aside. “Gargantuan is gonna save us.”

“Gargantuan?”

“He came to me in my dreams,” he said excitedly. “He’s gonna get us out of here. It’s his job.” Asher untangled himself from the covers, nearly tipping over the edge of the bed in his rush to get off it. He ran over to the small table.

“Hey,” I said, “Slow down, you’re not all the way better yet. And who’s Gargantuan?”

He turned to me with a gasp. “You don’t know who Gargantuan is? He’s a Freedom Fighter. The library has all their books. I like libraries,” he said, getting off track. “Gargantuans’ job is to rescue the Small Bones.” Asher climbed onto the chair, and I jumped from the bed to catch him when it tilted to the side.

“Okay, please slow down and tell me what’s going on?” Adrenaline raced through me so fast I thought I might throw up. Asher went from being too tired to use the bathroom on his own, to bouncing around and talking a mile a minute about being rescued by some person in charge of bones.

“Gargantuan is a Freedom Fighter,” he started, now standing on the floor again. “They’re superheroes, and they each have a job to do. Gargantuans’ in charge of saving the Small Bones. He told me he would save us.” He turned back to the chair.

“What does that have to do with you standing on a chair?”

“Because I have to keep an eye on the sky. He’ll come through a portal, then I’ll wave so he can see me.”

Superheroes weren’t my thing, but I’d at least heard of most of them. I didn’t know who the Freedom Fighters were, but I was sure they weren’t going to leap from the pages of their books to save us. Sometimes I forgot how old

Asher was, and how much younger than six he could sometimes seem.

"So who are the Small Bones?" I sat on the chair he wanted to stand on again.

Asher blew out a breath, sending his curls fluttering. "They're kids, like you and me. All kids are Small Bones in Galasia, because our bones are small."

I assumed Galasia was the world the stories were set in.

"Bad things happen in Galasia. Kids are taken for their raw powers. Gargantuan finds them and brings them home. He's strong and powerful."

"Okay," I said, following along now. "So what happens if a kid's bones aren't small?"

"Uh, I don't know. If you're a kid, you're a Small Bone. It doesn't matter."

"Asher—"

"Are you scared that you aren't a Small Bone?" he asked, stepping in to squeeze my biceps. "Because you are."

"Hey, I was in the middle of a growth spurt before I got here. I had some muscles." My mom always said I'd grow to be as big as my dad. I had a couple pictures of him.

"Well, they're gone now," he said, brows furrowed. "You're coming with me." Asher yanked on my hands until I stood. I helped him onto the chair this time, then held the wobbly table still while he stepped on it. He stared into the sunshine wearing the biggest smile I'd ever seen, and I decided then not to steal his hope. Maybe this was the only way his mind could handle everything going on. Now I just needed to find a way for my mind to stop feeling like it was being ripped apart. Maybe pretending to believe in Gargantuan would help, the way pretending to be unafraid and strong for Asher had helped for a while.

"What about the girls that came here with us?" I asked, settling onto the edge of the bed closest to the shaky table. "Will Gargantuan save them too?"

"No," Asher said sadly. "They're too old. He only saves the Small Bones. But maybe Ferian will help them." He brightened up at the idea. "She takes care of the grown-ups. The Big Bones." His voice went low. "Ferian can't wake the sleeping Bones, though. Only Gargantuan can."

"Wake them?"

"Yeah. If Gargantuan can't get to the Small Bones in time, he has the power to wake them. Children of Galasia are innocent, and the innocent get to come back. They just won't have their powers when they do." He shrugged. "But who cares about powers when you get to come back?" He turned to the porthole again.

I swallowed. "This sounds pretty morbid for a children's book."

"What's morbid mean?"

"It means something disturbing, or spooky. Like *Coraline*," I said when his confused expression didn't change.

He shivered. "That movie is scary. The Other Mother is mean. Gargantuan isn't scary or mean."

My throat no longer hurt and my headache had vanished days ago, but I couldn't shake the heaviness in my body, or the strange thoughts bouncing around my head. I felt empty on top of feeling sad, and my stomach kept flip flopping around. I took the half dose of medicine I'd been taking, because maybe after enough days it would fix all the other things still wrong with me.

I listened to Asher hum for a little while, then I curled around a pillow and started listening to the voices in my head.

CHAPTER 28

Malcolm

Asher spent a lot of time at that porthole, and I let him. I was too busy staring at the walls to stop him. As long as the sun was up, he only moved for bathroom breaks, or to huddle in close to me whenever the bolt slid back on the door. Sometimes, if I wasn't too numb to move, I'd wrap my arms around him protectively.

"Gargantuan is on his way," Asher said, getting down from the table to sit with me on the bed. He sounded less hopeful with every sunset, but he hadn't given up completely. "I think the water makes it hard for him to find us, but he will."

"Yeah, I'm sure he will."

"What's wrong? You don't talk as much as you used to. Is it because I said you talk too much?"

"No, I'm just tired." I lifted my arm so he could settle into my side.

"So why don't you sleep?"

"I sleep when you sleep."

"No you don't, you talk when I'm asleep."

"That's because I talk in my sleep."

Asher didn't buy it. He gazed up at me with worry in his eyes. "You're coming with me and Gargantuan, right?"

"Of course," I breathed, forcing a smile. "We go together."

"We go together," he repeated. "Malcolm and Asher forever." He balled my fingers into a fist before bumping it with his like I'd taught him.

Asher fell asleep, and I began talking again, only he wasn't the one I spoke to. Not anymore.

EVEN WITH EVERYTHING going on in my head, I thought I'd been doing a good job at keeping track of the days. Either I was off, or we'd docked earlier than the man in the suit said we would.

"Time to go," Declan barked, storming into our room and tossing our shoes at us. Asher startled awake, yelping when one of his shoes hit him on the shoulder.

"W-where are we going?" I asked, slipping my shoes on after telling Asher to put his on.

"No questions, now turn around."

It was still dark out, but through the porthole I spotted a hint of light in the distance. The sun would be up soon.

Declan yanked on us until we stood side by side facing away from him. I took Asher's hand as he started to cry. I wanted to hit Declan, to give him a matching scar on his other cheek, but the last time I did something stupid, they took Asher away from me.

Declan jerked our hands apart, first tying my wrists behind my back, then Asher's. "It's okay," I whispered to Asher, but I couldn't control the trembling in my body.

The whole ship sounded alive, orders were being shouted, and footsteps sounded from every direction. Asher and I were gagged next, and I nodded at him, trying to reassure him with my eyes when I couldn't with my words.

Young men and women were being herded above deck. It hadn't been just the four of us held prisoner on this ship. There were at least twelve more.

"Move it," Declan ordered from behind us when I froze. Asher and I started walking again, faster this time as I searched the new faces for the two girls who'd been in that basement with us.

The morning air was cool, and I almost tripped over a crate as we hurried to keep up with the small crowd ahead of us. Declan continued to shove at our shoulders impatiently.

There were other boats docked along the port, and a huge warehouse and crane up ahead. We were the only ones around, though, and it felt like we were hurrying to make sure it stayed that way.

The sky began to brighten as the ramp was lowered and more orders were yelled. Two men appeared, each carrying one end of a body bag. I'd seen enough of them lined up behind caution tape in my neighborhood to recognize them now. Two more men appeared carrying another one. I remembered something the man in the suit said.

"You've already cost us two packages."

I looked around again and still didn't spot the girls. I became dizzy, the voices filling my ears, the visions I'd started having last night popping up in front of me. Asher bumping into me snapped me out of it, and I continued to keep pace with everyone else.

Nothing looked or felt familiar to me, and the signs along the dock were all written in symbols. I dry heaved behind the cloth covering my mouth.

"Round that group up and load them in there," Declan told a tall, skinny man once we'd cleared the walkway. The man nodded, grabbing two young girls I'd never seen before and shoved them into a truck that already had a driver seated. A few other men dragged more girls that way.

"You two go in here," Declan said, forcing us into a box truck with images of fruits and vegetables on the sides of it. Asher and I hurried into a corner and crouched down together. Men rushed over, stocking it with crates to hide us, then Declan rolled down the door, locking it.

Asher and I stared at each other as the engine started up and the truck began to move at high speed. We fell to our butts, and one of the crates nearly toppled over on us. I pushed myself up quickly, using my shoulder to keep it steady. Doing so must have caught the knot Declan made on the rope tying my wrists, because it loosened a fraction.

I sat back down, twisting my hands until my wrists felt like they were on fire, until I got one of them free. I tugged down the cloth tied over my mouth, then pulled Asher's from between his teeth too.

"See," he whispered through his tears, "you are a Small Bone."

"Yeah, I guess I am." I didn't tell him it wasn't the size of my wrists that helped me, but Declan's poor knotting skills. "I'm going to loosen your rope, and then cover our mouths again. We have to pretend we can't get out of them, then when the time is right, we run as fast as we can."

Asher didn't like the sound of that idea. "B-but what if we get caught again? W-we s-should just wait for Gargantuan." He hadn't said his superheroes' name with much faith this time. It was more of a desperate plea for me to not get us taken away from each other again.

"We have to try," I said, feeling my blood pulse in my veins. "This might be our only chance."

"But y-you said you wouldn't try anything. You promised the man with the glasses." His body shook with his quiet sobs. The truck turned sharply, slamming us into the corner we were in.

"I have a bad feeling," I said in a hushed tone, letting my fear slip free in front of him. Asher either hadn't seen the bags holding the dead bodies, or he was too young to understand what they were. "We go together," I reminded him of our pact. "Malcolm and Asher forever."

Asher nodded, tears sliding down his cheeks as I fixed the cloth back over his mouth. I loosened his ropes, then slipped back into mine. We sat with our heads pressed together, my mind feeling like a strand of loose thread unraveling.

The crates went blurry in the truck, and suddenly I was looking into the watery eyes of my mother. "Momma?" I mumbled behind the damp cloth, straightening and squinting. She mouthed something, but I couldn't hear her. Her body took on a more solid shape then, her voice louder.

"Come home, Malcolm," she cried, and my heart pounded.

"Momma," I repeated. My grandpa showed up next, his coughing rag in his hand. He didn't look so good.

"We miss you, Mally," he said, and I whimpered his name even though it was muffled.

Asher nudged my leg, startling me, and the crates returned. I glanced over at him, seeing worry mixed in with his tears. I turned back to the crates, craning my neck to see around them. My mother and grandpa were gone. I fell back against the wall of the truck, closing my eyes. Asher rubbed his cheek up and down my shoulder to console me.

There was a loud boom, followed by the truck swerving and tires screeching. It sent me and Asher crashing to the other side as crates fell all around us. Declan and another man cursed from the cabin of the truck, while Asher and I groaned from the impact. I kicked a couple of crates off of us as we struggled to sit up.

The passenger side door slammed, and I could hear Declan yelling for the other guy to call for an extraction. The rolling door went up, and Asher and I squinted against the sunlight hitting us in the face. Satisfied that we were still alive, Declan slammed the door closed again, picking up his conversation with the other guy.

"Did you make the call?"

The guy answered in another language.

"English!" Declan shouted.

"I said I was about—"

"Give me the damn phone," Declan growled.

A moment later the door rolled up an inch. Declan hadn't locked it in place. Asher and I turned to each other, then I listened to Declan explaining that the truck had caught a flat. He yelled for someone to get there now.

"We've got a drop-off scheduled in two hours!" he shouted. "We can't be caught out here on this road, do you understand me?" He continued to yell as I hurried out of the ropes again. I tip-toed around the crates, then lowered to my stomach to peek under the door. I removed Asher's ropes next.

"What are you doing?" he whispered, panicking, when I pulled the cloth from his mouth.

"We have to go. Look," I pointed to the rolling door. "Gargantuan made a way for us. We have to take it."

He looked unsure but also curious.

"There's a field straight ahead, with a tree line at the other end of it. We just need to make it into the trees." The field was huge, the tree line so far away I could barely see it. We needed to make it much further than that too, but I just needed to get him moving. We'd run and figure out the rest later.

"O-okay," he whispered, eyes wide with terror.

I lifted the door in small, slow movements, sweating by the time I got the gap wide enough for us to slip under. I went first, then helped Asher down. Declan was still shouting orders into the phone. I couldn't see or hear what the other guy was doing.

Asher and I gripped each other's hand as we started to walk slowly, moving faster when Declan's voice grew more distant. After a while I stopped checking over my shoulder to see if they knew we were gone. All my focus went to the forest up ahead, to my mom and grandpa standing there waiting for me with smiles on their faces.

"*I knew you'd come,*" I mouthed as my lungs burned and my legs started to ache. My mom reached for me, urging me to move faster, and my grandpa sat at my piano, smiling while he pretended he could play. He liked to do that.

The world around me moved in slow motion as the trees melted away and my bedroom appeared. My poster of Florence Price still hung above my bed, and my piano sheets had been changed to the ones with musical notes on them. My mom knew they were my favorite. Our kitchen, which could only hold the three of us comfortably, appeared next. My grandpa's big silver pot sat on top of the stove, and I could smell the jambalaya on the breeze. I ran faster, even when my legs began to feel like noodles, even as Asher's tiny hand began to slip from my grasp.

I turned back to find Asher on the ground, reaching for me, crying my name. Declan chased after us, screaming his fury. I looked back to the tree line, to my mother's urgent shouts for me to hurry, to my grandpa's body slumped over my piano. He didn't have much time. I had to get back to him.

"Asher, you have to get up," I begged, falling to my knees in front of him.

"I-I can't," he breathed, both of us watching as Declan, and now the other man, ran for us.

"*Please*," I cried, helping him to his feet. "They're waiting for us."

His legs were much shorter than mine, and he was tired, weak, and still a little sick. We both were. He tried to run again, sweat and dirt soaking through his shirt, tears falling down his face as I shouted to my mother for help.

We trampled over wild flowers, purple and yellow and white. All beautiful, none of them ugly like this moment. Asher stumbled again, and I tried to carry him, tried to drag him home but I couldn't. I may have been bigger than him, but my bones were still small.

"I-I'm going to get us help, okay?" I stammered, seeing the two men get closer and closer.

"No!" Asher screamed, latching onto my shirt. "Please don't leave me. Please don't leave me."

"I-I'll be back. I promise. I'll come back for you." I peeled his fingers off me, my tears blinding me from the sight of his pain, but I could feel it. My heart broke under the force of it.

"No, no, no, no," he pleaded. "We s-stay together." He crawled toward me as I backed away, my gaze bouncing between him, the men, and my family waiting in the trees. "Malcolm, *please*!"

"Gargantuan will be here soon. He'll keep you safe until I get back," I sobbed. "I'm so sorry." I turned, looking toward the trees. "I'll find you. I'm s-sorry." I ran as fast as my body would allow, driving me closer to the forest.

"Malcolm!" Asher screamed, my name ripped from somewhere deep inside him. "Malcolm! You said you would keep me. *Please* don't leave me. *Please,* Malcolm." The fear in his voice shot through my heart.

I'd spent so much time trying to be brave that I'd forgotten I was just a boy. All the fear I'd been hiding wrapped around me now, and all the courage I'd been pretending to have floated away as I ran for the safety of my mother's arms. I couldn't do this anymore, couldn't survive this any longer. I wasn't strong enough, my mind had taken all it could take.

I was so close now, each step giving me the strength to move forward, every breath fueling the fire in my lungs. My mother smiled wider and my heart felt torn in two different directions. She stretched her arms out toward me, and I could feel her happiness crash into me.

I'll come back for him. I'll come back for him, I told myself.

Asher's voice reached me again in the distance, almost too faint now for me to make out. I hesitated for a second before my feet crossed the tree line, stumbling when his last words pierced my heart.

"Malcolm and Asher forever!" he screamed, right before a gunshot rang out.

CHAPTER 29

William

Present Day

We stood there with the truth out in the open now, the candle flames surrounding our pain, and the outside world forming a wall of snow around us. Neither of us could run from this. Not anymore.

"Asher," I whispered, letting the pain of hearing his name consume me. I needed something to hold on to, something to give me strength, because nineteen years later I still lacked it.

Asher was close enough to be the pillar I needed, and as though sensing that, he went rigid, letting me know he couldn't be my anchor.

"I-I thought you were gone. I thought he killed you because I ran. I saw him standing over you. You were so quiet, so still." I flinched, hearing the gun go off again in my head.

"I wished he had, instead of leaving me to live with the pain of losing you. The pain of what would happen to me next."

My knees wavered, and I willed the oncoming tears to recede. I didn't want anything blocking my view of him.

"It was a warning shot." He stood with his hands behind him. As though wanting to project stoicism, but his eyes gave away the emotions he tried to hide. He may have been angry, but he was also hurting.

I took a second from my heartache to appreciate every facet of him now—

even the pain-filled parts—before I lost him forever. He crept closer, stopping before getting close enough for me to do something idiotic like touch him, but he was near enough to read my gaze, which he seemed to do now. Did he see regret? Fear? Did he see the inner workings of my heart, and how it bled for him? Or did he only see the worst thing I'd ever done to him?

I thought about last night, about the urgency in his need for me to make love to him. He hadn't faced the truth yet. Hadn't sat with himself—or his therapist—and weeded through the mess of our past together. But he knew he'd have to today, and maybe he hadn't been sure we could survive it.

"How could you think I wouldn't figure it out? Your name? Did you think I was too young when I lost you to—" he paused to rub at his throat, "to recognize you now? Or maybe you were hoping I'd forgotten the most painful moment in my life altogether."

"Any or all of the above," I admitted. "I prayed every night you'd forget me. That the memory of me hadn't haunted you, the way your memory *relentlessly* haunted me." Why hadn't I done this sooner? Why hadn't either of us done this sooner? Because losing him now would be a much harder blow to my heart than it would've been in that hospital room.

"And if you had remembered what happened between you and Malcolm, I prayed you never knew that Malcolm was really me." I let out a shallow breath and rubbed at the sudden ache in my chest. Asher's hand twitched at his side as though he fought not to reach out for me.

"Why William?" His voice sounded rough. Either from losing the hold on his act of indifference, or the physical pain of speaking. Maybe both.

"William was my grandfather's name, and my middle name. He died shortly after I got back." I didn't say "home" because nothing ever felt like home again. I'd returned to a new and strange world, one I could no longer trust to be kind to me. One that hadn't been kind to Asher.

"I couldn't hear the name Malcolm without hearing your screams, without feeling or seeing your fear. I had to be someone different in order to survive, even if it was only in name." My legs were on the verge of falling now as I stood there, waiting for him to either destroy me or save me. He took in my stance, arms to my side, palms up. I stood there open to him, ready to take whatever he thought I deserved. I wouldn't close myself off from the pain. I wouldn't run from this.

"You're good at that," he breathed, his own emotions getting the better of him.

"Good at what?"

"Making me hurt for you." A single tear ran down his cheek, he blinked toward the ceiling to hold on to the others. "I'm so *angry* with you, but yet you make it so hard for me to hate you. You've made it hard since I got here. I thought I could let the past go. I wanted to let it go, because I knew if I dealt with it, I'd also have to deal with the anger and hate I still had for you. It's so... complicated, because I also don't hate you. Life has never been good for me, so that means you've been the best thing that's happened to me, both then and now. How am I supposed to feel about that?"

His words gave me hope, but I cautioned myself not to get excited. We weren't out of the woods yet. "Not a day went by that I didn't think about you, Ash—"

"You didn't think of me," he snapped.

"Yes, I did."

"No, you thought about what you did to me. Your pain was about *you,* it had nothing to do with me." He jabbed a finger at his chest, still trying to blink away his vulnerability. I couldn't let his lie stand. Couldn't allow him to shape the truth into something that would make walking away from me justifiable.

I took the two steps needed to enter his space and cup his cheeks. He recoiled with a sharp breath, but I held on. "You don't believe that. You've looked into my eyes for months now. The truth has been right in front of you."

Asher shook his head, rejecting my words.

"You *feel* the truth, Asher. While my pain has been self-serving at times, it has *always* been about you. My dreams were no longer mine when I returned. My ambitions and everything I fought to achieve at breakneck speed was all about you. All about your honor. All about making a difference because your life mattered. Everything I do, everything I've done from the moment I met you is with you in mind. *Always*."

He'd closed his eyes, not wanting to see the honesty in my gaze. It didn't matter. The truth tended to find us in our darkest corners anyway. I traced the outline of his face, then his lips, which quivered and parted under my touch. Tears flowed past his long lashes, and when he opened his eyes, I became hypnotized by their beauty and openness.

"How could I ever forget you?" he whispered, like not forgetting me was the real tragedy.

"Trauma can make you forget things, people. Some of that can be age, or circumstances surrounding how the memory was imprinted." I'd spent enough time researching the subject.

"That's because you've never had a Malcolm in your life. You're unforgettable." It didn't sound like a compliment.

"I can't remember the color of my mother's hair, or even if I have her name correct. But I remembered that your eyes were the color of leaves in the spring." He raised his trembling hands to my face, holding them suspended, like he was scared of what touching me would do to him. I leaned into them, closing my eyes as his fingertips rested on my wet cheeks. He mimicked the trail I'd taken across his features, grazing his digits over my lips, feeling my breaths wash over them.

"I remembered that your hair was brown, a few shades darker than your skin, and that it was soft like mine but... spongy."

A mixture of silk and wool my mother would say. Asher slid his hands over my short hair, sighing.

"I remembered how young you were, but how much older you seemed. Not much has changed there." His fingers skimmed over the flat bridge of my nose. "And I remembered how good it felt to be cared for by you, to be protected by you, and then to have that feeling ripped away. I could never forget you. *Never,*" he swore.

"I'm so sorry," I rasped. "I wasn't strong. I was only pretending to be. My inner voice was eating me alive, telling me things that weren't true. Sleep deprivation made me see things that weren't there. I tried my best to cope, but I was just a kid then too. I was falling apart. I had no business trying to keep you together."

Asher lowered his head but kept his hands on me. I kept mine on him too. I felt something shift in him, sensed a wall coming down. "I know," he said. "I know."

I exhaled in relief, pressing my lips to the top of his head. "I can't believe you're alive." I'd wanted to say those words for months. I'd wanted to celebrate, to spin him in my arms and jump for joy, to fall to my knees and beg for his forgiveness.

"Can... Can you tell me what happened to you?" In a way it felt too soon to ask. Just a few minutes ago he said he still hated me. But it had been on my mind for weeks. Since I first laid eyes on him again. If I was still going to lose him, I had to know everything first. "When did you become Ryan?" When he hadn't responded to seeing the name Asher on my back, I thought maybe he didn't even remember his own name.

He nodded, looking around as though searching for a place to start. I led him to the couch, sitting and pulling him down to straddle me.

"I was sold into slave labor," he whispered after several false starts. I held him at the waist, my grip steady but gentle to keep him physically moored to the present while his mind traveled into the past.

"My first owner asked me my name, but I couldn't speak. I'd gone somewhere in my head when you left, and I stayed there." There was no accusation in his tone. My heart throbbed with guilt anyway. "He... beat me until I passed out when I wouldn't answer."

Asher hissed when my grip tightened. I relaxed my hand and my jaw, apologizing.

"He kept me chained in a dark, cold cellar room while I healed, then did it again. I spent weeks healing down there. One day he finally gave up and said he'd call me Ryan, the name of the boy he bought me to replace. The boy who died screaming, he'd said. The name followed me to my next owner."

He removed his shirt, his hair falling over his face. I brushed the strands back as I took in the scars lining his torso. "My next owner liked to h-hurt me." He looked down at his chest, face awash with pain. "And so did his customers. I'd fall asleep wishing I could go back to the dark, cold cellar I'd spent the last few years in."

Asher shivered, holding his breath when I ran my fingers over the rough patch of skin on his back. "That was done little by little over time," he choked out. "Some of them liked to take their time with us."

"*Jesus,*" I breathed, my vision blurring from rage, a lot of it directed inward.

"You think you're in hell until you realize it can get much worse, then you start to think what happened before wasn't so bad." He swallowed a few times, exhaling before continuing.

"I was sold into the sex trade next, my body given to men who had a thing for young boys." Asher averted his gaze, the familiar look of shame filling his face. "I can still feel their hands grabbing at my skin, forcing me into position."

I removed my hands, thinking I may be making matters worse.

"Don't," he said, lifting my hands to his chest. "The closest I ever come to forgetting about them is when you touch me."

I leaned forward to press my lips to a rogue tear falling down his cheek, and he wiped mine away in return.

Drug dealers profited off of a sale once. What made human trafficking so lucrative, was the endless revenue stream the victims brought in. And when they were no longer of use, they could be resold or traded.

"I was a favorite because I didn't scream." He bit his quivering lip and wrapped his arms around me, his mouth now close to my ear. I squeezed him tight, feeling the pain in my heart spread to other parts of my body. "I lost count of how many nights I wished I could go back to the monster who had me before." His words were labored, and it tore me apart to make him relive his worst nightmares. I came close to stopping him, but as hard it was, it also seemed like something he needed.

"But being a favorite didn't mean all that much, because I was sold over and over again. No one kept me. No one ever keeps me," he whispered. His words triggered a memory, taking me back to another promise I hadn't kept.

"I'll keep you."

I gently urged him off of me so I could stand. I needed room to break, needed to get down on my knees to tell him once again how sorry I was for what happened to him. No matter how many times I said it, though, unrest remained deep inside of me, like I would never be free of this burden. Like we'd both been condemned to live a hollow existence because of it.

"I spent days getting lost in those woods before someone stumbled across me. I thought you were dead. I thought..." I paused to take a breath. "I sent help. I told them about the ship, about the truck, about Declan and the others. Too much time had passed, though. Everyone was gone. It was like it never happened. They never caught them, but I tried. I'm so sorry, I'm so sorry, I'm so sorry..." I cradled my head in my hands, feeling myself sink, unable to cope with the constant ache.

Asher got to his feet, trying to hold me up, but we were both too broken in that moment. We sank to the floor, both of us crying and holding each other. My fingers ached with how hard I gripped him. The terror of him being taken away from me, of losing him, was still fresh after all these years.

"Once I'd decided to deal with our past, all the anger and bitterness rushed to the surface," he whispered in my ear. "I couldn't make it go away. It had never really gone away to begin with, but it became easier to ignore when I started feeling... different feelings for you." He let out a ragged breath. "Tonight, I tried hugging you and kissing you like I had so many times before. Nothing worked. It only reminded me of what you'd done, of what I thought you'd cost me. I had to get the rage out of me somehow."

I kept my sobbing as quiet as possible, not wanting to miss a word of what he whispered to me.

"So I spoke my first words, and the more I talked the more pain you seemed to feel. It felt good at first, because I wanted someone to pay for everything that happened to me. But I realized that when you hurt, I hurt. I don't want us to hurt anymore, William. I want us to be free."

I froze, my tremors ceasing as I waited for what he'd say next. His heart pounded against my chest, and mine against his. Asher squeezed me tighter, nearly cutting off our air supply. His next words came out hoarse, like it took everything in him to let them go.

"It wasn't your fault," he said. "It was never your fault."

I could feel my remaining chains break free, feel life bloom inside of me.

"I blamed you all these years because I needed to survive, and hating you is what kept me going. It was how I coped, the one thing that gave me the strength to go on, the hope I'd see you again one day. In the end, you were my Gargantuan. You were the one who saved me, and you keep saving me still. Now it's my turn to save you. Let it go, William. Please, let the pain go."

The sound of sobs echoed around the room, increasing in volume and intensity as I cried his name with a mix of sadness and gratitude. Asher squeezed his arms and legs around me, shuddering through his own release of old and weary pain.

We stayed there for as long as it took, both of us drenched in salty tears by the time we pulled back to gaze at each other.

"You wear your heart everywhere," he breathed. "On your sleeve, in your hands, but mostly in your eyes. Just like I remembered." He kissed the corners of them, the candlelight making his own eyes shimmer. "You look at me like I'm special. That's how you make me feel." He shook his head. "But you're the special one."

I would've argued with him if I could have, but I was still trying to process everything he said.

"You... You forgive me?" I whispered in a ragged breath.

"You never needed my forgiveness. We were just boys, and you did more for me than most people ever would. More than anyone ever has."

"Y-you don't hate me anymore?"

"I wanted to believe I hated you, especially when I first got here. You seemed to have so much, and I had nothing. But you were so sad, always so sad. I realized you hadn't gotten off easy. It was too hard to hate you when I knew you were in just as much pain as I was. I know leaving me that day hurt you so much. Even with everything that happened to me, none of that was your fault, but you were forced to live with a choice no kid should've had to make."

I took my first real breath in years. Until recently telling my mother, I'd never told anyone what I did, or what Asher meant to me. I'd been too ashamed to. I'd told the authorities about a little boy named Asher, and about the other victims I'd seen, and the names and descriptions of the people who had a hand in trafficking us. Never more than that, though. Keeping the whole truth locked inside kept me a prisoner of my past, but I'd welcomed it. Not anymore. Now I wanted to be free, and I wanted to share my freedom with Asher.

Slipping my hand up his back, past his nape and into his hair, I brought him down for a kiss. It was tender, sweet, and I savored it, feeling other parts of our bodies come to life.

"When did you know?" I asked against his lips. "When did you know it was me?"

"In the hospital room. At first I couldn't be sure because of how foggy my head felt, and just the years we'd spent apart. You were bigger than the last time I saw you too. But then you told me about your foundation. Freedom Fighters. And the way you looked at me... I was sure of it then."

"How did I look at you?"

"Like you were guilty. Like you'd done something wrong."

Because I had. I couldn't look at him without seeing him crying in that field. "You knew, and yet you came home with me anyway."

Asher looked torn, just as torn as I imagined he felt that day. "I had no choice. You were the only thing familiar to me."

"Why didn't you say something then, or any time after?"

"I was confused. And I wasn't ready. Not to talk to you, to talk about my feelings or what happened to me. I wasn't ready for any of it."

I nodded, opening up for his kiss. "I had a feeling it was you who waited at the hospital before I even arrived." I touched his beauty mark. "Davidson had given me a description of you." Davidson saw my need for irrelevant details as a trauma response, a need to know exactly what I was walking into. So he indulged me. "I thought you were gone, but without a body there was always this hope." I closed my eyes, and Asher slid his hand under my shirt, his fingers brushing over my plea to Gargantuan again. *Bring him back.*

He already knew why I hadn't said anything. Already knew I'd hoped he didn't remember me or what I'd done, so I didn't bother explaining that any further.

"Did a part of you like my silence?"

"Yes, because as much as I wanted to hear you speak, a part of me also feared it, because I knew what happened tonight would come next. I feared you talking to Davidson, and once you went to Safe Haven, I feared your therapy sessions too. The idea of your weekly vision boards both awed and terrified me." I'd wanted him to deal with his trauma. I wanted the people who hurt him caught. But I was afraid that reliving his life might've triggered his memories of me. I struggled with wanting him whole, but not wanting to be pushed away.

"Looking back, though, I can see all the little mistakes I subconsciously made on purpose. Tests, I guess, to see if you truly hadn't remembered me, because I couldn't ask you outright. I was petrified when you remembered your favorite childhood meal, because it proved how far back your memories went." When nothing else came of it, though, I figured it was something that carried into his adulthood, and he had no recollection of how or why.

"There were other instances that proved you held on to some of your younger memories, like you knowing how old you were when you stopped speaking. But I told myself you either didn't know I was Malcolm, or you only remembered pieces of your past, and the pieces that included me weren't a part of it. Still, sometimes you'd look at me with such contempt, and I'd think 'he *knows*.' I'd then convince myself it wasn't true, but the truth is, I felt protected by your silence."

Asher scraped his fingers along my scalp, nestling deeper onto my lap and my burgeoning erection. It was my turn to kiss him again, this time deeper than I had before.

"How did you end up with my mother's violin?"

"You knew?" I couldn't keep the surprise out of my voice.

"Yes. I remembered leaving a scratch inside one of the openings near the strings. It was my proof that it belonged to me if one of the other boys ever stole it."

"Clever little thing," I grinned. Asher smiled at that, two clefts appearing in his cheeks. I'd spent too much time reflecting on his sadness to remember what his joy looked like, to remember it came with a set of dimples.

"My mother took me to St. Joseph's after they were informed about what happened to you. They let me have the violin."

"You gave up the piano for it."

"Yes," I breathed. Most prodigies started playing around age five. At twelve I was practically a senior citizen. It just meant I had to work harder to master it. "How did you end up back here?" I slid my hands to his hips.

"I was sold again. All of us who made it back were. But this time to someone who said they would help us. I don't remember much. We were out of it for most of the trip here."

"Will you talk to Davidson about all this?"

"Yes," Asher sighed after considering it for a while. "But will you *please* make love to me first?"

I tossed my head back on a laugh, the sound replacing the heartache hanging over our home like a dark cloud. "Yes," I said, smiling up at him. "With pleasure."

CHAPTER 30

Asher

I waited in the living room like William asked me to, biting down on my thumb nail and staring out into the snow. The night started with me thinking this would be the last time we saw each other, but now it would end with us making love. My heart wanted it, but I was scared my mind would get in the way. Flashes of the past played out in my head. The rush the men were always in. The way they treated my body. The pain. *The blood.*

A hand squeezed my shoulder, and I jumped, turning to find William watching me with soft green eyes. "Don't say we don't have to do this," I warned. It still felt strange to speak. My voice sounded weird to me and all the crying made the burning in my throat worse.

"I won't." He placed his hands on my cheeks. His palms were wide, his fingers long, and his body large. It made his touch feel like a shield around me, keeping me safe.

"I'm scared, but it doesn't mean I'm not ready."

"I trust you, Asher."

I didn't know what he meant by that at first, but I'd come a long way from that night in the hospital. He trusted me to know what I wanted.

William pressed his soft, full lips against mine, his tongue entering my mouth slowly. His hands slid down my neck and shoulders to my chest. My body heated in places that used to go cold when anyone touched me.

I fought against the shame creeping in, and the voice in my head saying what happened to me was my fault. Telling me he's just like the others. I wanted so many things. To cry, to scream, to hold him close, to push him away. Would it always be so hard?

The first time I'd let William touch me was hard, and I took a long hot shower afterward, scrubbing my skin because I couldn't scrub away the painful things in my head. Being the one to touch him first helped, because I'd had time to prepare my mind for it.

Now he kissed and touched me—within reason—whenever he wanted to. I loved it, but sometimes it took me back to those dark rooms and chains, times when I couldn't fight back.

"I still can't believe you're here." He made it sound like he held a gift in his hands instead of a broken man. "After everything..." He shook his head. "I'm just in awe of you." William's voice was deep and rumbly, but gentle and patient too. It made me excited, nervous, and impatient.

"What now?" My lips still tingled from his kiss. I knew what came next in the past, or rather, what came first, because the others never kissed me. This wouldn't be like that, though. William would take care of me.

He chuckled. "I love it when you do that."

"Do what?"

He shrugged. "Say exactly what's on your mind. You're the same over text, or when you're in the mood to kiss me. You don't ever try to play it cool."

I never thought about it like that, but now I wondered if it was something I did wrong. He said he loved it, so I decided to believe him.

My hands began to shake a little, and the warmth I'd felt a second ago started to melt away.

"Look at me," he said, tracing my ear. "Please."

Swallowing, I lifted my head.

"What are you thinking?"

"Do you think I'm dirty?"

"I would never think that. *Never.* I think you're beautiful and brave." He held my head firm when I tried to lower it again. "Think about where you were, and take a look at where you are now. You're strong, that's what you are. You're the strongest person I know, Asher."

"Thank you." I pushed past the lump in my throat.

"Tell me what you need from me. You set the pace tonight."

I didn't know what to say, didn't know what I wanted, because no one had ever cared about my needs before. For as long as I could remember, I'd been owned. With William, I now got to choose. "Slow," I whispered. "No one's ever taken their time before." I squeezed my eyes shut against the memories this time, blocking out images of bruises covering my body.

William leaned in, taking his time kissing both of my cheeks, the tip of my nose, my forehead, and then my lips. Time stood still as he breathed me in, stroking my jaw before pulling back. I sighed, my eyelids fluttering open. "This time will be different," he promised.

"Do you need a minute to yourself first?"

"Yeah. I think so."

"Okay. Meet me back here when you're ready."

I closed myself inside my bedroom, then headed for the closet mirror. I tried to see what William saw when he looked at me. Tried to see past the basic things I still needed to learn, like how to date without turning the night into a mess of anxiety and insecurity. Or how to talk to people, because even though I'd found my voice for William, I wasn't sure if I could share it with the rest of the world. There was safety in my silence, a part of me protected from harm.

I hurried to take a quick shower. My second one for the day, but maybe the warm water would help the nervous chill leave my body. I tied my hair up to keep it from getting wet. I'd straightened it again for William.

A few minutes later I stood in the closet again, wondering if getting dressed was pointless, but I did it anyway. Because maybe William would want to do something romantic like take off my clothes. That's how it was in *His Eternal Love.* And maybe I wanted romance for a change.

William was pacing the end of the hall, and turned at the sound of my footsteps. I smiled, liking the way his eyes sparkled whenever I did.

"Were you waiting for me?"

"Yes," he confessed, coming in to poke my dimples. "I was."

I hated being shy around him. I wanted to seem confident, mature. But it was because he seemed so amazed by me, even though I didn't find anything about myself amazing at all.

"Take a shower with me."

"Oh, I, uh, already showered." Was this a rule I didn't know about? Were we supposed to shower together before sex?

"This isn't to get you clean, it's to make you feel treasured."

"I... I don't know what that means." I felt stupid.

"Come, let me show you." He linked our hands, his gaze soft, not holding me responsible for what I didn't know yet.

William's shower was twice the size of mine, and I waited nervously as he turned the shower heads on at both ends. His sleeves and bare feet were wet by the time he turned back to me. "Guess I should've taken my clothes off first."

"Let me." I stopped him before he could unbuckle his belt. He dropped his hands to his sides, his smile encouraging.

I knelt, keeping my eyes on his as I removed his belt, then dragged his pants down his legs so he could step out of them. His cock was hard in his underwear, the length of it unreal. I licked my lips.

William groaned, gripping my hair. The band I'd used to keep it up snapped, sending strands tumbling past my shoulders. "I wish you could see how you look."

"Tell me." My heart pounded. I spread my knees wider on the bath rug, my own cock growing hard. I breathed through the urge to feel ashamed. It never quite went away. "Tell me how I look."

"Hungry. Desperate."

"I am," I whispered, tugging down his underwear. His dick sprung free, and I leaned back on my heels, leaving him room to kick out of them.

"I won't hurt you, Asher."

"I know." My mouth went dry as my gaze wandered over him, taking in his muscles and tanned skin. I'd seen him naked before, but I didn't think I'd ever get used to it.

I pushed up onto my knees again and cupped his sack, looking up to be sure what I did felt good to him. His mouth parted, and with more confidence I swirled a finger over his wet tip. William trembled, and I thought I could get used to making him feel this way. I placed a kiss on his shaft, then nuzzled my cheek against its warmth.

"Fuck, Asher," he grunted.

My gaze fell to his scars, and I looked up at him, making sure it was okay before I kissed them too. His eyes filled with pain, and he brushed the back of his hand down my cheek.

He helped me to my feet, wrapping his arms around me. I lifted my arms so he could remove my t-shirt. My hair fell over my face, the strands curling from the steam. William combed it back with his fingers.

"I tried to keep it straight for you."

"You could be bald and you'd still be handsome, Asher." William had never seen me naked, and I was scared that when he did, once he saw what I'd been used for, he wouldn't want me. But his words made me feel brave, more confident in my own skin, so I let go of the waistband of my sweats, allowing him to untie the drawstring.

"Ready?"

"Yes."

It was William's turn to drop to his knees, his hands touching every inch of exposed skin as he dragged the sweatpants down. I shivered, waiting for his reaction.

"Just as beautiful as the rest of you." His fingers trailed up and down my legs, his warm breath blowing against my hard cock. I grabbed onto his shoulders for support as his words hit my heart, soothing the ache there. "How did I get so lucky?" His words were full of worship. I blinked away the tears blocking my view of him.

"Can I kiss it?" His eyes dropped to my cock before returning to me.

"Please," I whispered, nodding.

He wrapped a hand around me, then kissed the tip of my cock.

"More," I breathed when he pulled away. He leaned back in, his dark chuckle traveling all the way to my balls. I felt my face grow hot, which only amused him more.

"Can I put it in my mouth? Just a little bit?"

I felt lightheaded from the sound of his voice, by how much it turned me on. "O-okay."

I touched myself a lot these days, but nothing compared to him taking me halfway into his mouth. He applied a little suction, moving up and down as his tongue alternated between stroking the vein on the underside and circling over the head. I arched, fingers digging harder into his skin. I tried to back away, but he held me to him with a palm on my ass cheek. I trembled as lights exploded behind my eyes right before I came.

"I'm s-sorry." My brain felt fuzzy, making it hard to speak. "I didn't mean to... that fast."

"It's okay." He stood, bringing my gaze back to him. "I'll have you ready again in no time." He licked cum from the corner of his mouth. "You taste delicious, by the way."

In a daze, I slid my palm to the back of his neck, pulling him in for a kiss. His mouth tasted salty, the texture creamy. I kept my mouth parted when he pulled away. I wanted more.

William grinned, bringing his fingers to my mouth. I licked up the drops of cum there.

He turned for the shower door, giving me the perfect view of his tattoo. It was the first time I could look at it without having to hide how much it meant to me.

"Wait," I said, catching him before he stepped in. I smoothed my fingers over the trees, the wildflowers, and finally the bones. "Seeing this made me angrier with you, but only because it was harder to be mean to you after. I didn't want to forgive you, or feel your pain, but you made it impossible not to."

"So you did watch me that night." He said almost to himself, looking over his shoulder.

"Yes." My skin heated thinking back to the night I watched him jerk off in his bathroom. I'd only seen the lower half. His shirt covered most of it, but it was enough.

"How did seeing me fuck my fist make you feel, Asher?"

I thought back to that moment outside his door, hearing him groan as he came over the sink.

"Confused."

"Why?"

"I'd never felt turned on before. Never felt anything close to that." Up to that point, I'd always fought against anything that felt even a little good. I'd felt something other than shame that night—or something else in addition to the shame. I kissed his shoulder, spreading my hand over his plea to Gargantuan.

"We were just Small Bones back then." His voice sounded scratchy, like mine. "Sometimes I think we still are."

I nodded, but he couldn't see me. "You once asked me who you were to me. Do you remember?"

"Yes," he breathed as I kissed a path from one shoulder to the next.

"What is this?" he'd whispered. *"This thing between us. Who am I to you?"*

I pulled him around, finding hope and love in his eyes, hoping he found the same in mine. "You're *everything* to me, William. You always have been."

William led me into the shower and showed me what he meant by "treasured." He started with my hair, tilting my head back to massage the shampoo in, my curls springing back to life. I moaned while he took his time soaping up my body, fingers pressing into my tense muscles as he skipped over my cock to work his way down to my toes. Water hit us from left and right, steam surrounding us.

"Close your eyes," he whispered, his fingers stroking across my hips to my dick. "Block everything else out. It's just us here." His words helped with the panic setting in.

I felt for the wall behind me, leaning back and breathing steadily until the past faded away and only the present remained.

"That's it," William praised from down on his knees. "How does this feel?" He circled my rim with a soapy finger. I searched for the right words to say.

"Like I'm at the beginning of something."

"Your adrenaline is slightly elevated. And now?" he asked, stroking my cock. My stomach muscles clenched, my fingers scraping along the tile at my back.

"Like... like I'm speeding, like I'm about to crash." My breaths started coming faster.

"That's the dopamine rush," he said. "And now?" His hand still moved up and down, but his thumb swiped over my rim and my tip now too. My legs shook.

"I'm gonna co—"

William stopped, and I sucked in a breath, my eyes snapping open.

"Not yet. I want to be inside you when the oxytocin kicks in," he whispered. "Turn around."

I complied, feeling hot and unsteady, hungrier and more desperate than I had before.

"Is it okay if I touch you here?" He squeezed my clenched ass cheeks, but I knew he meant the place in between them.

"Yes." I closed my eyes, resting my forehead against the wall and trying to relax. William spread me open and paused. I couldn't see his face, couldn't hear him move or breathe, but I winced when his hands tightened on me. He made a wounded sound then, bringing back the sting in my eyes.

"It's not your fault." My voice sounded thin, weak. "It's not either of our faults." The reminder was for the both of us.

William's breathing picked up speed, blowing across my wet skin. My blood rushed to my ears, the pounding of my heart making it difficult to think. I forced myself to stay in this moment, to focus on William's hands on me. I wasn't sure of what to say, but then I thought back on something he once said to me.

"Don't let them win, William. *Please*. Don't let them win."

I relaxed when his hold on me loosened, but I tensed up again when his tongue flattened over the scar tissue, followed by his lips pressing against it. I wanted to cry, I wanted to be fucked, but most of all I wanted to thank him for making me feel wanted, even with my scars.

He continued to lick and kiss me, pushing his tongue in and sending me up onto my toes with a shout that scraped against my raw throat. I backed into his mouth, grinding, my body moving on its own.

William stood in a sudden movement, spinning me to face him and kissing me hard and deep. "I need to be inside you." He cut the water off and led us out of the shower, drying us off before linking his fingers through mine. He walked us to the living room, where the coffee table had been moved, and the couch shoved away so his mattress could take their place. I hadn't even noticed it was missing from his bed frame.

"When did you do this?" The flowers were now in the living room too, their vases positioned along the floor.

"While you were in your room getting ready." He relit a couple of candles, then stood there watching me while I stared at him.

"You're sexy," I blurted out, wanting to give just as much as I got from him.

"Oh, yeah?" His voice sounded low and warm, his grin doing things to my insides. "What about me do you find sexy?" He grabbed hold of his cock, stroking slowly as he licked the pad of one finger before rubbing it over one of his dark nipples. He was good at this.

"Your body, for sure." I followed his lead, gripping my hard cock. William's eyes lit up, his gaze eating up my every move. "Your soft skin, your wide shoulders, your strong thighs, and... the size of your dick." We both picked up our pace, but I didn't have the same self-control William did, so I slowed down when my spine began to tingle. "None of that would matter though, if your mind and your heart weren't sexy too. They're the first things I see when I look at you."

He held himself at the base of his cock, bringing his breathing under control. "Get on the mattress, Asher."

I nodded, a sheen of sweat blooming on my skin as I settled onto my back. William prowled over to me, his long cock tapping against his stomach muscles. He crawled on top of me, his forearms planted on either side of my head, caging me in. I tensed up for a second, and William pulled away. "No, it's okay." I held him there by his waist. "I want you like this."

"If something doesn't feel good, you tell me," he whispered. "If you want to stop, we stop."

"Okay." I lifted my head to kiss him as he reached for a foil packet and bottle of lube I hadn't noticed.

"Just you and me. If y-you want that." I looked at the condom then back to William, second guessing my decision for a split second until I met his eyes. *This is William. I'm safe. We're safe.* Removing the doubt from my voice, I asked, "Do you want to?"

"More than anything," William sighed, setting it aside. We kissed until we were breathless, and I was ready for him to do anything and everything to me.

"Hold your legs open for me." He sat up, spreading lube over my hole and both our cocks before coating his fingers with it. He settled between my legs again, holding himself up on one arm while circling a finger at my opening.

"Stroke your cock for me. Not too much pressure. I want you aroused, I want you to open up, but I want my cock to be the reason you come. Understand?"

I nodded, letting go of the sheet to reach for my dick.

"That's it," he praised, lowering his lips to mine as he pushed the tip of a finger in. I groaned, using my heels to push myself back. "Relax, Asher. Breath." With his other hand, he gripped my hair, his fingers tugging until I felt the pull on my scalp. The sting took my mind off the fear and discomfort of him pushing into me. I refocused, keeping my eyes on his as I used both hands to hold our cocks together and lightly stroke them.

It took a while, and a lot more lube before three digits moved in and out of me with ease. Sweat covered our bodies, precum covered my hands.

William removed his fingers to line the tip of his cock up with my hole. I bunched the sheets in my fists again.

"Stay with me, Asher."

"Always," I breathed. I'd been about to close the door in my mind on all that happened to me in the past, but instead I chose to leave it open. I let it all in. I knew that after this, none of it would matter anymore. This would be my first time. This would be the only time that counted.

William sank into me slowly, air hissing from between his clenched teeth. I felt so stretched when he bottomed out. I didn't know where his body began and mine ended. We were one in that moment. I wrapped my legs around him, and he lowered his forehead to mine, giving me time to adjust to him, time to be sure of what I wanted.

He ran his hand up and down my thigh, and the hands of the men who'd taken me with no right to, fell away. Their bruises faded with them. William kissed his way to my neck, and the hands that had brutally wrapped around it disappeared. The marks often left behind went too. And when he whispered how beautiful I was, how proud of me he was, the voices that said I was nothing, only worth what I was used for, went quiet. My head and heart were clear for the first time in my life. I never knew freedom could feel like this.

"I'm ready." I hoped he knew those words went beyond this moment. I was ready to live.

William eased his hips back until I thought his cock might leave me altogether. I dug my heels into his lower back to stop him when all I had left was the tip. He sank in deep again, pushing me higher up on the mattress. I moaned, heat prickling my skin as he repeated the slow torture, grinding into me like he wanted to climb inside of me.

I held onto his forearms, meeting his slow thrusts.

"Fuck, you feel good," he moaned. "Tell me it feels good to you too."

"Yes," I whimpered, no longer afraid to admit how much I wanted this, how much my body needed it. "I... I..."

"I know," he panted, pulling back slowly, then punching forward with force this time. The mattress shifted over the floor. The way his body moved with strength and confidence turned me on, made me want to ask for things I didn't have the words for.

I felt my orgasm coming, I recognized the signs now, understood my body in a way I hadn't before thanks to William. I enjoyed the steady build up, the fire coming to life under my skin. I focused hard on staying there, on making this last as long as possible before the crash and then the fireworks came.

He brought his lips down onto mine, our tongues dueling as we groaned and clawed at each other. We couldn't stop until the kiss stole our last breaths, until my fingers melted into his flesh, and until his hands and cock imprinted on my body.

"Harder," I breathed. "Faster." We'd done the slow thing long enough. I needed to feel how much he wanted me. Needed to feel him let loose on me. He gazed at me with worry in his eyes, and I shook my head. "No, William. This is different, I promise." I was clear on that now, and I refused to let any more fear or doubt left in my mind come between us. "This is you. It's only been you."

One end of the mattress was now pressed against the couch and William pulled out, positioning me on my knees and instructing me to hold on to it. I slid my hands under the cushions, gripping the frame.

"*Oh fuck,*" I moaned, bracing my elbows to keep from falling forward when he entered me from behind. I felt so full like this. William folded his body over me, placing his hands on top of mine.

His pace started off slow, building speed with every thrust until the sound of our sweaty bodies coming together filled the room. "Your ass feels so fucking good," he hissed into my ear, licking the shell of it before biting down on my lobe. I whimpered, my cock bouncing as he fucked me harder and harder. "I'm gonna fill you with my cum, then I'm gonna to fuck you again, Asher."

"Yes. *Please*, yes."

William's chest brushed against the scars on my back while his dick rubbed against the ones around my opening. They didn't make me feel dirty and ugly like they had before. They told a story of survival.

I rocked my hips back to take his cock, my arms trembling as I stared down at my shiny crown. I wanted to touch myself, but I knew once I did this would be over.

"You're so fucking tight," William panted, "and warm." His breath swept over my sweat-soaked skin, giving me goosebumps. "It's never felt like this before. *Never.*"

With the exception of that brutal night we shared in his dining room, I wasn't used to hearing him curse or speak like this. He'd been much tamer then, though. I was no longer dealing with the man, but the animal in him.

"I don't think I'll ever get tired of this." He thrusted into me hard then, my arms buckling as I cried out for more. William pulled me back onto his thighs with a fist in my hair, tugging my head to the side so he could suck on my neck. I'd worn his hickey's before, but this time I wouldn't hide them like I did at Safe Haven. This time I wouldn't feel dirty about it.

"Oh, God. I can't. I can't..."

His cock felt too big for my body in this position.

"Don't tell me you can't unless you mean it, Asher." He'd stopped fucking me, but I bounced frantically on top of him.

I nodded, pressing his face into my neck again, moaning when the tug on my skin there went straight to my dick.

"Not yet," he growled when I slid a hand around my cock. He pulled me off of him, and I winced from the sudden loss.

"Get on top. Fuck me." It was an order. One I knew I could refuse but didn't want to. He squirted more lube onto his dick, spreading it around as I straddled him. I felt nervous. I'd dry humped him until I came after our night at The Daisy, but this was different. I'd be taking him inside me. This position would show how little I knew. I couldn't hide the insecurity in my gaze from him.

"You're perfect," he said. "There's no way you can get this wrong, Asher. Fuck my cock. Make me come."

The way he spoke to me... god, I couldn't do anything other than moan and whimper at his words. My hair clung to my face and neck, and the patch of skin he'd sucked on throbbed. He reached up to trace a finger there, his eyes darkening, cock pulsing at what he saw.

I lined his dick up with my hole, sinking onto it until my hot slick skin pressed into his thighs. I slapped my palms onto his chest, trying to catch my breath. William gritted his teeth, the veins in his neck bulging.

He held still while I took a testing thrust, then another, finding my rhythm and my confidence. Feeling bold now, I pinched and twisted his nipples like I'd seen him do.

"I need to move," he bit out, arching into my hands.

"Yes," I told him, feeling a rush of sensation flow through my body. "I'm not gonna l-last long."

"We've gotta make these seconds count then." He launched himself into a sitting position, pushing a hand into my hair to hold me still for a teasing kiss. He alternated between nibbling at my lips and plunging his tongue deep into my mouth before backing away. His grip on me prevented me from chasing him.

He did this a few more times as I rocked on top of him, until I eventually took my frustration out on his dick, fucking him harder and clenching around him. He settled back, gripping my hips as I slammed down onto his thighs.

"Fuck!" I cried out when he lifted me until only his crown rested in my hole before dropping me down onto him. He repeated the process while bucking into me with all his strength. I wanted more, so much more.

I felt out of control, head fuzzy from the heat and the pleasure.

"That's it," he whispered when I grabbed my cock, his own throbbing inside of me. I pumped myself in long quick strokes, the tingling at the bottom of my spine winding tighter as we fucked harder and faster, our bodies slapping together.

"Asher!" William slammed me onto him one last time, holding me still as he came inside me. I threw my head back, mouth wide as I followed him with a soundless scream. William thrusted a few more times, trembling beneath me, his cum making a squelching sound from within my hole.

I let my dick go and slumped on top of him, smearing my cum between our chests. William didn't let me lay there long. He rolled me onto my back, throwing my legs over his shoulders as he dropped down and lapped at my hole. I held him there with my hand on his head, circling my hips even while trembling through the aftershocks of my orgasm.

"God," I moaned, feeling drained. William licked his way up my body, getting as much cum as he could. His eyes were wild and desperate, and when he was done cleaning me he stole another kiss, rolling us across the mattress until we landed on the floor.

He panted above me, brushing back the hair sticking to my face. "Please tell me you're okay. Tell me if you're not okay too."

"I'm okay." Emotions hit me from every direction. Anger at having missed this for so long, sadness for the same reason. But mostly, I was happy.

"But what I really want to know," I grinned, "is who was *that*?"

"Who was who?"

"That sexy alter ego who came out during sex. We should give him a name."

William groaned, burying his face in my neck. "Don't embarrass me."

"At least I won't be the only one embarrassed for a change."

"You should be happy to know I've never gotten that carried away."

That did make me happy. There wasn't a dry spot on the mattress, so William moved us to the couch. I lay on top of him as we cooled down. I swept my fingers along his smooth chest, and he squirmed, snatching my wrist and placing an apologetic kiss to my palm.

"I'm ticklish in certain places."

"Where else?" I smiled, thinking of all the fun I could have.

"I'm not telling you." He kissed the top of my head, and I nestled deeper into his side. "When did you learn how to draw?"

I shrugged. "As far back as I can remember. At one time it was the only thing I was allowed, but then even that was taken from me." Basic needs like food and water hadn't been the only things used to control me. My love of drawing had been used against me too.

We lapsed into silence, content to watch the snowfall within our candlelit bubble.

"Is today the hardest day for you?" I asked a while later.

He laced our hands together. "Not just today. There's the day we were taken, the day I left you, and... June fifth."

I frowned at the unfamiliar date. "June fifth?"

"The day you lost your mother and nonna. I learned about all the days that meant something to you. They're all hard for me."

It seemed he knew more about me than I knew about myself, things I knew once but couldn't remember. I felt both sad and a little angry that I missed out on him all these years, and grateful about finding him again. "How do you do that?"

"Do what?"

"Make me happy-sad." I didn't have the words to better explain it yet.

"I don't know, but let's see if I can make you happy-happy."

You already do, I wanted to say, but I didn't think I could without wanting to cry.

He eased out from under me and crossed over to the Christmas tree, returning with a gift.

"Happy birthday, Asher." He pecked my lips before stretching out next to me.

"What's this?" I tore the paper off. It was a picture frame. I stared at the two people in the photograph, my hand shaking. "Is this..." It couldn't be. *How* could it be? I sat up, tears filling my eyes.

"That's you and your mother. It was after a performance with her band. I tracked down one of the members some years ago. He let me have it."

I couldn't have been any older than five, maybe a little younger. I ran a finger over her hair. Her curls were loose and did what they wanted to do, just like mine.

"It's black, just like yours." He tucked my hair behind my ear.

"I can't remember the color of my mother's hair, or even if I have her name correct."

"A-and her name?"

William smiled. "Isabella."

"I knew it," I cried softly, pressing the photograph to my lips. "I knew it." I looked at William who seemed to be barely holding himself together. I threw myself on top of him, hugging him with all the gratitude I felt in my heart.

"I love you, Asher." The words were low. I would've missed them if he hadn't spoken them into my ear. I pulled back, my happy-happy tears falling all over him.

"I loved you first," I breathed, and when he laughed, I joined in.

"So it's a competition now, huh?" His joy glued together some of the remaining broken pieces in me.

I set the picture frame aside, picking up the lube before straddling him. I got us both ready before lowering onto him. I waited there, running my fingers over his lips, before trailing them down my neck, right over the hickey he'd given me. William sat up, running his nose along my throat and across my collarbone, inhaling the scent of my skin the way he loved to do. He settled back down after that, and I started to move.

I rode him slowly this time as we gazed into each other's eyes, neither of us wanting to miss a second of it. I promised to spend the rest of my life loving him, to do the work needed to make that happen. My suffering hadn't been for nothing, not if in the end it brought me to him.

"They didn't win," I whispered, rolling my hips. "They didn't win."

EPILOGUE

William

Five Months Later

The bells above the entrance chimed as I walked into The Daisy. Franky smiled over at me while removing his tool belt near the bar. "They're in the back competing like children," he said, shaking his head.

"As expected," I chuckled, making my way to the art studio.

The Daisy was one of only a few places where Asher felt safe. After we'd frequented it enough times, he took Leland up on his offer to host the art brunch every first and last Sunday of the month. Somehow it always turned into them dividing the room and making the event a competition.

The bar was intimate, less overwhelming during the afternoon, which made it easier for him to give it a try. He'd made both Franky and Leland aware of his background, without going into too many details. They'd become protective of him because of it. That made things easier on me too, because I still lived in fear of something happening to him, or him being taken again.

I slipped through the studio door and watched quietly from the back.

"I'm winning this time," Leland said, crossing his arms while one of the waitresses took on the role of judge. She scanned the finished pieces, checking to see which side did a better job—therefore deciding who did the better job instructing them.

"You never win," Asher reminded him, laughing when Leland glared.

The small crowd held their canvases up with pride, each side of the room good-naturedly trash talking the other.

Asher was crowned the winner, and Leland led the losing side in a chorus of boos. I clapped from my spot near the door, drawing Asher's attention.

He hopped off the stage, weaving through the tables to get to me, throwing his arms around my neck. "I missed you," he said, accepting my kiss.

"Get a room!" Leland shouted.

Asher shook with silent laughter. "Ignore him. He's just a sore loser."

"How was your session with Dr. Shwartz this morning?" Today was a big day. We had two important stops to make before heading to my mother's house for dinner. I'd spoken to my therapist about it, which helped with some of my anxiety. Asher was supposed to do the same.

"It went okay, I guess. She encouraged my decision, but I'm not sure how much it helped. I still feel unsure about it."

I knew from our joint sessions that it could be hard to break through to Asher immediately. Sometimes rationality didn't kick in for him until much later. He was like that outside of therapy too.

"You'll be fine. And I'll be right there with you." We stepped out of the way so the patrons could exit the studio. Asher said bye to them all as they passed.

"What about you? What did Dr. Stein think?"

"She thinks it's long overdue, and so do I."

"So why are your shoulders so tense?"

"I didn't say it would be easy, or that I'm not nervous. Just that it's overdue." I dropped my forehead to his.

"You know I'll be in a bad mood later," he warned.

"I know." I sank my hands into his hair. Pushing himself past a limit always resulted in a bad mood, with him dwelling on the past and how it affected his present life. Dealing with his anger came with the territory of loving him, just like dealing with my guilt came with loving me. We were a work in progress.

"So I'm saying sorry in advance."

"You don't have to say sorry at all, Asher. Are you done here?"

"Yeah," he sighed. "Just let me grab my backpack from Leland's office."

"Okay. I'm double-parked, so meet me in the car." I held onto his fingers when he backed away, only letting go when he smiled at me. "I love you."

"I love you more." He turned, disappearing through a side door.

Leland and Franky were locked in a heated kiss at the bar, so I headed straight outside. Asher joined me a few minutes later. We linked hands across the center console before I pulled off. We didn't speak during the drive into Brooklyn, but we squeezed each other's hand when our thoughts allowed us a moment's peace.

"We're here," I whispered, stating the obvious. We'd already been sitting in front of the park I was abducted from for a while. Asher hadn't rushed me either. He'd just stared at the entrance right along with me. Getting out of the car, he came around and took my hand again.

It wasn't an urban park, but when compared to the size of other neighborhood parks, this one was on a much grander scale. There were several entrances, and plenty of areas where one could go unseen. Areas perfect for kidnapping.

"This is where I saw her." I pointed to the bench the woman responsible for my disappearance had sat on. It was close to the entryway we'd parked at. It had been simple to make a grab-and-run. "They never found her," I murmured. I wondered where she was now. I looked around as if maybe she was here with us, strolling the grounds for her next victim.

I hadn't stepped foot in a park since that day, and walking around now with Asher felt both light and heavy. Like reliving the pain while also shedding it. Asher remained a supportive presence at my side.

Kids played without a care in the world while their parents kept an eye on their surroundings. I'd once been innocent like them, believing a stranger taking interest in my pursuits was a good thing. Now I had more in common with the adults who knew the horrors that lurked nearby. Hopefully their children wouldn't have to learn their hard lessons by living them like I did.

"How do you feel?" Asher asked once we'd exited park.

I inhaled the cool spring breeze, exhaling while I considered his question. "I feel free." I leaned back against the passenger side door, pulling him with me and wrapping my arms around his waist. "I mean, I'm not suddenly ready to run the Central Park Marathon, but they can't hurt me anymore." I shrugged. "They didn't win."

"That's right," Asher said, rubbing a thumb over my cheek. "And anyone who wants to hurt you now has to go through me first."

I gripped his ass, pressing his lower body into mine and stole a kiss. "Are you ready?"

"Yeah, let's do this."

I lifted my gaze to the gray clouds rolling in. "Like storm clouds on a rainy day," I said, reminding him of what his mother used to tell him.

"I wish I could remember that."

"Who knows. Maybe you will once we get there." I opened his door, shutting it once he settled inside.

We arrived at the cemetery, following the instructions given to Isabella's gravesite. His grandmother was buried beside her, but while Asher remembered a few things about his mother, he had no recollection of his nonna. If it weren't for me, he wouldn't have even known he called her that.

We'd stopped to buy flowers, and I knelt at their graves with him, helping to lay them below their tombstones. The clouds parted then, sunshine returning.

"They know we're here," he said before turning his smile to the warm rays of the sun. "It feels like I should've been here sooner."

"It happened right on time." I reminded him of something we learned in one of our sessions. Breakthroughs didn't happen late, they happened when they were supposed to.

We spent the next hour chatting with the two people he once loved most. I filled them in on all the hard work he'd been doing to obtain his high school equivalency diploma, and he told them about my plans to bring Gargantuan to the big screen.

"I've been learning to play your violin. William named her after you." His voice thickened with emotion. "You'd love him. You too Nonna. He takes good care of me." He kept his gaze on me, and my heart swelled until I thought it might burst from all the love it contained.

"I love your son." I smoothed my fingers over his mother's engraved name. "And your grandson." I reached over for his nonna's tombstone next.

"And I love him more," Asher said predictably. I rolled my eyes, and he laid his head on my shoulder.

The sun dipped behind the clouds again, the wind stirring up the fallen leaves. "I think they're telling us it's okay to go," he said, laughing through his sadness. It began to drizzle, picking up speed as we dashed hand in hand to the car. We were out of breath from all the running and laughter by the time we shut ourselves in. The skies opened up then, pouring down around us.

I leaned over to kiss all the parts of his face that I loved—which meant every inch of it. "Do you want to head home? My mother will understand."

"No." Asher stared pensively into the rain. "I need..." *A mother right now*, he didn't say.

"Okay, let's go. She'll be happy to see you."

We pulled up to my mother's Brooklyn Heights home thirty minutes later.

It may not have been nestled in the neighborhood she'd envisioned before I was taken, but her dreams of owning a brownstone had come true.

"My babies are here!" She was already holding the door open, allowing us to run in from the rain. She must have been watching for us through the window.

"Momma," I said, coming in for a hug, but she nudged me out of the way to get to Asher.

"Is today a good day for a hug?" she asked him, because being touched by anyone but me was still a problem sometimes. Asher embraced her instead of answering. They rocked from side to side as she mothered him, rubbing soothing circles along his back.

"Gee, I remember when I was the favorite," I muttered dryly.

"I remember when I was the second favorite," Davidson said, stepping in beside me. He looked at my mother like she walked-on-water. It'd taken a couple months to get used to the idea of them dating. Mostly because I'd been the only man in her life since my grandfather died. Apparently, she and Davidson grew closer after the Freedom Fighters charity gala last year.

We moved out of earshot. "How's it going between you two? Without any intimate details," I tossed in. I knew things were rough at the beginning. Neither of them had been in a serious relationship for some time, and Davidson was the protective, provider type. Neither of which appealed to my fiercely independent mother. She wanted love and companionship. She wanted someone who treated her as an equal, not a delicate thing to be kept on a shelf away from harm.

"She puts me in my place when needed. I just want to take care of her, but I'm learning the best way to do that is by standing by her side, not in front of her. No more gilded cages." He winked. That was how his marriage ended, and he'd cautioned me against losing Asher the same way.

"Yeah, no more gilded cages," I agreed. "Anything new?" Asher had told Davidson everything after the Christmas holiday, which led to the FBI busting a trafficking ring with ties to Asia. The men and women taken into custody were underlings, but a few of them turned state's evidence, leading the bureau to someone a little higher up on the food chain. Aisling Murphy—the man I once knew as Declan.

"Murphy's being extradited here as we speak." He'd been living out his retirement in Ireland.

"And everyone else who hurt Asher? The man who brought him here?"

"We're working with our partner agencies abroad on all that, but everything's classified right now. Don't worry." He rested a hand on my shoulder when I sighed. "We're going to get these fuckers, and all the sick, powerful people protecting them." Sick people who couldn't afford to be exposed. People who ran the risk of losing their political positions by having their affiliation to the trafficking underworld revealed.

I thought about the lady from the park, the one responsible for me and Asher's abduction.

"Don't worry about her either," Davidson said, reading my mind. "We'll drag her from whatever hole she's hiding in." The FBI had received new information on her too, but she'd since gone underground. I nodded, putting it all to the back of my mind for now.

My mother patted my cheeks and gave Davidson a peck on the lips once she was done with Asher, then we all headed for the kitchen. She helped Asher tie his apron while I grabbed a bottle of water from the refrigerator. Davidson snagged a beer before leaving us to go watch Sunday football.

"Okay now," my mother started when I swooped between them to kiss Asher on the cheek. "You get started on the potatoes while I season the chicken tenders. Be sure to—"

Her words were cut off when, after grabbing an apple from the fruit bowl on the counter, I swooped back in to kiss Asher on his nose. I jumped out of the way of her swatting hand. Asher grinned like a lunatic.

"Like I was saying, be sure to cut the fries nice and thin. We want them cris—"

I squeezed between them again, reaching for the knife block and kissing him on the corner of his lips. "Okay I'm done." I moved out of reach to dice my apple on the other side of the kitchen.

"We want them crispy," she finished. I settled onto the island as they talked and worked, but now I realized I needed a plate. I set my apple and knife down before sneaking over to the cabinet to the right of Asher. My mother was too busy showing him the perfect squash she found at the farmers market to notice me there. I quietly pulled a plate out, then kissed Asher on the other cheek.

I held my plate up when my mother shook her head at me, trying her best not to smile. "I needed a plate."

"Can't you eat an apple like normal people do?"

"But then I wouldn't be able to do this." I slid my free hand around his nape, and he turned my way for a more meaningful kiss.

"Boy, get off him, he can't breathe." She laughed, but I did this partly because she enjoyed seeing us happy and together after all we'd been through. She moved around the kitchen collecting pots and pans while I gazed down at him. His cheeks were pink, his eyes glassy. I knew if I felt behind his apron I'd find him hard.

"Show some respect," I whispered playfully, then to my mother I said, "I can't help it." I brushed my mouth across his smile. "I love him too much."

"But don't forget I loved you too much first," he quipped.

I groaned. "Hurry up with the food, Momma. I think hunger has made him delusional."

"Have I said how adorable you two are?"

"All the time," I told her.

She walked over with a pile of ingredients in her hands. "Okay, while we're getting the chicken tenders and fries ready, you mix the batter for the double chocolate fudge cake. That oughtta keep you busy." She set everything on the island, then pulled the recipe from her apron pocket. I got to work, me and Asher stealing glances at each other.

We ate and joked around the dining room table, but decided it was time to leave once my mother and Davidson put the record player on and began slow dancing as if we weren't there.

After all the stolen glances and kisses Asher and I shared, there was an unspoken rush to get home anyway.

A tangible wave of lust filled the car, but a dark cloud hovered over the interior as well. I turned to Asher at a red light, taking in his folded arms as he stared out his window. I understood his need to descend into his thoughts. We'd had an eventful day, and with all the distractions now out of the way, it was time to process it all.

I pulled into our building's parking garage less than an hour later. Asher exited the car first, and I took a deep breath before trailing behind him to the elevator.

"You're in a bad mood," I said as we stepped on. We moved to opposite sides of the cabin, and I couldn't keep my eyes off him.

"No. I've just been thinking. No more bad moods for the wrong reasons. What we did today deserves a celebration."

"Oh? What kind of celebration did you have in mind?" Nothing made me weaker than Asher dressed in all black, and when he reached up to let his hair loose I wanted to fall to my knees. The strands were longer now, the curls more out of control. A corner of his mouth lifted in approval when my cock pitched a tent behind my zipper.

"The kind that starts and ends with you fucking me." He was more brazen now. He didn't shy away from waking me at all hours of the night for a quick fuck, or sometimes a long, drawn out one. He made no apologies for demanding sex often. I wouldn't have accepted those apologies anyway, because I wanted him just as often and as feverishly as he wanted me. His body was my safe place, my home, my place of reverence. *Mine to protect.* It went both ways, because my cock was his to do with as he pleased.

"Do you want to talk about today first?" I tried not to let my arousal overrule my number one need—to make sure he was alright.

"No, I don't. When we get inside, I want you to fuck me and not be nice about it. Then we can talk, and then you can make love to me. Okay?"

"Okay," I breathed.

Asher started unbuttoning his shirt.

"Don't," I said, with an edge to my tone. "I plan on ripping it off of you."

He swallowed, nodding before stepping off the elevator.

"Head to the dining room," I said once we entered the apartment. "I'll be fucking you over the table."

I grabbed the lube from my bedroom, pulling my cock through my zipper and slicking myself up as I prowled to the dining room. Asher waited by the window, turning at the wet sound of my hand stroking my dick. I stuck the bottle in my back pocket, freeing my hands to do what I promised I would.

Without a word, I approached him, gaining satisfaction from the widening of his eyes. My ego would never grow tired of how my cock affected him, never get enough of the tight fit whenever I slid inside of him. My dick tapped my stomach as my long strides ate up the distance separating us.

"Malcolm," he breathed as I tore his shirt open. He unconsciously called me that sometimes, in moments when he wasn't thinking, only feeling. The name no longer bothered me the way it used to. I was even okay with my mother's occasional lapses now too. It felt like a little piece of me carved out just for them.

Yanking the sleeves off his arms, I grabbed him by the waist to hold him steady. "How many inches do you want tonight?" I ripped open the button at his fly, crouching to roughly remove the skin tight jeans. He wore nothing else underneath.

"How many?" I growled, his erection nearly slapping me in the face when I rose to grab a fistful of his hair. I stroked him from root to tip while he tried to formulate words.

"All of it," he panted, blushing a brilliant shade of red.

"You think you can handle all of it tonight?" I whispered, biting down on his cheek. "Or are you in the mood to hurt for it?" Talking like this didn't trigger him. He was clear on my intentions, clear about who I was, and who we were to each other.

"T-two fingers." He moaned, his nails digging into my forearm. "N-no more than two fingers." It typically took at least four to get him ready. He wanted a tight squeeze. He wanted to choke on his pleasure as I entered him.

"God, you're fucking beautiful." I slammed my mouth against his, prying his lips apart with my tongue as I backed him into the table. "Face down," I bit out, turning him before shoving him down. His palms slapped against the surface, his hair falling over his face.

Pouring lube into both hands, I reached around for his cock while slipping my other hand through his cleft. "You're so hot, Asher."

"Hurry," he gritted out.

Regardless of what he asked for, I'd never hurt him, so I took my time working one finger in, and then two. His palms slid over the wooden tabletop, and his moans came from somewhere deep inside. I could feel the vibrations against my fingers pumping in and out of his opening.

"I-I'm gonna c-come," he panted, as I jerked his cock while filling his hole with my digits.

"Good, because this is gonna be hard and fast. Don't be surprised if I come as soon as I shove into you."

I kicked his ankles apart. "Are you ready for my cock?"

"Y-yes. Give it to me."

We were both shaking by the time the first half made it in. I breathed, counting to three before giving him a little more. My orgasm was well on its way by the time I was fully seated, and the way he cried my name said his climax was barreling down too.

His ass was so tight I could hardly move, it felt as though we were glued together. I leaned over his back, bracing one hand on the table, the other still fist-fucking his cock. I pumped my hips in quick, short jabs until he loosened around me.

"Fuck, William," he groaned, resting his forehead on the table. "Your dick is... *everywhere*." He sometimes said that was how it felt to be fucked by me. Like I'd taken over every corner of his body. The feeling was mutual, because he owned every part of me.

I picked up the pace, fucking into him, his whimpers cranking up my need for him. I should've taken off my clothes, because it felt like I was being burned alive from the heat of him. I dragged my cock out to the tip, then rocketed my hips forward, causing the table legs to scrape along the floor. Asher went rigid beneath me, his cock pulsing in my hand, his cum hitting the floor.

"No!" he said when I slowed, unsure if continuing after he'd orgasmed would hurt him. "K-keep going. Finish inside of me." He bucked into me, fucking me as he finished spilling in my hand.

Biting down on his shoulder, I closed my eyes, fucking him until I came seconds later.

I stayed inside of him until my cock softened and slid out, my cum spilling from his hole, coating his inner thighs. After catching my breath, I straightened, helping him up. Moving his sweaty hair out of his face, I checked to make sure he was okay. Checked to make sure *we* were okay.

"I'm okay," he breathed. "*We're* okay."

I lifted him by the hips, setting him on the table and pushing between his legs.

"Now will you talk to me?" Now that the fog of lust had cleared, I needed to know what was on his mind.

Asher slid his arms around my neck, staring up at me with big, sad eyes. "Today reminded me of how alone I am in this world without you. I have no family, no friends."

We'd done some digging around and learned that his mother and grandmother came here from Italy not too long before he was born. I'd hoped to uncover some long-lost family members, but it seemed they came here alone. Isabella had dreams of becoming a famous, American musician.

"You'll find friends," I promised. "You're already loved by Franky and Leland. And there's my mother and Davidson. You have your whole life ahead of you. You'll eventually meet so many people you have things in common with, you might forget all about me."

"Not a chance." One corner of his mouth kicked up before he grew serious again. "I'm still that boy who needs you. The boy who sees forever in your eyes. The boy begging on hands and knees for you not to go. I *need* you. All the therapy in the world won't fix that."

I understood what he meant, because I'd always be the boy who abandoned him. The boy who'd never get over leaving him. I'd accepted that no matter how old we got, our bones would forever be small. No matter how much we healed our wounds, those little boys would remain.

"The pain is less now," he said, "but the past still isn't painless."

Our love was dark and intense sometimes because of the lingering pain, but there was light to be found too. We were men on a mission to be whole, and that journey wasn't an easy one. Some days we fucked with the past on our minds, anger and betrayal seeping through every roll of our hips, every violent kiss. And sometimes we made love to the sound of our tears and words of forgiveness. Regardless of how we came to each other, the undercurrent was always love, always a need to understand and let go. We'd be letting go and attempting to understand each other for the rest of our lives. No matter what, we'd stay devoted. That was our vow to each other.

"Life will never be pain free, but I'm going to love you anyway, Asher."

"And I'm gonna love you more." His response filled my heart, my soul, and the room with laughter the way it always did.

"I can't wait to see you try." There was nothing I wanted more than I wanted him. Nothing I yearned for more than I yearned for us. Together we would weather any storm, climb any hill or mountain life put in our path. Asher was my person, and I was his.

I pulled him to the edge of the table, and he wrapped his legs around me. I sank into him slowly, the lovemaking portion of our night beginning. I lowered my mouth to the tattoo scrawled beneath his collarbone, and he kissed my matching one in return.

Asher whispered the four words we would now live and die by in his mother's native language, his Italian getting better and better each day.

I whispered the English translation into his ear as we molded our hearts together, as we promised to love each other for eternity, as we became one. I then repeated it in my head until it felt engraved there, until it became a promise I'd never forget or break again.

Malcolm and Asher forever... Malcolm and Asher forever... Malcolm and Asher forever.

THE END

• Bonus Scene •
William

Three Years Later

The mouthwatering scent of jambalaya hit me before I opened the apartment door. After much debate between his love of art and cooking, Asher had decided to go to culinary school. When I'd told him he could do both, his response was: *"Oh, I plan on it."*

Anita Baker's sultry voice blended with the sounds of the kitchen drawers opening and shutting. My mother's taste in music appealed to Asher. They discovered they had similar tastes in movies too. Now they spent their Sundays' cooking, picking through her record collection, and crying over old black and white films.

Stepping inside, my heart filled with warmth and joy at the sight of all the balloons covering the ceiling.

"Please don't make a big deal about my birthday this year. I just want a quiet night in with you."

"Okay," he'd said without argument. I should've known not to trust it. Then again, he was cooking, so maybe this was exactly the night I'd asked for.

I pushed past the curling ribbons dangling from the balloons and quietly set my satchel on the hall table. I fought to hold in my laughter as he belted out, "...giving you the best that I've got..." He was good at a lot of things, but singing wasn't one of them.

I winced when the closet door hinges creaked, but Asher kept singing like he hadn't heard anything. I hung my coat up, then crept toward the missing piece of my heart.

I wasn't expected to be home for another hour, so I thought I'd have some fun and take him by surprise. Turning the corner, I nearly stumbled. Asher moved around the kitchen barefoot, in nothing but his favorite pair of skinny jeans. He didn't even have the decency to button them. They hung low on his hips, the waistband of his sexy Valentine's Day underwear peeking out.

Most days I still found it hard to believe he was real, that he was here, and he was mine. I'd roll over in the middle of the night reaching for his side of the bed, exhaling once I made contact with his warm skin. I'd haul him into me, sometimes tucking his head beneath my chin before drifting back off, other times fucking him until the fear of losing him vanished.

Standing on the kitchen threshold, I debated swooping in behind him to plant a kiss on his bare shoulder. Or something more comical like tip-toeing over to snap the elastic on his boxer briefs.

Asher made the choice for me, dipping a spoon into the stockpot before turning, wearing a grin that said he knew I was there all along. "You're back early."

"And you're no fun." I headed for the spoonful of jambalaya he held out to me.

"You can't surprise me. I *always* feel you coming." He wiggled his eyebrows suggestively.

"I can vouch for that." Because he'd clench around my cock, begging me to pump him full *every* time. I accepted the small serving, moaning as the savory combination of rice, meat, and seafood hit my tongue.

"Well?" He prompted. I took my time chewing, enjoying each delectable flavor. "How is it?"

I licked my lips, taking my time to lengthen the suspense.

"William," he groaned.

Pecking him on the lips, I whispered, "My great grandmother would be proud."

Asher beamed. He'd been working on mastering the recipe for months now.

"What's this?" I fingered the red ribbon tied into a bow around his neck. "Are you my birthday present?" I bit down on his bottom lip, my cock hardening.

"Nope. I'm your Valentine's Day gift."

Just then, a loud pop sounded, likely one of the heart-shaped balloons overwhelming the apartment. It was followed by a bark, then a low whine of distress before a tiny bundle of white fur shot into the kitchen.

"What the—" My words cut off when the puppy ran straight for me. The scared little furball scratched at the legs of my jeans while I turned my shocked stare to Asher. "You got me a *dog*?" I scooped it up, holding its trembling body against my chest.

"Happy birthday." Asher kissed me, taking his time with it.

"You got me a dog," I said again, smiling through my pleasant surprise. "And it's a Bolognese." I recognized the breed from all the research we'd done into Asher's family history. They hailed from Bologna, Italy. The place where Asher's mother was born. We'd managed to track down a few distant relatives and had plans to visit them next month.

"Her name is Sidney."

I couldn't help laughing. "You named my dog after Sidney Poitier?"

Asher shrugged, blushing. "Have you *seen* his performance in *A Raisin in the Sun*? He deserves way more than a dog named after him."

"Well, I guess we're even. I did name your violin." I held Sidney up in the air, talking to the puppy as if she were a baby. Asher watched, a smile spreading over his face. I set her down, watching as she ran out of the kitchen to the doggy bed I hadn't noticed in the living room.

I backed Asher into the counter, letting his bun down and smoothing his hair over his shoulders. "So this is why you insisted I didn't miss rehearsals for tomorrow's opening performance." I'd been asked to be a guest conductor for the opening night of Sailor's Moon.

"So... since I got my birthday gift, am I allowed to *open* my Valentine's Day gift?" I rubbed his satin bow between my fingers.

"Open me wide," he whispered, lowering my zipper. Asher had come into his own over the years. He was smart, funny, loyal, and loved predicting surprises. But he was also bold, carnal, and adventurous in the bedroom. These days it wasn't uncommon for him to fall into the chair across from my desk, jerking himself off until I called an end to my virtual meeting to suck his cock.

I tugged on the ribbon, unwrapping him, taking arrogant pride in the hickeys revealed. A matching set waited between his thighs.

Asher pulled my cock through the opening of my jeans. He weighed it in his hand, dropping his gaze to it before meeting my eyes again. "No need to fuck me with your fingers first. I've already made room for it."

"*Fuck*, Asher." I lowered to my knees, helping him out of his jeans before gripping his underwear.

"Uh-uh," he said, and I rose to my feet again, giving him a questioning look. Stroking my cock, he brought his lips close to mine and whispered, "Tear a hole into the back of them, then shove this all the way inside."

"I can do that." I shuddered as he worked my length.

"I know you can." He kissed me hard, slipping his stiff cock through the front of his underwear to rub it against mine. Abruptly breaking the kiss, I forced him around. His breaths flew from his lips, his palms slapping against the counter.

"You asked for it," I warned, kicking his ankles apart before kneading his ass cheeks through the tight boxers. I stepped in close, letting my dick slide up and down his cotton-covered cleft. "I'm gonna send you to your fucking toes, Asher. Then I'm gonna fuck into you *hard,* until you come all over the cabinets."

"Do it," he panted, dropping his head between his shoulders and backing his ass into me. "*Please...* do everything you just said."

I left him there trembling while I dug around the junk drawer for a bottle of lube. We kept them stashed everywhere. I slicked myself up, getting off on the impatient sounds he made.

"Hurry—"

I ripped his underwear open, spreading his ass cheeks apart as I aimed my cock for his hole, plunging all the way in. His command turned into a shout of pleasure.

As promised, my first thrust sent him scrambling to his toes. He shifted his grip to the counter's edge.

"Hold on tight," I bit out, securing his hips and fucking him roughly. The heat of him was too much to bear, burning its way through my whole body. My balls ached as the need to orgasm hit me so fast I grew dizzy. It was like I hadn't already fucked him before leaving, or last night, or twice the night before that.

We were constantly aroused and shameless about it. Constantly needing to fill and be filled. Our hands, our mouths, his ass, my fingers... Wanting him would never grow old.

The thought of it all lit the fuse on my orgasm, and I did nothing to hold back my release. The possessive part of me wanted him branded with my cum right now. The part of me obsessed with him belonging to me needed to see the proof of that spilling from his well-fucked hole.

"Are you c-close?"

"Yes," he hissed, turning his head and craning back for a kiss. "I-I was close before you got h-home."

I forgot he'd prepared himself for me. "Toys or fingers?" I growled.

"B-both," he moaned, rocking from the harsh impact of my thrusts. "Both."

That both turned me on and made me jealous. It always did, and he liked that. It wasn't out of the norm for me to step into a room to find him fucking himself on a dildo just for the pleasure of me tearing it out stuffing him with the real thing.

"Don't," I bit out when he reached for his dick. "You come from my cock or not at all." I bent my knees a bit, searching for his sweet spot. He cried out a second later, his fingers white-knuckling the edge of the counter.

"Did you try to come with your fingers inside of you?" I breathed heavily as sweat soaked through my shirt. "Or with that tiny cock inside of you?"

"N-no. I o-only want to come with you."

I picked up my pace, striking his gland as my ego swelled, my control slipping, and my climax raced through me. "Fuck. Come with me, Asher. Come." My pelvis crashed against his ass cheeks one last time, my cock spurting into him as my brain glitched.

"I can feel you," Asher moaned, pounding his ass back onto me. "Feels so fucking good."

His breathing quickened, grew louder as he took advantage of my cock, fucking me senseless as I painted his insides with my cum. "I'm coming, I'm coming," he chanted. "*Fuck*, I'm coming." Asher exploded with a strangled cry, his cum splattering against the cabinet.

We stayed there, recovering, my dick twitching inside of him.

My phone chirped from my back pocket. "What?" I muttered confused, staring down at the text from the concierge. "Leland and Franky are here." Before I could figure out why, another text came through. "And Noon and Solace." We'd all grown close over the years.

"What are they doing here?" I gazed suspiciously at Asher, who at least had the decency to flush with embarrassment at the predicament we were in.

I groaned at the next set of names that came through. "My mother and Davidson." They all must have shown up one after the other, thus all the messages. "She has the code to the elevator, and will bring everyone right up here." That was when I noticed how much food Asher made, and the three cakes lining the island.

"What happened to a quiet night home with just the two of us?" I couldn't help but laugh at the absurdity of our situation as I righted my clothes. We'd just had sex in our kitchen, and Asher was naked. "They'll be up here any minute."

"It'll be fun," he said, scooping up his jeans. His underwear hung around him in tatters.

"Fun? You're leaking cum everywhere."

Asher looked at the droplets hitting the floor. "Yeah, maybe this wasn't such a great idea."

"You think?" We both keeled over with laughter, Sidney barking and running into the kitchen again.

I sent my mom a text letting her know not to come inside yet. "She's going to know what we've been up to." I laughed harder when Asher's expression turned mortified. We wiped the floor and cabinet down before racing for the shower.

"I can't believe you." I shook my head, still chuckling as we soaped and rinsed in less than two minutes. Sidney watched her crazy parents from the bath mat.

Asher cut the water off, wrapping his arms around my neck as if we had all the time in the world. “Come on, did you really want them to miss the proposal?”

My eyes widened, thoughts going to my satchel and the ring inside. I’d picked it up while I was supposedly at rehearsal. “You *knew*? How?” I’d sworn everyone to secrecy.

“Heard you talking to Cole about it the other night.”

Cole was a classically trained pianist. He’d stopped by to help me put the finishing touches on something I’d been working on.

“You’re just as bad at whispering as Davidson.”

“No,” I laughed, cupping his cheeks. “You’re just nosy and hate surprises.”

Asher grinned, his dark eyes sparkling with enough love to mend everything broken in the world. “You planned to propose to me on *your* birthday.” It was his turn to shake his head in disbelief.

“There’s no greater gift than you agreeing to marry me.” I would’ve done it sooner, but I wanted to give him time to find himself, to discover all his likes and dislikes. I wanted to give him the space needed to dream dreams, to create and meet goals. Time for him to decide if choosing me was the right move, time to decide whether or not he wanted to stay.

Some may have thought we rushed into what we have. That he had no choice because I saved him. The truth was, he’d saved me.

I never held him back, never blinded him to all the options he had in life that didn’t include me. I allowed him to be free, and every day he’d come home excited to fill me in on all he’d done, on all he’d seen. And every night he’d remind me that nothing made him happier than being right there in my arms.

“You can stop holding your breath,” he’d once said. *“I’m not going anywhere. I can be my own person and still choose you.”*

We’d made plans for forever, but I loved him enough to let him go if his plans changed. Thankfully they hadn’t.

“Well?” I whispered, swallowing down my nerves. “Will you marry me, Asher Gray?”

“Yes,” he whispered back, as our phones rang in the distance, and our hoard of family and friends began pounding down our front door. “A million times, yes.”

• Bonus Scene •
Asher

Six Months After the Proposal

I sat perched on the kitchen island while William sat on the stool between my legs. He slid his hands up my bare thighs.

"You know the rules," I tsked. "No touching."

He frowned, dropping his hands back to his lap. "Can't we just go to bed now?"

"Nope. You have to guess all five correctly first." I chuckled when his frown deepened.

"Remind me again why I need to be blindfolded?"

"Because your other senses become heightened when you lose one or more. I need you to *really* taste the ingredients." I'd banned him from the kitchen after his mother picked up Sidney for the night, then spent the next couple hours cooking up options for him to taste-test, deciding to turn it into a tortuous game.

"But why tonight? We finally have the place to ourselves."

Taking care of a needy puppy was more work than either of us had realized. Sidney demanded all of our attention when she was home.

"We're getting married in a few weeks, and I still haven't narrowed down the desserts." I agreed to have everything else catered, even though cooking ranked in my top five favorite things to do. I refused to hand the dessert menu over to anyone else, though.

"Fine," he grumbled. "But you're going to have to make it up to me once this is over."

"Don't I always?" I used that husky voice he loved, my shoulders shaking with silent laughter when he perked up a bit. "See? I bet that sounded even better now that you can't see anything."

"It did," he said grudgingly.

"Open up." I brought a forkful of the next option to his mouth. William hummed as he chewed and swallowed. I licked the corner of his mouth clean, and he froze.

"Why must you be so cruel?"

I tipped my head back with a laugh, laughing harder when he covered his semi-hard cock with both hands, as if trying to hide it. His hands were big, but not *that* big.

"You could have at least let me put some clothes on. I'm at a serious disadvantage here."

I'd caught him as soon as he stepped out of the shower, allowing him to towel off but nothing else. What he didn't know was that I'd slipped out of the boxer briefs I'd been wearing before maneuvering onto the island in front of him.

"Well—"

"Let me guess," he cut in dryly. "Being blindfolded *and* naked heightens my sense of taste too."

"No, the naked part was completely selfish. I wanted something to look at while we played this game."

He scowled. "At least you're admitting this is a game. A way to torture me."

"You're stalling now. Guess what it is."

William tilted his head thoughtfully, lapping up what I hadn't gotten off the corner of his mouth. "I taste coffee, and..." He gestured for another bite, chewing slowly this time, and I resisted the urge to kiss his cocoa powder dusted lips. "Tiramisu," he whispered with a triumphant smile.

"I haven't even confirmed it yet."

"Yeah, but I know I'm right. Come on, give me the next one."

"Oh *now* you're excited."

"Hey, I got one right." This time I didn't argue when he placed his palms on top of my bare knees. His eagerness was too adorable, and besides, if his hands were on me, that meant I got to enjoy the sight of his dick.

I twisted toward the dish of desserts, choosing something he'd never had before. Something I knew he'd confuse with something similar I'd made a long time ago. I was also in the mood to make him suffer, so I traced a finger along the seam of his mouth to signal for him to open up. His hands tightened on me.

"Crème caramel?"

I leaned in, whispering into his ear and pulling a shiver from him. "Crème brûlée."

"That's ch-cheating," he breathed. "I've never had that before."

"Guess I'll have to make that up to you as well, won't I?" I rubbed my cheek along his jaw before straightening.

"I g-guess so." His hands slid higher.

"Uh-uh," I warned. "Not another inch higher." If he knew I was naked and hard too, he'd end things right then and there. "Only three more options to go."

William bit down on the sandwich cookie I pressed to his lips. *"Fuck,"* he moaned. This was an easy one. It was the one sugary pastry almost capable of making him orgasm. *"Alfajores,"* he whispered in reverence, powdered sugar coating his chin and chest. "You're going to pay for this." He fisted the base of his cock. In a daze, I reached for the precum leaking from his dark tip. William hissed when I swiped it up, spreading it across his lips before mopping up the mess with my tongue.

"I'm telling my mom to keep Sidney for the whole weekend. You've just earned yourself an uninterrupted two days of marathon fucking." The hand on my knee shot to my crotch area, causing me to suck in a surprised breath. William's brows raised above the silk blindfold. "You removed your underwear."

"Don't you dare," I panted when he reached for the blindfold. "You take it off and you'll be fucking your hand tonight if you do."

William hummed, his full lips spreading into a smug smile. "Pretty sure you mean that. But I'll play along." He parted his mouth, waiting for the next treat as he stroked my dick. I bit back a whimper. I used my fingers to feed him the next item.

"Baklava," he said immediately. "No one makes it quite like you do."

My cheeks warmed. I loved his compliments. I'd been about to thank him, but he leaned over to kiss my cockhead.

"That's what we were missing," he mused. "A little bit of salt."

"Who's ch-cheating now?" I asked.

"Next," he said, not looking the least bit repentant.

I closed my eyes on a silent sigh, wondering how he'd managed to turn the tables on me.

"You were right about my other senses being sharper," he whispered, inhaling deeply. "I can smell your lust."

The warm scent of baked goods was all I smelled. "You're imagining things." The tremble in my voice gave me away.

William teased my cock with gentle strokes. "Earth to Asher," he said, laughter in his tone. He pointed to his open mouth.

"Oh, right." I broke a piece of cake off, my hand unsteady as it traveled toward him.

“Mmmm.” William grabbed my wrist, holding my hand in place while he sucked my fingers clean. He swallowed, his smile blinding as he whispered, “Your favorite, and the winner, double fudge chocolate.”

He ripped his blindfold off, love pouring from his gorgeous green eyes. “Now I get to have my *real* dessert.” William shoved his stool away, and I wrapped my legs around him as he scooped me up, then raced for the stairs. His joy was infectious as we kissed and laughed all the way to our bedroom. I outranked cake and cookies. That’s how I knew his love was real.

THE END

About the Author

C.P. Harris writes emotionally charged romance with a dark edge. Her stories dive deep into flawed characters, and leaves you with hard-won, happily-ever-afters. When not writing, she's devouring the same intense, complicated romances she loves to create. If you crave angst, obsession, and endings that hurt before they heal, then C.P. Harris might just be your next favorite author.